HARVARD STUDIES IN COMPARATIVE LITERAT
VOLUME X

VIRGIL THE NECROMANCER

Studies in Virgilian Legends

BY

JOHN WEBSTER SPARGO
NORTHWESTERN UNIVERSITY

CAMBRIDGE

HARVARD UNIVERSITY PRESS

1934

PRINTED AT THE HARVARD UNIVERSITY PRESS

CAMBRIDGE, MASS., U. S. A.

In Memoriam

E · V · S

PREFACE

PART of Chapter I and most of Chapters V and VI of this group of studies are based on materials in my Harvard doctoral dissertation. My obligation is very great to the work of the late Domenico Comparetti (1835–1927), one of the most distinguished scholars of the nineteenth century. Those interested in his achievements will like to read the articles on him by Alessandro Chiappelli (*Nuova rivista storica*, II [1918], 239–252), Giorgio Pasquali (*Quaderni critici*, VIII [1929], 7–46), and Augusto Rostagni in the tenth volume (1931) of the new *Enciclopedia Italiana*.

The number is now legion of those who have persevered because of the encouragement and helpfulness of Professor George Lyman Kittredge. Of that number I am not the least grateful one. From the inception of these studies, Professor Archer Taylor has most generously thrown open to me the stores of his erudition. His watchfulness has prevented many a blunder. Professors Stith Thompson and A. H. Krappe have been kind in the matter of references, and Professor P. S. Allen gave me an indispensable book. Mr. George C. Vieh, Dr. Vernam Hull, and Dr. Ernest Simmons have assisted me in various ways. Without the support of Harvard University, of the Guggenheim Foundation, and of Northwestern University the work would not have reached the stage of publication for many years. I am particularly indebted to the staffs of the libraries at Harvard, Chicago, and Northwestern Universities, and of the Newberry Library and the British Museum. At the Museum, Mr. Arthur I. Ellis was especially helpful; and I would acknowledge also the friendly assistance of the staff of the Print Room. M. Robert Brun of the Bibliothèque Nationale was courteous and kind. The remarkable care and skill of the printers have contributed much. Finally, I must try to set down here what no words of mine can adequately express: my greatest indebtedness is to my beloved wife, high-hearted comrade and collaborator, whose eye will never see these pages.

J. W. S.

Evanston, Illinois,
May 15, 1933

CONTENTS

ILLUSTRATIONS

VIRGIL THE NECROMANCER

I

THE FIRST FOUR HUNDRED YEARS

EXCEPT among the initiated it is commonly felt today that the literary classics of Greece and Rome fell upon parlous times during the Middle Ages, that the luminous lamps of classical literature shone as through a glass darkly to the mediaeval mind. As the years pass, however, and we learn more about the period intervening between the decline of Rome and the rise of the Renaissance, we come more and more to believe that the historian in the not too distant future may be justified in regarding the centuries during and following the Renaissance as almost as unsympathetic toward life and thought and effort in the middle period as the "dark ages" themselves were toward classical antiquity. We are beginning to realize that this brilliant and exciting Renaissance, for all its fine and inspiring achievement, was fiercely and often unreasonably intolerant of almost everything mediaeval. In its eager haste to make the antique pagan world its own, the Renaissance was prone to forget that it was the humanly erring fingers of mediaeval men that had perpetuated the classics through centuries of patient toil. Out of a bewildering confusion of religious and political and social antagonisms was bred a contempt for the Middle Ages which endures to this day wherever those same antagonisms still flourish. Even now, with accurate knowledge of mediaeval times steadily becoming more accessible, learned men occasionally persevere in interpreting the Middle Ages from the point of view of these outworn prejudices. Such being the case in modern times, we can understand the better why the young men of the Renaissance turned from the doctrines of their fathers in such fierce revulsion that they were blinded to the fact that their birthright in the Middle Ages — theirs, whether they would or no — might conceivably be turned to advantage in their strenuous attempts to expand spiritual horizons. Cassiodorus and his helpers and successors passed into oblivion, but not without leaving behind them much of the material out of which the Renaissance built up its culture, a culture which ironically enough it took pride in regarding as utterly alien in spirit to whatever the Middle Ages could offer.

The remarkable thing is that the mediaeval tradition was so tenacious of life as to preserve what it did against the multifarious agencies of annihilation constantly at work. Somehow the tradition was strong enough to defeat the destructive influences of ignorance, of anti-pagan prejudice, of preoccupation with the life to come, and to pass on to later times the literary treasures of Mediterranean civilization.

Prominent among these treasures beyond price were the works of Virgil, which throughout the Middle Ages had enjoyed a reputation quite as lofty as during the days of Roman supremacy. His poems were studied in the schools, discussed in the cloisters, quoted by the more enlightened of the Fathers, like Augustine and Jerome, and in general may be said to have represented to the cultivated man of the Middle Ages much that Shakespeare represents to the cultivated English-speaking person of today. Dissenters there were about Virgil's greatness, just as there had been dissenters during classical times, but his literary reputation survived the vicissitudes of the Middle Ages in undiminished splendor, though in many respects different criteria came into force and emphases were curiously shifted.

It is to this shifting of emphases and perspectives that we must look for the reasons underlying the subject of these studies, — those remarkable products of the mediaeval imagination, the Virgilian legends which first appeared about the middle of the twelfth century. The story of Virgil's literary reputation has been discussed along with the legends by Domenico Comparetti. I shall touch upon it only incidentally in the course of the following pages.

When we are dealing with legends, strange shadows of the shadows of reality that they are, it behooves us to exercise particular care lest we turn legend-makers ourselves and wander blindly in the mists of our own imaginings. It is none too easy, for instance, to keep sharply differentiated the legend in its original form, with the objective facts about it — such as when, where, by whom, and under what circumstances it was told — from, on the one hand, subsequent occurrences of the legend with their corresponding facts, and, on the other hand, the inevitable conjectures which arise concerning the adumbrations of fact or fancy at work in the mind of the original narrator to produce the initial version. If a preconceived notion is brought to the consideration of the legend, one is too likely to pass over the primary and indispensable facts in order to indulge in the pleasant game of speculation concerning origins.

For nearly eight hundred years the Virgilian legends which we shall examine here have been known to large numbers of men in every generation, who have related them and in the past century studied them, with varying degrees of disgust, delight, disbelief, credulousness, stupidity, and intelligence.[1] Neither the number of the legends nor the number of narrators is small during the first four centuries, and their geographical distribution is virtually coextensive with the boundaries of Western Europe. Clearly, we shall wallow in confusion almost at the outset unless a systematic plan of some sort is determined upon and adhered to rigidly. After some deliberation I have settled upon following a strictly chronological order in drawing up as objectively as may be an exposition of the progress of the legends during the most important part of their history. In order to avoid, so far as possible, repetition and the appearance of merely rehearsing a catalogue, and to economize space and time, I append to this bare record a table which is designed to enable the reader to locate a given legend at a glance and to follow its development readily. Hence, when additional material is found, it can be easily placed with reference to other variants, and no matter how far afield I may wander in the following chapters, the reader will at all times have at hand a simple outline of the essential facts. It is anticipated that the table will be used especially in conjunction with the text of the present chapter.

The earliest of the more or less homogeneous group of legends with which we are concerned appears, not in a crude and unpolished form as if straight from the unlettered folk, but in a thoroughly sophisticated book that has been called "the aptest reflection of the cultivated thought of the middle of the twelfth century," written by a remarkably versatile churchman who was at once traveller, friend of Becket, Bishop of Chartres, diplomat, and "best classicist of his age," John of Salisbury.[2] In the *Policraticus*, finished about 1159, gossip has it that the Mantuan seer one day asked Marcellus which he would prefer to have, a bird that would capture other birds, or a fly that would exterminate other flies. After he had duly discussed the matter with his uncle Augustus, Marcellus decided that he should prefer the fly, so that Naples might be relieved of its otherwise interminable plague of flies.[3]

In a chapter "on hunting, both according to writers and according to its kinds, and on its use, proper and improper," [4] John introduces this extraordinary anecdote by a casual *fertur*, "it is said." Said to him during one of his numerous trips to Italy, perhaps in Naples itself? Comparetti would fain think so, but has to skip nearly two centuries to find dubious support in a fourteenth-century chronicle of Naples, the *Cronica di Partenope*, in which Marcellus is governor of Naples, and Virgil is his minister. Hence, Comparetti continues, the folk of Naples must have believed this same fiction in the twelfth century, and the story "is in all probability due to some monk who wished to give the popular superstitition an edifying turn." Obviously we cannot establish the existence of a popular tradition in this manner. Somehow John of Salisbury got hold of the story. Beyond that we know nothing. Graf sees literary antecedents for the little tale, but "il Comparetti non lo concede" — Comparetti won't admit it.[5]

The other pertinent allusion to Virgil in the *Policraticus* is even more ambiguous. A certain Stoic named Ludowicus made an exile of himself in Apulia (the province in which Naples is situated) for many years, and in spite of vigils and fasts and much labor finally failed in his effort to take back to France the bones, rather than the spirit, of Virgil, for he was striving for the impossible.[6] This passage will be returned to later; for the present we must pass on to one of the earliest Occidental representatives of a very widely disseminated collection of stories.

Dolopathos, sive De rege et septem sapientibus was composed in Latin prose toward the end of the twelfth century by a monk of Lorraine, in the bishopric of Nancy, Joannes de Alta Silva, who based his version of this branch of the *Seven Wise Masters* upon oral tradition. It was translated into Old French verse in the following century. Here neither Virgil's bones nor the products of his magic art are concerned; the worker of miracles and maker of talismans does not appear, as he does in the later legends. Virgil is "ille famosissimus poeta," but his powers transcend those of a mere bard, and in addition to being master of the entire seven liberal arts and teaching them to the sons of the nobility, he foresees the future when need arises, and also instructs his pupil Lucinius how to do so. When the other scholars, envious of Lucinius's progress, conspire to poison him, he sees their trick in advance, just as later he foresees his mother's death. The plot of this whole adaptation of the venerable type of story known as Potiphar's Wife turns on Virgil's foreseeing the imposture of the new stepmother and devising means to frustrate it. It is true that Virgil's prototype in the *Book of Sindibād*, the Eastern form of the *Seven Wise Men*, is not a magician, but a philosopher; yet he gains knowledge of the future by consulting the stars, as Virgil does. In any case, it is hardly safe to base inferences on other versions than *Dolopathos* itself, as it has been drastically altered in the course of oral transmission, like many another frame-story.[7]

That Virgilian legend should have come within the purview of the wandering scholars is but natural. We might wish for less allusiveness in the *Apocalypsis Goliae Episcopi*, wherein the author

tells us that upon going to a grove he sees Pythagoras and follows him to another land, where there
is a throng of people, each with his name on his
forehead. In an Elizabethan translation the story
continues:

> Here's Priscian busy beating his schollers hands;
> Beating the aire here Aristotle stands;
> Tully with words doth sharpest things assuage,
> While Ptolomee stares upon the starres so sage;
>
> . . . .
>
> Lucan's theire leader, to the war they passe,
> Virgill meanewhile is framing flies of brasse;
> With fables Ovid flockes of men doth feed,
> And Persius' pate doth biting satyres breed;
> Statius his mouth beyond all measure wide,
> With swelling style his matter doth out-stride;
> Terence with dances doth the people please,
> With drenches Hippocrates gives the people ease . . . [8]

Alexander Neckam, foster-brother of Richard of
the Lion Heart, and an ecclesiastic with wide and
varied interests, provides a fairly lengthy list of the
prodigies performed by Virgil, in *De naturis rerum*,
a prose work composed perhaps during the last
decade of the twelfth century. The Lucretian echo
in the title proves illusory, for the two books constitute a sort of manual of twelfth-century science, enlivened by numerous anecdotes. Chapter
CLXXIV of Book ii, in which the Virgilian material appears, is devoted to a discussion of schools
and universities both ancient and contemporary,

the author's general idea being that the fame of a
country may be gauged directly by the amount of
attention given to such institutions. After mentioning several earlier schools, Neckam passes to
those of the Romans. One of their best, it seems,
was at Naples, and its leader was none other than
the Mantuan seer himself. Too gifted to remain a
mere pedagogue, Virgil applied his genius in civic
matters, and freed Naples of a plague of poisonous
bloodsuckers by throwing into a well a leech made
of gold. When the butchers' meat took to spoiling
too rapidly, he relieved the merchants by inclosing
it in a meat-market through the power of some herb
or other, where it was preserved perfectly for five
hundred years. The "Virgilian garden," as made
by the seer, was protected by immobile air instead
of a wall; air, too, was the material out of which
Virgil made a bridge which took him whithersoever
he would go. In Rome — changing the scene of his
activity — he built a noble palace, in which were
wooden statues, each holding a bell in its hand and
representing one of the provinces of the empire.
Whenever trouble arose in a province, its represen-
tative rang its bell, and a bronze horseman atop the
palace brandished his spear and pointed it toward
the province in difficulties. Thus corrective mea-
sures could be taken before the situation got out of
hand. This "Salvatio Romae," Virgil told the ad-

miring populace, would endure until a virgin should
bear a child; so it looked as if it would stand forever, but at the birth of the Saviour it crumbled to
ruins.

Neckam refers to these marvels incidentally. In
discussing centres of learning he is reminded of the
one at Naples conducted by Virgil, and then by an
easy association he recalls these extraordinary phenomena, which, contrary to his wont, he leaves un-
explained, even asking the reader, in a rhetorical
question, to explain them. If the provenience of
John of Salisbury's tales must be left to conjecture,
that of Neckam's is even less sure, for not enough
is known of his life to justify asserting either that
he did or that he did not visit Italy.

Walter Burley, another Englishman, who died in
1337, says expressly that he is borrowing from
Neckam in his treatment of the legends. Perhaps
the influence of *De naturis rerum* itself was largely
restricted to England, but through Burley's work
De vita et moribus philosophorum the section on
Virgil reached a considerable audience on the Continent.[9]

Conrad of Querfurt, chancellor of the emperor
Henry VI and newly elected bishop of Hildesheim,
wrote a long letter from Sicily in 1196 to his friend
and subordinate, the prior of the abbey at Hildesheim, relating his joy at traversing ground hal-

lowed by classical associations. Conrad quotes
Virgil and other poets with evident relish, and includes a disquisition on his works and arts. It may
be worth noting that this learned man of action had
been selected by Frederick Barbarossa to be the
tutor of his son, the future Henry VI, and that
therefore Conrad was in a sense responsible for that
prince's wide reputation for classical learning.
Naples itself was the work of Virgil. A palladium
made in vain by him to preserve the city against
capture consisted of an image of the city inclosed in
a slender-necked glass bottle. Its efficacy was
proved, Conrad thinks, because after the city was
captured by his troops the glass was seen to have a
flaw. The bronze image of a horse made by Virgil's
magical incantations strengthened every horse that
looked upon it so that he could bear his rider. A
bronze fly placed in a gateway by the seer kept all
other flies out of the city as long as the talisman
remained intact. Virgil's bones were guarded in a
castle overlooking Naples, surrounded by the sea;
when they were exposed to the air a terrible storm
arose, — "which we have seen and tested," adds
Conrad. Medicinal baths, with statues indicating
what ills each bath cured, were constructed in the
neighborhood of Baiae. Virgil confined all of the
serpents beneath the Ferrean gate at Naples. A
flesh-market of his contriving preserved for six

weeks meat which spoiled if it was taken out before the expiration of that time. A bronze archer kept Vesuvius in check by threatening it with drawn bow; but a gaping farmer touched the string, the arrow shot into the crater, and at once the eruptions began again.[10]

Clinschor of *Parzival* fame was a nephew of Virgil, and therefore came by his black art honestly; he hailed from the "terra de Labur," and he accomplished many wonders.[11]

The Provençal poet Guiraut de Calanso, about whom not a great deal is known, supplies us with the second reference to the legends in a vulgar tongue, and at the same time mystifies us not a little. Writing about 1200 a jongleur's *vademecum*, — a long poem in which he lists allusively the stories and accomplishments which must fill out the repertory of the successful entertainer, — he includes among the stories those which tell "of Virgil, how he managed to protect himself against woman, and of the orchard and of the fishpond, and of the fire which he knew how to extinguish." [12] Wolfram von Eschenbach, the first minstrel whose knowledge of Virgil as a magician is recorded, is now joined by a second. The sowing of the first seeds of legend was bearing early fruit, and we shall soon see how abundant was the full harvest.

Yet another Englishman adds his testimony concerning the legends, but in this instance we are not left uninformed about the place where he learned them. Gervasius of Tilbury wrote about 1211 a compendium to amuse and inform and edify his patron, the emperor Otto IV. Perhaps he wrote it near Arles, where he spent his last years. Some of the material in it, including the Virgilian legends, he acquired during his residence of many years in Italy. He left England when he was yet a boy, studied and lectured at Bologna, apparently spent most of the last decade of the twelfth century in Sicily and thereabouts, and may have been an actual eye-witness of the subjugation of Apulia and Sicily in which Conrad of Querfurt played an important part. Since there is no complete edition of the *Otia imperialia*, and since no manuscript earlier than the thirteenth century is known to exist, there seems to be little to justify efforts to date the Virgilian parts of the work earlier than about 1211.[13]

In France, Gervasius tells us, there was a remarkable church, in the refectory of which no spider or fly could exist; and, similarly, no fly could stay in the refectory of a church in the neighborhood of Arles. This last fact Gervasius was sure of from personal investigation; and he knew, too, that at Naples Virgil set up a brazen fly "by mathematical art" which as long as it was intact permitted no fly to enter the city. These three phenomena, at Naples and at the two churches, seem to be regarded as parallel.[14] Here Virgil's meat-market preserved flesh indefinitely through the power of a piece inserted in its wall or side. Serpents he confined near the Nolan gate. The destiny of persons entering Naples by the Gate of Good and Ill Fortune was controlled by two images created by Virgil. If the stranger inadvertently entered by the arch presided over by the smiling image, prosperity awaited him; but if he entered by the arch where the frowning image glared down, misfortune and distress were in store. A statue of bronze made through the virtue of astrology stood in Virgil's herb-garden on Monte Vergine and kept in check a volcano overlooking the *terram Laboris* — Vesuvius, no doubt — by means of a bronze trumpet in its mouth. This figure is somewhat like the archer mentioned by Conrad, save that the trumpeter blew back the winds which otherwise would have brought volcanic dust and ashes to the garden. At Pozzuoli Virgil constructed medicinal baths, with inscriptions indicating the ills which each one cured; but the doctors of Salerno thought that the baths interfered with their business, and destroyed the inscriptions, so that the people were left in ignorance of the properties of the waters. By mathematical art, Virgil pierced a long passage through a mountain. In it no one could plot treachery.[15]

"Here is something new that happened in our own time," says Gervasius; an Englishman came seeking Virgil's bones in the time of King Roger of Sicily. The king gave the necessary permission, and since the people of Naples — "where Virgil had shown so many proofs of his power" — knew nothing of the whereabouts of his grave, they made no objection to what they thought would be a vain quest. Now this Englishman was a renowned writer, learned in the Trivium and in the Quadrivium, skilled in physics, profound in astronomy; and by his art he found the grave, and in it the dust and bones of Virgil, with his head resting on a book in which the *ars notoria* was written. The Englishman got the book, but the people would not permit him to have the bones, which were placed on exhibition behind a grating in the Castel del Mare. "I have seen some extracts from that book," concludes Gervasius, "and have made experiments satisfactorily establishing their value."

Of the *Chronicon* of Helinandus all but the last five books have been lost. Unfortunately the source of the Virgilian legends as they appear in the encyclopaedia of Vincent of Beauvais is among the lost material. Nevertheless Helinandus should be mentioned here because his serving as Vincent's informant with respect to the legends pushes the date of Vincent's version back, in a way, to the time of the *Chronicon*, that is, between 1204, the date at which it breaks off, and 1229, the year of its author's death. Any inferences about the origin of the legends would have to take Helinandus, through Vincent, into consideration. Thus it seems that the first three-quarters of a century saw considerable interest in and development of the legends in the hands of John of Salisbury, Neckam, Conrad, Gervasius, and Helinandus.[16]

Michael Scottus, who died perhaps in 1236, mentions in his *Liber introductorius* Simon Magus, Virgil, Peter Alexandrinus, Peter Abelard, and Solomon as magicians.[17]

In order to make the present exposition as clear as possible, it will be well henceforth not to list in the text every occurrence of those legends with which we are already familiar. Mere repetition will, then, be passed over; only when a new legend appears, or when an older one is changed in one way or another, will further notice be taken in the present chapter. Every significant occurrence of every legend will be found recorded in the table, however.

The author of the earliest versions, two in Old French verse and one in prose, of the *Image du Monde*, redacted about 1245 or 1246, repeats most of the previous legends — apparently he was familiar with both Neckam and Gervasius — and adds some of his own. Virgil founded Naples on an egg, and extinguished all the fires in a city in revenge for an insult by a great lady. He made two candles burning bright and a lamp with fire in it which burned everlastingly. A prophesying head which he made foretold his death, but so enigmatically that he failed to understand it.

Curiously enough, the same Virgil figures in an earlier chapter among the prophets of Christ and is even singled out for special admiration by St. Paul, who regrets that Virgil has died too soon to be converted to Christianity.

In the second verse version, in which the author declares that he himself has made a trip to Sicily and can vouch for the things he reports, more space is devoted to the relationship between the saint and the seer. It seems that after considerable searching St. Paul found in Italy a subterranean cave guarded by two men of copper each holding an iron hammer, and in the cave was Virgil's spectre seated before a table covered with books, reading by the light of two candles. In his right hand he held a book. When St. Paul entered the cave, the archer shot at the candles and instantly everything fell to ashes. The holy man hastily left those parts and sailed for Sicily, where he lost no time in converting to Christianity Virgil's pupil Lucinius, king of the region.

St. Paul's purpose in occupying himself with Lucinius seems plain, for the scribe has already told us that among Virgil's marvels was a book as small as his fist, in which he had written about the Seven Arts, but which could be approached only by one of his clerks who was son to the king of Sicily. Unfortunately the conversations between the saint and Lucinius are not recorded, but it seems not unlikely that St. Paul shared a common trait of human nature — when he failed to procure Virgil's book, he determined that no one else should have it!

A glancing reference to Virgil as one of the many philosophers who have travelled far afield in search of wisdom might be considered not altogether unhistorical.[18]

Vincent of Beauvais, protégé of Saint Louis, and as ravenous a book-worm as Pliny the Elder, contents himself in the main with repeating his predecessors. In his *Speculum naturale*, finished in 1250, Virgil is an alchemist, along with Adam, Noah, Moses, Cato, Aristotle, and many others; the necessaries of the art are "Sulphur, auripigmentum vituum, Sal Hammoniacum," and the like. The *Speculum historiale*, completed six years earlier, returns to the customary group of legends, with but slight variation. Virgil's bones were buried two miles from Naples. Virgil made a bell-tower which swayed as the bell rang. But, says Vincent, "this does not seem to be true, because the use of bells had not yet been invented." It never rained in Virgil's garden. The *Salvatio Romae* is not significantly different from the one described by Neckam; it is the first of the Seven Wonders of the world. Vincent goes to the trouble of denying a very ancient story, originally based on a widespread misunderstanding of the Fourth Eclogue, and not ordinarily narrated with the group of legends here under consideration, to the effect that Virgil prophesied the coming of Christ.

Vincent's work is of particular interest not only because it was a veritable *Encyclopædia Britannica* to its own time, but because it remained important for nearly four centuries. The complete work, not inappropriately sub-titled *Bibliotheca Mundi*, covers more than four thousand double-column folio pages in the last edition, that of 1624. The *Speculum historiale*, in which the chapters on Virgil appear, occupies about one thousand three hundred pages. A reliable indicator of the regard in which a work was held during the later Middle Ages is the date of the *editio princeps*. The art of printing was but a very few years old when the first edition of the *Speculum historiale* was printed, and before 1500 six more were called for. This huge work of general reference, accessible in one form or another to every literate person for centuries, exercised incalculable influence in the whole field of knowledge, and incidentally transmitted the Virgilian legends to all who could read.[19]

The *Perlesvaus*, written during the first half of the thirteenth century, introduces us to a new device of Virgil's making. It is a turning castle which will never stop whirling until a sinless knight of great courage comes.[20]

Jansen Enikel, with the exception of Wolfram von Eschenbach the first of the writers on these legends to charge Virgil with diabolism, shows some independence of his predecessors. Writing at Vienna, perhaps about 1280, a voluminous versified history of the world some thirty thousand lines in length, he relates a group of legends which we have not before seen. Virgil was wise enough to learn necromancy. He was a pagan, blind to the true faith, and a child of hell. His learning came to him when he found a glass bottle in a garden where he was working, according to his wont. The bottle was filled with devils, whom he released after they had taught him what they knew. His career began when he made a stone woman of magic art. The sight of this image dispelled unchaste thoughts in the minds of all who looked upon it. The statue did its maker little credit, for Virgil began to burn with love for a citizen's virtuous wife, who spurned his riches and his advances, and told her husband, who planned a trick. Virgil, deceitfully encouraged, kept a midnight appointment at the foot of a tower, and was drawn up in a basket; but the basket unexpectedly stopped half-way, and Virgil was left suspended until next day, in full view of the people of Rome. In revenge for the shame of it, Virgil extinguished the fires of the city by the devil's aid, so that the people could neither bake nor eat. The repentant wife was compelled to stand on all fours in public while the people kindled torches at her lightly-clothed person. Naples this child of hell built on three eggs in such a way that if one of them were broken the city would fall. A golden statue portrayed a man pointing with one hand toward a mountain, presumably Vesuvius, while he pointed toward his own stomach with the other. On the statue was engraved the inscription

"Where I point, there is a treasure."

The good people of the town dug about industriously but vainly in the direction of the mountain for this hidden treasure. Finally a drunken man, impatient at the delay, struck the statue and broke it, only to discover the treasure within the broken figure.

In this history of the world the section devoted to Virgil follows a reference to one "Anthyochus," ruler of Rome, the wisest man since Solomon, — a wholly fabulous personage, — and precedes a brief section on Tarquinius, who lived in Nero's Golden House and also ruled Rome. No source other than oral tradition is conjectured for these legends. Enikel's chronicle, then, provides evidence from a new quarter that Master Virgil's deeds were being told by many tongues. Enikel differs from most of the earlier writers in being unlearned. Instead of merely referring fleetingly to the legends, as his predecessors did, he devotes some five hundred lines of very bad verse to spinning the yarns into stories of a sort, and thus he is the first individual to attempt a sustained account of the legends or a consistent characterization of Virgil the necromancer.[21]

About 1280 also, Gérard d'Amiens wrote in the Picard dialect the *Roman d'Escanor*, an episodic romance of the Arthurian cycle in which Virgil's necromantic powers are mentioned in passing, as is the case in a Provençal poem by Guylem de Cervera in which the basket is alluded to, and Virgil is made a riding horse by a woman, in place of the more usual attribution of this experience to Aristotle.[22]

Cléomadès, by Adenès li Rois, is the first romance to relate the legends at length, but it is none the less fairly late, since by 1285, the approximate date of composition, they had been flourishing for more than a century. The legends are introduced by the way, as is often the case. Certain extraordinary gifts — all automata — have just been bestowed. Everyone is amazed at them. Those of feeble understanding ask how such things can be made; but the art of necromancy, everybody knows, is indeed a marvellous thing. Why, look you, Virgil did a great marvel when he founded two castles on two eggs at Naples. One of them is still standing. As a sort of equivalent to the *Salvatio Romae*, Virgil's magic mirror enabled the Romans to see by the reflection in it whether anyone was coming toward Rome or contemplated falsehood or treason. His benevolence prompted Virgil to make an ever-burning fire, which gave great comfort to many folk; but, as usual, there was a joker. Before the fire stood an archer of copper, with bow drawn and arrow aimed directly at the fire. Upon his forehead he bore the words

"If anyone strikes me I'll shoot."

One day a sturdy beggar passing by struck the figure with his club. At once the arrow was discharged and the fire extinguished for evermore. Very ingenious, we agree, were the four great men of stone made to represent the four seasons of the year. They were placed on towers at the four corners of the city, and at the change of spring to summer the statue named Spring tossed an apple of brass to his brother, Summer, and so on.

"Do you know why I have recorded these marvels of Virgil?" asks Adenès rhetorically. "Because," he says in effect, "you can then understand how these other automata came to be contrived; and, anyway, you don't have to believe me unless you like." [23]

Evidently Guiraut de Calanso was right in including the deeds of Virgil when he drew up his list of subjects which the complete minstrel must know, for that fanciful record of rivalry in song, the *Wartburgkrieg*, echoes Wolfram in referring to Virgil's association with Klingsor — now a minstrel — and in particular to the book of magic. It had been Zabulon's book, and Virgil got it at the cost of great trouble. We are told allusively of Virgil's voyage in quest of it to the magnetic mountain set in the sea amidst sirens and crocodiles and griffons. Zabulon, its maker, was a necromancer of Jewish-heathen stock who lived twelve hundred years before Christ. He worshipped a calf and was the first to devote himself to astrology. Virgil had a devil in the form of a fly which had been inclosed in a ruby by Aristotle in order to release the devil from the pains of hell.[24]

A thirteenth-century French manuscript tells the story of "a clerk named Virgil" who made many marvels in the town, including a series of moving statues which remind one of Alexander Neckam's *Salvatio Romae*.[25]

Again and again the Swiss writer of *Reinfrit von Braunschweig* returns to the subject of Virgil's books. In one place, the book, hidden under a stone at the feet of "Savilon," before whom burns a light night and day, was found by Virgil with the aid of the devil in the glass, whereupon an iron figure struck and killed Zabulon with a hammer. At the same moment Christ was born. This takes place upon the magnetic mountain, as in the *Wartburgkrieg*. The two stories are perhaps derived from a common source. In addition, *Reinfrit* alludes to the basket story. Yrkan, the heroine, would not treat her lover as Delilah treated Sampson, or as the lovely Athanata did at Rome when by her deception she caused Virgil to hang aloft.[26]

Virgil as a seer appears in a French song on the death of Edward I (1307).[27]

A scribal error is responsible for Virgil's appearing as an outraged father in *An Alphabet of Tales*, a collection of *exempla* dating perhaps from 1308.

Virginitatem in filia amissam pater aliquando crudeliter punit.
Valerius tellis how Virgillius slew his awn doghter in

þe markett, to þe intent þat hym had lere be callid þe slaer of a virgyn þan þe fadur of a strompett.[28]

Automata figure again in a *roman d'aventure* of the first third of the fourteenth century, *Le Romans de la Dame à la Lycorne*. On a revolving tree barring the way are two fencers of copper made by Virgil "par son bon livre." The tree is guarded by ten knights, and no one save the most loyal can pass.[29]

An Old French manuscript, dated 1311, in the University Library at Turin supplies two new incidents. Virgil prophesies to Nero that his palace will endure until a virgin bears a child. Virgil and Nero then indulge in a long combat of wits, Virgil apparently on the side of the angels, while Nero represents the devil. Virgil at last wins by force of brute memory, summarizing most of the Old Testament, and Nero, as the loser, is decapitated by Virgil. We are outside the usual drift of the legends here, and must ascribe these bizarre adventures to mere caprice on the narrator's part.[30]

One of the multifarious branches of as widely spreading a tree of story as one is likely to find has already embraced Virgil. The *Dolopathos* figure of Virgil came apparently from oral tradition; the one in the Middle English *Seven Sages* is hardly related to the earlier. Collections of tales in which the individual stories are not integrally held together by the plot have a tendency to shift markedly in content. The framework alone is not well calculated to prompt the memory. Random associations come into play, and tales seem to drop in and out arbitrarily. One of the fifteen tales in most of the Middle English and later redactions of the *Seven Sages of Rome* is the story of Virgilius, told by the emperor's wife. All three of the incidents we have already seen in one form or another. There is the ever-burning fire, threatened by an archer bearing on his forehead the words

> Whoso smytes me, knight or swain,
> Sone I sal smyte him ogayn.

A "Lumbard" took umbrage, and shot his crossbow at the archer, who in turn released his bow, and the fire

> Þan slokkend it for euer and ay.

On opposite walls of the town Virgil made two figures of brass which threw a ball to one another.

> Þis was a quaintise, verrayment.

Yet another image he made holding a mirror. In it the Romans could see for a distance of seven days' journey. Thus they were forewarned when anyone planned war. The statue's efficiency irked the king of "Poyle" (Apulia), for he could never catch the Romans unawares. He promised rich reward to anyone who could destroy the image. Two clerks undertook the task. They went to Rome, buried gold under the statue and under a gate of the city, and then told the emperor that they were treasure-seekers willing to share their discoveries with him. The emperor agreed to their request to be allowed to hunt for gold, and next morning accompanied them to the gate, where they dug up the money which they had buried. The emperor, impressed by this proof of their skill, permitted them to dig under the image when the clerks told him that Virgil had hidden his gold there. At night they returned and set fire to the props supporting the image, and it fell. The next day the enraged populace seized the greedy emperor

> And gold and silver þan þai melt,
> And in his mowth and nese it helt;
> in eres and eghen þai helt alswa,
> Ay whiles a drop in wald ga.

The oldest extant manuscript of the Seven Sages in English is dated about 1320. Its influence continued for nearly five centuries. Nine manuscripts are known, and thirty later versions, most of them printed, have been made, dating from Wynkyn de Worde's undated edition of about 1515 to 1814, and perhaps later. Thus there has been a continuity of many centuries in England.[31]

Cecco d'Ascoli, burned at the stake at Florence in 1327, is the first Italian to leave a record of his

interest in Virgilian legends.   In discussing the
proper way to make "images," that is, talismans,
Cecco cites as an instance the image which Virgil
made at Naples to keep the flies away. It was made
while the second aspect of Aquarius was in the as-
cendant, by cutting the likeness of a fly in the stone
of a signet ring. Thus is the marvellous fly ration-
alized! [32]

Virgil was known as both poet and seer to the un-
frocked priest of Troyes who prudently adopted
the disguise of Reynard the Fox in order safely to
satirize the life and manners of his time, the first
half of the fourteenth century. In the earlier part
of *Renart le Contrefait*, written in 1319, we are told
that Virgil was a physician; he wrote "Gioricques"
and "Bucoriques." The author's facts are a little
shaky. He is vague about one "Maro," and at the
next moment tells of Virgil's death at Brundisium
and burial at Naples. They say that of all poets
Virgil was the best. His works are taught to children, according to St. Augustine, because they are
not lightly forgotten. Certain chronicles say that
this Virgil made many marvels — and a list follows
which sounds very much like Vincent's. In the
later part, written between 1328 and 1342, there is
a discussion some three hundred lines in length of a
series of legends which in their turn remind one in
general of those already encountered in the *Image*

du Monde; in addition to these legends, it is said that Virgil made stone conduits underground which conveyed Greek wine from Naples to Rome, and that he made a bridge over the river. Nobody was wise enough to understand what the materials were, whence came the foundation, or how the stone was applied. Finally, Virgil having been buried in a castle "toward Sicily," his person is described, again after the pattern in the *Image du Monde*.[33]

The anonymous author of that part of the *Cronica di Partenope* which concerns us gives the longest list of marvels thus far. This record of early Naples, composed during the fourteenth century — the Virgilian section shortly after 1326 — and attributing some of its information about Virgil to Alexander and Gervasius, repeats most of the older stories — prominent exceptions are those of the basket and of the revenge — and adds a few unimportant ones. The talismans are increased by a copper grasshopper which relieved a plague of these insects. The figure quelling Vesuvius by a trumpet is here altered into one which prevents the wind's spoiling fruits in Virgil's garden. A marble fish serves as a decoy to supply Naples with fresh seafood. Virgil invented war games for the Neapolitans. His magic art was acquired from a book which he found beneath Chiron's head.

In this chronicle we have the first attempt in Italy to construct what might be termed a biography of the legendary Virgil. The author is not satisfied with mere allusions, like many of his predecessors, but goes to the trouble of expanding the laconic notices of some of the early writers into little stories. Virgil the magician is by way of developing into a personality in the hands of this Italian, as he has been already in the hands of Jansen Enikel, of Adenès li Rois, and of the author of *Renart le Contrefait*.[34]

In a sirventes-like satire on Naples, Cino da Pistoia refers to the fly which drove others away. He may have got the story from his friend Cecco d'Ascoli, but it is obvious that there were ample opportunities for picking it up elsewhere by 1330.[35]

With the accomplishments of Virgil described in such works as the *Seven Sages of Rome* and Vincent's encyclopaedia, it is not surprising that a collection designed in its beginnings to recite the deeds of famous Romans should give him his share of attention. The *Gesta Romanorum*, first composed probably not long before 1342 by an unknown clerical author in England, repeats one legend and introduces four new ones. Neckam's account of the *Salvatio Romae* is copied, and the source is acknowledged. A horseman made by Virgil assisted the emperor in enforcing the laws by slaying people who stayed out in the streets after curfew; one of three magical gifts, a piece of cloth made by Virgil's art, transported a person any distance in a moment. Fire fought fire when Virgil thwarted by means of a magic mirror the almost successful efforts of another necromancer, hired by an adulterous scholar, to slay the husband of a woman who would continue her amours unhampered. Finally, in some manuscripts Virgil replaces "a certain philosopher" of most versions in a form of the *Merchant of Venice* story.

A knight of the court falls in love with Emperor Lucius's daughter. For one hundred marks she agrees to permit him to pass the night with her, but the moment he enters her bed he falls into heavy slumber. His ready money gone, he hypothecates his lands in order to procure a hundred marks for a second effort, with the same result. At the end of his resources, the knight borrows a third hundred marks from a merchant, pledging the forfeit of as much of his flesh as will counterpoise the gold if the money is not returned on the date agreed. The knight then asks Virgil for help in the third attempt, and is told to remove a magic object made by Virgil which he will find in the bed clothes. This done, the third venture is successful, and the emperor's daughter begins to love the knight, who in his happiness forgets the term of the loan. Then follows a law suit with details very similar to those in the familiar story of *The Merchant of Venice*.[36]

In *El libro de buen amor* by Juan Ruiz, Archpriest of Hita, the Virgilian legends are introduced after the manner of *exempla*, to point a warning against the deadly sin of lechery. The wise Virgil, "as says the text," was deceived by a lady when she hung him up in a basket. Then comes the usual story of the revenge, but it is followed by two fresh episodes, derived from folk-lore or from the Archpriest's vivid imagination. Virgil made a shining copper floor for the Tiber. To so great an extent does lewdness dominate women folk that the scorned lady of the revenge episode had a circular stairway set with sharp knives, so that Virgil might be killed; but the magician learned of this particular piece of lewdness through his incantations, and all desire for her left him, and he came no more to her. The author, who wrote his *Book of Godly Love* about 1343, played several musical instruments and was thoroughly familiar with the calling of the *jongleur*. Thus his name must be added to the not inconsiderable number of minstrels who contributed to the spread of the legends.[37]

An anonymous German poem of the first half of the fourteenth century, supposed to be by "Klingsor," tells about an image in Rome which bit off the fingers of an adulteress. This image Virgil made by his magic art. A woman suspected of indiscretion could clear herself by putting two fingers into the mouth of the image and asserting her innocence. If she told the truth, all went well. If she did not, the mouth closed and bit off her fingers. The empress of Rome devised a scheme to evade the penalty of her amorous shortcomings. When her master, nervous at the thought of sprouting horns, taxed her with infidelity, she agreed to submit herself to the chastity test. Her lover she directed to clothe himself in rags, so that he could pass as a madman. As she went through the street to the place of the ordeal, the disguised lover pushed his way through the crowd, embraced her with both arms, and kissed her. Fortified by this experience, the empress proceeded to the test. She placed her fingers in the mouth and swore that the only man who had been as close to her as her husband was this fool whom everyone had seen. In triumph she withdrew her fingers unscathed from the mouth, and the emperor begged forgiveness for his false suspicions. The image now bites no more; its power gone, it fell into a thousand pieces. This *bocca della verità*, as I shall call it, is familiar to later writers.[38]

About the middle of the fourteenth century another Italian wrote down some of the legends known to him. In this commonplace book Antonio Pucci varies but slightly from his predecessors. Virgil made a set of chandeliers and a lamp which never wore out and could not be extinguished.[39]

Again toward the middle of the fourteenth century the *Chronique* of Bertrand du Guesclin mentions Virgil's education in necromancy at Toledo, the revenge episode, the speaking head, and the far-sighted mirror.[40]

In view of the wide prevalence of the legends, it is difficult to understand how Petrarch or any other person able to read could fail to know something about them. In spite of his reluctance to believe them — if the well-worn story of his telling King Robert that he did not recall having read that Virgil was a stone-mason is to be interpreted as an indication of reluctance — Petrarch betrays his acquaintance with the story that Virgil made by incantations a passage through the rocks near Pozzuoli, and he mentions the Castle of the Egg. A contemporary commentator on Virgil's *Aeneid*, Cionus de Magnalis, refers to the *Salvatio Romae* as another of Virgil's works, and bases his faith in Virgil's magical powers on the eighth eclogue. Petrarch is echoed by Benvenuto da Imola in his commentary on the *Divine Comedy*, the foundation of the Castle of the Egg being referred to casually. The passage through the rocks could not be taken in time of war, and no robbery could be committed there.[41]

Heinrich von Mügeln, Saxon Meistersinger at courts in Prague and Vienna, who died about 1371,

bases his story of Virgil and the magnetic mountain on the *Wartburgkrieg* account. Virgil was shipwrecked on a magnetic mountain, his ship having
been led thither by two birds called griffons. There
he found the devil in a glass, presumably liberated
him, and by his direction found the book of magic
under a corpse. Beset by eighty thousand devils
out of work, he set them the task of building a road
through solid rock.[42]

Petrarch's apparent aversion to the legends was
not shared by Boccaccio, who repeated certain of
them in 1373–4 in his lectures at Florence on the
Divine Comedy. Virgil, a profound astrologer, was
so fond of Naples that he made there, by astrological art, a fly of brass, a horse of bronze, and a
frowning and laughing face at the Nolan gate, all
for purposes with which we are already acquainted.[43]

Virgil's usual rôle is curiously reversed in the
Somnium viridarii (*Songe du vergier*), for there he
gives advice on the proper education of a prince.
The Lord God revealed that a young prince must
not make images or be an astrologer, and must not
devote himself to mechanical science, i. e. indulge
in manual occupations. A king must not be a rhet-
orician or a logician. Virgil tells the king of the
Romans that in order that his people may live in
peace and tranquillity he must see to it that they

are governed by wise, prudent, and educated men of good counsel.[44]

In his three great literary mirrors John Gower managed to reflect a surprisingly comprehensive view of the later Middle Ages, and the Virgilian legends were not omitted. In the *Mirour de l'omme* the *Salvatio Romae* appears in much the same way as in Neckam's treatise; and the *Confessio Amantis*, some years later, mentions Virgil three times, first in an exemplum against cupidity, where the story of the mirror and Crassus is repeated almost word for word from the *Seven Sages*, and later in two lists of humiliated lovers. In one of these, Love and Youth are depicted as leading their forces to the shrine of Venus. Virgil appears in the troop of Love:

> And there me thoghte I myghte se
> The king David with Bersabee,
> And Salomon was noghte withoute; . . .
> And over this, as for a wonder,
> With his leon which he put under,
> With Dalida Sampson I knew,
> Whos love his strengthe overthrew.
>   I syh there Aristotle also,
> Whom that the queene of Grece so
> Hath bridled, that in thilke time
> Sche made him such a Silogime,
> That he foryat al his logique;
> Ther was non art of his Practique,
> Thurgh which it mihte ben excluded
> That he ne was fully concluded

To love, and dede his obeissance.
And ek Virgile of Aqueintance
I sih, wher he the Maiden preide,
Which was the doghter, as men seide,
Of themperour whilom of Rome;
Sortes and Plato with him come,
So dede Ovide the Poete.[45]

An amusing burlesque of legal procedure at the
end of the fourteenth century in Italy is afforded by
The Lawsuit of Belial against Jesus, a popular mix-
ture of theology and jurisprudence by Jacobus Pal-
ladini de Teramo, churchman in high office in
several Italian cities. The story runs that when
Christ descended to harrow hell he was regarded as
a trespasser and interloper, and was prosecuted as
such by Belial before the celestial court. Witnesses
were of course needed, and various guests of Belial's were summoned. Moses, defending attorney,
lamented when certain witnesses were barred.
Belial inquired why he should lament, since their
testimony would have been thrown out, anyway,
for he knew from a first-hand source of information that Abraham was in hell as an adulterer,
Isaac as a perjurer, David as a murderer, Hippocrates as the slayer of his nephew, Aristotle as a
thief who stole Plato's writings, and Virgil as one
who showed himself a fool when he permitted himself to be exposed by a woman to public mockery.
The case is one to rejoice the lawyer's heart, for

Judge Solomon finally awards the decision in such a way that although Jesus wins, the issue is so befogged that both sides claim the ".moral" victory.[46]

There are no less than five several Virgils in the immense history of the world compiled by the Belgian cleric, Jean d'Outremeuse, about the end of the fourteenth century. These five are Virgil, son of Hector king of Athens; Virgil, king of "Bougie" in Libya, son of Gorgile; Virgil, king of Sicily, son of Alienus; Virgil, son of the prophet Virgil; and Virgil, son of a senator Johans who became the sixty-second pope about the middle of the sixth century. This list alone might conceivably arouse suspicion in an historical mind; but when the deeds of the second, Virgil, king of Bougie, are described, in some thirty-six folio pages scattered through several hundreds, we see plainly that we are in a never-never land devised by the chronicler to divert the readers of his vulgarization of history. To mediaeval romance in general many pages are devoted, and in this author's treatment the Virgilian legends become quite similar to romance.

Virgil, the great scholar, was born at Rome, where his parents had come from Africa, on May 6, 519 — the era is unimportant. On March 6, 526, he went to school on an island, for at that time no one could become a king unless he was a learned man.

In 543 he finished his schooling in Libya because he had learned all that his masters knew. By now a very handsome young man, he set out for Rome, arriving there February 18, 544. He was a great scholar in every branch of knowledge, expert in the Seven Arts, a great philosopher and scientist, and so well versed in Holy Writ that he was able to prophesy the coming of Christ. He was of noble family, and had as fair a body as one may see, — tall, well-proportioned, — save that he was a little stooped in the shoulders, and bowed his head. He had been well taught above all others, was gentle, debonaire, generous, and withal humble; and he cared only about study. Great festivities were held in his honor at Rome, especially by the emperor Julius and the senators, for many of them were of his blood. Virgil understood the amenities of court life, and was much praised by the Romans. News of his perfection came to Phebilhe, daughter of Julius Caesar, and she was straightway sorely smitten with the love of him.

I analyze these details, which occupy approximately one of the total of thirty-six scattered pages devoted to Virgil, in order to indicate something of the nature of Jean's treatment. It is evident that Jean regarded Virgil as a kind of hero of romance, whose *enfances* and accomplishments are of vital interest. This amusing succession of tales would delay us too long were the analysis continued. The stories will be found listed in the table, and some of them will be discussed later. Jean has been bitterly condemned for his untrustworthiness, for, to the student of sober history, as may be easily inferred from the brief analysis above, he is no better than an exasperatingly elusive and versatile liar. Yet if he be regarded as a romancer rather than as an historian he will be found amusingly imaginative. His precise dates for things that never happened, and his extremely exaggerated coloring of actually historical incidents, remind one vividly of Rabelais's method of parodying just such works as Jean's. Perhaps the author had no idea that he was writing romance, not history; but I suspect that his verve and sureness of touch betray his real intention of writing *con amore* to amuse rather than merely edify. After all, some more recent efforts to prank out the dull dry bones of history have been hardly more successful.[47]

In a chronicle finished in 1400, Giovanni Sercambi used the basket story as an *exemplo morale*, the lesson being that humility, in the person of Virgil, conquers pride, in the person of the lady, "Ysifile." The story of Virgil's revenge, the usual complement to that of the basket, is omitted here. As Virgil is being led to execution, he pronounces an incantation over a basin of water, and is whisked away by "spiriti maligni." This story might well fit in a collection like the *Gesta Romanorum*.[48]

Ruy Gonzalez de Clavijo, ambassador of Don Enrique of Castille and Leon to Tamerlane, touched at Gaeta on his journey and saw on the island of Ponza "grand edifices erected by Virgil." [49]

We are now able to survey the progress of our Virgilian legends during two centuries and a half, or from their inception to 1400. With the attempt made by Jean d'Outremeuse to write a complete biography of the thaumaturge extending from his birth to his death, we reach what must surely be the farthest flights of the human imagination on this topic. Certainly the group of legends here under special consideration has developed as far as it can and still retain the coherence which has frequently thus far been characteristic of it. The legends as they occur for the century and a half after 1400, then, will be treated much more summarily. It will be remembered that, in the interest of lucidity, conjectures regarding sources and influences are deliberately excluded from the text of the present chapter. Chronological order — rigorously adhered to also by Jean d'Outremeuse, but with infinitely merrier results — will be maintained so far as possible, and national and linguistic boundaries will be noted only in passing. They are relatively unimportant in the present instance, as the record thus far shows. The four most extensive discussions of the legends have been in the works of a Viennese, of two northerly Frenchmen, and of an Italian.

The unimportance of such boundaries is emphasized by the work of the first Dutchman to hand on any of the legends. In 1411–12, Dirc Potter, in some respects the "moral Gower" of Holland, spent some time on a mission in Rome. When he returned to Holland he had completed his long didactic poem in praise of love, *Der Minnen Loep,* in the course of which he relates the story of the basket and its corollary, the revenge. Potter's influence in Holland may be compared with Chaucer's in England, and the subsequent adaptations of these stories will require discussion later.[50]

Italy again contributes to the history of the legends in a particularly interesting quarter. A versified history of Mantua, finished about 1414 or later by Bonamente Aliprandi, devotes nearly seven hundred lines to the life and works of Virgil, of which approximately two-thirds recount the legends in which we are interested. Aliprandi knew that Virgil's birthplace had something to do with Mantua, and he therefore devotes more attention to the poet and seer than any of his predecessors save Jean d'Outremeuse. The stories of the basket and of the revenge are told as usual, but after the consummation of the revenge Virgil is jailed and makes his escape in a ship which he draws on the wall of his prison. Hospitably received by a poor peasant and his wife, Virgil presents them with a cask which will always supply wine. At a banquet, Virgil causes the dishes on Octavian's table to fly through the air. Melino, his pupil, he sends to Rome from Naples to fetch his book of magic. Melino of course opens it, and a cloud of devils clamors about him. He puts them to work building a road from Rome to Naples. This "Melino" is the Arthurian Merlin. Aliprandi changes the fly-talisman slightly by combining two earlier accounts. Virgil enchanted a fly into a piece of glass, and no flies entered Naples; and by magic also he made a fountain which provided a constant supply of oil.

It is very difficult even now to draw a definite line between actual and legendary biography of Virgil; there is little reason for condemning Aliprandi because he could not, and certainly no reason for condemning him because he included with such biographical details what information he had about Virgil the magician. As a chronicler of Mantua he recorded whatever he could learn about one of Mantua's most famous citizens.[51]

During the second quarter of the fifteenth century a Spanish hero-worshipper wrote a prose *chan-*

son de geste celebrating the deeds of his master. *El Vitorial* of Gutierre Diez de Games depicts the Count of Buelna as first in war, first in peace, and first in the hearts of his countrywomen. By the way is introduced the edifying tale of Virgil's needle. Julius Caesar, disturbed at the ephemeral nature of human glory, consulted with the sage Virgil on ways and means of preserving both glory and mortal remains. The glory was easily assured by naming the month of July after him. An ever-during place of sepulture was more difficult to come by, but it was not beyond the magician's powers. It happened that Solomon, king of Judea, had caused to be made an enormous obelisk as tall as a tower; on its summit his bones were to have been placed in an apple of gold. But somehow his plans had gone awry, and Virgil knew that the shaft lay in a field at Jerusalem. When he offered to buy it a shrewd bargain was struck by which Virgil was to pay a large sum of money for each day that it took him to transport the unwieldy column to Rome. Virgil made strong engines and carts, paid through the nose for a time, but finally, to the amazement of the disappointed vendors, got it all the rest of the way in a single night, and set it up in the square, with the golden apple in place, in which eventually, they say, the remains of Caesar were inclosed with great honor.[52]

In elegiac verses on the departed glories of Rome, John Lydgate, monk of Bury, apostrophises the Eternal City:

> Wher is the temple / off þi proteccioun
> Made bi Virgile / moost corious off beeldyng
> Ymagis errect / for euery regioun
> Whan any land / was founde rebellyng
> Toward þat parte / a smal belle herde ryngynge
> To that prouynce / thymage dede enclyne
> Which bi longe processe / was brouht on to ruyne.

Once again we meet the familiar *Salvatio Romae* in much the same form in which it was described by the first writer to attach these automata to the name of Virgil, Alexander Neckam.[53]

Feminism was just as interesting in the Middle Ages as it is now. It inspired literature of all kinds, then as now. An author was sure of an audience if he wrote against or in defence of women, then, as now. Bad women excited abhorrence; good women excited praise — then, as now. Any author who wrote on feminism during the later Middle Ages was very likely to use Virgil as an example, horrible or otherwise. If he was indulging in a diatribe against women, the treachery of Virgil's lady in suspending him in the basket was to the point; if he was defending them against unfair treatment by men, then her fate in the story of the revenge served his purpose.

Alfonso Martínez, Archpriest of Talavera, in 1438 devoted a work to the exposure of feminine malice. Even a man of Virgil's acuteness and knowledge, which extended to magic, was deceived by a woman — and the basket story follows, accompanied by the revenge, which is here included apparently because of the satisfaction which it gave the author to show a woman being treated as she deserved.[54]

As what might be termed a counter-irritant to the *Roman de la Rose*, Martin Le Franc, regarded by a respected authority as one of the most considerable French poets of the fifteenth century, wrote in the years 1440–42 at Basle *Le champion des dames*, a long poem of which the object is explained by the title. In the course of the lengthy dispute between the Champion and Evil Thought, the latter seeks to prove his point by relating several stories showing that man should flee from womankind. One of these is the double tale of the basket and of Virgil's revenge. "And whoever doesn't believe this had better go and look at the Colosseum at Rome," Martin adds, implying that there the basket episode occurred.[55]

The perennial charm of the *Tale of Two Lovers*, written in 1444 by Aeneas Sylvius, the future Pope Pius II, helped to assure the continued popularity of the most widely known of the Virgilian legends.

In his attempt to answer his own question, "O wretch, whye stryve I agaynst love?" the lover proceeds, in the words of the first English translator:

Loke . . . upon Poetes, Vyrgyll drawen up by a roape, honge in the mydwaye to the wyndowe, trustynge to have enbraced hys love.[56]

An early Swiss humanist and lawyer of Italian training, Felix Hemmerlin, whose name was latinized as Malleolus, used in 1444-45 the Virgilian legends in an original way. In a long satirical dialogue between "Nobilis" and "Rusticus," the former interests the latter in Virgil by implying that the poet had leanings toward the simple life as well as toward necromancy. The nobleman describes the finding of the book of magic, which was written in Chaldaic characters, through the aid of an uncommonly malignant and withal clever spirit which had been shut up in a glass by the seal of Solomon. The spirit offers to teach Virgil how to read the book of magic in return for his freedom, but Virgil is guileful enough to obtain the secret and then to inveigle the spirit into returning inside the glass, which he shuts up forever in a mountain to prevent everlasting trouble. Thus Virgil introduced the art of necromancy in Italy — an art invented by the Persians. It seems that both Solomon (who knew the signs and characters by which demons are put to flight) and Abraham spoke the Chaldaic tongue. Virgil made at Naples, by means of magic, a great round palace, very tall, which still stands; Nobilis saw it himself. Then there are the famous baths which Virgil made of varying colors and odors and properties, the passage under the mountain, through which Nobilis has wandered personally, the fly, the meat-market, the garden, and, in the deep sea near the city, the strong fortress called *Castrum Ovi*. In the midst of this Castle of the Egg is a round bronze pillar with an egg elegantly placed on four columns. Virgil erected it years ago and put a spirit in it. If the egg should be broken in any way, the fortress would sink in the sea, and hence to this day the egg is sedulously guarded. Rusticus is well satisfied with these proofs that Virgil was his kind of man, and the discussion passes on to the Trojan War.[57]

About 1450 John Capgrave, Austin friar of King's Lynn, wrote in *Ye Solace of Pilgrims* an account of a pilgrimage to Rome, in the course of which he describes the *Salvatio Romae*. In the Capitol

uirgile mad a meruelous craft þat of euery region of þe world stood an *ymage* mad all of tre and in his hand a lytil belle, as often as ony of þese regiones was in purpos to rebelle ageyn þe grete mageste of rom a non þis ymage þat was assigned to þat regioun schuld knylle his bell. . . .

and so on, just as Alexander Neckam tells the tale.[58]

With the advent of the printing press, and the consequent relatively cheap production of reading matter, the literature of the later Middle Ages was ransacked in an effort to keep pace with the tremendously increased demand for books. Hence the works printed during the first quarter-century or so following the invention of printing represent in large degree the subjects which interested the men of the thirteenth, fourteenth, and fifteenth centuries — centuries during which, as we have seen, the Virgilian legends flourished. It is not remarkable, then, that these legends should reappear in works published during the "cradle" period of printing, in incunabula.

A compendium of knowledge which in one form or another occupied the attention of printers for three-quarters of a century after its initial publication in 1475 is the *Rudimentum novitiorum*. The Virgilian legends are taken from Neckam; the biographical comments on Virgil and his works are similar to those in the history of Vincent of Beauvais.[59]

In a group of Italian tales about women who have deceived men, of uncertain date, the story of Virgil in the basket of course has its place.[60]

In his famous *Liber chronicarum*, Hartmann Schedel illustrates how close were the biographical

ideas current about Virgil to the conception that
Virgil was a magician. Schedel says that Virgilius
Maro was a great physician, much devoted to the
study of medicine and of mathematics.[61]

Any properly educated young man may be
trusted to fall in love. Once in love, what will be
the proper attitude for him to take toward women?
The rogue in Stephen Hawes's *Pastime of Pleasure*,
finished in 1506, argues against trusting them, and
strives to carry conviction by citing as object
lessons Troilus, Aristotle, and Virgil; the last of the
luckless three is depicted in the two adventures of
the basket and the revenge.[62]

It is something of a surprise to find Virgil's hot
and cold baths reported in a French translation of
Orosius, but the surprise abates when we learn that
the translator expands his source and brings the
book up to date.[63]

Many of the more interesting of the legends were
combined to form the Virgilius *Romance*, written in
prose of perhaps the first quarter of the sixteenth
century, which appeared, with certain variations,
in English, French, Dutch, and, later, Icelandic.
Inasmuch as little is definitely settled about the
Romance, including the date, I refer the reader to
the special discussion in Chapter IX.

Some thirty years ago Professor Johannes Bolte
discovered a hitherto unknown fragment of a Ger-

man chap-book in verse entitled *Von virgilio dem zauberer*, printed about 1520. As Virgil was digging in his garden one day he turned up a glass filled with eighty devils, who promised to watch over him and teach him magic if he would liberate them. The bargain was consummated and Virgil went to Rome, where he applied his new knowledge in the fabrication of a statue of a woman in stone. The basket and revenge episodes follow. Virgil founded Naples on three eggs, and made a statue on which in red gold was the inscription "Where I point is a treasure." One hand the statue held on its mouth; the other pointed in the direction of a mountain. There was a delicate differentiation in this pointing, however; the mountain was indicated by the index finger; with the second finger the statue pointed at its own stomach. Finally, after much digging about in the direction of the mountain, a drunken man, out of patience, struck the statue on the neck, broke it, and found the treasure inside — a piece of luck which the author piously hopes will come to him.

No great difficulty is presented here; obviously the ultimate basis is Jansen Enikel, read in haste or perhaps in a fragmentary text, for there follows immediately the tale of the *bocca della verità*; Virgil has women brought to the statue which he had made long before, and the usual *bocca* story follows.

It seems clear to me that the presence of the first statue in this version is due to the fact that Enikel describes the statue which dispels unchaste thoughts. Somehow the detail escaped the adapter. He introduces the first statue, but does not know what to do with it, and therefore refers to it when he turns to the story of the *bocca*, which does not occur in Enikel.[64]

Possibly as early as 1492 or before is the Spanish *Romance de Virgilios*, a story different from the others that we have seen. Virgil has wronged a lady of the court, and has been sentenced to prison. After seven years the king inquires after him at dinner. The queen is touched with pity, and refuses to eat until the prisoner is released. He is discovered to be a most patient soul, and since the lady whom he wronged still loves him, the two are married forthwith.[65]

An anonymous French "Secret of Natural History" of about the same time depends largely on Gervasius, by the author's own statement, but with certain variations. The ever-burning fire, with archer threatening it, is attributed to "Plinius"; and to the same worthy the author acknowledges indebtedness for a story that in Apulia near Naples there is a palace full of treasure hidden under a mountain "by diabolical knowledge." Such devices are the tricks of the devil to ensnare the avaricious.[66]

Sebastian Franck, partisan and opponent of Luther, humanist, geographer, historian, student of popular literature, traveller, devoted some part of his tremendous energy to the writing of a chronicle in which he surveyed the deeds of Virgil. The account sounds much like that of Vincent, with the addition of the stories of the basket and the revenge.[67]

As his contribution to the perennially interesting strife between the sexes, Gratian Dupont published in 1534 *Les controverses des sexes masculin et femenin*, in which the "bon homme" Virgil, a man of great honor, is shown in the basket — as true as the gospel! Such is the duplicity of womankind.[68]

Published about the middle of the sixteenth century, a collection of tales in English which has been hitherto little noticed provides some of the legends. *The deceyte of Women, to the instruction and ensample of all men, yonge and olde,* is a series of "ensamples" drawn from ancient and modern times to illustrate the devices by which woman evades the shackles imposed by man. Anyone preparing such a collection during the centuries through which we have been progressing would be likely to include the horrible example of Virgil.

An Olde Deceyte of Vergilius

Vyrgyll was a very Wyse and experte man, and was
a mayster of many dyvers sciences ye whiche (as some
men say) the deuel had learned him, and also he was a
wise man of council, in so muche that ye Emperour chose
him to be one of the lordes of his counsell. This Vyrgyl
did many meruayles Wyth Nicromaci for he made a
garden Wherein Were al maner of trees of al fruyte and
fruytes, *and* What time that he Wolde / there they
found euermore rype frute, fayre floures and sede And
also there Was in the garden all maner of birdes, the
whiche songe, nyght and daye. And this garden had no
inclosing but onely the lyght that shone ouer it, and yet
there could nobody come in. Also he made in Rome an
Image of gret light, the which might not fal And they
of Rome might not open nother dore nor window, but
they must nedes se the Image. And who soeuer had
sene that ymage, ye day he shoulde haue had no pleasure for to haue doone the Workes of the flesshe, of the
which the women of Rome wente and shewed Virgilius,
the which at last cast downe the Image. and than the
women had their pleasure agayne. Also this Virgilius
had made in the myddes of Rome to the profyte of the
common people, a lampe of glasse the which shone *and*
lyghted all Rome ouer and ouer, in so much that there
was neuer so smal a strete but it was as lyghte of that
lampe as though there had ben two torches burnynge,
and some men say it stode well .iii. C. yere. And not fer
from thens in an other place he had made a man of copper wyth a bow in his hande, poyntynge wyth hys
arowe to the Lampe. And so it fortuned upon a tyme
the doughters of Rome wente a sportynge in an euen-
ynge, and there came one of the maydens of Rome the
which smote uppon the strynge of the bowe wyth her

VIRGIL IN THE BASKET
From *The Deceyte of Women*, London, 1550?
(Courtesy of British Museum)

finger, and so the arow sprong louse, and shot the lampe in peces the which was greate pitye. . . .

The revenge and basket stories follow, and then that of the *Bocca della Verità*. "Here may ye se how the Mayster Virgilius that was so wise and so crafty in al thynges: and yet he was deceyued of a woman, ye of more then of one, as is rehersed afore." Of these, the magic garden is taken from the English or Dutch version of the Virgilius Romance, the revenge is from a text of the *Image du Monde*, perhaps the translation published by Caxton, and the basket is from the French or Dutch version of the Virgilius Romance.[69]

We come to a close on a sceptical note. Sebastian Conrad, commentator on the first book of the *Aeneid*, does not believe that Virgil was hung from a tower, or that he wished to have his poem burned after his death.[70]

Our brief outline of the development of the legends during the first four hundred years of their existence is now completed. The essential facts are in large part before us. It is easy to perceive that the most influential early contributions are those of Alexander Neckam, Gervasius of Tilbury, Vincent of Beauvais, the *Image du Monde*, and Jansen Enikel; yet, even if other names and works be added to the list, many interesting questions must remain unanswered. Of the answerable ones, a few will be discussed in the following chapters, each devoted to one phase or another of the legends. When the pertinent facts as I have been able to gather them prove insufficient, conjecture will be resorted to, but care will be taken to distinguish facts from hypotheses.

TABLE OF LEGENDS TOLD ABOUT VIRGIL*

John of Salisbury. *Policraticus. Ca.* 1159.

>1. Fly. 2. Virgil's bones sought.

Joannes de Alta Silva. *Dolopathos.* About end twelfth century.

>1. Virgil has a school. 2. Virgil has the gift of prophecy.

Apocalypsis Goliae. Ca. 1180.

>1. Bronze fly.

Alexander Neckam. *De naturis rerum.* Last decade twelfth century?

>1. Virgil's school. 2. Gold leech. 3. Meat-market. 4. Garden with wall of air. 5. Flying bridge of air. 6. *Salvatio Romae.* 7. Virgil's prophecy that *Salvatio Romae* would endure until a virgin should conceive.

Conrad of Querfurt. *Epistola.* 1196.

>1. Naples built by Virgil. 2. Palladium. 3. Bronze horse makes riding-horses strong. 4. Bronze fly. 5. Virgil's bones, in castle overlooking Naples, cause sea to rise if disturbed. 6. Medicinal baths. 7. Serpents

---

* Every occurrence through 1300 is listed. After 1300, casual allusions are not listed.

confined under Ferrean gate. 8. Meat-market. 9. Bronze archer keeps Vesuvius in check.

Wolfram von Eschenbach. *Parzival.* Beginning of thirteenth century.

 1. Virgil a magician.

Guiraut de Calanso. *Fadet joglar.* Ca. 1200.

 1. Virgil protects himself against a woman. 2. Orchard. 3. Fish-pond. 4. Virgil extinguishes fire.

Gervasius of Tilbury. *Otia imperialia.* Ca. 1211.

 1. Brazen fly. 2. Meat-market. 3. Serpents confined near Nolan gate. 4. Two images at Gate of Good and Ill Fortune. 5. Bronze statue with trumpet holds in check volcano overlooking Terram Laboris. 6. Garden. 7. Medicinal baths. 8. Road through mountain. 9. Englishman finds bones of Virgil.

Helinandus. *Chronicon.* Ca. 1216 (1204–29). (See Vincent of Beavais.)

Michael Scottus. *Liber introductorius.* Before ca. 1236.

 1. Virgil a magician.

Maître Goussouin? *Image du Monde.* 1245–46 ff.

 1. Bronze fly. 2. Bronze horse heals sick horses. 3. Naples founded on an egg. 4. Fire extinguished in a city in revenge for insult by a lady. 5. Flying bridge. 6. Garden with wall of air. 7. Ever-burning lamp with archer threatening it. 8. Prophesying head; Virgil's death through ambiguous oracle. 9. Sea rises when Virgil's bones are disturbed. 10. Hammer-men. 11. St. Paul.

Vincent of Beauvais. *Speculum historiale.* 1244.

 1. Virgil buried two miles from Naples. 2. Bronze fly. 3. Meat-market. 4. Swaying bell-tower. 5. Garden in which no rain fell. 6. Baths. 7. *Salvatio Romae.* 8. Virgil not a prophet of Christ.

—— *Speculum naturale.* 1250.

> 1. Virgil an alchemist.

Perlesvaus. First half thirteenth century.

> 1. Turning castle.

Jansen Enikel. *Weltchronik. Ca.* 1280?

> 1. Devils in bottle freed when they teach Virgil necromancy. 2. Female statue curbs lust. 3. Basket. 4. Revenge. 5. Naples built on three eggs. 6. Gold statue of man pointing to Vesuvius and to own stomach; treasure in latter.

Gérard d'Amiens. *Roman d'Escanor. Ca.* 1280.

> 1. Virgil a necromancer.

Guylem de Cervera. "Proverbes." End of thirteenth century.

> 1. Basket. 2. Virgil a riding-horse.

Adenès li Rois. *Roman de Cléomadès. Ca.* 1285.

> 1. Castle at Naples built on two eggs. 2. Medicinal baths. 3. Horse of metal on column heals sick horses. 4. Mirror. 5. Fly. 6. Everlasting fire with archer of copper threatening it. 7. Automata representing four seasons throw apple each quarter.

Wartburgkrieg. Ca. 1287.

> 1. Quest of magic books in magnetic mountain. 2. Virgil has fly-devil in ruby.

MS. B. N., fonds fr. 19525. Thirteenth century.

> 1. Automata resembling *Salvatio Romae.*

MS. B. N., B. R. 6186. Thirteenth century. "Nero's Daughter."

> 1. Basket.

Reinfrit von Braunschweig.   Ca. 1300.

>   1. Quest for magic books in magnetic mountain. 2. Fly-devil in glass. 3. Hammer-man. 4. Basket.

French song on death of Edward I.   *Ca.* 1307.

>   1. Virgil knows magic.

Le Romans de la Dame à la Lycorne.   First third of fourteenth century.

>   1. Automatic fencers of copper.

Turin University MS. L II 14.   1311.

>   1. Virgil prophesies Nero's castle will stand until a virgin conceives. 2. Virgil decapitates Nero when the latter loses flyting contest.

Middle English *Seven Sages.*   Ca. 1320.

>   1. Ever-burning fire with archer threatening it. 2. Two figures of brass throw ball to one another. 3. Mirror undermined.

Cecco d'Ascoli.   *Alcabizzo.*   Before 1327.

>   1. Astrological fly-image.

Roman de Renart le Contrefait.   (A) 1319.   (B) 1328–42.

>   1. Conduits of stone bring wine to Rome. 2. Marvellous bridge over river. 3. Bronze fly. 4. Bronze horse heals sick horses. 5. Mirror. 6. Basket. 7. Revenge. 8. Prophesying head; Virgil's death through ambiguous oracle.

Cronica di Partenope.   Shortly after 1326.

>   1. Subterranean aqueducts. 2. Gold fly. 3. Gold leech. 4. Metal horse heals sick horses. 5. Copper grasshopper. 6. Meat-market. 7. Copper statue with trumpet prevents wind's spoiling fruits. 8. Magic garden with all manner of herbs. 9. Marble fish as de-

coy. 10. Images of Good and Ill Fortune at Nolan gate. 11. War games for Neapolitans. 12. Four prophesying heads. 13. Serpents confined under Nolan gate. 14. Medicinal baths. 15. Road through rocks. 16. Castle founded on egg in glass. 17. Magic book found under Chiron's head. 18. Englishman seeking bones.

Cino da Pistoia. *Rime.* 1330.

1. Fly.

Gesta Romanorum. *Ca.* 1342.

1. *Salvatio Romae.* 2. Automatic horseman patrols streets. 3. Cloth as magic carpet. 4. Magic mirror. 5. Cure for insomnia; *Merchant of Venice.*

Juan Ruiz. *El Libro de Buen Amor.* *Ca.* 1343.

1. Basket. 2. Revenge. 3. Tiber floored with copper. 4. Virgil learns of stairway with knives through his incantations.

"Klingsor." German poem of fourteenth century.

1. *Bocca della verità.*

Antonio Pucci. Common-place book. *Ca.* 1350.

1. Fly. 2. Horse. 3. Castle on egg. 4. Revenge. 5. Bridge over river. 6. Garden. 7. Two inextinguishable chandeliers. 8. Ever-burning lamp. 9. Prophesying head. 10. Virgil's bones.

—— *Contrasto delle donne.* *Ca.* 1350.

1. Basket.

Petrarch. *Itinerarium Syriacum.* *Ca.* 1360.

1. Road through rocks. 2. Castle of the Egg.

Benvenuto da Imola. *Comentum. . . .* *Ca.* 1360.

1. Castle of the Egg. 2. Road through rocks.

Heinrich von Mügeln. *Ca.* 1371.

> 1. Virgil finds devil in flask at magnetic mountain; releases him on promise of help in finding (2). 2. Books. 3. Street made by devils.

Boccaccio. *Comentum.* . . . 1373–74.

> 1. Fly. 2. Horse. 3. Faces of Good and Ill Fortune at Nolan gate.

Somnium viridarii. *Ca.* 1374.

> 1. Virgil teaches prince.

John Gower. *Mirour de l'omme.* *Ca.* 1375.

> 1. *Salvatio Romae.*

—— *Confessio Amantis.* *Ca.* 1390.

> 1. Mirror. 2. Basket.

Jacobus de Theramo. *Processus Beliali.* End fourteenth century.

> 1. Basket.

Jean d'Outremeuse. *Ly Myreur des Histors.* *Ca.* 1400.

> 1. Virgil prophesies the coming of Christ. 2. Two bronze statues mark the weeks. 3. Mirror. 4. *Salvatio Romae.* 5. Copper horseman with balance for weighing. 6. House built in one night. 7. Virgil a lawmaker. 8. Ever-burning fire with archer threatening it. 9. Virgil teaches agriculture. 10. Bronze fly. 11. Virgil converts senators to Christianity. 12. Basket. 13. Virgil shifts shapes. 14. Virgil enchants temple so that women proclaim misdeeds aloud. 15. Virgil slays three kings in battle. 16. Virgil has Caesar's body burned and ashes put in globe atop obelisk. 17. Virgil conjures up armies. 18. Dog appears like Virgil. 19. Revenge. 20. Naples founded on egg. 21. Marvellous bridge. 22. Magic garden with wall of air. 23. Virgil

causes people to shift shapes. 24. Virgil makes invisible walls, mystifies peasant, resuscitates dead asses. 25. Two ever-burning lights and ever-burning lamp. 26. Prophesying head of copper like *bocca*. 27. Automatic horseman patrols streets. 28. Wine and oil conducted from Naples to Rome. 29. Road through rocks. 30. Horse of brass heals sick horses. 31. Castle guarded by flail-men. 32. Virgil makes astrological calculations for Egyptians. 33. Virgil is baptized a Christian. 34. Virgil founds Pozzuoli. 35. Medicinal baths. 36. Shows by enchantment. 37. Magical dinner of eighteen courses. 38. Virgil foresees his death; ambiguous oracle. 39. Virgil makes garden. 40. Virgil makes deceptive chair. 41. Virgil dies, protected by flail-men, in chair, so as to appear alive. 42. Virgil's bones, in castle at Naples, cause sea to rise when disturbed.

Giovanni Sercambi. *Croniche.* 1400.

1. Basket. 2. Virgil's escape by incantation over basin of water. 3. Revenge.

Dirc Potter. *Minnen loep.* Shortly after 1412.

1. Basket. 2. Revenge.

Bonamente Aliprandi. *Cronica de Mantua.* 1414 or later.

1. Basket. 2. Revenge. 3. Escape from prison by drawing ship on wall. 4. Ever-flowing wine-cask given to hospitable couple. 5. Octavian's dishes made to fly from table. 6. "Melino" sent for Virgil's book, opens it. 7. Resulting devils build road from Rome to Naples. 8. Castle of the Egg. 9. Fly-talisman in glass. 10. Ever-flowing fountain of oil.

Gutierre Diez de Games. *El Vitorial.* 1425–50.

1. Obelisk.

John Lydgate. *Fall of Princes*. 1430–40.

1. *Salvatio Romae*.

Alfonso Martínez.   *El Corvacho*.   1438.

1. Basket.   2. Revenge.

Felix Hemmerlin. *De Nobilitate*. . . . 1444–45.

1. Book of magic. 2. Devil sealed in glass. 3. Round palace made at Naples. 4. Medicinal baths. 5. Road through mountain. 6. Fly. 7. Garden. 8. Castle of the Egg.

Stephen Hawes. *Pastime of Pleasure*. 1506.

1. Basket.   2. Revenge.

Les faictz merveilleux de Virgille. First quarter sixteenth century?

1. Marvels at birth of Virgil. 2. Virgil learns magic at Toledo. 3. Virgil walls estates of enemies with air. 4. Hostile army fixed immoveable by magic. 5. Hostile army made powerless by wall of air. 6. Basket. 7. Revenge. 8. Ever-burning lamp with archer threatening it. 9. Garden with singing birds surrounded by wall of air. 10. Fish-pond fed by fountain. 11. Treasure-house underground guarded by hammermen. 12. Female statue curbs lust. 13. Bridge in air over sea. 14. Daughter of Sultan of Babylon visited by means of flying bridge. 15. Virgil makes river of Babylon seem to appear in sultan's palace. 16. Castle of the Egg. 17. Virgil founds schools at Naples. 18. Medicinal bath. 19. Marvellous bridge. 20. Bronze serpent = *bocca della verità*. 21. Virgil by magic spoils water when emperor besieges Naples. 22. Virgil disappears in tempest at sea.

[Additions in Dutch and English translations:] 2a. Devil under board. 7a. *Salvatio Romae*. 7b. Automatic horseman patrols streets. 21a. Virgil attempts rejuvenation.

Von Virgilio dem Zauberer.   1520?

> 1. Glass filled with devils. 2. Female statue curbs lust. 3. Basket. 4. Revenge. 5. Naples founded on three eggs. 6. Statue points to mountain with one hand, holds other in mouth; treasure inside statue. 7. *Bocca della verità.*

Romance de Virgilio (Spanish). 1525 or earlier?

> 1. Virgil is imprisoned for seven years because he wronged a lady. He is released and marries her.

The Deceyte of Women.   Ca. 1550?

> 1. Garden with fruit always ripe and birds singing; no visible protection, yet nobody could enter (= wall of air). 2. Statue curbs lust. 3. Ever-burning lamp threatened by archer. 4. Revenge. 5. Basket. 6. Brazen lion (= *bocca della verità*).

II

THE TALISMANIC ART

EVERY conscientious magician makes talismans. In the days before the head man, the high priest, and the medicine man had sunk to the low estate of master of legerdemain, the talismanic art was piously cultivated. From time immemorial, any effort of man to avert evil or to procure good has been and still is likely to proceed through the use of some concrete object more or less closely resembling a talisman. A survey of talismans in general is thus obviously far beyond the scope of the present chapter.[1] Fortunately, the talismans made by Virgil are of such a nature that we may limit our field of observation to the sort described by the *Oxford English Dictionary* as being, "especially in Byzantine Greece, and in Asia, a statue set up, or an object buried under a pillar or the like to preserve the community, house, etc. from danger." The bronze fly, the gold leech, the meat-market, the palladium at Naples and the enchanted egg, the horse, and the grasshopper — to mention no more — may be broadly regarded as talismans in this more restricted sense. In order to examine these in an effort to determine how the writer of the *Aeneid* ever came to be accused of fabricating them, it is most practical to isolate them and to study the more significant ones separately. Since the fly which kept all other flies out of Naples is the first of these in the order of occurrence, I shall begin with it.

I. MUSCA

It will be recalled that John of Salisbury, the earliest writer to imply that Virgil was a magician, provides the initial version of the fly-talisman story (p. 8, above). Thirty-odd years later it is alluded to in the *Apocalypsis Goliae Episcopi*. Neckam, perhaps significantly, as we shall see, omits it, but all of the other earlier writers mention it — Conrad, Gervasius, Vincent of Beauvais, and the author of the *Image du Monde*. Of these, all who add other legends mention the fly first, with the exception of Conrad, who puts it after the palladium and the horse. The fact that in most of these instances the fly leads off confirms in some degree a suspicion that the story of the fly as told by John of Salisbury may actually have been the first of the Virgilian legends to come into existence.

The variations among these six versions throw disappointingly little light on the question. John of Salisbury is the only writer to elaborate a story about the fly; aside from the by-play of Marcellus and Virgil a-hunting, he says merely that the manufactured fly (*musca*) exterminated other flies. The Goliardic author gives us but a brief glimpse of Virgil "framing flies of brasse." Conrad has it that the bronze fly was placed on the gateway of Naples; as long as the fly remained intact, no fly could enter the city. Gervasius follows rather closely, omitting the reference to the city gate, and adding that Virgil made the fly by mathematical art. Vincent, as always, simply paraphrases: in the gateway of Naples Virgil is said to have made a bronze fly which expelled all of the flies from the city. Finally, the *Image du Monde* introduces a slight variation to the effect that when the fly was set up in the square, it hunted the other flies so hard that they could not come near; if they came within radius of two bowshot, they died.[2] It is not difficult to infer what has happened in this slight progression. Once the fly has been put on the gate of the city (Conrad), the first idea of extermination is somewhat altered, and we have the flies expelled from the city. If they are expelled (Vincent), then comes easily the effort at rationalization in the *Image du Monde*: they are "expelled" by being chased out; but at the same time, the old power of the talisman is retained, for they die if they return. The virtually insignificant changes which took place in this particular legend during the first century of its existence help not at all in an effort to understand what causes prompted its coming into existence; the legend appears to be a unit. Therefore it will be best to return for a moment to its first narrator, John of Salisbury.

In depth and breadth of reading John of Salisbury surpassed most other men of his time. This is another way of saying that he may be expected to have read many of the Latin authors whose works were known in the twelfth century. Among these, Pliny the Elder, author of one of the greatest storehouses of fact and fancy ever brought together, the *Natural History*, was certainly prominent. Occasionally the fly question fell within Pliny's roving vision. It appears that whenever plagues of flies brought pestilence to the people of Elis, they invoked Myagros, "the hunter of flies," by means of a sacrifice, and at once the flies died. While commenting on the absence of birds in some communities, Pliny is reminded that at Rome neither flies nor dogs entered the Temple of Hercules in the Cattle Market. In connection with honey in Crete, it must be told that not a fly is to be found on Mount Carina, and no fly will touch the honey made there.[3]

The reason for the absence of flies in the Cattle Market becomes clearer when we learn that Solinus

says that the flies stayed away because Hercules
had prayed to the Fly-chaser (*Myiagrus*) during
sacrifice there. This explanation is confirmed by
the testimony of Pausanias:

> They say that when Hercules, the son of Alcmena,
> was sacrificing in Olympia, he was greatly plagued by
> the flies; so either out of his own head or by the advice of
> some one else, he sacrificed to Zeus Averter of Flies, and
> thus the flies were sent packing across the Alpheus. In
> the same way the Eleans are said to sacrifice to Zeus
> Averter of Flies at the time when they drive the flies out
> of Olympia.[4]

Both Solinus and Pliny were readily accessible to
John of Salisbury and his contemporaries, and some
relationship between these passages and the fly-
talisman may exist. From banishing flies through
propitiating the fly-god by means of sacrifice, it is
but a step to banishing them by means of the image
of a fly, and it is entirely possible that just this step
was taken at some time or other; but there are no
facts to bear out such an assumption. One bit of
negative evidence is that Pliny and Solinus had
been available throughout the Middle Ages; if they
were the ultimate inspiration of the fly-talisman,
why should its appearance have been delayed until
the middle of the twelfth century?[5]

Not so accessible as Pliny and Solinus to John of
Salisbury, who probably read no Greek, but cer-

tainly comprehensible to many a person in Southern Italy and Sicily, the *Magna Graecia* of earlier times, was an anonymous chronicle-like work of about A.D. 1000 on the sights to be seen at Constantinople, Πάτρια Κωνσταντινουπόλεως.[6] In the discussion of the great number of noteworthy objects at the Byzantine metropolis, certain of them are reported to have been made by Apollonius of Tyana, traveller, philosopher, and thaumaturge of nearly a thousand years before. The particular ones which are of interest in the present connection are brazen insects, among them a gnat (κώνωψ) and a fly (μυῖα). It may be inferred that until they were broken these talismans were efficacious in keeping actual insects under control; but the text is confused. In addition to the gnat (κώνωψ), a mosquito-bar (κωνωπίων) appears also.[7]

If a person who knew Latin read this Greek text, his rendering of the word for gnat, κώνωψ, would be *culex*. Now it happens that one of the poems generally regarded in the Middle Ages as written by Virgil bore precisely this title, *Culex*, — a fact of little enough significance in itself, as there is no hint of talismans in this youthfully pedantic celebration of the heroic deed of the gnat in sacrificing its life to awaken a slumbering shepherd threatened by a serpent; but if we turn to what was in varying forms during the Middle Ages the standard biog-

raphy of Virgil, the life attributed to Donatus, we
find a statement of some interest. The author gives
a list of Virgil's works; among those of early youth
are the *Catalecton*, the *Priapea*, the *Epigrammata*,
Ciris, *Dirae*, and *Culex*. These poems have always
been much overshadowed by the major works of
Virgil, and it is doubtful whether they were more
familiar to mediaeval readers than they are to the
average educated person of today. Vincent of
Beauvais, for a typical mediaeval instance, mentions in his encyclopaedia article on Virgil only the
three great poems. If through lack of association
with their contents the unfamiliar titles of the
minor poems meant little, their predominantly
Greek and learned flavor would tend to diminish
even that little, and when a none-too-well-lettered
reader came to the expression — which actually
appears in the biography —" and he [Virgil] made
a gnat" (*fecit et culicem*), that reader would seize
upon it as at least one fact with which he had an
association.[8]

We might, then, have Virgil pictured as making a gnat; but how associate Virgil with the kind
of talisman-gnat made by Apollonius? In the
Πάτρια Κπόλεως the sixth-century Pope Vigilius
is mentioned as having consecrated one of the
monuments at Constantinople. We have already
observed how Jean d'Outremeuse made a slip —

after all, quite an easy one — between the names
of Virgilius and Vigilius. The latter name would
have been known to relatively few save professed
church historians by the twelfth century, whereas at least the name of the Roman poet was
known to everyone with any pretence whatever
to learning.[9]

One of the difficulties with this hypothesis is that
in the Virgilian legends there is no gnat; the insect
is invariably called a fly — *musca*; but Apollonius,
of course, made a fly, too; and Virgil's fly might
have been patterned after it.

Another possibility is that Virgil's fly was inspired by the presence at Naples or elsewhere —
thus far we have seen no conclusive reason why the
original fly should have been Neapolitan — of a
giant figure of a fly which lacked a satisfactory explanation. If this were associated with the *fecit et
culicem* passage, the same result might be expected.
No such Neapolitan figure is mentioned, however,
until it appears in the fourteenth-century *Cronica
di Partenope*, where the fly is of gold and is as large
as a frog; without the object itself the theory seems
superfluous. It is true that a great variety of
images of human beings, animals, and insects, including flies and bees, can be found engraved on
Egyptian scarabs; and the ubiquitous beetle might
have been misinterpreted as a fly. That scarabs

should turn up in Southern Italy and throughout the Mediterranean region in the twelfth century would not be remarkable, and if such were the case, the necessary materials for the fly-talisman as made by Virgil would be ready.[10]

We have already noted that more than a century and a half after John of Salisbury, Cecco d'Ascoli interpreted Virgil's fly-talisman as an astrological image engraved on the stone of a ring, and related how it was made; but Cecco was applying fourteenth-century talismanical lore, as was Aliprando later when he referred to the fly which, when enchanted by Virgil in a glass, drove the other flies away. Apparently it was not until the latter half of the twelfth century that the art of constructing astrological talismans even became known in Europe. Nearly a century after the appearance of the first Virgilian legends Vincent of Beauvais mentions no talismans of this description. Through these potent images the influences of the stars were controlled, or rather directed in the proper channels, by the magician-astrologer, who made them of prescribed materials at the astrological moment when the conjunction of the planets was favorable to his design. There is little likelihood that the fly as described by John of Salisbury and the other early writers on the Virgilian legends had anything to do with astrological images.[11]

Perhaps it is the Apollonian fly and gnat which turn up, differently attributed, in Evliyá Efendi's seventeenth-century *Narrative of Travels*. In the section "On the wonderful Talismans within and without Konstantíneh" we are told: "At the place called Altí Mermer (the six marbles), there are six columns, every one of which was an observatory, made by some of the ancient sages. On one of them, erected by the Hakím Fílíkus (Philip), lord of the castle of Kaválah, was the figure of a black fly, made of brass, which, by its incessant humming, drove all flies away from Islámból. . . . On another of the six marble columns, Iflátún (Plato) the divine made the figure of a gnat, and from that time there is no fear of a single gnat's coming into Islámbúl (*sic*)." Here there is no question of astrological images, but apparently of figures of giant insects mounted aloft, as in the case of Apollonius and of Virgil.[12]

Probably Aliprandi's idea of the fly came directly from the series of flies reported of Virgil by John of Salisbury and the rest, and had nothing to do with another tradition which seems to have been largely German. Enikel's account — followed closely in *Von Virgilio dem Zauberer* [1520?] — of the discovery of the book of magic involves Virgil's digging up in his garden a glass full of devils, whom he at first takes to be worms. In the *Wart-*

burgkrieg the devil is a fly imprisoned by Aristotle in a variety of "glass," a ruby. In *Reinfrit von Braunschweig*, again, the devil is shut up in a glass vessel; "Savilon" imprisoned him, and Virgil released him only to trick him into reëntering the glass; the precise method by which Virgil fooled him does not appear in the source which he is using, adds the author. Heinrich von Mügeln repeats this story, omitting the ruse by which the devil is once more imprisoned in the flask, but Felix Hemmerlin retains it.

All of these versions call to mind the famous story of the fishermen in the *Thousand and One Nights*. Especially close are the versions in *Reinfrit von Braunschweig* and in Hemmerlin's *De Nobilitate*, where the devil is liberated, divulges his secret, and is then cajoled into returning to his glass cell. In the *Thousand and One Nights*, it will be remembered, the demon had been shut up by Solomon, a personage who in hermetic literature is interchangeable almost at will with Aristotle, the magician who according to the *Wartburgkrieg* confined the fly-devil in the ruby.[13]

II. MACELLUM

The meat-market which preserved flesh presents a curious problem in that it is very nearly unique. So far as I can discover, no other magician ever

thought of fabricating such a highly practical device. Neckam is the first to describe it. Since the
Neapolitans had trouble with spoiling meat, Virgil
shut it up in the market and spiced it with herbs,
and as a result it remained unspoiled for five hundred years. Neckam, be it noted, does not mention
the bronze fly. Conrad includes both. The *macellum*, he says, will keep the flesh of animals killed
in it for six weeks. Gervasius specifies no length of
time, asserting merely that a piece of meat will
remain fresh as long as it is inside the market.
Vincent of Beauvais laconically summarizes, and
remarks that meat did not spoil there. The *Cronica
di Partenope* elaborates. An east wind caused the
meat to spoil, so Virgil suspended pieces of various
kinds of meat in an arch near the old market where
the meat was sold, and as a result all of the meat for
sale kept for more than a week. Sebastian Franck
borrows from Neckam.

It has no doubt been observed that these accounts do not agree with one another. One sup-
poses that Neckam and the rest may have experienced the same difficulty as the modern reader in
visualizing this marvellous agent of preservation.
With no parallels to assist in explaining how the
legend came about, one is driven to consider what
the earlier fly-talisman can have had to do with
this impeccable meat-market. Flies, real ones, and

meat-markets have a very definite, if unpleasant, association. Anyone who has handled or seen meat under other than ultra-modern conditions of cold storage knows that the presence of flies and decomposition has a striking relationship of cause and effect. If Virgil's fly-talisman kept the flies out of Naples, then the meat would remain fresh, if not for five hundred years, at any rate for a few days longer than if the flies had been permitted inside the city. Perhaps this mysterious and unique forerunner of modern refrigeration had its origin in some such process of thought.

The close similarity in spelling of *macellum* and *Marcellum*, especially in the oblique cases, has led to a conjecture that the idea of the meat-market is due to confusion between the two words. If Virgil made a bronze fly for Marcellus, as John of Salisbury affirms, then some such as yet purely imaginary phrase as *muscam aëneam pro Marcello* might have been used. Omit the *r* from *Marcello* by an easy slip in copying, and you have *macello*, "meat-market." Or, again, if we infer that there must be a tradition — as yet not discovered — behind the assertion of the relatively late (1326 or later) *Cronica di Partenope* that Virgil was Marcellus's master, that is, tutor or instructor, then another purely imaginary remark may be conjured up, to the effect that "Virgil taught Marcellus": *Virgilius*

Marcellum instruxit. Omit the *r* here and you have *Virgilius macellum instruxit*, "Virgil built a meat-market." These speculations are both amusing and seductive. Nobody who understands the technique of mediaeval manuscripts will deny that such things could take place; but in the absence of facts in support it is wise to regard these as but happy conjectures at best, and to guess a little more conservatively that the *macellum* is a corollary of the bronze fly with its background in the fly-less Cattle Market of Pliny.[14]

Once Virgil was reputed to have made one talisman, there is obviously no difficulty in extending his imaginary powers to other magic objects, particularly, of course, to talismans. Neckam records a gold leech made by the Mantuan seer. When it was thrown to the bottom of a well, a plague of leeches was relieved at Naples. The plague broke out afresh as soon as the talisman was withdrawn, and only ceased upon its restoration to the well. The *Cronica di Partenope*, nearly a hundred and fifty years later, also mentions "a frog or indeed a leech" of gold which Virgil made under certain constellations — thus, the leech, like the fly, has become an astrological image. The immediate origin of this talisman is probably to be sought in an effort to account for the zodiacal signs and leeches which ornamented the marble top of an actual well, the *Pozzo bianco*, at Naples in the twelfth century. This is perhaps a satisfactory explanation for the legend of the manufacture of the object, but it does not tell why it was Virgil, rather than another magician, who made it. His association with it seems best accounted for by considering the fly-talisman as coming first, and the leech as simply a transfer of the powers which he had already shown in the case of the fly. The fly-talisman is, to be sure, the first of the lot.[15]

Precisely what Virgil did to control serpents at Naples is not clear. Conrad speaks of the Ferrean gate, in which Virgil shut up all the serpents of the district; they were very numerous because of subterranean buildings and vaults, and Conrad's troops feared to destroy the Ferrean gate lest the serpents escape and cause trouble. Gervasius, in a fuller account, mentions a paved street leading to the Nolan gate; "under the seal of this street" (*sub huius viae sigillo*) Virgil shut up all of the dangerous reptiles, whence it happens that poisonous worms are never found within the city. The *Cronica di Partenope* follows Gervasius rather closely in the matter of the paved street and the seal under which were shut up all kinds of serpents and harmful worms, so that they were never seen at Naples unless they were carried in accidentally with litter.[16]

A definite talisman is the copper cricket, mentioned only in the late *Cronica di Partenope*. This cricket imitated the fly and drove other crickets away from Naples. Solinus may have had something to do with Virgil's manufacturing this insect, for he reports that once upon a time, when Hercules was asleep, God silenced forever the crickets of the district.[17]

More interesting to writers who discussed the Virgilian legends during the first two centuries of the life of those curious tales was the bronze horse, first mentioned by Conrad of Querfurt, who says that it was constructed by Virgil with the aid of magical incantations in such a way that, so long as it was intact, no horse would suffer from swayback, — a malady so prevalent in the country that, both before the talisman was made and after it was broken, any horse which bore a rider was sure to develop a broken back.

The *Image du Monde* refers more briefly to the horse; it healed ailing horses of every ill as soon as they looked at it. In *Cléomadès* it is necessary to tie the sick horses to the pillar on which stood the image, which by its healing powers interfered much with the business of the horse-doctors. *Renart le Contrefait* repeats the *Image du Monde* almost word for word. The *Cronica di Partenope* expands to include circumstantial details. Infirm horses had but to look at the bronze horse to be healed. The veterinary surgeons of Naples, much grieved at their loss of custom, broke open the belly of the statue one night, and its virtue departed. In 1322, the *Cronica* goes on, the bronze of the image was melted down to make the bells for the largest church in Naples.

The development of this legend seems pretty simple if the lead given by the ubiquitous Pliny can be trusted. In discussing the *hippomanes*, a substance of widely varying nature, he says that it exerted a powerful sexual stimulus upon living horses when it was mixed with the molten bronze poured into the mold when the statue of a horse was being cast. The finished statue, we gather, was a sovereign remedy against equine impotence.[18]

According to the sixth-century chronicler Joannes Malalas, Apollonius of Tyana made a horse-talisman, and Malalas is corroborated by the geographer Harun ibn Yahya, writing three centuries later, who describes both the talisman and its influence: three bronze horses made by Apollonius were placed on columns at the emperor's gate to prevent the living horses' whinnying and making disturbance. They were so effective that it was not necessary for grooms to hold the mounts outside the palace or even to tie them.

The tradition of this talisman was tenacious, for it is referred to again by Nicephoros Callistos Xanthopoullos in the fourteenth century.[19]

Given a great number of bronze horses surviving from distant times, and the tradition of the *hippomanes* as perpetuated by Pliny, the legend of the talisman made by Virgil is easy enough to understand without having recourse to the similar statue attributed to Apollonius of Tyana; but if we take Pausanias into consideration, it is obvious that the Byzantine thaumaturge probably owed his bronze horse to that same tradition of the *hippomanes*, and therefore possibly both Virgil and Apollonius were credited with such figures because the *hippomanes* story was current, and was of course likely to adhere to the reputation of any famous magician.

The Virgilian legend of the bronze horse does not appear to me to be one of the original legends related of Virgil. Before it could be attached to the name of the poet he must have acquired some reputation as a necromancer. In the development of this legend, therefore, I look in vain for light on the question why Virgil came to be regarded as a magician.[20]

III. OVUM INCANTATUM

An unusual sort of talisman was the egg supposed
to have been made by Virgil to protect the fortress
thence called *Castel dell' Ovo*. Since its nature has
been ill understood, a careful examination of this
egg is in order. The legend appears for the first
time about the middle of the thirteenth century,
almost a hundred years after the beginning of the
whole cycle of legends, and it is therefore of slight
importance in the search for the reasons underlying
Virgil's metamorphosis from poet to magician.
From the *Image du Monde* we learn that Virgil
founded a great city on an egg in such a way that
when anyone moved the egg the whole city shook,
and the more the egg was shaken the more the city
trembled. The cage in which the egg was kept is
still shown at Naples, say those who have been
there and seen it.

No clear idea of the egg results from these remarks. There seems to be a contradiction: the city
was founded on an egg, and yet that egg was kept
in a cage. If the city had been founded literally
upon an egg, we might infer that the egg would
have been buried in the foundation somewhere, and
not kept above ground in a cage where people could
see it.

A few decades later, Jansen Enikel says that Virgil built a city named Naples and hung it on three eggs, so that if anyone broke them the city would sink. They preserve the egg — the number shifts unexpectedly — carefully in the city. Whenever anyone tried to seize the egg, the city trembled from top to bottom, houses and all. If the city was *hung* on three eggs, there is no question of their having been used as the foundation; they must have been elevated somehow. The fact that *three* eggs are mentioned may be significant, although the number immediately shrinks to one when the guarding of the talisman is mentioned.[21]

Confusion becomes worse confounded in the *Roman de Cléomadès*: Virgil made a great marvel when he set two castles on two eggs in the sea and arranged them in such a way that if one of the eggs were broken, the corresponding castle would sink. Somebody tried the experiment, and one of the castles did sink. The other one is still at Naples, and so is the egg on which the castle is founded. If these eggs had been sunk deeply in the foundation, as the text seems to imply, how could they have been easily susceptible of breakage, or easily visible?

Antonio Pucci refers casually to the egg, but we again have occasion to be grateful for the circumstantial details supplied in the earliest part of the

Cronica di Partenope. The rubric for the passage on the Castle of the Egg runs: "How Virgil conserated an egg, had it put in a bottle, and conserved it in the Castle of the Egg, and how the said castle should endure as long as the egg." In the sea, on a rock near the city of Naples, Virgil built a castle, which is still there and is called *castello marino*, or of the sea. By means of his arts he consecrated in the castle an egg, the first laid by a certain hen, and this egg he inserted in a bottle through the very slender neck. This bottle he then put inside a cage, and the cage he put in a little room placed under the castle. This room, secret and well closed, was guarded with great solicitude and diligence, and from this egg the castle takes its name. The ancient Neapolitans maintained that upon the egg depended the fate and fortune of the castle, which would last as long as the egg was kept safe and sound; and therefore it is well guarded.

Now this series of things within things — the egg within a bottle, the bottle inside a cage, the cage inside a guarded room, the room inside a castle — does not give the impression that the egg had much to do with the foundation of the castle. In fact, the implication may be that the talisman was placed thus elaborately *after* the castle had been built. Another local source, an anonymous Neapolitan manuscript roughly contemporary with the *Cro-*

nica di Partenope, fails to point to a relationship between the egg and the foundation. It is said, runs the manuscript, that Virgil shut up an egg in a glass bowl, and that the fate of the city of Naples depends upon it.[22]

In the fourth part of the *Cronica di Partenope*, written not long after 1382, the story is carried farther, with no mention, however, of Virgil — although any reader of the work would be certain to recall the circumstantial details just summarized. Queen Joanna I, it seems, had the "Castello de Louo" rebuilt; for prophecy had it that in the aforesaid castle was an egg, placed inside a bottle; and if the bottle and the egg were broken, the castle would fall. It very nearly turned out so, for when Messer Ambrosio, bastard son of the Duke of Milan, escaped from this castle, where he had been imprisoned, he broke the aforesaid egg. Thereupon the ancient battlements of the said castle fell with a crash; but Queen Joanna had them erected again, firmer and more beautiful than before. And since she was mindful of the name of the castle, she had the egg (miraculously made whole again?) inclosed in a glass container fairer and more subtly wrought than before.[23]

Pucci, Petrarch, and Benvenuto da Imola refer to the egg only in passing, but the genial and garrulous Jean d'Outremeuse gives more precise information. In the year 551, on the eleventh of July, Virgil commenced to found the city of Naples by the sea. It was magnificently built on a harbor and on an ostrich egg. This egg he placed afterward on a carved pillar in a castle which he founded near Naples,[24] and which he called the Castle of the Egg. It is still there, and they say that the city trembles if anyone moves the egg. Again the talisman seems to have a double function, as something of power for the construction of the city, and, the construction completed, as an object of virtue in the castle itself. It will be noted that this ostrich egg was kept on a pillar, presumably where it could be seen.

Aliprandi and Benvenuto da Imola again merely allude to the castle. Felix Hemmerlin, however, who had lived in Italy, elaborates. At Naples, near the city, in the sea, he writes, there is a very strong castle called the Castle of the Egg. In the centre of it is a round bronze ball or egg elegantly placed upon four columns. This egg was cleverly set up by Virgil, and it contains a demon (*spiritum*), for if the egg should be broken in any way, the castle would straightway sink into the sea; therefore to this day the egg is very carefully guarded. Here there is no implication that the egg was used in the foundations in any way; it was exposed on high, and therefore, since the safety of the castle was bound up in it, a watch had to be maintained. Yet the tradition is far from consistent, as has already been seen, and as the Virgilius Romance shows further.

In the French version of this Romance we are told that the city of Naples was founded on an egg by Virgil, and that the same worthy built a square tower at the summit of which he made an *ampulla*, or vial, by enchantment, and a piece of iron-work so that no one could take it away without breaking it. Inside this piece of iron-work he put a device of some kind, and inside that he put an egg. Then he suspended the *ampulla* by the neck in a chain, and it still hangs there. If it should be moved, the city would tremble, and if it were broken the city would sink. In the Dutch version — translated closely in the English — some amusing changes occur which illustrate how legends may alter in mystifying ways, and how at least one mind met some of the problems which we are attempting to solve. The Englishman wrote:

Than he [Virgil] . . . thought in his mynde to founde in ye myddes of the see a fayer towne with great landes belongyng to it And so he dyd by his cunnynge, and called it Napells. And the fundacyon of it was of egges and in that Towne of Napells he made a tower with .iiij. corners and in ye toppe he set a napell upon a yron yarde and no man culde putt a waye that apell with out he brake it. and thorowghe that yron set he a bolte, and on that bolte set he a egge And he henge the apell by

THE CASTELLO DELL'OVO TODAY

the stauke apon a cheyn and so hangeth it styll And whenne the egge styrreth so shulde the towne of napels quake and wha*n* the egge brake than shuld the towne synke. . .

Not understanding what an *ampulla* was, the Dutch writer converted it into something that he did understand, an apple. If you hang up an apple, the obvious thing to hang it by is the stem; so what was the neck of a glass bottle or vial becomes the stem of an apple. The usual contradiction prevails between the founding of the city upon an egg or eggs, and the subsequent transference of the same egg to act as a talisman protecting the castle. As in the *Cronica di Partenope*, the egg is protected by various coverings, and is hung up in an elevated position.

This detailed examination of the stories told about the egg demonstrates that the various writers were passing along a tradition which they did not themselves understand. From its inception in the *Image du Monde*, in the middle of the thirteenth century, to its last retelling in the Virgilius Romance, nearly three centuries later, confusion and contradiction prevail. If we can see through these versions to a common idea or core of fact, we seem to visualize, somewhat hazily indeed, an egg as a talisman first involved in the foundation of Naples, and then elevated or suspended somehow in a castle the safety of which depends upon the scrupulous preservation of the egg against damage and even against being touched. In some instances, the egg is protected by inclosure inside a series of receptacles within receptacles, much after the manner of safeguarding saints' relics. The similarity, however, provides no clue, since, in spite of the extraordinary versatility of mediaeval saints and of the wide variety of the relics which they left behind them, there is no record of venerated eggs.

Historically, there was, and for that matter still is, a building at Naples called *Castello dell' Ovo*; but unfortunately for the purposes of this inquiry, the present name of the building in question is not mentioned until the middle of the fourteenth century, a full hundred years after the beginning of the legend in the *Image du Monde*.[25]

Evidently the difficulty about the egg is not solved by historical evidence; but before we abandon it to the fate of Humpty Dumpty, a second glance at the legends may enable us to proceed a little farther. We have one egg, three eggs, two eggs. The author of the *Cronica di Partenope* thinks that it was the first-laid egg of a hen; perhaps he considered it as important to distinguish the egg in some manner, and the first-fruit of a pullet might possess a magic quality lacking in other eggs. The idea is not found elsewhere with reference to

Virgil's egg, however, and I have not pursued it. Jean d'Outremeuse, the only other writer to specify the kind of egg involved, says that it was an ostrich egg. At first sight, such a statement seems quite as arbitrary as that in the *Cronica*; but the fact is that there is a considerable body of tradition and myth about ostrich eggs. So considerable is it, and so confused, that the skill of the practised mythologist would have to be applied before the twisted strands of bygone beliefs could be arranged in sufficiently orderly fashion to present a clear picture, or series of pictures, of what the ostrich egg stood for in the minds of men in the past.

In ancient Greece and Italy, ostrich eggs are known to have been placed in tombs; for what purpose, is not quite clear. One scholar has conjectured that they were supposed to give strength to the dead.[26]

Whatever the intention in ancient Greece and Italy, somewhat similar customs prevailed, and continue to prevail, in the Mohammedan world. In pre-Islamic Arabia, near Mecca, a sacred tree was worshipped at a yearly festival, when ostrich eggs and other offerings were hung upon it.[27]

For some centuries ostrich eggs suspended in dark mosques, churches, and mausoleums have been observed by the sharp eyes of travellers in and about the Near East. The earliest testimony which I have seen is that of Laurence Aldersley, in 1581, included by Hakluyt in his collection. "There is also the chappell of the sepulchre, and in the mids thereof is a canopie as it were of a bed, with a great sort of Estridges eggs hanging at it, with tassels of silke and lampes."[28] Sir Thomas Browne reports having seen such eggs, "some painted and gilded," hanging in Greek churches.[29]

A survival of Mohammedan influence in another quarter is recorded about 1730 by a Spanish writer on folklore, who says that it was the custom in Spain to hang up an ostrich egg or two above altars in churches. He cites two at Burgos.[30]

At Mount Athos

From the drum of the cupola hangs an elegant brass coronal, and from this are suspended silver lamps, small Byzantine pictures, and ostrich eggs, which are said to symbolize faith, according to a strange but beautiful fable, that the ostrich hatches its eggs by gazing steadfastly at them.[31]

Another probable survival of Mohammedan influence occurs in Coptic churches in Egypt, where the eggs appear in great profusion. We are told that in the choir of a church between Cairo and Old Cairo,

Before the sanctuary-screen hang six silver lamps ... with ostrich-eggs over them: there are twenty eggs without lamps but mounted in metal with a little metal cross above and pendants below. ... The ostrich-egg is a

curious but common ornament in the religious buildings
of the Copts, the Greeks, and the Muslims alike. It
may be seen in the ancient church of the Greek convent
in Kaṣr-ash-Shamm'ah, and in most of the mosques of
Cairo, mounted in a metal frame and hung by a single
wire from the roof. In the churches it usually hangs before the altar-screen. . . . Here and there it hangs above
a lamp, threaded by the suspending cord, as in the
church of the Nativity at Bethlehem: and sometimes it
hangs from a wooden arm, as in the Nestorian church of
At-Tâhara at Mosul. . . . Sometimes instead of the
eggs of the ostrich, artificial eggs of beautiful Damascus
porcelain, coloured with designs in blue or purple, were
employed. . . . The 'griffin's egg' [= ostrich egg?] was
a common ornament in our own mediaeval churches.
In an inventory of 1383 A.D. no less than nine are mentioned as belonging to Durham cathedral . . . hung up
before the altar or round St. Cuthbert's shrine. . . . In
some chancels special aumbries with locked gratings
were provided for them. . . . Some think that the egg
was regarded as emblematic of the resurrection. An entirely different explanation of the symbol, current
among the Copts themselves, was given to me by the
priest of Abu'-s-Sifain. In contradiction to common belief, he said that the ostrich is remarkable for the cease-
less care with which she guards her eggs; and the people
have a legend that if the mother-bird once removes her
eyes from the nest, the eggs become spoiled and worth-
less that instant. So the vigilance of the ostrich has
passed into a proverb, and the egg is a type reminding
the believer that his thoughts should be fixed irremov-
ably on spiritual things.[32]

Perhaps as satisfactory an explanation as can be
given for the suspension of these ostrich eggs is that
advanced by F. W. Hasluck, whose brilliant infer-

ences have contributed much to our knowledge of
the folklore of Asia Minor:

The original purpose seems to have been prophylactic,
... though, as often, more elaborate explanations have
been invented. Primarily an egg is said to be sovereign
against the evil eye because it has no opening and is, so
to speak, impregnable; ... ostrich eggs mounted as
charms are generally held in a metal frame, not pierced
for a string. ...[33]

Certain similarities — perhaps purely accidental
— may now be noted between things said about
Virgil's egg and the observations of travellers concerning ostrich eggs in buildings. The authors of
the *Image du Monde* and of the earliest part of the
Cronica di Partenope say that the egg was in a cage.
Two modern writers have noticed that the ostrich
eggs are suspended in frames of metal, and one of
these speaks of "griffin's eggs" in cages.[34] If we
make sufficient allowances for garbling in transmission, it seems possible that something like the
metal frames designed to hold ostrich eggs may
have become transformed into the cages referred to
by the writers of the legends; and if the metal
frames themselves were placed *on* objects, instead
of being suspended, we might have the starting
point for the stories of Jean d'Outremeuse and
Hemmerlin, to the effect that the egg was set on a
pillar or a platform supported by pillars, or of the

Romance, which refers darkly to the egg as reposing on a bolt running through "a yron yarde."
There is also the definite statement by Jean d'Outremeuse that the egg *was* an ostrich egg; yet we are
far from proof that he spoke truly, for I have been
unable to turn up any authentic record that ostrich eggs were suspended in buildings during the
thirteenth or fourteenth century, when the legends
were being written.   It might be assumed that
ostrich eggs continued to possess some power or
other in the eyes of men from pre-Islamic times or
earlier to the sixteenth century; but assumption is
not proof.

No more convincing proof can be adduced in
support of another theory, to the effect that Virgil's
egg was originally intended as a foundation sacrifice
to insure the safety of a building. Attractive and
perhaps more inherently probable at first sight
than the other hypothesis, the case for Virgil's egg
as a substitute for human sacrifice becomes unconvincing when we learn that the evidence for such
substitutes is slight, scattered, and of no great age.
Moreover, the legends themselves, if all of them are
considered, bear out this conjecture very slightly.[35]

The most interesting of the Virgilian talismans
have now been considered, and we pass on to another kind of story.

III

SAINT VIRGILIUS?

IF IT is true that every conscientious magician makes talismans, it is just as true that no reputable saint ever departs from this mortal world without leaving behind him for the consolation of the faithful a number of relics, great or small. According to half a score of writers, Virgil's bones were regarded with considerable respect and interest by Neapolitans during the later Middle Ages. Does this indicate that Virgil was regarded as a saint?

John of Salisbury, earliest reporter on Virgil the necromancer, alludes twice to the extraordinary proclivities of the poet-seer. We have already examined the fly-talisman, and turn now to John's preachment on the illogicality and hence sinfulness of attempting the impossible, for only to the Most High are all things possible. The moral is pointed by the folly of a certain Stoic named Ludowicus, who made an exile of himself for many years, and, in spite of vigils and fasts and much labor, finally failed in his effort to take back to France the bones, rather than the spirit, of Virgil.

This allusion informs us merely that Virgil's
bones were supposed to have been regarded as valuable and accessible by a Frenchman at some time
before 1159. We are not even told whether Ludowicus found the bones. The point of the passage in
John's eyes was that the man was attempting the
impossible. The chief interest for us John ignores.

One of the sights of Naples about which Conrad
of Querfurt wrote in his letter to the people at home
in Hildesheim was the bones of Virgil, which were
kept in a castle surrounded by the sea. If these
bones were exposed to the air, clouds came up, the
depths of the sea were disturbed, the waters rose,
and a tempest raged. These things Conrad does
not attempt to explain. "We have seen and tested
them," he says, and that is all.

Much greater detail we find in the *Otia imperialia*
of Gervasius.[1] During the reign of King Roger of
Sicily (historically, 1130–54) an English scholar
obtained from the king letters authorizing him to
seek for the bones of Virgil. The people of Naples
made no objection to the search, as they thought
the bones could not be found; but through his art
the scholar found them beneath a tumulus in the
middle of a mountain. At Virgil's head was a book
in which was written the *ars notoria* along with
other similar matters. The Englishman took the
book and the bones, but the Neapolitans feared

that, in view of the special affection which Virgil once upon a time had for the city, some awful disaster (*enorme damnum*) might befall, and they elected to risk ignoring the king's wishes rather than to expose the city to·destruction by obeying them, for they were of the opinion that Virgil had planned to be buried secretly in the tumulus, lest the removal of his bones cause the destruction of his works of artifice. So the "magister militum" and a mob of the people gathered together the bones in a bag, and transferred them to the Castle of the Sea at the edge of the city, "where they are shown through an iron grill to anyone wishing to see them." To inquiries concerning his intentions if he had actually got the bones, the scholar answered that by means of his conjurations the bones would have divulged the whole art of Virgil, and that he should have been content to have control of the bones for forty days. The scholar departed with only the book, "and we ourselves have seen certain excerpts from that book through the aid of the venerable John of Naples, cardinal in the time of Pope Alexander, and have made experiments satisfactorily establishing their value."

We may well wish that we could share some of the experiments of Gervasius, if only to learn the real facts about these legends. We may perhaps question the absolute veracity of this author, but the facts remain that his is the fullest account that we have of this matter, that his reasons for falsification of his source here — if he does falsify — are not plain, and that his story can be related to historical facts with some small degree of plausibility, as we shall see later. His source was not the same as Conrad's, for we may be sure that Gervasius would hardly have omitted some reference to the storm attendant upon the disturbance of the bones, if he had known of it.

The first version in verse of the *Image du Monde* conveys the impression that Virgil was buried outside Rome somewhere in a castle near a city and near the sea, in the general direction of Sicily. His bones are still there, rather more carefully guarded than the bones of most people. Move them, raise them in the air, and the sea rushes toward the castle. The higher the bones are raised, the higher the waves leap, until the point is reached where the castle would be overwhelmed unless the bones were lowered; and the moment the bones are replaced the sea subsides. This has often been tested; the power yet endures; "so say those who have been there." The second version in verse of the *Image du Monde* adds the story of St. Paul which has been mentioned in Chapter I. All that Vincent of Beauvais knew about this question was what the Middle Ages in general knew, the statement in

Donatus's biography that Virgil was buried two miles from Naples. Then there is silence for nearly a century. Andrea Dandolo, writing a Venetian chronicle about 1339, repeats in brief summary what Gervasius said.[2]

We can see how the vagueness of the *Image du Monde* might give the impression that Virgil's tomb was near Rome, in the general direction of Sicily. Antonio Pucci's commonplace book says that Virgil was buried in a castle outside Rome, and that his bones are still there. Like others before him, he goes on to tell the story of the storm.

The *Cronica di Partenope* also puts Gervasius under contribution, changing only a few details. King Roger's letters are to the *university* of Naples, and demand that the institution turn over the book and the bones. When they were found, the bones were deposited in a leather bag in the "Castello dell' Ovo," where they were shown, "like the relics of a saint," behind an iron grating.

The *Image du Monde* perhaps furnished Jean d'Outremeuse with information, for in the great Belgian mirror we see that St. Paul declared Virgil to be a believer, after he had read a letter left by Virgil in his cabinet. He took over all of Virgil's books, put his bones and the letter in a coffer, and ordered the people of Naples to guard it carefully and never to look inside. The coffer was deposited in Virgil's house, which he had built on the sea in the manner of a castle. There they are still, and produce storms in the way that we have already seen described by earlier authors.[3]

In these legends of the power of Virgil's bones, it is apparent that there are but three at most that are independent, — those written by John of Salisbury, Conrad of Querfurt, and Gervasius of Tilbury. The combination with the St. Paul story in the *Image du Monde* and later does not affect materially the legend that we are examining. Now these three writers are all rather early, the latest of them writing within fifty years or so of the earliest, — a fact which is worth noting here, for to examine a tradition which is moderately clear and at the same time has had a productive life of only half a century is a relatively simpler task than to unravel the centuries-old confusion of some of the other legends.

Although we look in vain for historical substantiation of the Virgilian legends, certain material preserved by twelfth-century historians can perhaps be brought to bear effectively upon the legend concerning the power that resided in Virgil's bones.

Alexander, abbot of Telese (some forty miles northeast of Naples), devoted a chronicle of the years 1127–35 to the deeds of Roger II of Sicily — that same Roger, apparently, from whom Gerva-

sius of Tilbury says the English scholar received
letters authorizing him to search for Virgil's bones.
The chronicler knows nothing, or at any rate says
nothing, about Virgil's bones. He does remark, in
the dedication to King Roger, that Virgil had received the reward of Naples and the province of
Calabria for writing a pair of verses.[4]

Roger celebrated his coronation at Palermo in
1130 with most elaborate ceremonials, which impressed Alexander greatly. During the same year
he received the submission of Naples from its
"magister militum," Sergius, who feared the power
of Roger. Naples, says Alexander, had since the
decline of the Roman Empire scarcely ever been
subdued by force of arms — and now it yielded
merely at Roger's word![5] But Southern Italy was
in such a state of guerilla warfare, with the balance
of what power there was fluctuating incessantly,
that Naples, and with it the whole province of
Apulia, rebelled once more in two years against the
power of the Norman ruler of Sicily. Roger ravaged the rest of Southern Italy almost at will, but
Naples seemed somehow exempt from the general
rule, and defied the invader repeatedly. A fleet of
sixty vessels attacked Naples only to be repulsed;
but Roger's Saracens had wasted the countryside
so severely that Sergius thought best to make a
"voluntary" peace with the Norman.

In the spring of 1135, Naples revolted again. The city's reputation for impregnability encouraged the inhabitants of the country round about to take refuge inside the walls. Again the surrounding territory was pillaged and burnt, and siege was laid to the city itself. But summer heat came on and brought with it plague and pestilence, and Roger found it impossible to hold his murmuring soldiery longer at the walls.[6] In the following September Roger made another naval attack in apparently invincible force, but a sudden storm scattered his fleet, and yet again Naples was providentially saved from armed entry.[7] During much of this time, and through the year 1136, Naples remained blockaded. Another voluntary submission was made in 1139, and at last in 1140 Roger made his solemn entry; but once again the sting of defeat was avoided, for the king ornamented his triumph by dispensing favors to the nobles of the city.[8]

Such, in brief, were the vicissitudes of Naples during this decade of contests with its unwillingly acknowledged overlord, whose train of mercenary Greeks and Normans and Saracens pillaged and burned the rest of Southern Italy mercilessly and almost resistlessly, while the city of Naples seemed to bear a charmed life, and time after time escaped fire and the sword through the merest accidents. We have no record, of course, of the effect of the

experiences of this extraordinary decade upon the
people of the city; but that some means would be
devised to account for the continued immunity of
Naples we can be sure. The people would have done
so in the twelfth century as they would in the twentieth. Roth, in the article already referred to, believes that the story told by Alexander of Telese is
sufficient to explain the growth of the legendary
effectiveness of Virgil's bones. Alexander thinks
that Virgil had been lord of Naples, Neapolitans felt
the need of accounting for the immunity of their
city in its struggles with Roger, and so the story
arose.

We are distinctly in the realm of conjecture here,
and when Roth goes on to suggest that Roger really
did send the Englishman to steal the benevolent
bones of Virgil, so that Naples would then fall an
easy prey to the Norman king's mercenaries, we
are inclined to agree that, lacking a more plausible
hypothesis, this one is not untenable; but there is
another possibility which in my opinion tends in a
manner to substantiate Roth's suggestion.

When the father and the uncle of Roger II,
Roger I and Robert Guiscard, invaded Sicily in
1061, they embarked on a struggle which lasted for
almost thirty years. Mohammedan rule had become decentralized, and thus their conquest was
made possible through a combination of bravery

and scheming. The "Norman domination" of which the historians speak involved a relatively small number of Normans. It was through courage and leadership that they were enabled to make headway, both in Italy and in Sicily. Lack of numbers, then, to a certain extent, imposed upon them of necessity the chief glory of Norman rule in Sicily — broad toleration of creeds and races.

Uniting under their strong rule the Saracens of Sicily, the Greeks of Calabria and Apulia, and the Lombards of the south-Italian principalities, the Norman sovereigns were still far-sighted and tolerant enough to allow each people to keep its own language, religion, and customs, while from each they took the men and the institutions that seemed best adapted for the organization and conduct of their own government.[9]

Sicily, the meeting ground of many races from prehistoric times, continued to harbor peoples of many tongues and many religions during the later mediaeval centuries. One of these tongues was Arabic, and one of the religions the Mohammedan; but when Arabic came in it did not eliminate Greek elements, nor did the Norman invasion in its turn obliterate either Greek or Arabian customs. Sicily, then, in a peculiarly vivid sense illustrates the truth that folklore consists of "the wrecks of all the cultures of the world." One bit of tradition in Sicily is pertinent here.

For the year 972, an Arabian chronicler writes

that at Palermo there was a mosque, once upon a time Christian, in which was to be seen a great sanctuary.

I have heard said by a certain logician that the philosopher of the ancient Greeks, or Aristotle, lies in a wooden box hung in this sanctuary, which the Mussulmans have changed into a mosque. The Christians greatly honored the tomb of this philosopher, and used to invoke rain from him, believing the tradition left by the ancient Greeks about his great excellence in intellectual matters. The logician said that the box was always suspended there in mid-air, because the people would run to pray for rain, or for the public safety, and for deliverance from all of the calamities which induce man to turn to God and propitiate Him; such things happen in times of famine, pestilence, or civil war. In truth I saw up there a great box of wood, and perhaps it contained the tomb.[10]

Roger II, the most powerful enemy of Naples, had himself crowned at Palermo. Palermo possessed the bones of Aristotle. In these bones resided supernatural powers which could be called into use in time of civic emergency. To anyone familiar with the ways of the folk, the next conjecture is inevitable. In Aristotle, "the master of those who know," the city of Palermo, and hence its ruler, possessed indeed a redoubtable tutelary genius. Naples needed help more than human; it appeared to owe its exceptional security to some such assistance. The natural demand for an ex-

planation would force the name of some great Neapolitan to the fore; and whose name could it be,
save the name of him who had justified the ways of
Rome to Greece, who had sung the triumph of Italy
over the land of Aristotle, who once on a time was
overlord of Naples itself? [11]

Whether Roger actually suspected that Naples
owed its impregnability to the protection afforded
by Virgil's bones, and sent an Englishman to steal
them away, as Roth thinks, or the demand in
Naples for a local equivalent to Aristotle's bones in
Palermo resulted in the supply of relics assumed to
be Virgil's, is open to question. In either case, the
cause would be the same: Aristotle's protectorate
of the rival city resulted in the discovery of bones
attributed to Virgil.

It has no doubt been observed that this method
of accounting for the origin of the legend points
pretty definitely to the decade 1130–40 as the probable date of formation; and therefore a tacit assumption must be made that the legend remained
in circulation until 1196, when Conrad of Querfurt
wrote it down, and until about 1211, when Gervasius of Tilbury penned his circumstantial account. One difficulty here is that the only positive
date of these three writers is that of Conrad. John
of Salisbury may well have picked up his story at
some time before 1159, and Gervasius of Tilbury is

known to have been a student at Bologna as early as 1177, although his closest personal contact with Naples occurred perhaps just before and during 1189, when William II of Sicily gave him a house at Nola. We cannot argue soundly on the absence of evidence, whether the absence be in John of Salisbury's tantalizingly brief allusion or in documents between 1159 and 1196; but we can point to one more historical fact which, it appears to me, may bear correlation with other historical facts and with some of the material in the legends.

In 1191 Henry VI of Germany directed his triumphal march south from Rome toward Naples. His Norman enemies were concentrated within the city, and almost no resistance was met on the journey. Siege was laid to Naples, but in the course of the summer an epidemic arose in Henry's army and the siege had to be abandoned. The city actually was captured three years later by Henry's forces,[12] and, as we have seen, to Conrad of Querfurt was assigned the task of rendering the walls defenseless.

This experience of Henry's army in 1191 is a duplicate in almost every respect of the experience of the army of Roger II sixty years before. If the legend of Virgil's bones did arise in the 1130's, we may be sure that the occurrence of 1191 caused its enthusiastic recall, with, perhaps, the embellishments that we see in Conrad and Gervasius. The evidence of John of Salisbury, while slight, is sufficient to make me hesitate to assign the origin of the story to 1191 or later, although Conrad was certainly on the ground very shortly after that, and Gervasius may have been there at the time. It should be remembered that John of Salisbury, Conrad, and Gervasius are our three main sources of information about this particular legend. Alexander Neckam's failure to mention it has little significance, since, although his work was written presumably between 1190 and 1200, the precise date is unknown, and no one can say whether he was ever in Italy.

I now turn to another matter which may be related to the legendary power of Virgil's bones. Conrad of Querfurt alone among all of the retellers of the stories about Virgil refers to a palladium which Virgil made to preserve the city of Naples. Even the wide-ranging and inventive Jean d'Outremeuse knows nothing of it. This palladium, says Conrad, was an image of the city shut up by Virgil's magic in a glass vessel (*ampulla*) with a very narrow opening. As long as the vessel was unbroken the Neapolitans felt that the city was safe. Their confidence was vindicated, for when the city fell into Conrad's hands he found a small crack in the vessel.

This unique occurrence of the story gives us little to go on. Comparetti [13] thinks that there is a relationship between this palladium and the famous egg of the Castel dell' Ovo. It will be remembered that the *Cronica di Partenope* and the Virgilius Romance mention a glass vessel as one of the things inclosing the egg; but these are too late, I think, to provide evidence reliable enough to use.

There is perhaps a clearer relationship between the story of Virgil's bones and the egg-talisman, if we can trust Gervasius to report any facts at all. He says that the military commander of Naples and a mob of the people gathered together the bones of Virgil in a bag, and took them to the Castle of the Sea, "where they are shown through an iron grill to anyone wishing to see them." Now this Castle of the Sea is none other than the fortress-like building later called the Castle of the Egg. The presence of Virgil's bones there presumably protected the building, at the same time making it a sort of mausoleum. Some Moslem, or person familiar with usage in Moslem countries, hung up an egg there, because of an association between ostrich eggs and mausoleums in Mohammedan lands; and thus came about the attribution to Virgil of the egg-talisman. Such is my conjecture as to the origin of the legend of the egg.

Was Virgil, then, actually regarded as a saint? A

century or so ago, certain scholars, perceiving the similarities between some of the Virgilian legends and saints' legends, decided that the great poet never could have been regarded as a wonder-worker, and that the legends about Virgil were originally meant to celebrate the deeds of some thaumaturgic St. Virgilius. This idea, tenable only before serious investigation of the legends had begun, was nevertheless held only a score of years ago.[14] It will suffice to say that of the saints bearing the name of Virgil now known, none displays sufficient similarities with either Virgil the necromancer or Virgil the poet — I distinguish the two arbitrarily for the moment — to make this old conjecture worth considering.[15]

Virgil, I think, was no more regarded as a saint — to use the term in its accepted Christian sense — in twelfth-century Naples than Aristotle was at Palermo. Nowhere until we come to Jean d'Outremeuse, writing in Belgium about 1400, do we find an attempt by the narrators of the Virgilian legends to relate the story of Virgil's bones to that other legend, by the twelfth century some seven hundred years old or more, to the effect that by writing the Fourth Eclogue Virgil became a prophet of Christ.[16] The transition from the conception of Virgil as a prophet of the coming of Christ to a conception of Virgil as a saint by anticipation would have been easy, especially if we recall St. Paul's reported visit to Virgil's tomb; but that transition was never made, in the legend of the bones or in any other of the legends. As a foil to Aristotle, then, Virgil was simply at first the Neapolitan or Italian "master of those who know," who in his wisdom knew ways of protecting Naples, just as Aristotle knew how to protect Palermo. We cannot say that Virgil was the patron saint of Naples, a successor of St. Stephen and a predecessor of St. January; rather he was, like Barbarossa or Charlemagne elsewhere, a benevolent guardian protecting his own.

IV

THE PNEUMATICAL SAGE

WE NOW turn to a story of which the development, in so far as any took place within the Virgilian legends, was quite simple. Alexander Neckam is the first to attribute the construction of the famous *Salvatio Romae* to Virgil, and therefore Alexander must be regarded as responsible in large measure for the change in scene of many of the later legends from Naples to Rome.

At Rome, according to Alexander, Virgil built a noble palace, in which stood, with a bell in its hand, a wooden image of each province. Whenever a province plotted against the power of imperial Rome, the image of that province struck its bell. Immediately a brazen soldier astride a brazen horse on the roof of the palace brandished his spear and turned in the direction of the offending province, and troops were dispatched to control the situation. When Virgil was asked how long this edifice would last, he replied, "Until a virgin shall conceive." Those who heard this applauded the philosopher, thinking that this meant that it would last forever; but it is said that at the birth of the Saviour it fell to ruins.

Vincent of Beauvais also mentions the *Salvatio Romae*, omitting the brazen horseman. Each statue had suspended from its neck a bell which it caused to ring when a revolt occurred in the province which it represented. The variation is not important, for all of the later occurrences of this legend, — including a thirteenth-century French manuscript,[1] the *Gesta Romanorum*, the *Historia septem sapientum* branch of the *Seven Sages of Rome*, Jean d'Outremeuse, Lydgate, the *Rudimentum novitiorum*, and the English Virgilius Romance, — seem to derive directly from Neckam's version.

The *Salvatio Romae*, then, as it appears in Neckam's account and occasionally elsewhere, was a collection of statues of human beings capable of moving themselves when a certain thing happened. These figures are therefore classifiable as belonging to a kind of machinery in great vogue in mediaeval romance, — namely, automata.

Arturo Graf devotes a score or so of pages to the study of the *Salvatio Romae*,[2] and traces the legend back as far as the eighth, or perhaps even the seventh, century — this *consecratio statuarum* having no maker, however, until Alexander Neckam ascribed it to Virgil. Graf is inclined to believe that the legend is due partly to the presence in Rome of numerous statues the origin of which was unknown to the people during the Middle

Ages — hence the tendency to place the *Salvatio Romae* in the Campidoglio, in the Pantheon, in the Colosseum, and so on — and partly to a belief common to most peoples in the sympathetic magic residing in figures. These inferences appear to me very probable, but they neglect one important attribute of these figures, — their power of moving themselves, their virtue as automata. Actual statues surviving from ancient times at Rome were of course not self-moving, and the ordinarily small doll-like figures used in sympathetic magic do not usually move. Is it possible to point to a third element in the origin of these statues which was responsible for their ability to move?

Before I attempt to answer this question I should like to pass in review certain other automata created by Virgil.

Conrad of Querfurt takes us back to Naples in his description of a brazen archer holding a drawn bow. A peasant wondered why the archer did not let fly, and smote the bowstring. The arrow struck the crater of Vesuvius, and fire and stinking ashes once again belched forth. We infer that a kind of taboo was broken by the peasant. This automaton has in common with the figures of the *Salvatio Romae* its power to move when a certain thing happened.

Conrad's archer of bronze holding Vesuvius in

check does not reappear later; but an archer closely resembling him is mentioned in the second version in verse of the *Image du Monde*. St. Paul found Virgil's body with candles burning on either side and an archer aiming with bent bow at a lamp. When St. Paul stopped the motions of two hammer-wielding automata at the entrance, the archer shot his arrow and broke the lamp, and all fell to dust in the darkness.

The *Roman de Cléomadès* tells of. Virgil's ever-burning fire at Rome threatened by a copper archer bearing the legend "If anyone strikes, I'll shoot." A ne'er-do-well happened along and struck the archer with a club. At once the arrow leaped forward and extinguished the fire. The *Seven Sages of Rome* duplicates this story, and so does Jean d'Outremeuse.

In the *Faictz merveilleux de Virgille* and in the Virgilius Romance in English the lamp illuminates the entire city of Rome. The copper figure holds an arbalest. After Virgil had left Rome, and the city had been only partially rebuilt after its destruction, the citizens' daughters were amusing themselves one day, when one of them approached the bowman and struck the string with her finger. The bolt sped away and struck the lamp. It had lasted for three centuries after Virgil's death. The girls were badly frightened, for the bowman disappeared suddenly and was never after seen. The version in *The Deceyte of Women* is very similar to this one.

These tales all seem to preserve the idea of a taboo. As long as the archer is unmolested he remains motionless, and the fire or lamp burns on. Strike him, touch his bowstring, and straightway the charm and with it the lamp are broken. To put it in another way, the archer is a mere motionless statue until a specific thing happens; not until then does he become an automaton. Like the figures of the *Salvatio Romae*, the model for this archer might well have been some ancient statue or other surviving in mediaeval Rome, except that the figure which we are studying had the power of movement.

An archer similar in function appears in William of Malmesbury's chronicle of the kings of England, completed during the fourth decade of the twelfth century, and thus antedating by some sixty years the first of the Virgilian archers. In the Campus Martius at Rome stood a statue pointing with its index finger. On its head was the inscription "Strike here!" It was understood that the head of this statue contained Octavian's treasure, and so it had been damaged by many blows dealt by people seeking the gold. Gerbert, who later became Pope Sylvester II, tried another method. He marked the spot touched by the shadow of the finger at high noon, and returned at night with a slave bearing a lamp. By means of his magic art he caused the earth to open, and descended into a room all of gold, filled with golden figures and precious objects of all kinds, and illuminated by a carbuncle opposite which stood the figure of a child with drawn bow. When Gerbert or his companion reached toward anything, the figures seemed to start toward them. Gerbert refrained from touching things, but his boy picked up a knife. Immediately the little bowman shot his arrow and extinguished the carbuncle, and the two seekers were able to make their way out through the darkness only after the knife had been replaced.[3] I note here in passing that the "Strike here!" statue reappears later in Enikel's *Weltchronik*, in *Cléomadès*, and in the Middle English *Seven Sages*.

Gervasius of Tilbury knows of another automaton, also of bronze, which held at its mouth a trumpet. Erected by Virgil in his garden, it blew back unfavorable winds and the destructive fumes issuing from a neighboring mountain. Its power had departed, however, either from the effects of age or of damage. The *Cronica di Partenope* contains an allusion to this trumpeter which blew back harmful winds.[4]

Especially familiar to readers of mediaeval romances are automata which guard entrances. The second version in verse of the *Image du Monde* depicts two hideous men of copper fashioned by Virgil to prevent entry to his tomb by striking the earth with hammers. *Reinfrit von Braunschweig* has a single hammer-man. Jean d'Outremeuse turns the hammers into flails, and in the English Virgilius Romance there are in addition to the hammer-men twenty-four flail-men who by their constant beating keep intruders outside Virgil's castle. They could be controlled by a person who knew where were hidden the "vyces" which started and stopped them. The whirling castle in *Perlesvaus* which will never stop until a spotless knight comes is an automaton. The means of stopping it reminds one of Neckam's story that Virgil told the Romans that the *Salvatio Romae* would remain intact until a virgin should bear a son.

Time-telling images were made by Virgil, too. *Cléomadès* attributes to him four statues which mark the changes of the seasons by tossing an apple one to another. The *Seven Sages* fathers on him two figures which toss a ball to mark the passing of the weeks. Jean d'Outremeuse draws from his horn of plenty statues which similarly mark the weeks, the months, and the seasons.

Thus far Virgil's automata have been sufficiently conservative to stay in one place; while they can move their arms or turn in their positions, they do not have power of locomotion. The *Gesta Romanorum* and Jean d'Outremeuse, however, tell of a brazen horseman who scours the streets after curfew each evening, and slays all those who disobey the law by straying abroad.

These automata cannot be studied profitably within the texts of the Virgilian legends alone. It was pointed out by the late Professor Bruce twenty years ago that those which are attributed to Virgil appear in texts which are considerably later than certain romances in which similar automata occur, and therefore that "the Virgil legend was influenced by the romances — probably more than vice versa."[5] Yet to transfer the automata merely from the Virgilian legends to romances that antedate them by a few score years explains little about the origins of these automata. For instance, it is interesting to know that the *Pèlerinage de Charlemagne,* written during the first half of the twelfth century, describes two children of copper which turn about and blow horns of white ivory when an eastern breeze strikes them; that lamps are put out by archers, very much as in the Virgilian legends, in *Eneas* and in the Thomas *Tristan*, dated approximately 1160 and 1170; and that in two other romances dated about 1170, the *Roman d'Alexandre* and *Huon de Bordeaux*, there are two children who guard a bridge with hammers, and two copper men with iron flails who guard the entrance to a castle built by Julius Caesar.[5]

We cannot account for all of Virgil's automata, including the *Salvatio Romae*, by those in romances; moreover, not all of those in the later romances can be accounted for by automata appearing in the earlier ones. We must look elsewhere for a common origin of all of them.

The actual existence of automata, not merely their presence in the imagination of authors of romance or legend, is demonstrated for the middle of the thirteenth century by the book of travels of the Flemish friar, William of Rubrouck. He tells us of the marvels at "Mangu Chan's" palace at Karakorum, in what is now Eastern Siberia. Among them was a silver tree on top of which stood an angel with a trumpet. A man concealed beneath the tree blew through a pipe, and the angel raised the trumpet and sounded it.[7] Tartary lies far from our province; but the connection will appear later.

An Arabian treatise of the tenth century refers to many remarkable objects, among them the figure of a man on horseback brandishing a sword with which any person approaching with hostile intent was killed, and figures of copper which also slew with their swords anyone who came near the bridge which they were guarding.[8]

Still earlier is the famous account of the ceremonies with which an ambassador was received at
Constantinople in the ninth century. A philoso-
pher-artisan made for the emperor a throne called
the throne of Solomon. As an ambassador approached the throne, lions and griffons on the
steps arose and roared, birds in golden trees sang,
and other remarkable things happened.[9]

We have now glanced at automata appearing in
twelfth-century Naples, thirteenth-century Siberia,
tenth-century Arabia, and ninth-century Constantinople. The *Salvatio Romae* has been noted as
going back to the eighth or perhaps the seventh
century. It would be possible to add many more
from sources outside romances, but my desire here is
to seek an explanation of these real and imaginary
phenomena rather than to multiply examples.

That explanation lies, I think, in the treatise on
pneumatics by Hero of Alexandria, who lived at
some indeterminate date between the second century B.C. and the middle of the first century of the
Christian era. The devices which he describes were
not necessarily invented by him, as he inherited
much from predecessors; but my purpose will be
achieved by citing one or two of the machines discussed in his treatise.[10]

On Hero's birds made to sing by flowing water,
and to turn in their places, we need not dwell, al-

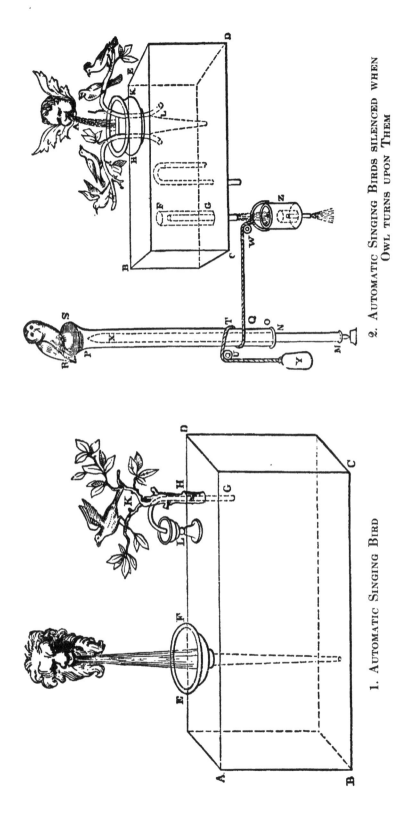

1. Automatic Singing Bird

2. Automatic Singing Birds silenced when Owl turns upon Them

AUTOMATIC SINGING BIRDS

From *The Pneumatics of Hero of Alexandria*, trans. J. G. Greenwood, London, 1851, pp. 29, 31

(Courtesy of British Museum)

though it is interesting to note that this may be an
ultimate source for many a charming spring garden
full of singing birds in the romances.[11] More to the
point here is Hero's theorem xli, "On Hercules and
the Snake." The problem which he sets himself to
solve is this: "When an apple is lifted, Hercules
shoots a dragon which then hisses." [12] The solution
follows easily. Given a small tree round which a
snake is coiled, an apple lying near-by, and a figure
of Hercules, bow in hand, facing the tree. All of
this must be placed on a box-like structure, beneath
which are two water-tight and air-tight compartments one above the other. The upper one is filled
with water; the lower one is empty. An opening
from the upper to the lower tank is closed by means
of a cone-like stopper which is attached by a cord to
the apple above. Also attached to the apple is another cord which runs along or beneath the top of
the box-like structure to the figure of Hercules, up
inside the figure and down the arm to the hand,
where it terminates in a smaller trigger-like finger
capable of holding the bowstring and releasing it
when pulled back. To the lower compartment is
attached a hollow pipe which runs up the tree-
trunk and terminates in a small whistle. Now all is
set for the experiment. The forbidden apple lies on
the ground. Pick it up, and the cord releases the
trigger, the bow springs, and the arrow is shot. At

the same time, the stopper at the bottom of the upper compartment is lifted, and water rushes into the lower compartment, forcing the air out through the hollow pipe and causing the serpent to hiss. As long as you retain the apple, the serpent continues to hiss. Replace it, the stopper settles back into the hole, the air pressure stops, and the snake hisses no longer. Hercules alone is left in disrepair. To enable him to work again you must put the arrow back on the string and place the string again on the trigger. When the lower compartment is filled with water, it must be emptied.

This illustrates the principle by which Hero's automata operated in general. It is clear that apparently miraculous noises could easily be made in this manner, and a long series of events could be brought about by employing a large number of compartments or tanks. The possibilities would seem to be limited only by the resources of the experimenter. Thus it is easy to see how trumpets could be sounded in the same way, and Hero shows how it is done in his theorem xvi.[13]

It appears from this that it would be perfectly possible to set up after this fashion a table pranked out with the furnishings of the cave into which Gerbert and his slave made their way. You would have an ever-burning lamp arranged in the way that Hero describes fully in theorems xxii, xxiii,

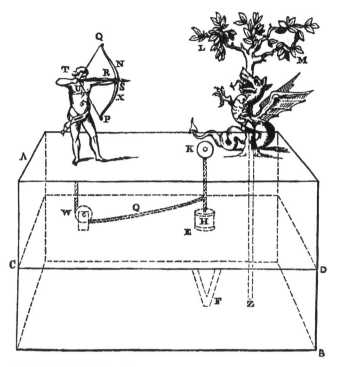

SNAKE HISSES AND HERCULES SHOOTS ARROW
WHEN APPLE *K* IS LIFTED

From *The Pneumatics of Hero of Alexandria*,
trans. J. G. Greenwood, London, 1851

(*Courtesy of British Museum*)

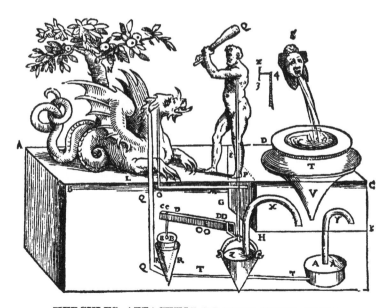

HERCULES ATTACKING DRAGON WITH CLUB

From *Gli artifitiosi et curiosi moti di Herrone, tradotti da M. Gio. Battista
Aleotti d' Argenta . . .*, Ferrara, 1589, p. 89

(*Courtesy of British Museum*)

xxiv.[14] As the hand of one of the two intruders
reaches out toward an object, the proper cords
cause the figures arranged about the walls to bend
forward, or to clash their weapons on their shields.
When the slave finally picks up the knife, attached
like the apple to the archer's hand, the bow is released and the arrow shoots toward the inextinguishable lamp, which, however, *is* extinguished
this time by the force of the air issuing from a tube
connected with a tank below into which water
started running as soon as the knife was lifted,
carrying up with it the stopper. The hullabaloo set
up by as many tanks as we have chosen to supply,
attached to whatever noise-making devices our in-
genuity has been able to contrive, will continue in
the darkness until the slave replaces the knife,
when the stopper will settle back into its opening
and all will again be peaceful.

There is yet more in Hero's treatise, however.
He demonstrates how to construct an automatic
theatre in which the story of Nauplius can be
enacted entirely by automata.[15] Twelve people
appear and make a ship ready for a voyage. Some
saw, some hammer, some swing axes, and some use
drills. There is much noise. The scene closes, and
next we see the ship of the Achaeans drawn into the
sea. Then ships sail by, with dolphins playing; but
a storm comes up. In the next scene Nauplius

stands with raised torch, Athena beside him. The torch begins to burn. Then there is the shipwreck, with Ajax swimming. Athena appears in the air. Thunder peals. Lightning flashes and strikes Ajax, who disappears.

All of this we are told more or less specifically how to do by Hero.[16] In any case, here is employed a general principle which might account for many of the automata which appear in the earlier romances, such as the flail-men or hammer-men; and when we come to the later, more versatile figures which are able to move from a fixed base, like the brazen horseman in the *Gesta Romanorum* who policed the streets after curfew, we may infer that the imagination, grown familiar with the ordinary automata, found it no great leap to pass from fixed to unfixed figures. After all, what we must suppose as taking place here is the development of the idea of actual automatic figures operating on Hero's principles. Once seen, these would work strongly upon the imagination. Hero himself says that "the ancients called those who constructed such things thaumaturges because of the astounding character of the spectacle." [17] If the relationships here suggested are correct, mediaeval men saw such apparatus at work, or heard of it, and took it over as part of the furnishings for their tales. In size there seems a discrepancy, for certainly in the romances,

AUTOMATIC HAMMER-MEN STRIKING ANVIL,
WITH AUTOMATIC FORGE

From *Gli artifitiosi et curiosi moti di Herrone, tradotti da M. Gio.
Battista Aleotti d'Argenta . . .*, Ferrara, 1589, p. 93

(Courtesy of British Museum)

and we may infer the same in the Virgilian legends, the figures were frequently of normal human size, while the "experiments" of Hero and his successors were probably on a very small scale. Mediaeval sense of perspective — or the lack of it — may have played a part here.

The precise line of transmission between Hero and the later Middle Ages is not clear. Everyone knows of the clepsydra, or water-clock, with its moving figures which Harun-al-Rashid presented to Charlemagne; the story is told by Eginhard *sub anno* 806. At Constantinople, Leon, Archbishop of Thessalonica, made automata during the ninth century.[18] Somewhat more to the point here is the water-clock of King Roger II of Sicily, possibly made by a mechanic from Malta, which struck the hours by throwing a ball into a basin.[19] With such a contrivance at Palermo during the first half of the twelfth century, we may be sure that it was known at least by reputation at Naples. Thus it can be shown that mechanical devices which did the same sorts of things as those described by Hero were known west of Greece; but in view of the receptivity of the Arabian world to Greek science and thought, it is possible that the avenue of transmission may lie there, for in the first decade of the tenth century the famous Persian poet Firdawsī described automata in his Shāhnāma.[20] In any

case, the theorems of Hero may well serve as the
ideas behind the automata of European romance
as well as those which appear in the *Thousand and
One Nights*.[21]

Perhaps to be classed with Virgil's automata is
the speaking head which he made. According to
the first version in verse of the *Image du Monde*,
this head gave him an ambiguous answer concerning his death, and as a result he died of sunstroke —
Virgil thinking that the image meant that *it* should
be protected, rather than his own head. In the
Roman de Renart le Contrefait the head is of brass;
Pucci says it is of copper. The *Cronica di Partenope* multiplies the number by four; they are human heads which reveal to the Duke of Naples
what happens in the four quarters of the world.
Jean d'Outremeuse reduces the number to one;
Virgil gives it powers of speech by placing within it
privy spirits.[22]

The construction of the speaking head was attributed to Gerbert before it was to Virgil. Recently
the whole subject has been ably and fully discussed
by Arthur Dickson,[23] who decides that the speaking
or oracular head is "a continuation of the earlier
story of the Oracular Idol. . . . Like the idol, the
head is inhabited by a demon which gives responses
. . . sometimes . . . the head is destroyed, and its
possessor forsakes magical studies. But a new
factor has evidently entered in, which has trans-

formed the Oracular Idol into a mere head; . . . and this appears to be the custom, widespread throughout the world at various times, of using severed human heads for purposes of divination." [24]

These inferences impress me as being thoroughly sound, as far as they go; and they go very far toward solving any question likely to arise in connection with the prophesying head. The one unsettled possibility is whether this piece of apparatus has anything to do with the principles underlying the theorems of Hero of Alexandria.

In the thirteenth century Albertus Magnus was interested, to the extent of attempting to explain how they worked, in automata which could move and speak; and he had good precedent, for he quotes Aristotle on the figure of a man which was caused to emit sounds by air forced through a pipe. It was no doubt this interest of Albert's which resulted later in the attribution to him of the manufacture of an automaton which moved and spoke, and of a speaking head very similar to the one ascribed to Virgil. [25] The Universal Doctor explains how a statue of Minerva could move and sing by means of apparatus similar in general to the machinery employed by Hero; he does not talk about demons inhabiting these figures, and it is plain that the heads are mechanical contrivances, not human heads of which the powers of speech have been preserved by magical means.

The famous statue of Memnon, which Strabo says opened its eyes and emitted a cry at sunrise, was converted by the simple magic of oral transmission into a figure capable of human speech. Maimonides knows of similar figures which held converse with human beings. Early in the seventeenth century Baptista Porta was convinced that such figures could be made to operate by means of air-pressure, and in the middle of the century Athanasius Kircher actually made one.[26]

The ultimate origin of the mirror which Virgil made at Rome may lie in the same quarter. Immediately it is surely modelled after the famous lighthouse at Alexandria, for centuries regarded as one of the Seven Wonders of the World, as we perceive easily in the earliest form in which it appears, in the *Roman de Cléomadès*, where the mirror showed anyone approaching Rome with treason in his heart. In the Middle English *Seven Sages of Rome* a statue holds the mirror in its hand; the safety of the city is bound up in it, for when it is destroyed the city falls. The mirror appears to be a continuation of the *Salvatio Romae* idea. In the *Roman de Renart le Contrefait*, in the *Confessio Amantis*, and in the *Myreur des Histors* it is similar, but in the *Gesta Romanorum* it is simply used privately by a magician to show matters happening afar.[27]

Hero of Alexandria discussed the science of optics and the uses of mirrors, and the tenth-century Arabic *Abrégé des Merveilles* alludes to them repeatedly in the same general spirit as the authors of the Virgilian legends of the mirror.[28]

The lighthouse at Alexandria threw its beams far and mystified mankind. Its use as a mere lighthouse was eclipsed in the popular mind, apparently, and it was regarded as an instrument which could "see" as far as it threw its beams — a misconception easily understood. Part of the popular attitude was perhaps associated with the knowledge that it had a reflector, a mirror; and thence came the multitude of mirrors in the fiction of the later Middle Ages and Renaissance.

The *Salvatio Romae*, the other automata made by Virgil, the speaking head, and the magic mirror all would seem to owe their existence to the effects upon the non-mechanically-inclined mediaeval mind of scientific and pseudo-scientific experiments of the Greeks as handed down in one way or another. When distance in both time and space had cast a romantic haze over these mechanical toys of past ages they lost their cogs and pulleys and water-tanks, and became wondrous creations of that incomparable mediaeval Wizard of Oz, Virgil the necromancer.

V

VIRGIL IN THE BASKET

THE most familiar of the tales that clustered about the name of Virgil the necromancer is the story of his ill-starred midnight tryst with his lady-love. Virgil fell in love with the emperor's daughter — any emperor will do — who pretended to reciprocate his affection, and arranged for a meeting which could be brought about only by Virgil's ascending her tower in a basket drawn up by a rope, since normal access to her was carefully guarded. The rejoiced lover entered the basket, but his crafty mistress drew him only half way up, and left him hanging there all the next day, to the great merriment of the people. Released after hours of torment, Virgil resolved on revenge. He extinguished all of the fires in Rome, and when after three days the emperor approached him to learn how they might be restored, the magician replied that the only means of relief lay in the public humiliation of the emperor's daughter. She must appear naked in the public square and permit the populace to kindle their torches at her person. Moreover, the enchantment would continue until everyone in Rome had visited the lady, for one torch kindled from her would not light another.

It is plain that this tale consists of two distinct parts, the basket incident itself, and the revenge. That the parts were originally distinct is certain, for the two stories are found told separately of other individuals earlier than they were told of Virgil. In the present chapter the story of the basket will be examined.

I. EARLIER FORMS

If we reduce this basket story to its simplest terms, we have an outline something like this: a lover attempts to visit his lady, who is kept away from him in a tower, by means of a basket; the lady does not wish to receive him, and leaves the unfortunate lover suspended in mid-air.[1]

Oriental literature supplies a parallel or two of some interest. One occurs in the *Katha Sarit Sagara*, a famous collection of Indian stories completed in 1070. The wife of a merchant falls into evil habits when her husband leaves her for a journey, as he discovers upon his return.

As it was evening, he went into the house of an old woman in that place. . . . And at night he asked that old woman, who did not recognize him, "Mother, do you know any tidings of the family of Dhanadeva?" When the old woman heard that, she said, "What tidings is there save that his wife is always ready to take a new lover? For a basket, covered with leather, is let down every night from the window there, and whoever enters it, is drawn up into the house, and is dismissed in the same way at the end of the night." [2]

Another parallel is in the *Thousand and One Nights*.

The musician Ibrahim Abn Ishak slips out of the caliph's palace to visit a slave girl. On his way through the streets he sees a large basket, draped with gorgeous material, hanging by silken ropes. He enters it and is pulled up to a flat roof, where he is received by beautiful slaves and conducted below to a palace of royal splendor. Abn Ishak seats himself on a divan, and shortly a lovely lady places herself opposite him. Songs, feasting, and story-telling follow, and Ibrahim passes a wonderful night. The lovely lady tells him he is the most interesting man she has ever known. Ibrahim protests that he has a cousin in comparison with whom he is but as a drop of water to the ocean. He makes his departure in the basket, returns for a second night, and is invited to bring his cousin for a third. Two baskets are let down, and Ibrahim brings the caliph, who discovers the lady's identity, falls in love with her, and marries her.[3]

This famous collection was edited in its present form about 1450 in Egypt. An earlier date cannot be assigned, although it, or a similar collection, was mentioned in 943 and 987.[4]

In another Oriental collection of later date appears a long and involved love-story in the course of which the lover reaches an enchanted garden, where his beloved is kept under a spell, by means

of a basket attached by a rope to the summit of a
ruined castle. The hero is finally successful, the
enchantment is broken, and he marries the princess.[5]

Again in the *Katha Sarit Sagara* we find two
other stories which contribute to the Oriental history of this type of tale. They do not involve the
use of baskets, but they present similar features.
In one of these the lover is hoisted through the
window by a rope; in the other, the rope carries a
wooden seat on which he ascends. In the latter
there is an additional parallel with the story of
Ibrahim; the man pulled up aids his master to
marry the occupant of the room which he enters.[6]

From these tales we may infer that baskets were
used as vehicles between lovers and their mistresses. Thus far, the similarity of these baskets
with the one in Virgil's adventure is not compelling.
The mere employment of baskets is not sufficient
to convince us of a relationship; the resemblance
might easily be fortuitous.

There is a famous basket story in that most
charming of mediaeval romances, *Floire et Blanceflor*. In the various discussions of its sources satisfactory parallels have been indicated for many of
the episodes, including the successful effort of the
hero to have himself introduced in a basket into the
heroine's quarters in an Oriental harem.[7] Of the

groups in which the several versions of the romance have been classified, numbers I and II are most familiar to the average reader, for here fall two Old French, the Middle English, the Icelandic, and the Danish versions, among others.[8] In these, Floire bribes the porter of the tower in which Blanceflor is imprisoned to conceal him in a basket of flowers and have him carried by two manservants up the stairs.[9] A strikingly similar episode occurs in an ancient and very popular collection of Buddhist *exempla* dated about A.D. 430.

The king of Benares, fond of casting dice with his chaplain, won invariably by pronouncing a charm to the effect that "given opportunity, / All women work iniquity." On the verge of ruin, the chaplain interrupted playing at dice with the king during the time required to rear a baby girl whom he never permitted to see any man but himself. The girl grown, the chaplain challenged the king and won continually by adding after the king's charm, "Always excepting my girl." The king guessed what had happened, and hired a scoundrel to corrupt the chaplain's paragon. The fellow managed to pass himself off to the girl's simple nurse as her long-lost son, and kept in her good graces by supplying her with flowers and perfumes for her charge, while the nurse pocketed the money which the chaplain gave her for them. When the time seemed ripe, the fellow feigned illness for love of the girl, and, with the girl's consent, the nurse carried him, concealed in a flower-basket, into the sevenfold guarded house, where he succeeded in wrecking the girl's virtue and hence the power of the chaplain's counter-charm.[10]

In another group of the *Floire et Blanceflor* romances the basket episode is rendered differently. In the Spanish, popular Italian, Dutch, and Greek versions, and Boccaccio's *Il Filocolo*, the lover, concealed as before in a flower basket, is *hoisted* to the lady's window by means of a rope.[11]

Scholars generally agree that the first version of this romance was composed between 1160 and 1170, and Arabian, Persian, and Byzantine sources have been advocated.[12] It is scarcely necessary, I think, to point out that the parallels above cited between Oriental tales and the romance are very close. Possibly this romance was the vehicle of transmission between the East and the Virgilian story, for that the tower in the romance was originally an Oriental harem seems well established;[13] and, as we shall see later, Virgil's lady is usually housed in a tower — an essential feature, for, unless her place of abode could be easily guarded, there would be little motivation for the episode.

There is yet further evidence that baskets as aërial vehicles were known in the Orient in the Middle Ages. In his edition of *Li Romans des Sept Sages* Keller prints a basket story from a manuscript of *Le Markes de Romme*.[14]

Darius, king of Persia, had his beautiful daughter carefully guarded in a tower by eunuchs, and permitted no man to see her. One of the king's seneschals had a son named Ysocars, handsome, versed in astronomy, and a brave knight withal, whose fame had come to the ears of the king's daughter and had caused her to love him desperately; but Ysocars knew naught of it. One day when the princess was taking the air Ysocars happened along and fell asleep in an orchard near-by. Her maidens recognized him, and the princess having confessed that he was the man she had loved before she had ever seen him, one of the maidens suggested that since a meeting could be arranged only in the greatest secrecy, a letter should be dropped down to him summoning him to appear at the foot of the tower that night. The suggestion was followed, and the rejoiced Ysocars appeared, entered the basket which the princess's maidens had lowered, and was pulled up to the welcoming maiden. The visit was entirely satisfactory to both people concerned, and was repeated frequently until it was discovered that the princess was with child. Ysocars was then captured, but escaped punishment.

That the basket story was floating about and was likely to be attached to almost any name that happened to come into the relater's mind is illustrated by an early Italian diatribe against the perfidy of women, *Proverbia qui dicuntur super natura feminarum*, dating perhaps from the thirteenth century. The basket adventure is merely referred to as befalling Antipater, one of a long series of unfortunate lovers,—Adam, Solomon, Helen, Charlemagne, Samson, Pasiphaë, Dido, and so on.[15]

One more tale, that of Hippocrates, remains to be considered before we turn at last to the versions

HOW PHILOCOLO WAS PUT IN THE ROSE-BASKET

From *Ein gar schone newe histori der hochen lieb des kuniglichen fursten Florio vnnd von seyner lieben Bianceffora,*
Metz, 1499, fo. xcix, r°

(*Courtesy of British Museum*)

which name Virgil as the occupant of the basket. The story of Hippocrates appears in one of the least likely places, *L'estoire del Saint Graal.* It is forced into the narrative in typically loose romance fashion apropos of nothing at all. Certain characters of the Grail story are shipwrecked on a rock where was the tomb of Hippocrates, inscribed in letters of gold

CI GIST YPOCRAS LI SOVERAINS PHILOSOPHES QUI ONQUES FUIST: ET QUE SA FEMME ENGINGNAIT ET LIVRAIT A MORT PAR SON MALICE, ET IL, LEI APRES.

Evidently the scribe had a story on his mind of which he needs must be relieved, for he goes on to say that it is only fitting and proper that the tale should be told. Then follows a long relation of the life and doings of Hippocrates: how he was a great philosopher and physician, and healed the nephew of the Emperor Augustus of a mortal illness, and so on. What is of interest here is his adventure with a fair dame come from Gaul, who resented the fame of Hippocrates, and boasted that no man was so wise as to be able to withstand her wiles.[16] The beauty of this lady was so striking that when the emperor saw her he ordered that she become one of his household, and gave her quarters. She set herself to attract Hippocrates, and succeeded so well that he fell ill for love of her. She healed him by a kind word, for within a week he was able to return to the rejoicing court.

The scheming woman took him to one side and pointed out that he could visit her by being pulled up to her chamber in a vessel which was used by the son of the King of Babylon, imprisoned in that tower, to carry up food. Hippocrates appeared at midnight, was pulled up by the lady and her maid, and left suspended. The next day all Rome saw him there in shame. Finally the emperor came back from a day of hunting and ordered that Hippocrates be taken down. The sage disclaimed all knowledge of how his predicament was brought about, but the beautiful lady from France took care to spread the news far and wide.

At this time the information came to Rome that Jesus had raised Lazarus from the dead. Hippocrates determined to become a disciple of Jesus since the Nazarene was more powerful than he. He got as far as Persia on his trip, and there healed the apparently dead child of the king, who took Hippocrates with him to visit the King of Syria, with whose young daughter Hippocrates fell in love. He married her and took her to his home, building for her a beautiful château "en l'isle fort." [17]

Now the story of Darius's unfortunate daughter names her lover and the occupant of the basket Ysocars. He has in common with Hippocrates (always called *Ypocras* in the Grail texts) his knowledge of the stars, and is probably a development from that philosopher. These matters are dark and past clear grasping, but it is not impossible that manuscript errors or imperfect eyesight or hearing might account for the change.[18]

cele maison qui iadis fu si riche
et si bele estoit ensi decheorte.
Ensi que ypocras fu ... pen
dus en le tour de ... me
... les gens li veïrent ... anc

ours fu ce dist li contes
et lestoire des philoso
phes le tesmoigne q̃
ypocras fu li plus so
uerains clers del art de phisique

YPOCRAS IN THE BASKET

From MS. B. M. Add. 10292, fo. 45, rᵒ

(Courtesy of British Museum)

Possibly the earliest instance of Virgil's association with the basket story occurs in a thirteenth-
century Latin manuscript in the Bibliothèque
Nationale, of which an extract was printed by
Du Méril.[19]

Virgil is enamoured of Nero's beautiful daughter and
begs for her love. She invites him to appear at night at
the foot of her tower, where, divested of his clothing, he
enters a basket which she has lowered, is pulled up half-
way and left suspended until the next day. The news
gets about even to the emperor, who is greatly enraged,
and, following the custom of the times, passes sentence
of death upon Virgil. The magician makes his escape to
Naples by muttering an incantation over a basin of
water, and then exacts his revenge.

Nero's daughter, too, lived in a tower, no doubt
a survival of the Oriental harem. We have the
Oriental basket quite as plainly as before, up to the
humiliation by suspension.

The next adapter of our tale is Jansen Enikel,
who in his *Weltchronik*, a compilation of universal
history dating from the last quarter of the thirteenth century, devotes some six hundred lines to
Virgil the necromancer.[20]

Prosperously established as a magician in Rome,
Virgil was imprudent enough to woo the wife of a citizen.
She was not interested, but became worried when Virgil
pointed out that he should infallibly die unless she
yielded, and consulted with her husband. The latter
advised that the basket humiliation be resorted to as a

means of getting rid of the troublesome suitor. "Tell him," he counselled, "that I watch you so closely that he could not come to you by the ordinary means." The lady sent for Virgil and proposed the basket scheme as a means of getting together. Of course the delighted wooer agreed, and that night he appeared and signalled his arrival by throwing a pebble against her window. With the assistance of her husband, the lady let down the basket, pulled Virgil up part of the way, and left him hanging. She was a pure woman; chaste and beautiful was her life.

Here the mistress of the harem has become a chaste wife and the lord of the harem has become her husband. Only the lover, here Virgil, and the tower, the reminiscence of the harem, remain. Virgil's casting a stone at her window is a minor and natural change. Perhaps the most interesting addition is the element of chastity in the wife, which may possibly have been influenced by the punishment of suspension in a basket, as will appear in a moment. Chronological difficulties make it impossible to determine whether Enikel got the story from the Latin manuscript which tells of Nero's daughter. I am inclined to suspect that the tale was floating about, now attached to Virgil's name, now attached to the name of some other worthy, and that it cannot be said what his actual source was.[21]

II. BASKET LAW

The careful reader will have noticed a discrepancy between the Oriental basket stories, including their immediate Occidental offshoots, and the similar stories told of Hippocrates and Virgil. In order to account for this discrepancy, a considerable excursus from the immediate subject is necessary.

After Hippocrates had been duped by his lady-love, and left suspended in the basket halfway up the tower, the unknown author halts his story long enough to tell us that the vehicle used by Hippocrates was not used to convey food, but was of a shameful and contemptible nature, for it served to expose to the public view just before their execution criminals condemned to death. Hence when Hippocrates appeared in it, the Romans thought that he had been convicted as a malefactor, and the philosopher himself was ashamed accordingly.[22]

Similarly, in other versions we find the victim's shame at having been suspended in a basket so great as to motivate the terrible revenge wreaked upon the faithless lady. In the story of Nero's daughter, the emperor passes sentence of death upon Virgil, because it is the custom of the country and of the empire to do so in the case of victims suspended in a basket. In Enikel's history, the citizens of Rome ask Virgil how it happened that he is in such a plight. He answers merely that it is his own will, but his female tormentor above tells the crowd that he hangs there because of a shameful deed.

So it runs in many versions which it would be needlessly tedious to repeat here. The point which I wish to bring out is that the punishment of the lover by exposing him in the basket does not seem to be merely a practical joke, but that it humiliates him to an unbearable point. Why should it humiliate him? Why should the people of Rome scorn him as a result of it? Certain it is that the thwarted suitor's thoughts turn from love to revenge; the mighty Virgil, whom we have already seen play the rôle of magician, summons up all of his skill to avenge the insult. Instead of a vain fond lover he becomes again the magician of supernatural power, bent on securing vengeance for injury now that it is too late to gain success in love.

I have just pointed out the similarities between the episode of Virgil in the basket and certain Oriental tales. In these latter, however, no punishment is found. They concern themselves merely with getting the lover to his lady by means of a basket. The venture succeeds, and there are no unpleasant consequences conditioned upon the use of the basket. The basket is merely a vehicle for transportation between the ground and a high window in a tower or the like. However other details may vary in the Oriental and semi-Oriental versions, the basket itself remains merely an instrument to the lovers, a means of their getting together. There is no hint of shame or ignominy in its use. Yet when we turn to the Virgil story and related tales, we find the basket developed into a means of punishment and humiliation to the lover, a means of exposing him to public shame and ridicule. Surely we may infer that the use of the basket as a means of access to the lady is Oriental in origin. Whence the second element?

I have taken the hints in the story of Nero's daughter and in that of Ypocras concerning the use of this basket. We are told there that it was a means of humiliating condemned criminals on their way to execution. In addition, F. H. von der Hagen suggested long ago that the basket of Ypocras had nothing to do with Roman law, but had some connection with the laws of the Germanic folk.[23] I shall therefore devote the next few pages to a discussion of precisely what this basket of Ypocras has to do, if anything, with ancient law.[24]

In the great German dictionary of the Brothers Grimm we learn of a punishment for fraudulent bakers, who were pulled up in a basket and then dumped out in such a way as to fall into a pool or mud-puddle.[25]

The second municipal code of the city of Strassburg, written during the years 1214–19, stipulates that anyone who serves a false measure of wine shall undergo the punishment of the *schupfe* — "de scupha cadet in merdam." [26] Thirteenth-century Livonia knew the punishment, for one way of avoiding a fine of ten silver marks was to take the dive from the *scuppestol*. [27] Defalcating merchants suffered the same penalty in Brandenburg during the thirteenth century, [28] and according to a Strassburg codex of 1270 wine-sellers who gave short measure were subjected to it. [29] At Rostock, too, it appears at about the same date. [30] The punishment itself is not mentioned but the instrument, *schuppestüel*, is referred to in a matter-of-fact way as a fixed point at Cologne in 1269. [31]

Most of these texts use Latin, and the fact that the Germanic word is used would indicate that there was no Latin word available, thus pointing, I think, to the inference that the instrument was not new, for otherwise some effort would be made to explain the Germanic term employed in a Latin text. Similarly, in Augsburg, a German text *sub anno* 1276 refers repeatedly to the *schuphe* as a punishment for bakers who bake below the legal weight. [32]

A few years later the city of Zürich was damaged in a conflagration set by a baker who had been subjected to this punishment because of fraudulent dealings. He deserved a worse fate, but clemency was extended to him.

Beside the water was an apparatus with a basket in which criminals were placed before sentence was executed. The basket was hoisted up and the occupant had to jump into the water below to get out. When the baker Wackerbold leaped into the water he was roundly laughed at by the bystanders, who thought he had got only what he deserved. But Wackerbold, enraged at his shame, plotted how to turn the tables on them. By virtue of his trade he was allowed to collect firewood, so he stored his house full, awaited a favorable wind, and fired it. The wind carried the blaze to other houses, and a great conflagration started quickly. Two women found Wackerbold on a height where he could enjoy the spectacle, and reproached him for running away from the city when there was so much need of him to help fight the fire. "Go back and tell them," said the baker, "that I needed a fire to dry myself by after my wetting. Now that I am comfortably dry, I can laugh at them as they laughed at me. Let them sit by their fire and laugh or weep, as they will." [33]

During the first quarter of the fourteenth century the penalty of the basket was in force at Regensburg. "In accordance with ancient law" bakers and "rüffian" were subjected to it, "in the presence of a great multitude"; [34] and, in 1326, a baker so treated, desperate upon emerging from the filth into which he was precipitated, stabbed the village priest and was torn to pieces by the mob,

in spite of taking sanctuary.[35] We pass to the city
of Jansen Enikel, and find that a Viennese statute
of 1340 directs that bakers "shall be ducked, after
the fashion that has descended from the ancient
law of princes." [36] If only fifty years after Enikel
an ancient law is spoken of casually, would not that
law have been in existence a generation or two
before, when Enikel was writing?

A particularly tantalizing variety of this punishment is described as in force at Magdeburg in 1346.
The baker is pulled up in a basket attached to a
pillar, and given a knife with which he must cut
himself out, only to fall into the filth below.[37]

I have listed these examples in order to make
clear my point that the basket punishment was in
some form or other very widely known in mediaeval
Germania; but the reader may object that although
that point is now clear, the transition between
short-changing bakers, wine-sellers, and the like
and Virgil is not easy. After all, whatever the local
situation may be, baking a loaf of bread a little
smaller than legal specifications, or pouring out a
short pint of wine is not a dastardly crime for which
the perpetrator would be put to death; and we have
seen that one reason why Virgil or Hippocrates was
so badly humiliated was that each knew that the
ogling crowd thought that he was on the way to
execution for some serious crime. From a legal

point of view, I suppose the crime or criminal intention of Virgil or Hippocrates to have been—depending upon the version of the story which is used — that of adultery or fornication.

It happens that the legal records of the city of Lübeck furnish us with just such an example. The municipal code of 1240 provides that adultery shall be punished by the *scuppestol* and by banishment from the city; and half a century later the crime was similarly punished,[38] and in Utrecht and Haarlem in Holland, the like was the case.[39]

With these facts set forth, I wish now to consider the possibilities of a relationship between the basket punishment as it appears in the Hippocrates and Virgil stories, and the historical punishment itself.

In the course of the discussion of Virgilian legends in the *Image du Monde*, written in the neighborhood of 1245, reference is made to an offence against Virgil committed by the woman whom he humiliated in the episode of the revenge, which I shall study in the sixth chapter. What the offence could have been other than the exposure in the basket I do not know. The basket story is told in full in the Latin account of Nero's daughter, in the Ypocras legend, and in Enikel's *Weltchronik*, the first two of which are dated thirteenth century, while Enikel's work is assigned to the last quarter of the same century. If I am correct in guessing that the *Image du Monde* refers to the basket, then 1245 would be the earliest of these dates. Presumably the story might have been in existence before that, as otherwise one would expect the *Image du Monde* to be more specific; it would seem that both author and audience were familiar with the story. Yet, since Vincent of Beauvais, writing at about the same time, omits both the basket and revenge stories, whereas he includes enough of the legends to show that he was keenly interested in Virgil the necromancer as well as in Virgil the poet, I am inclined to believe that not far from the middle of the thirteenth century is the date of formation of the Virgil-Ypocras basket story. If, now, we compare actual dates, we find that the second municipal code of Strassburg was drawn up between 1214 and 1219; it will be remembered that it contained a provision for the basket punishment. It may of course be mere coincidence that the author of the *Image du Monde* is believed to have been a native of Metz, barely eighty miles away from Strassburg. Augsburg and Zürich are in the same general district, and it is well known that these municipal codes were formulated the one from the other.

Facts do not carry us to our destination. I am inclined to turn to fancy, and to hazard the guess then that some version of the Oriental basket story

— similar, say, to that in the Spanish, popular Italian, Dutch, and Greek versions of *Floire et Blanceflor* or to that of Darius's daughter — drifted within earshot of some individual familiar with the Germanic punishment basket. When he heard about the basket as a vehicle, he read into it his own connotation, and saw a means of improving the story.

To that improvement we shall now return, but not before we make a succinct summary of results thus far. As I see it, the punishment motif, derived immediately from the municipal codes of mediaeval German cities and ultimately from ancient Germanic custom, was spliced with the tale of the Oriental love-basket, and the two, blended as a more or less homogeneous unit, were disseminated all over Europe, surviving to this day in the manners and customs of the folk. The Germanic part has a natural tendency to revert when it remains upon its native soil, as we shall see, while the purest reminiscence of the Orient, the harem-like tower, becomes just as essential; for the two chief points of the story are attained first by emphasizing the lady's inaccessibility and thus bringing about the introduction of the basket, and secondly by indicating the commission of a crime which would justify the disgraceful punishment of exhibition.

III. LATER FORMS

In or near Switzerland, about the year 1300, an anonymous author wrote the romance of *Reinfrit von Braunschweig*, of which the heroine, he says, did not behave as Delilah behaved toward Samson, nor yet as the beautiful Athanata at Rome did to Virgil.[40]

New details of some interest appear in the *Roman de Renart le Contrefait*, wherein the basket story was written between 1328 and 1342.[41]

Virgil fell in love with a lady of the country, who lived in a tower higher than ten lances. Virgil grew depressed over unrequited love, but his messenger returned with hopeful tidings. But the lady was tricky, and the basket ruse followed. The next day Virgil was humiliated before all Rome, but when the basket was let down the lady persuaded him to re-enter it, and once again he swung aloft, all the while rendered even less at ease by the fact that he had removed his clothing.

The Latin tale, which for convenience I shall hereafter call the tale of *Nero's Daughter*, has certain similarities with this story which incline me to believe that a relationship is possible between the two. The motivations are similar. In *Nero's Daughter* the girl is imbued with feminine malice; here she has a spiteful heart. Moreover, in both versions Virgil dispenses with his clothing. If there is a relationship, I do not know why merely a lady of the country has replaced Nero's daughter. In any case, it would seem reasonable to infer that the story was in the air, and that versions now lost were in circulation.

Further evidence of the widespread dissemination of this episode is provided by its inclusion in Juan Ruiz's *Libro de Buen Amor* as an *exemplum*. Ruiz says that he found it "in a text," a fact which need not affect adversely a conjecture that by this time (1343) the tale was part of the repertoire of many a wandering minstrel.

No matter how racy the substance, any story genuinely current during the Middle Ages is likely sooner or later to turn up in allegorical dress. It need not surprise us, then, to find that Virgil's name has been changed to Fausse-Amour in a fourteenth-century French manuscript preserved at Copenhagen. The King of the Vices, Fausse-Amour's chief, is named Pride, *Orgueil*. He is engaged in attempting to conquer King Modus and his queen, Racio.

Fausse-Amour dons as a disguise the habit of a pilgrim, and betakes himself to the city of Esperance, the capital of the virtuous crew, where the hostess at his inn tells him that King Modus is away. Delighted, the bogus pilgrim persuades the hostess to gain him audience with Queen Racio so that he may communicate matters of importance to her. When the queen admits him, he insists on having a secret conversation. She recognizes him as one of the enemy, but takes him to her room and seats herself on the foot of her bed for the audience. The essence of Fausse-Amour's lengthy discourse is that he desires to be Queen Racio's lover. The latter realizes that she must do something to be rid of him, and tells him to wait until night in a room near-by. Then she calls together her attendants and orders a large basket to be brought to her. When night has come, she retires and orders the pilgrim to be brought in. The queen's maid assists him to remove his clothing, and he is just ready to retire also, when the queen's servants announce in well simulated consternation that the king has returned. Fausse-Amour has to flee precipitately just as he is. He takes refuge in the basket and is swung out the window, let down a short distance, and left there. With this problem off her hands, Queen Racio sends letters to the king, who returns at once and mocks Fausse-Amour. The latter is induced to confess his true identity and his motives for visiting the city of Esperance, and the king then returns his clothing and recommends that henceforth Fausse-Amour be governed by Abstinence. "Think," proclaims the king, "how false lovers are always deceived. Virgil was hung at a window just as you are. Women are extremely subtle. Adam, the most perfect of men, Samson, the strongest, and Solomon, the wisest, were deceived by them; and so you may be comforted." Finally Fausse-Amour is dumped out of the basket.[42]

The author was independent-minded enough to retell the story in an original fashion, and his precise sources are therefore difficult to discover. The lover's being merely let down in the basket and left hanging, instead of being pulled up and so left,

FAUSSE-AMOUR IN THE BASKET

From MS. Thott 415, Royal Library, Copenhagen

(Courtesy of Royal Library, Copenhagen)

is not satisfactory evidence for rejecting a connection with the Virgilian story, since King Modus himself makes clear that a relationship is intended. The collaboration between the queen and her household reminds us somewhat of Enikel's version, where the husband assists his wife in duping Virgil, and the naked state of the lover reminds us of *Nero's Daughter* and the *Roman de Renart le Contrefait*. We can scarcely expect to find one single source when there were probably a great many versions in circulation.

The most versatile adapter of our story, the one most keenly aware of the need of smoothing out motivations in order to make a plausible narrative, is one of the greatest of the mediaeval historical romancers, Jean des Preis, "dit d'Outremeuse," who wrote at Liége about 1400. He makes Virgil a love-pirate of blackest hue.

As a natural result of the magician's good works, Virgil was much admired at Rome, among others by Phebilhe, daughter of the Emperor Julius, whose love mounted until she could bear it no longer, although she had never seen him. She sent for him and told him all. By reason of her position, not to speak of her beauty, Virgil found it impossible to refuse her, especially since she was not particular about her status. Virgil made it plain that he was not interested in matrimony, but that friendship would be welcome. So they spent much time together, and such is the way of a maid with a man that Phebilhe determined to marry Virgil. It would have been all over with Virgil if he had been an ordinary man, but since he was a magician he dared gainsay the lady, with the natural result that she was furious, and set her mind on revenge. Virgil did not object to her being furious, as he was interested only in study and in demonstrating his power to the Roman people. Anyhow, he told her, there was no woman alive he loved more than herself, and she ought to be content, since if he ever should marry she would be his choice. But Phebilhe was now a woman scorned, in her own eyes at least, and she began to talk about her reputation, for it seems that she had let it be known that she was going to marry Virgil. The magician contemplated a moment and knew that she lied. "He who takes a wife is destroyed," said he, "I know I should be unlucky in marriage; but if you wish to go on with things as they are, I shall be very happy." Phebilhe decided to trick Virgil, and pretended to be mollified. "But father says I mustn't see you any more," she said, "and so when you want to see me you will have to be pulled up in a basket which I'll let down to you from my window; but don't bring anyone with you." Virgil agreed, first warning Phebilhe not to permit anything shameful or dishonorable to happen, and returned at night with several senators whom he had rendered invisible. Phebilhe appeared at her window surrounded by a laughing throng of attendants, who made merry together at the shame they were going to put upon Virgil. Virgil and the senators heard this, so the magician made a figure resembling himself, put it in the basket, and left. Phebilhe had the basket pulled up half way and tied thus, while she relieved herself of all the rage and scorn of the past weeks. The figure had an evil spirit in it which enabled it to carry on an extensive conversation with Phebilhe, which I shall not repeat here. In the morning the women made a great outcry, and all Rome came to see, among them the emperor, who ordered that the basket be lowered so that he could cut off the miscreant's head; but when the emperor struck at the figure's head, a thick, stinking fog came forth from its mouth, whereat the crowd was much dismayed. The figure then performed many marvels to divert the crowd, one being to raise and lower itself at will the height of the tower, another to paralyse the emperor and his barons so that they could not strike him. Finally it entered Phebilhe's tower, where the spirit quit the semblance of Virgil, which the emperor's henchmen found was but a bundle of rags.[43]

Put an imagination like that of Jean d'Outremeuse to work on a plot, and almost anything can happen. Yet a feature of this writer which should be respected is that his conscience as a story-teller did not permit him to retain unmotivated turns in the plot; he smoothed out the illogical sequences. We know precisely why Phebilhe devised the basket ruse, and at the same time we get Virgil's point of view well enough to understand why he felt that a terrible revenge was justifiable. Perhaps the predominant trait of the mediaeval Virgil is his omniscience, which he has achieved through magical aid. Jean d'Outremeuse is the first recorder of the tale to perceive the incongruity of depicting the mighty all-seeing magician as the simple dupe of a scheming woman. Jean moulded the heterogeneous medley of scraps which came to his hand into something more nearly resembling a coherent biography of the necromancer than Enikel was able to do. Although the latter calls Virgil a child of hell, he does not retain him in that character so well as Jean d'Outremeuse does. The alterations here are so considerable that it seems to me quite as satisfactory to say that Jean may have seen several of the earlier versions here considered as to say that he may have seen none of them. It is known that he was familiar with the *Image du Monde*, at any rate, but he must have found a full text of the basket episode somewhere.

An early Icelandic reworking, dating from perhaps the fourteenth century, shows interesting variations.

Virgil, a magician of the South countries, falls in love with the daughter of a powerful noble, who repulses him and threatens him with dire consequences. He counterthreatens, and she pretends to yield when Virgil agrees never to expose her. The ruse this time does not include a basket. Virgil is pulled half way up to the girl's window by a rope, where he is bidden stay until dawn. He ties his jewelled belt to the rope and lowers himself a little, but when he lets go he falls to considerable injury below, leaving the belt to the triumphant lady. After his recovery the intrepid wooer returns and permits the lady to ride him up hill and down dale until he has to take to his bed again.[44]

This last episode is the well-known *fabliau* of Aristotle and Phyllis shifted to Virgil. Aristotle was humbled in all the pride of his wisdom by one of the women at Alexander's court. She pretended to reciprocate his love for her, and promised to accept him as her lover if he would permit her to saddle and bridle and ride him. Aristotle agreed and was ridden, to the great satisfaction of Alexander and his court.[45] The first part is plainly the Virgil-basket story with the basket lost somehow, as the revenge story, also slightly altered, proves conclusively. The exhibition is omitted. The fall to the rocks below, with the resulting injury, will be considered later.

Mere allusions to the basket story are not interesting enough to discuss *in extenso*.[46]

Bonamente Aliprandi, the first Italian to tell the basket story, included a versified biography of Virgil in his fifteenth-century *Cronica de Mantua*. The lady in this case was the daughter of a knight, and her suitor was about thirty years old. The scheme to humiliate Virgil originates with the lady's father, to whom she tells all. The plan is for the lady to move to a palace with a high tower, and to tell Virgil that she is carefully watched, so that the only means of entrance will be in the basket. Virgil is pulled up and left suspended until next day, when the crowd mocks him. Finally Octavian orders him taken down, and reproves him.[47]

Here there are scattered resemblances to several earlier versions. The Emperor Augustus has

Ypocras taken down and scolded, as Octavian does here. In both, the humiliation of being exposed to public view is emphasized. In Enikel's *Weltchronik* the citizen's wife proposes the ruse; here the girl's father proposes it. In both Enikel and Aliprandi the lady is to pretend that she loves Virgil, and to make it clear that the basket is the only means of access to her. In *Renart le Contrefait* a messenger is employed, as in Aliprandi; the lady, "of that country," is unmarried, as here; and, again, the emphasis of the humiliation by exposure is common to both. These points in common with earlier versions are not sufficiently numerous or convincing to outweigh certain differences. Here the lady is merely the daughter of a knight; she is not confined in a tower, but for this special occasion lodges in one which her father fortunately happens to have handy. The messenger may be a reminiscence of the harem go-between; compare the porter in *Floire et Blanceflor* and the hostess of the inn in the allegorical Old French version. The introduction of Octavian indicates, I think, a garbling in transmission which would corroborate my impression that many of these versions are due rather to the widespread dissemination of the story than to any single version. A vague recollection that some emperor was concerned with Virgil's descent from the basket might account for the use of Octavian's name.

We find another Italian, Giovanni Sercambi, relating the same story in yet different dress a few years later. In his *Cronaca, sub anno* 1420, he has an *exemplo morale* which is of interest in our growing collection.

Before the birth of Christ there lived in Rome an emperor named Hadrian, who had a daughter, Ysifile, whom he kept night and day in a most beautiful tower. It happened that at this time Virgil, poet and great necromancer, was banished from Mantua and came to Rome. In the month of May he fell in love with Ysifile, a tricky one, who agreed to submit to Virgil's will. It was troublesome to get to her, however; the only way she could think of was to take advantage of permission she had from her father to have a rose basket pulled up to her window. If Virgil would enter that, she would pull him up, and afterward let him down again. Virgil agreed, and was pulled up half way and left there for sixteen hours. Ysifile sent for her father and told him a false story — that Virgil had tricked the man who was bringing the roses, and had hidden himself beneath them in the basket; but as she pulled it up she became suspicious of the weight, and perceived the villain lying in wait for her. The emperor ordered Virgil to prison, and eventually condemned him to death, but Virgil escaped on the way to execution by reciting an incantation over a basin of water, and was immediately whisked away by evil spirits.[48]

Here the rose basket immediately arrests the attention. It will be recalled that one branch of the romance of *Floire et Blanceflor*, including Boccaccio's *Il Filocolo*, brings about the meeting by means of a basket of flowers in which the lover hides and which is pulled up to the harem where Blanceflor is kept. Probably Sercambi knew Boccaccio's romance, but he must also have known the Virgil story, too, for otherwise we cannot account for the basket's stopping on its upward journey. It is of particular interest, then, to note that Sercambi apparently perceived the similarity between the Virgil basket story and that in the romance. We have new protagonists again in the Emperor Hadrian and his daughter Ysifile. The girl devises the basket ruse by herself, apparently without motivation (as in *Nero's Daughter* and *Renart le Contrefait*); and, more vindictive than her sisters in other versions, she calls her father to witness Virgil's exposure and then lies about it so as to procure the sentence of death upon the doubly unfortunate lover, whom her father does not seem to know.

At roughly the same time that Sercambi was writing his *Cronaca*, Dirc Potter was working on his *Minnen loep*, which contains the first Dutch contribution to our cycle, and thus begins the interesting record of Holland's adaptations of the tale.

Lucrecia was a proud young woman, and was seldom permitted to go out, and so Virgil, much in love with her, used to go at night and stand at the foot of the tower where she slept. Lucrecia would sit at her window and converse with him. They arranged for the basket in course of time, and Virgil entered it. When it stopped half way up, the lover decided that she was tired, and was but resting a moment; but the whole plan had been thought up by another lover, who was with her, and Virgil was left hanging, unbecoming though it was for a man of his dignity to appear so. When the basket was at last lowered, he slunk home.[49]

No emperor is present. Motivation for the trick is brought about in a new way. Although the lady was proud and rarely ventured forth from her tower (note the persistence of the Oriental harem in such traces as this; but for our knowledge of the provenience of the tale, such a feature would be considered as merely a random remark), she had a lover with her there all the time, and it was this lover, one Berthamas, who brought about the humiliation of Virgil. Like Sercambi's Ysifile, Potter's Lucrecia deluded Virgil into thinking that his suit was welcome. With the tale in the air everywhere, one need not be surprised to find slight variations occurring. The main plot persists, essentially unchanged. The victim, Virgil, remains, because everyone knew his name as that of the poet most conspicuous in the mediaeval world. The other characters vary, simply because no sufficiently well-known figures were ever called upon to play their rôles.[50]

More ingenious is the manner in which René I, Duke of Anjou, Lorraine, and Bar, Count of Pro-

vence and Piedmont, King of Naples, Sicily, and
Jerusalem, who lived from 1409 to 1480, and probably did most of his writing after 1450, brings in
the story of the basket in his allegorical romance,
Li livre du cuer d'amours espris, which is frequently
reminiscent of the *Roman de la Rose*, as well as of
much purely romance material. Bel-Accueil con-
ducts Cuer to a sort of chamber of horrors for
lovers, where as trophies hang the spoils of love
gone wrong. First is pointed out an ancient basket
of willow twigs which is suspended by a golden
chain; then a pair of shears a foot and a half long
(the kind with which they shear sheep in Berry)
containing a great piece of coarse black hair from
the head of a man; then a bridle, saddle, spurs, together with several other objects. These are explained as being Virgil's basket, Delilah's shears,
and Aristotle's riding equipment. Virgil was treated
thus, we are told, because he prized Love's power
lightly; and so the basket will hang there as a
memorial as long as the world shall endure.[51]

Probably the oldest form in which the romance of
Virgilius exists is the French *Faictz merveilleux de
Virgille*, printed during the first quarter of the
sixteenth century. (For details see Chapter IX.)

Virgil loved the daughter of a great lady of Rome,
member of one of the best families. When Virgil so-
licited the daughter through an old sorceress, she told

him that there was great danger; that the sole way to reach her was to come to the foot of the tower where she slept and enter a basket which she would have ready for him. The tower was at the market-place, and the morrow was market-day. When she had pulled up Virgil — who had removed his clothing — and fastened the rope, the lady informed him that he would remain there so that everyone might know his wantonness in wishing to lie with her. The emperor was much chagrined when he heard of Virgil's plight, and commanded the lady to release him.

The "great danger" to which the lady alludes is no doubt a faint suggestion of the closely guarded tower which we have seen so frequently before. The complete lack of motivation for the ruse recalls the similar lack in *Renart le Contrefait* and in *Nero's Daughter*; and Virgil's entering the basket unclothed is paralleled in the same two versions. The lady's taunting Virgil reminds one of the scolding of the citizen's wife in Enikel and of Phebilhe in Jean d'Outremeuse. The circumstance of the emperor's knowing the victim is not usual, the only clear cases being in the Ypocras story, in the allegorical version, where the victim is not Virgil but Fausse-Amour, and in Aliprandi's chronicle. It is possible that the writer of the romance knew the tale as it appeared in *Renart le Contrefait* or in *Nero's Daughter*, or in both; but this is far from certain.

The conspicuous fact, I think, which emerges from this examination of mediaeval variants of the

basket story is that it seems to have been transmitted habitually in skeleton form. That is to say,
hardly more than the bare essentials of the plot and
the name of Virgil are common to more than two or
three of them. Were this not the case, we should
find more features in common. A conspicuous and
clever development like that by Jean d'Outremeuse
would exert more influence. That such skeleton
forms existed would hardly need demonstration,
but I have listed a dozen or more. Just such casual references as Gower's or Machaut's, to select
at random, must have served as the media of transmission, for transmission there certainly was, and
in abundance.

The German *Von Virgilio dem Zauberer* (1520?)
includes the basket story, but as it copies Enikel
almost word for word there is no reason for considering it further, and the case is similar with the
version in *The Deceyte of Women*, which is taken
from the French or Dutch form of the Virgilius
Romance.

For convenience in treatment I shall now abandon the general chronological arrangement which I
have been following, and classify subsequent contributions according to the respective languages in
which they are written.

IV. HOLLAND

The versions produced in Holland after 1550 are, if not numerous, of great interest. At first the old patterns are followed without significant change. Casteleyn's *Conste van Rhetoriken* contains a poem on the power of love called *In 't Amoreus*, of which the third stanza is a list of unfortunate lovers. The mention of Virgil in the basket reminds Casteleyn of Dido.[52] Other such lists appear in a play and a poem by J. B. Houwaert, *Jupiter en Yo* and *Pegasides Pleyn, end Lyst-hof der Maeghden*.[53]

In 1657 appeared what amounts to a one-act play built round the basket, — Joan van Paffenrode's *Klucht van Sr. Filibert, Geen Mal boven Oud Mal*, a diverting and animated treatment too lengthy to analyze in full.

"Sr. Filibert" is heavily smitten with love for the beautiful Laurette, whom he wooes through his manservant Weerhaen and Laurette's maid Bely. A passionate love-letter the lady tears to bits as she inveighs against the presumption of Filibert. Off stage Weerhaen is instructed by Bely and Laurette what to tell his master. He follows orders implicitly, and as a result Filibert enters a basket let down by Bely, who pulls it up half way and leaves it suspended. Two members of the night-watch happen along and discuss Filibert's presence in the basket, deciding that he is a thief, and fetch a ladder so as to take him down; they will do with him what it is customary to do with "such birds." Bely pretends sympathy for Seigneur Filibert and tells him that her lady has taken his misfortunes very seriously. She goes on to persuade Filibert that it is her lady's pleasure that Filibert take back into his service his manservant whom he has dismissed for suspected complicity in the recent disgrace. Now Filibert thinks he has his eyes open at last, for Bely makes him believe that his own stupidity and the accidental arrival of the night-watch were alone responsible. Through a long stage-direction we learn that the two men happening along were not the night-watch at all, but were paid by Laurette to masquerade as such in order to bring about Filibert's disgrace. To add to the hilarity, Filibert must satisfy Weerhaen's injured dignity with money, and pays the bogus night-watchmen for their kindness in fetching a ladder to get him down and in refraining from reporting him as a thief to the authorities. At last light begins to dawn on the poor gull when he learns that Laurette is betrothed "to her Gedeon" and Bely likewise to Weerhaen. The playlet ends with a soliloquy by the victim on the power of "Cupidoos," and the appropriate apophthegm "Semel insanivimus omnes." [54]

If we make due allowance for the necessary changes involved in converting narrative verse into drama, there can be little doubt that van Paffenrode got his ideas from Dirc Potter. The names are changed; Virgil has dropped out completely, but the details are virtually identical. Potter motivated the trick by means of introducing the lover of the lady's choice and keeping him with her throughout the episode, although the reader does not know this until the adventure is nearly over. In the play, van Paffenrode follows Potter very closely in this respect, thereby attaining a higher degree of dramatic suspense than would have been possible if he had cleared up the entire plot at the beginning. To create an artificial preliminary motivation he has Laurette tear Filibert's love-letter to pieces while she gives Weerhaen a "speak for yourself, John" message. It will be remembered that Potter's contribution to the story was this new motivation, and the dramatist followed his example in postponing the solution to the end. The introduction of the pretended watchmen and of the secondary plot of the servants is van Paffenrode's own.

Probably the piece was successful, for but two years later appeared an obvious imitation of it, Melchior Fokkens's *Klucht van de verliefde Grysert*. Oliver, the lady's brother, induces the unwelcome lover Wolfert to enter the basket, pulls him up, and laughs at him when the watch come along and accuse him of being a thief.[55]

These plays were built on literary sources. Not so is it, however, with a version collected from the folk two hundred-odd years later in the little town of Audenaerde.

On the gable of a fine house there was a few years ago an old story hewn in stone about a magician. It has disappeared now, but the story still circulates among the folk. Once upon a time a fine young man lived at Audenaerde who loved the daughter of one of his neighbors, but in vain. She did not reciprocate his love. At last her heart seemed to soften, and she agreed to pull the young man up to her window in a basket if he would appear at midnight. He came, bringing the basket himself, and attached it to a rope which the young lady let down. Half way up the gable the basket stopped and whirled about in a dizzy manner. Next morning workmen on their way to the day's labor saw him hanging there and mocked him. Late in the day the basket was lowered, and the young man made his shamefast way home.[56]

I discern no trace of van Paffenrode's play here. Whether the tableaux cut in stone kept the story alive at Audenaerde, or the tableaux themselves were the result of the story's existence in oral tradition, we cannot know. The lover is a lad of the town, no magician. Hence later when the magical revenge is brought about, an additional character must be found to provide the magic. Virgil has been split up into two people, — a common enough occurrence in folk-tales, — one the young lover, the other the old magician. Motivation, amply provided in van Paffenrode's version, here reverts to its pristine flimsy state. The girl does not reciprocate the young man's love, and humiliates him to be rid of him. Almost all trace of the punishment basket has been lost, although the crowd seems to know instinctively why the lover is suspended, and

THE BASKET SCENE IN *FEUERSNOT*

From *Almanach der Bayerischen Staatstheater*, München, 1931, p. 26
Editors Knorr und Hirth G.m.b.H., München

they hoot and jeer at him as lustily as their mediaeval forbears.

From this folk-tale Ernst von Wolzogen got the
plan for the libretto upon which Richard Strauss
based his opera *Feuersnot*.

The lover's name is Kunrad; his lady-love, the daughter of the mayor, is named Diemut. Kunrad, a studious
recluse and magician, seizes Diemut in a moment of un-
controllable passion and kisses her before the towns-
people. In reprisal for this insult Diemut pretends to
desire a meeting, and Kunrad is left hanging before the
mocking citizens. He summons his diabolical magic to
his aid and extinguishes all fire and light in the city of
Munich. The citizens beseech Diemut for pity. Finally
she helps Kunrad into her chamber, but evidently the
lover's reception is a cold one, for the fires remain black.
At last she heeds the prayers of her people. The Volks-
chor, supported by the Straussian orchestra, sings,

> All' Wärme quillt vom Weibe,
> All' Licht vom Liebe stammt,
> Aus heissjungfraulichem Leibe
>   Einzig
> Das Feuer uns neu entflammt,

and the obdurate lady is finally won, as the audience
perceives during a five-minute orchestral interlude
while the lights gradually come on.[57]

V. FRANCE

In France interest in our story dwindled almost
to nothing during this period. A conventional list
of humiliated lovers includes a reference to the
Virgil-basket episode,[58] and Charles Desmaze re-

lates it as occurring to Maurice-Quentin de la Tour at Cambrai, where de la Tour is supposed to have wooed a merchant's wife. She pulls him up part of the way and leaves him suspended, while she and her husband laugh. Next morning passers-by jeer at him. Probably the story was taken by the biographer from some source which it is impossible to define. I have no suspicion that it was current among the folk of Cambrai.[59]

On December 31, 1733, a *commedia dell' arte* in which two baskets are concerned was played at Paris. A doctor is pulled up in a basket five or six feet from the ground. A second lover is then pulled up, also.[60]

During the first third of the nineteenth century, in the general region of which Nevers is the principal city, several versions of the basket story were collected.

A tailor presents gifts to a servant with whom he is in love. The girl lives in a hay-loft, and offers to pull up the gallant in a willow basket by means of a pulley, if he will appear at midnight. The lover appears, is pulled up divested of his clothing, and left hanging at the second story, to the derision of everyone.

Another version depicts a shoemaker as undergoing the same experience.[61]

Some two hundred miles to the northeast, in the district of Trois-Évêchés, was collected about 1860 another version which bears uncertain evidences of being genuinely popular, a product of the folk.

A married baker courts the wife of a writer. For a consideration of fifty *louis* the lady hearkens, promising an appointment for the morrow, when her husband will be away. Since the stairway is closed at night, the lover must needs content himself with a basket as a means of entry. The lady informs her husband of the affair, and he rejoices at the trick. With his assistance the wife pulls up the basket and attaches the rope. An apprentice perceives the crowd mocking at his master and runs to his mistress, who begs the writer and his wife to leave the baker where he is until the next day, when she and the apprentices beat him soundly.[62]

Now this "chant populaire," if such it be, presents a curious problem. With regard to the subject matter I would note these significant features: (1) The wooer, the victim of the basket scrape, is a *baker*. I have already called attention to municipal law-codes of mediaeval Germany which prescribed precisely this punishment — public exhibition suspended in a basket — for fraudulent bakers. (2) The husband of the lady is a writer, an *écrivain*. Not in any previously cited version has this been the case; but if one takes into consideration the facts that Virgil himself was a writer, and that a whole cycle of German and perhaps English popular ballads (which will be referred to below) on the love-basket story makes the wooer a writer, something approaching a case for the genuine folk quality of this song seems to emerge. (3) This version was picked up in the village of Retonféy, in Trois-Évêchés, a district which includes the cities of Metz, Verdun, and Toul. Earlier in this chapter I have referred to the possible significance of basket penalties prescribed in the civil code of Strassburg during the thirteenth century, while the author of the *Image du Monde*, a citizen of Metz, was writing his chronicle which seems to refer to the Virgil-basket story.

If these facts can be accepted at their face value, then we are drawn to infer that in this *chant populaire* we have evidence again of the splicing of the two basket motifs — the Oriental love-basket and the Germanic punishment-basket. The time is long — six hundred years and more — between the date of composition of the *Image du Monde* and the date of collection of this popular ballad. Unless three reciprocally independent circumstances have here coincided to mislead us, the subject matter of this ballad is truly popular, — the result, so to speak, of a six-hundred-year gestation among the folk in the neighborhood of Metz. In striking support of this inference is a passage found in the *Chronique de Metz* of Philippe de Vigneulles, in which under the year 1511 the events of a day of celebration are recorded. One of the events was a procession of *chairiots*, perhaps the sort of vehicle used in the presentation of mystery plays.

After the Nine Worthies came eight or nine wagons in each of which was a wise or famous man of ancient times who had been deceived by a woman. First came King Solomon and his wife bringing him to worship idols. In another wagon was Samson being shorn by Delilah. In still another Judith was cutting off the head of Holofernes. In another were Hercules and "Sairdanapolus" spinning. Then came Virgil suspended in a basket, and finally Aristotle ridden by a woman.[63]

If the story was well enough known in Metz to be used in a street procession, we may well believe that it was folk property.

The most recent contribution to the basket story in France appears in *La descente de Marbode aux enfers* in search of Virgil, in Anatole France's *L'île des pingouins*. Frère Marbode is warned by a fellow monk, in sound mediaeval fashion, against the dangers of reading Virgil, for he was a magician, and in spite of his power was deceived by a courtesan of Naples, who pulled him up and left him suspended all night in a basket used to pull up provisions.[64] Now Anatole France has done two things here which it never occurred to any other writer to do. He has transferred the scene of the basket story to Naples, and he has reverted to the basket of the Ypocras story, which, it will be remembered, was reported to Ypocras as being used to pull up food to the captive son of the king of Babylon. The combination is of course a simple one, and is probably due to France's reading a version of the Ypocras story as well as the Virgilian legends. Thus, with a purely literary retelling, this chronicle of the life of a tale originated by Frenchmen and related by Frenchmen for seven centuries comes to an end so far as France is concerned.

VI. ITALY

After 1550 Virgil's importance as hero of the story diminishes, and almost every version substitutes some indefinite person or other for the poet and necromancer. So it was in Italy, for example in the case of a verbose and wearisome *novella*, the fifth in the collection by Pietro Fortini, in which we are told of a credulous pedant who would lie with a gentlewoman and suffers deception. The only character named is the pedant Giovambatista. Motivation is brought about chiefly by his personality. He is so insufferable that one is glad to see any misfortune befall him. Then, too, the lady's chastity is a matter of some concern to her father confessor. The pedant comes directly from the property room of the *commedia dell' arte*, and has no virtues to recommend him. Fortini worked with a free hand, for he dispensed with the basket and made the priest the chief contriver of the pedant's disgrace, which consists in first being made drunk and then being hung up to ridicule.[65]

Also in the sixteenth century appeared Andrea Calmo's farce *La spagnolas,* in which lovers are again suspended in baskets. Spectators of the *commedia dell' arte* no doubt saw similar episodes frequently in comedies of which written versions have not survived. I suspect a relationship between this play and *I Vecchi scerniti per amore,* played at Paris in 1733.[66]

An interesting version collected not actually in Italy, but in an Italian-speaking community in the eighties of the nineteenth century, makes the poet Ovid the occupant of the basket.

> The poet fell in love with the emperor's daughter and violated her. Her father heard of it while he was hunting, and returned in a rage. Ovid's friends attempted to let Ovid down in a basket, but the emperor came while he was in transit, and the basket had to remain where it was. After pondering for a day and most of a night, the emperor decided that he did not have the heart to execute him, and so he had him let down and saved him from the furious mob, only to banish him to an island, where the poet died shortly after.[67]

Perhaps subterranean survival is responsible for this version. The connection between the basket and the lover's designs on the lady is all but lost. It has become merely episodic. In the Ypocras story the emperor learns of his favorite's plight when he returns from hunting, somewhat as here. The kernel of real fact is interesting. The banishment of "the most capricious poet . . . among the Goths" and his death in exile are biographical facts.

The basket adventure is supposed to have befallen Leo the Wise, Byzantine emperor from 886 to 911. As a result of his infatuation for a lady he was well laughed at by his people.[68] Solomon, too, suffered like Virgil, according to a Bulgarian collection of tales gathered in the eighties of the nineteenth century.

A virtuous lady refused to become one of Solomon's concubines in spite of the repeated importunities of the king's courtiers, but she became frightened when the king threatened to have her removed from her house by force. Accordingly she agreed to permit him to visit her providing her reputation be saved. He came at night, entered the basket prepared for him, and was pulled up part way. When he begged for mercy, the lady read him a lecture on his conduct, and demanded whether he preferred to be dashed to pieces below or to be left suspended as a spectacle for the people next day. Solomon promised rich gifts and the utmost respect if the lady would liberate him. When he swore on his crown to love her only as a sister, she lowered him, and the chastened king returned to his home.[69]

This lady's unique achievement in becoming Solomon's sister may, indeed, be a folk-tale, for the fame of Solomon attracted every imaginable kind of story; but this version, like the preceding one, is very late, and I suspect that the Bulgarian story is a literary adaptation of the widespread story of Virgil in the basket.

VII. GERMANY

Circumstances compel us once more to retrace our steps, this time to inspect the work of Germany's earliest "columnist," Hans Sachs, whose eager curiosity led him at one time or another to most tales told by mediaeval writers, particularly to those of a humorous nature and those having to do with women. As the basket story lays claim to both of these distinctions, it is not surprising to find Sachs using it again and again. He knew both the Virgil story and its forerunner, the Germanic punishment-basket. First he treated the former in *Der Fillius im Korb*. This differs in no considerable degree from earlier versions, and such is the case with a rehandling of the same theme by Sachs eight years later, *Der Filiüs im Korb*, with a moral attached. *Der Fillius* has been shown to be based upon Enikel, and perhaps upon Sebastian Franck.[70]

His handling of this material having apparently been successful, Sachs turned the story about and made a woman the occupant of the basket, thus in a way reversing the process which took place when the basket story passed from the Orient to Europe, for here the woman is pulled all the way up and ac-

complishes her object. *Die pürgerinn im korb* is a
pious married woman whose early morning de-
partures from the marital bed turn out to be visits
not to church but to a lover, who pulls her up in a
basket to his chamber. The husband spies upon
this German Wife of Bath, and when she returns
tells her that he has seen her conveyed to heaven in
a basket, and that therefore she must be an evil
spirit, and he will have none of her. A moral rounds
off the tale. Sachs here must have used his imagination freely, for so far as I know there is no similar version.[71]

The actual basket punishment itself is described
by Sachs in *Dreyerley straff zw Frankfürt*. A baker
whose loaves were too small was hung in a basket
suspended from a pole over a pool of stinking water
and given a knife with which to cut himself out. A
throng of people stood about and jeered the baker
as he crawled out of the filth.[72] Sachs was doubtless
describing a scene which he had witnessed himself.[73]

How deeply the use of the basket as a means of
punishment sank into the consciousness of the
German folk is indicated by the existence of certain
proverbs, in use for centuries, and still current.
"To get a basket," *einen Korb bekommen (kriegen)*,
is equivalent to our "flunking" an examination,
that is, to fail. Perhaps it is a development from an

LUCAS VAN LEYDEN: VIRGIL IN THE BASKET

(*Courtesy of British Museum*)

older, more specialized meaning which we can more readily understand in the present connection: "to fall through a basket," *durch einen Korb fallen*, to fail to secure the lady of one's choice,[74] a meaning well illustrated by another of Hans Sachs's pieces, *Der jung Gesell fellet durch den Korb*, the moral of which is that young folks must be careful when they a-wooing go. Sachs saw a painting on the wall of an inn and describes the scenes there depicted.

A young lady holds a young man suspended in a basket attached to a pole which projects from her house. The bottom of the basket is loose. On the youth's head is a legend to the effect that other young men should beware of wooing treacherous women. Then the basket gives way and the wooer falls into a pool of filth below, to the accompaniment of the jeers and laughter of the bystanders, a group of young women, who tell him that he is an object lesson to those who are not faithful to their loves.[75]

These proverbs, and this illustration of one of them, refer to a kind of informal folk justice designed to protect morality. Similar customs are represented by the English skimmington or stang, and by the American custom of riding immoral or otherwise objectionable people out of town on a rail, the ride frequently being terminated by the application of a coat of tar and feathers.[76]

It is likely that this precipitation through a basket as a punishment for wayward lovers is a reminiscence of the penalties prescribed in mediaeval German municipal codes rather than of the Virgilian adventure, although the definite association here with amorous misconduct may owe something to the latter.

Sachs wrote a counterpart of *Der jung Gesell fellet durch den Korb* entitled *Die stoltz jungfraw fellt durch das sib*. Here a young lady falls through a sieve as a punishment for presumption in love. He asserts fancifully that he beheld the lady in the sieve at Cologne when he passed through that city on a journey.[77]

A cycle of German ballads of which the earliest come from the late fifteenth or the sixteenth century is based upon either the Virgil-basket story or the punishment-basket. For convenience I shall refer to the cycle as *Der Schreiber im Korb*. Some of the songs have a title like *Heinriche Kunrad der Schreiber im Korb*.

A writer goes a-wooing in the market-place, where the object of his affections lives. An appointment is made, and toward midnight the lover returns and is told that the only way he can reach the lady is by means of a basket. Against his will he enters it, is pulled up, and then falls down, injuring himself. He gives bribes, evidently fruitlessly, in an effort to prevent the singing of songs about it.

The association of this ballad with the matters here under consideration is obvious, and does not re-

LUCAS VAN LEYDEN: VIRGIL IN THE BASKET, 1525

(*Courtesy of British Museum*)

quire emphasis. With slight variations, the song appears in a great many collections of *Volkslieder*.[78]

Closely related to *Der Schreiber im Korb* in all save the use of the basket is a series of ballads of which the earliest example I have is that of Ulrich von Lichtenstein, writing in 1255. Ulrich is pulled up to the lady's apartment by a rope made of sheets tied together; but the lady is obdurate, and finally tricks Ulrich as he departs by means of the improvised rope, and he has a nasty fall.[79] The Icelandic *Virgiless-rímur*, which telescopes the stories of Virgil and of Aristotle and Phyllis, also dispenses with the basket. To all intents and purposes, the lover suspended by a rope is equivalent to the lover hung in a basket attached to a rope. So it is in Oriental stories, and so it would seem to be here. If in these ballads the lover has a fall similar to that which he suffers from the basket in other versions, then the analogy is even closer.

A dozen or more students' songs have been collected from Germany and Holland which belong to this last general type. The lover is seized, bound, and thrown out a window.[80]

Der Schreiber im Korb and related ballads have some connection with the Virgil-basket story, for both lovers are smuggled in — or, rather, expect to be smuggled in — by a basket or rope, both come to grief in essentially the same manner, and in ad-

dition there may be some significance in calling the
victim of the German ballads a *Schreiber*. Certainly that word would characterize Virgil well. It
may possibly be to the point to recall here that the
first person to report the Virgilian legends in Germany was Conrad of Querfurt, chancellor of the
Emperor Henry VI of Germany, who took part in
the conquest of Southern Italy, and at the end of
the twelfth century wrote a letter to friends in Germany in which he reported a number of the Virgilian legends. It is true that he says nothing of the
basket affair, which as we have seen was first attached to Virgil about the middle of the following
century. Yet stranger things have happened in
folk-tales than that the association of the name
Conrad with Virgil's name somehow should have
stuck with the association of Virgil's name and the
craft of writing, and thus contributed to produce
this cycle. Further, this group of ballads is at
home where the punishment-basket was developed,
and that punishment was still in force during
the centuries when the *Schreiber im Korb* first
appeared.

There is yet another group of stories which may
have some connection with our subject. A monk
in love with a married woman is with her when the
husband unexpectedly returns home; he is forced
to take refuge in any handy hiding place, fre-

GEORG PENCZ: VIRGIL IN THE BASKET

(*Courtesy of British Museum*)

quently in a cheese-basket. The tale as told by Schumann is typical.

The young wife of an old man wants help in her "housework." A young monk performs satisfactorily, but one day when the husband enters suddenly the former betakes himself, naked, to a cheese-basket hanging out the window. The husband, who already knows the facts, cuts the rope and throws the basket into the Danube, then hears the monk moaning, and fetches the abbot to exorcise the devil from the basket.[81]

Probably the similar tale in the *Historie of Frier Rush*, "How Rush came home and found the priest in the Cheese-basket, and how hee trayled him about the town," is taken from an earlier German version of the monk in the cheese-basket. It is lacking in the German versions of *Bruder Rausch*. Friar Rush cuts the rope holding the basket in which the priest has hidden, and drags the basket several times through a pond; thence to town, where he opens it before the people.[82] Eulenspiegel and Skelton are reported to have amused themselves in somewhat the same fashion.[83]

Mediaeval chronicle and allegory did not leave the basket out of account; but we must bear in mind that the Renaissance showed just as lively an interest in the Virgilian legends as the preceding period. It is but fitting, then, that a typical Renaissance genre, the emblem book, should include the basket story. Theodor de Bry tells it briefly in his *Emblemata Nobilitati*, 1593, in order to explain an illustration.[84]

The last of the German versions of this cycle to which I wish to direct attention is that of A. F. E. Langbein, who reversified *Heinriche Konrade der Schreiber im Korb* as he found it in *Des Knaben Wunderhorn* into smoothly-flowing couplets.[85]

VIII. ENGLAND

Late in date but old in story is the Scottish popular ballad *The Keach i' the Creel*, which in some respects resembles the Virgil-basket episode.

A bonnie young clerk falls in love with a fair maid, but they cannot meet because the maid's father locks the door carefully. The clerk's wily brother brings a ladder, and they climb to the top of the maid's house, whence the clerk is let down in a basket through the chimney to the girl's room. The father, aroused by voices, rushes to the girl's bed. She has covered the clerk, and tells her father that she is holding the Bible. The father, content, returns grumbling to bed, but the mother hears more noise, rises to see for herself, gets her feet entangled in the basket and rope, and is pulled up the chimney by the clerk's brother, who thinks he felt a signalling tug at the rope. She gets a good jolting, and thinks the devil has got her —

> And every auld wife that's sae jealous o her dochter,
> May she get a good keach i the creel![86]

The clerk's journey *down* a chimney to his lady-love is none too similar to Virgil's journey *up* the side of a tower, or, to go a step farther back, to Floire's journey; but the oldest analogue of *The Keach i' the Creel* puts the matter differently. In *Le chevalier à la corbeille* the lover orders his squire to secrete himself so as to have access to the roof, whence he pulls the knight up in a basket and then lets him down the chimney in the same basket.[87] I find it impossible to claim a clear relationship between the *Chevalier à la corbeille* and any of the basket stories listed above; but in view of the evidence collected in this chapter of the very wide dissemination throughout Southern and Western Europe during the twelfth and thirteenth centuries of tales in which lovers are pulled up to their ladies in baskets, I find it just as difficult to deny relationship. The essential difference between the two would seem to lie merely in the *direction* in which the baskets go, down or up; and the evidence that we have of the versatility, brilliance, and imaginative powers of various writers of romances and fabliaux in these two centuries appears to me to be sufficient to account for this relatively slight change in plot. The following similarities may be noted, at any rate: (1) both Virgil and the chevalier love a lass forbiddenly; (2) in both stories a basket is the lover's means of transportation to his lady; (3) in both the lady is watched jealously; (4) in both the basket is a means of punishment or humiliation, in the Virgil story to the lover himself, in the other to the meddler. The differences, while not inconsiderable, seem to be slightly more than balanced by the similarities, particularly if we note that the Scottish lawyer John Rolland supplied a possible link between the *chevalier* and the clerk in *The Court of Venus* (1575):

> Als it is red in storyis ancient,
> Thocht it be not in ald nor new Testament.
> How that Vergill that worthie wise doctour,
> In latin toung was most faculent,
> Nane mair pregnant, facund, nor eminent,
> To writ or dyit, he was of Clerkis flour:
> Throw ȝour defait, and Inflammit ardour,
> He was deiect be daft delyrament:
> Become ȝour slaif to his greit dishonour.
>
> Quhair ȝe him hang ouir ȝour wallis in a creill
> Howbeit efter he was reuengit weill.

The association of Testament, clerk, and creel in Rolland's verses, and of Bible, clerk, and creel in the ballad may be significant.

There are certain Elizabethan, or more accurately Jacobean, basket stories which may be related to some of the foregoing tales. In *Dobson's Drie Bobs*, 1607, we are told that one Malgrado, a student at Christ's College, loves the daughter of a laundress and entertains her in his room against the rules. When anyone enters, he puts her into a large basket and pulls her up by a rope to a rafter, where she remains concealed.[88] Deloney's *Thomas of Reading* (1632) gives an anecdote closer to our theme.

Cuthbert of Kendall loves the "Oastesse" of Bosom's Inn. In dalliance, with the host looking on from a dark corner, they sing one of the few Elizabethan jigs which have survived. The host determines to dissemble a little longer, and announces that he will ride afield. Cuthbert and the hostess retire to a warehouse and lock the door. The husband's spy sees them and reports to him. He returns and calls to have the lock broken. Cuthbert and his companion hear the command and open the door, remarking casually that they went in for a cheese and the door blew shut. But the host is skeptical. Cuthbert is bound, placed in a basket, and drawn up into the "smoky Lover" of the hall, there to hang in the smoke and heat until next day.[89]

The basket appeared on the London stage in William Haughton's *Englishmen for my Money* (1616), in the second scene of the fourth act. Vandal, unfavored Dutch suitor of Laurentia, has been led to impersonate the favored lover, Heigham, at a basket rendezvous. The scene is developed at some length, but the upshot is that Vandal is pulled up half way by Laurentia and her sisters and left suspended.[90] Vandal's nationality turns one's speculations toward Dutch treatments of the tale of Virgil in the basket. The *Klucht van Sr. Filibert* is forty years later than this play, but in view of the close relations between England and Holland during the sixteenth century it appears entirely possible that Dirc Potter may have been the inspiration for Haughton's scene.

In a note on *Virgilius in de Mande* J. E. Gillet directs attention to what he considers a basket suspension in John Lacy's play *The Dumb Lady*, first acted in 1669 and printed three years later.

The unpopular lover, Squire Softhead, is got out of the way by a stratagem: Mrs. Nibby: "Your father's bringing of him [Softhead] in to woo you again; fall to your madness, and let me alone to dispose of the Squire. I'll have him drawn up with an engine, and there he shall hang i' th' air in a cradle til you're married or run away."

The fact that a cradle is used instead of a basket is sufficient to rule the passage out as a parallel. Dramatic necessity requires that the troublesome squire be kept out of the way until Olinda, the heroine and the object of his affection, is safely married to someone else. The incident is more likely to have been developed from some such ruse as that of Nicholas in Chaucer's Miller's Tale.[91]

What seems to be a late echo of the punishment-basket turns up in the mid-eighteenth-century chapbook *Simple Simon's Misfortunes and his Wife Margery's Cruelty which began The very next Morning after their Marriage.*

MARGERY CRUELLY PULLING UP SIMPLE SIMON
IN THE BASKET

From *Simple Simon's Misfortunes . . .*, London, 1750? p. 8
(Courtesy of British Museum)

Simon sought surcease from his wife's scolding the day after their wedding. He went to an ale-house, but Margery found him there, drove him out, and got drunk herself. When Simon got back home his shrew was already there, and "she invented a new kind of punishment; for having a wide chimney, wherein they used to dry bacon, she taking him at a disadvantage, tied him hand and foot, bound him in a basket, and by the help of a rope drew him up to the beam in the chimney, and left him there to take his lodging the second night after his wedding; with a small smoaky fire under him; so that in the morning he was reezed like a red herring. But at length he caused his wife to shew him so much pity as to let him down:

> In Love release me from this horrid Smoke,
> And I will never more my Wife provoke:
> She strait did yield to let him down from thence,
> And said, Be careful of the next Offence." [92]

The "new punishment" invented by Margery has little novelty for the reader of this chapter; and a clue to the precise source of it is yielded by the fact that a chapbook version of *Thomas of Reading* printed and sold, like *Simple Simon's Misfortunes*, in that great chapbook factory, "Aldermary Church-Yard, Bow Lane," boasts the identical woodcut used to illustrate Simon hanging in the chimney.[93]

Last in the line of English uses of our tale is Bulwer-Lytton's in *Pelham* (Chapter XVII), written apparently during one of the author's lapses into journalistic style. A woman throws her glove out of the window purposely, to test the love of M. Margot. She insists that he recover it in the same manner in which it left her, through the window, but by means of a basket and rope. Clad in a sea-green dressing-gown, M. Margot is left hanging, "to his extreme mortification."

We have now followed the love-basket from India to Flanders, from the *Katha Sarit Sagara* to *Feuersnot* and *L'île des pingouins*. We have seen the tale come from the East to Italy and France, there retaining for a time its Oriental form intact, but, soon becoming attached to the Virgil legends, joining with a Germanic custom which found expression in municipal codes of the later Middle Ages, and then undergoing dissemination throughout the length and breadth of Europe, now in literary, now in popular form, and occasionally retaining such vitality as to survive almost to the present day. In no one elaborate treatment of this tale are all features of any previous version repeated identically, for the nucleus of the plot was so familiar to story-tellers that any narrator felt free to alter a detail here and there to suit his fancy, just as to-day ancient humorous tales from Chaucer and elsewhere keep turning up in new dress to suit the times. With the essential elements of the plot in mind, we have been able to follow the story from age to age and from people to people. Fortuitous material has been added and dropped. At one time it is simply the anecdote of the promiscuity of a man's wife, at another an episode in the most delightful of mediaeval love-stories, at yet another an object lesson on the chastity of the matrons of Rome. Almost every literary form is represented and a great variety of redactions is reflected in the half-hundred or so of versions here collected. Perhaps the most striking revelation of the search is the apparent coalition of an Oriental love-story with a Germanic legal custom in producing a new tale having an independent life of its own extending over six centuries.

VI

THE MAGE'S REVENGE

MORTIFIED and humiliated by his exposure in the basket before the people of Rome, Virgil employs his magic art to turn the tables on his false mistress, who soon discovers that hell hath no fury like a magician scorned. By means of his occult powers he extinguishes all the fires in Rome. When the emperor, rendered desperate by the clamor of his famishing people, begs Virgil for relief, the seer replies that the fires can be restored solely upon condition that the lady who has humiliated him (the emperor's daughter) expose herself naked in the market-place and permit the people to kindle their candles and torches at her person. The enchantment will continue until every householder in Rome has visited her, for one torch will not light another.

The story is not a pretty one. Variants are strange and not too easily understood. I shall limit myself to a brief consideration of the possibilities as I see them. Since I have already printed in note 19 of Chapter V an early version, *Nero's Daughter*, in which the story is complete in all of its essentials, there is no need to introduce a detailed summary here. What slight variations occur from one version to another have no bearing upon the question of origin.

Earlier than *Nero's Daughter* is Guiraut de Calanso's cryptic mention of the fire which Virgil knew how to extinguish. I am inclined to suspect that the fire here is not the fires of Rome which Virgil extinguished in reprisal for his humiliation, but is possibly the ever-burning fire or lamp which was finally put out by the automatic archer when the taboo placed upon it by Virgil was violated. In the *Image du Monde* the matter becomes clearer. A lady insults Virgil, and therefore he extinguishes all the fires in a city; the revenge story follows. The insult, I assume, was Virgil's suspension in the basket, although the text is not explicit. Jansen Enikel, like most of his successors, uses the revenge as a natural sequel to the basket episode. The lady nearly dies of shame. In Jean d'Outremeuse's highly elaborated version she actually does die. Jean makes other changes also. The lady has to appear in the window whence she lowered the basket (instead of in the market-place), and, as a subsidiary revenge, Virgil enchants the church where she attends mass, and she is compelled to confess aloud her misconduct with Virgil. Other accounts I list in a note, for their variations are not significant. Finally, in Strauss's *Feuersnot* the business is changed so as to make the scene stageable, as I have already remarked. [1]

Like a great many of the Virgilian legends, this one was told earlier of another person. St. Leo the Thaumaturge, Bishop of Catania in Sicily, who died in 780, is reported to have caused a competitor named Heliodorus, a versatile trickster and magician, to be burned; but before divine retribution was thus visited upon him, Heliodorus performed several feats later attributed to Virgil, among them the humiliation of a woman who called him a liar and spit in his face. He extinguished all the fires in the city by magic, and told the emperor that they could be rekindled only from the woman. The life of St. Leo containing this tale was translated in 1626 from a Greek manuscript written probably before 787. [2] A story similar in most respects to the Virgilian episode turns up again in Greek in the history of the world by Dorotheos, Metropolitan of Malvasia, in the eighteenth-century publication referred to in Chapter V. It is probable that the Virgilian legends had become known by that time in Greece, rather than that the Heliodorus story remained latent for ten centuries and then suddenly reappeared, for the basket episode precedes that of the revenge. [3] A similar tale was collected from the Serbian folk in 1869.

The woman in the case is a witch and a rival of the wizard who extinguishes the fires and humiliates her. I can draw no inference concerning this small group of variants scattered over eleven centuries, save that Greece would appear to be as likely a centre for them as any.[4]

The *Rigveda* may put us on the right track for a solution of this puzzling story.

King Tryaruna angered his domestic priest Vṛśa and the latter departed. As a result the heat of the king's fire disappeared, and the offerings thrown upon it were not cooked. So the king sought out Vṛśa and brought him back. It remained for the priest to restore the fire. He found a female demon acting as wife to the king. "Having seated himself with her upon the cushion on a stool, he addressed her with the stanza,

'Whom do you here?' [*sic*!]

Speaking of the heat in the form of a boy, he addressed her thus. And when he had uttered the stanza

'Far with light'

the fire suddenly flamed up, repelling him who approached and illuminating what was already bright; and it burned the Pisācī [the demon] where she sat."[5]

Here fires are extinguished by magic art in reprisal for offence, and rekindled in some manner through association with a woman. The parallel is not exact and is therefore not altogether convincing; but it does provide some elements from which the Virgilian story and its analogues may have arisen, for the *Rigveda* was current in India for many centuries from 1000 B.C. on. It seems possible, then, that the association of revenge, extinguishing fire, and rekindling it through the agency of a woman might have had some effect upon this type of story. Oddly enough, the priest's name, *Vŕśa*, is not unlike *Virgilius* in sound!

In the Virgilian legend we fail to perceive a religious element; yet the best suggestion that I know is that somewhere in the maze of myth developed about the origin of fire lie the beginnings of the revenge which Virgil inflicted upon the emperor's daughter. A French observer of the last century records a religious ceremony which he saw performed in Syria. The occasion is the annual renewal of the sacred fire.

Fire just descended from heaven is passed from one part of the church to another. The tumult in the church becomes indescribable. Pilgrims rush to illuminate their candles at the sacred torch, and the one who first obtains it is certain to go straight to paradise, no matter what sins he may have committed. . . . They pass the divine flame over their faces and legs; the women pass it under their skirts, and burn themselves severely in order to remove all traces of their sins.[6]

This rite appears to have its origins in pagan ceremonies involving purification or atonement through the extinguishing of all fires and rekindling them from a single fire of sacred origin. One thinks of the carefully-guarded fire of the Vestal Virgins at Rome and of fires fetched from Delphi in Greece. Perhaps the most famous example is the annual expiatory rite at Lemnos performed by women in memory of the misdeed of their feminine ancestors.

Because the women of Lemnos neglected the worship of Aphrodite, the goddess made them intolerable to their husbands by afflicting them with an evil odor. When the husbands brought in other women, the afflicted ones slew their spouses in rage, whereupon the ancient divinities of Lemnos withdrew from the island. Then the Argonauts happened along and were received with festivities by the Lemnian women, suddenly recovered from their ailment. Each year these events were commemorated. Husbands withdrew from their wives for a day, and for nine days all of the fires in the island were extinguished, to be rekindled only when a ship returned from Delos with fresh, sacred fire, which was distributed amid rejoicing.

Now this sort of rite, involving extinction of fire and separation of the sexes, then rekindling of fire and the reunion of the sexes, is known all over the world as a method of inducing fertility in the spring. Such is presumably the origin of the Syrian ceremonial.[7] This Eastern rite kept appearing constantly in the West throughout the Middle Ages, in spite of repeated efforts to suppress it, and continues to this day in certain places, notably in Florence. We come closer to the beginnings of the Virgilian phase of the story when we learn that

Pope Gregory IX in 1238 forbade its celebration. Needed, of course, are clearer echoes of this type of festival than we have thus far seen in the Virgilian legends. The sole writer to provide such an echo is Jean d'Outremeuse, who says that when the people had the fire restored to them they held a great festival.[8]

It will be remembered that Maître Gossouin — if he be the author of the *Image du Monde* — is the first to link Virgil's name with the revenge. It would seem that Gregory IX's decretal came at just the proper time to project the idea into Maître Gossouin's consciousness, for the first version of the *Image du Monde* as we have it was written probably in 1245, when the recollection of the Pope's order may well have been fresh. Furthermore, we must not rule out the possibility that Heliodorus's revenge may have remained current in Sicily and Southern Italy, where Greek was read steadily, and where Maître Gossouin says he travelled.

The soundness of this conjecture does not depend upon the fact that the combination of the basket story with that of the revenge was made after both stories reached Europe, and after the basket story had become attached to Virgil; for the first incident is told, without the second, in the *Saint-Graal* biography of Ypocras or Hippocrates.

Yet in this latter the author apparently felt that the magician should wreak some kind of vengeance on the tricky lady, for the renowned physician is said to have bribed a hideous crippled beggar to touch the lady with a magic herb which had the property of an aphrodisiac, working through the sense of touch. The moment the beggar touched her with it, she fell violently in love with him. Ypocras spied upon her, and when he saw her enter the beggar's hovel he called the emperor and his court to see her shame. At first Augustus ordered that they be burned as found in bed together, but on second thought he forced her to marry the beggar and become the chief laundress of the palace.[9]

Why did the author of *Nero's Daughter*, or Enikel, or Maître Gossouin — whichever of the three first attached the story to the Virgilian cycle — consider that it was appropriate to Virgil? Virgil, to be sure, was regarded as a magician; but this is not sufficient, for he was not a magician in love until after the basket story joined the legends. The impetus may have begun with the fire which was associated with him first in this same *Image du Monde*. Perhaps the *Roman des Sept Sages* provides a clue here, for in several versions the poor women of Rome are said to have got warmth from the ever-burning fire made by Virgil.[10]   Thus we have Virgil controlling a fire which has something to do with women. The attribution of the basket adventure to Virgil supplies the final necessary link — the fire-controlling magician is placed in conflict with a woman. In the rites, all fires are extinguished for a period. They must be rekindled at one source only, the new, divine fire freshly sent by supernatural powers. This new fire is expiatory; its application absolves sins. Virgil the magician has supernatural powers. The lady who suspended him in the basket is his mistress, and has therefore presumably committed the sin of adultery. The fires are extinguished, and can be rekindled at one source only, the person of the lady who has sinned. The Virgilian fire, then, would originally have been conceived as purification from carnal sin. The new idea introduced is that the public exposure of the lady constitutes a humiliating revenge for her obduracy and trickery.

From religious rites, pagan or Christian, celebrating the purifying influence of a sacred fire, to the unsavory tale of Virgil's revenge is indeed a long step; but whether the story is Christian or pagan or merely Virgilian, the basic idea is the same — that of fire as an agency for the expiation of sin.

VII

LA BOCCA DELLA VERITÀ

VIRGIL'S legendary trials with women were not restricted to the subjects of the last two chapters. He made several contrivances designed to regulate that most unpredictable of variables, the conduct of women, only to learn that even a magician may have to admit that he has attempted the impossible. The regulatory device of which the failure is here to be recorded is the *bocca della verità*, the mouth of truth, which was so constructed that it bit off the fingers of an adultress when she placed them in its mouth and swore a false oath. Even this admirable invention was circumvented by the wiles of womankind, for the empress of Rome planned an equivocal oath frequently resorted to in story. She arranged with her lover that he should dress as a lunatic and embrace her as she proceeded to the test. Then she swore that the only man who had been as close to her as the emperor was this madman. The oath was of course true, and the triumphant empress withdrew her fingers unharmed. The emperor, it should be noted, first became aware of his wife's infidelity when a horn grew from his forehead.[1] So runs the tale about Virgil and the *bocca* in its earliest version, a German song of the fourteenth century.

Before we proceed, it is well to observe that this story, though well integrated, is not an inseparable unit. The two parts are clearly discernible. First there is the story that Virgil made a stone image of which the mouth would clamp down on the fingers of a perjurer in conjugal matters; and second, there is the story of the ruse, based on an equivocal oath, by which the guilty women eludes the justice dealt out by the truth-tester.

The second of these two parts is a widely-known tale in both Orient and Occident, and has been carefully investigated. In every instance some truth-testing apparatus is used, but the equivocal oath does not occur in connection with the *bocca della verità* before the anonymous fourteenth-century German story just summarized. The numerous devices — fountains that produce clear or muddy water, hopping or motionless seeds, hot iron, relics of saints, and so on — need not detain us, as it has been satisfactorily established that the ruse is of Oriental origin.[2] It is the *bocca della verità* which I wish to examine here.

Jean d'Outremeuse knows of a head of copper which Virgil contrived in such a way that it could detect falsehood in adulterous women. He directed the Romans, who had come to Naples expressly to beg him for assistance in such matters, to place the head in the wall of the tower from which Phebilhe had attempted to suspend him. They did so, and the *bocca* worked well, for no ruse is mentioned.

In the next version, in Jean Mansel's *Fleur des histoires*, we return to the earliest extant form of the episode, that in fourteenth-century German. According to Mansel, Virgil made at Rome a throat of copper, which always detected feminine duplicity until a young woman devised and carried out the ruse; then in a rage Virgil destroyed it, because he himself knew the truth of the case.[3]

Felix Hemmerlin presents a fresh rendering in the fifteenth century. The wife of Emperor Antonius, suspected of infidelity, was conducted to the stone of truth (*lapis veritatis*) fashioned by Virgil. She prearranged the ruse and successfully withdrew her hand from the mouth of the stone after the equivocal oath. The Senate doomed her accusers to death.[4]

Johannes Pauli used the story in his *Schimpf und Ernst* in 1522, and from his great collection it was repeated many times, notably by Hans Sachs, who devised an additional chastity-test in the adulterers' bridge constructed by Virgil to relieve an agony of doubt in King Arthur's mind. Whenever a person guilty of adultery rode upon the bridge, Virgil spied from a tower in its centre and rang a bell, whereupon the sinner slipped into the water. The casualties were heavy, but the queen survived the test without difficulty. This device I regard as a combination of the cold-water punishment for adultery with the idea of a chastity test. There is also a faint echo of the *Salvatio Romae*.[5]

In the *Faictz merveilleux de Virgille* the instrument is a brazen serpent, as it is in the English and Dutch versions of the Romance. The ruse occurs in due course, and Virgil smashes the serpent.

Von Virgilio dem Zauberer, otherwise a duplicate of Enikel's *Weltchronik* with respect to Virgilian legend, adds the *bocca*, including the ruse. The emperor whose wife undergoes the test first becomes aware of the need of it when a horn sprouts from his forehead. This feature is sufficient to remind us of the initial Virgil-*bocca* story in the fourteenth-century song, and close examination shows conclusively that the writer of *Von Virgilio dem Zauberer* had before him, in addition to a manuscript of Enikel's *Weltchronik*, either the manuscript of the first version of Virgil-*bocca* or a close copy of it.[6]

Finally, the version in the *Deceyte of Women* must be glanced at. In this mid-sixteenth-century English text the *bocca* for the first and only time is a lion's mouth:

And also Vyrgill made to the profyte of the Romayns (to thende that they myghte haue short lawe *and* that euery man myght incontinent know whether his cause wer trewe or false) by the crafte of Nygromancy a Lyon of brasse, and Who that put hys hande in the throte of the lyon, and swore that his cause was true, and good and his othe being false lost his hande. . . .

The woman here is Virgil's own wife. She employs the ruse, succeeds, and Virgil in wrath smashes the lion. I am uncertain where the English author found the lion, but I am inclined to suspect that it may be due to a description of the stone called *la bocca della verità* in the Church of Santa Maria in Cosmedin at Rome. One of the many things which it resembles slightly is a lion with a mane, as we shall see later.

Of these versions, clearly the most important is the first one, which may have exerted even more influence than can be demonstrated. The very brief and sketchy outline by Johannes Pauli may be based upon this original, or upon that in the printed *Von Virgilio dem Zauberer*, of which the conjectural date of printing is 1520. Whatever the relationship, Pauli's tale did more than any other version to popularize the story, though its brevity makes it virtually useless when we attempt to decide what the *bocca* originally was.

It seems plain to me that it was at the start a stone with a hole in it. So says Hemmerlin, who of all the narrators of the story is the only one who certainly travelled in Italy, so says Johannes Pauli, and such the *bocca* is to this day at Rome. So it is also in a tale about the Emperor Julian which appears in the *Kaiserchronik*, an anonymous German chronicle of the first half of the twelfth century.

Julian, not yet emperor, embezzled money confided to his care by a widow, who in her impoverished state was compelled to bake and launder for a living. One evening as she was washing clothes in the Tiber she came upon a stone image which the heathen had hidden there so that they might pray to it in secret, and she beat the clothes against it. A devil within it protested against such usage, identifying himself as the god Mercury, and promised to help her regain her money from Julian if she would complain to the emperor and require that Julian swear upon the image. The widow complied. Julian cheerfully appeared at the image and inserted his hand in its mouth, but before he could carry out his intention of swearing that he had never seen the widow's money his hand was stuck fast. At once he agreed to return the money, but his hand continued to stick fast. Finally, when the bystanders had departed, the demon in the image agreed to assist Julian in every way provided he would abjure the Christian faith.[7]

So far as the *bocca* is concerned, the trail of the story is lost here. In the biography of Julian in a Syrian manuscript of the sixth or seventh century, he is said to have embezzled money from the widow, but he swears on the crucifix and by the

Holy Communion that he has not done so. Then the demon advises the widow to have Julian swear "by that image which protects the hours of the city, and I will take him, and he will not be able to save himself from my hands, until he has returned to you everything that he has taken from you." Before this oath is taken, the demon converts Julian from Christianity, and the widow is forgotten.[8] In the earlier version the localization of the *Kaiserchronik* image in the Tiber is missing, and there is no *bocca*. Thus if there is a relationship between the *Kaiserchronik* story and that of Virgil and the *bocca* — and there may be — the probability that the *bocca* was originally made of stone is enhanced.

It is enhanced still further by a pair of legends in which Virgil is not mentioned but the *bocca della verità* is. Dirc Potter, who we know visited Rome, included in his *Minnen loep* the entire story, ruse and all, save that no magician is concerned and that after the successful ruse the *bocca* does not fall to pieces. The *bocca* was a great round stone made like a head, and it bit off the hand of a perjurer as neatly as if it had been cut.[9]

Similarly, Juan de Timoneda describes the *bocca* as a stone like a millstone, with a face in the middle half of a lion and half of a man—a description which would well apply to the *bocca* as it exists today.[10]

Now there is reason to believe that taking an oath on a stone here is not merely the product of a mediaeval writer's vagrant fancy, for mankind frequently has used stones for this purpose, in ancient classical as well as in modern times. Apparently some quality was attributed to stones which made oaths taken on them binding. Every variety of stone seems to have been employed, from small ones held in the hand to huge monoliths, and oaths taken on or through stones having holes in them were peculiarly efficacious.[11] In ancient Rome oaths by *Juppiter Lapis* were resorted to;[12] but a better clue is provided by the fact that the Church of Santa Maria in Cosmedin at Rome, in the portico of which a stone called *bocca della verità* leans today, stands upon ground holy before Christianity reconsecrated it; for here was the *Forum Boarium*, here traders dealt in cattle, and here they had from time immemorial erected temples sacred to Truthtelling and to Fair Play, even one to Chastity.[13]

The precise location of these temples is a matter upon which doctors disagree violently. That they stood near Santa Maria in Cosmedin, or *in Schola Græca*, is a matter of fact.

The earliest and most important of these temples was that of *Herculis Invicti Ara Maxima*. It was the primitive centre of the cult of Hercules in Rome, and ancient tradition claimed that it was built immediately after the retribution forced upon Cacus for his deception regarding Hercules's cattle, and the recognition of the hero's divinity by King Evander.[14]

It was here that the Romans were taken to swear their most solemn and binding oaths. The task of cleansing the Augean stables would be slight compared with that of blazing a clear trail through the maze of myths centered about one or another or all of the forty-odd heroes named Hercules-Herakles known to classical antiquity,[15] but from certain trustworthy guides various seemingly pertinent facts may be gleaned about the cult of Hercules in ancient Italy. Those about to undertake a journey sacrificed to Hercules on the *Ara Maxima*, and this god was recognized as the patron of merchants and hence of mercantile transactions, so that his cult encroached on that of Mercury to such an extent that Hercules came to be regarded as the deity presiding over fair play, over correct weights, over the genuineness of coins. In this manner, presumably, the *Ara Maxima* came to be a place where oaths were sworn and transactions were solemnized. From it women were rigorously excluded.[16] This aspect of Hercules as the god of oaths, of the plighting of troths, of the sanctity of pledges, is regarded as native to Italy, for it was probably transferred from a Sabine deity. To Hercules was consecrated a tithe of all profits, as to the earlier deity, Sancus, in whose care also lay the restoration of lost property to its rightful owner. Now Hercules and Juno seem to have borne a relationship to one another, possibly because of the fact that, since women were excluded from the *Ara Maxima*, Hercules must have been regarded as a peculiarly masculine god; thus Juno, as the *Bona Dea* to whom women resorted, came into antithesis with Hercules, and men were excluded from her adjacent altar. Juno and Hercules together, moreover, were revered as the gods of marriage. Finally, *Bona Dea*, whose cult appears to have merged at times with that of Juno, was regarded as the daughter of Faunus, whose cult also was associated with the *Forum Boarium*; she was the mistress of feminine wisdom, and was so chaste that she never left her chamber, her name was never heard in public, and she herself never saw or was seen by any man save her husband.[17]

These ancient divinities and semi-divinities were quite as much all things to all men as their saintly successors; but from this abundance of pre-saints' legends we may draw suggestions concerning the possible background of the *bocca della verità*, since fragmentary ideas of these ancient cults had a fitful existence during the Middle Ages. To the story of Julian and the widow's lost gold, we may apply the

old faith in a god to restore lost property, a faith
which descended to Hercules and would thus have
merged with other beliefs attached to Mercury.
Hence the willingness of the god Mercury in the
stone image to help the widow regain her money, in
the *Kaiserchronik*. To the *bocca della verità* as we
find it in Virgilian legend we may apply the conception of Hercules and Juno as the deities of marriage, the swearing of oaths, and perhaps the noteworthy chastity of the daughter of Faunus, to
account for the interest of the *bocca* in feminine
chastity. Thus we seem to perceive most of the
elements involved in the *bocca* story as existent in
ancient Rome. If they had been scattered about
at random in the city, any argument in which they
were forced into relationship with our tale would
be a waste of time; but the fact is they were not
scattered about, for every one of them had a centre
in common with the others, that centre being the
Forum Boarium, the site to which the legend of
the *bocca della verità* still clings and to which it has
given its name, the *Piazza della Bocca della Verità,*
the site upon which stands to-day the church now
sheltering the *bocca,* Santa Maria in Cosmedin.

Of the *Ara Maxima* there appears no trace to-
day. It may have stood near the charming little
round temple known now as the desecrated church
of Santa Maria del Sole, formerly Santo Stefano

Rotondo or delle Carozze, and erroneously called the Temple of Vesta.[18]

Near the *Ara Maxima* stood the temple of *Hercules Invictus*.[19] In the time of Pope Sixtus IV (1471–84) the ruins of an old temple between Santa Maria in Cosmedin and Santa Maria del Sole were destroyed. A bronze image of Hercules, now in the Capitoline Museum, was found there, and since that time it has been surmised that here was the temple of *Hercules Invictus*, although this temple could have been only a later reconstruction of the primitive one.[20] It has also been thought, and with some reason, that the shrine of Hercules was none other than the round church of Santa Maria del Sole itself.[21]

During the Middle Ages this small church was considered to have been the temple of the Sybil from which her oracular statements were issued.[22] At the time of the earliest versions of the *Mirabilia Urbis Romae*, during the twelfth century, it was known as Santo Stefano Rotondo, and is referred to as having formerly been the Temple of Faunus.[23] Faunus, god of fertility, was identified in Rome with Pan. He was a wood-spirit, taking on also the character of an incubus, of whom women must especially beware; he appeared in dreams, and so became an oracle. His was one of the oldest cults in Rome, and it lasted until the end of paganism.

In many respects it was confused with the cult of Hercules, and we may perhaps see in this intermingling the reason for the identification of the round temple.[24]

In the same version of the *Mirabilia* there is another remark which leads us in a different direction: "Ad sanctam Mariam in fontana templum Fauni, quod simulacrum locutum est Iuliano et decepit eum." [25] The story referred to in this passage is that told above, about the widow who entrusted her property to Julian the Apostate, and found an idol in the Tiber which was none other than the devil Mercury (patron of merchants, god of eloquence and trickery).

The round temple of Mercury on the Aventine near the *Forum Boarium* was one of the oldest in Rome. It was deeply venerated, and merchants were wont to expiate there the sins of lying and perjury. It is celebrated by Ovid, and mediaeval documents mention its presence in the neighborhood.[26] The twelfth-century version of the *Mirabilia* contains a reference to a temple of Mercury on the Aventine, "et fons Mercurii ubi mercatores accipiebant responsa," which seems to indicate oracular attributes of the divinity.[27]

Another temple of interest to us is that known as the *Sacellum Pudicitiae Patriciae*, or the shrine of chastity frequented by patrician women. This altar, about which very little is known, may have stood near that of *Hercules Invictus*.[28] For centuries scholars and travellers occasionally thought that the church of Santa Maria in Cosmedin might itself have been constructed upon the site of the shrine of *Pudicitia Patricia*, just as others have considered it to be the successor of the *Ara Maxima*.[29] That Santa Maria in Cosmedin, which was in existence by the sixth century, was constructed over ruins of other edifices has been made clear by excavations, but the exact nature of the ruins is doubtful.[30]

At some moment as yet undetermined, the round stone called the *bocca della verità* was taken from its ancient resting place and rolled up against the church of Santa Maria in Cosmedin. In 1615 a French traveller says that he saw it in that place. Its presence there during the sixteenth century is perhaps most forcefully witnessed in contemporary sketches by Étienne du Pérac, Martin Heemskerk, and an anonymous Dutch painter. A Spaniard writing in 1551 says that it was leaning against the church. In the fifteenth-century Latin and German *Mirabilia* and in the travel-book of Capgrave dating from the middle of the century, the *bocca* with its marvellous qualities is placed at Santa Maria in Cosmedin. Earlier than this there is apparently no direct and conclusive evidence, unless

LA BOCCA DELLA VERITÀ TODAY

we accept as valid the canon Crescimbeni's statement in 1715 that for many centuries before its removal inside the portico in 1632 it had stood leaning against the side of Santa Maria facing the Marmorata. Most interesting is a guess made by Giovenale in his thorough study of the church. He reproduces an "oceanic mask" painted in 1123 upon a wall of the court at Santa Maria, which he suggests may have been an imitation of the *bocca della verità*. If such be the case, the stone had been unearthed long before the date of our earliest version of the *bocca* story.[31]

The actual provenience of the stone has never been discovered. Theories there are and have been for centuries, but so far none of them has been proved.[32] It has been variously thought to be the image of Jupiter Ammon; of the *Pallore* or *Terrore* worshipped in Rome; of some other god, perhaps Pan, perhaps a river-god; an unidentified oracle; part of the *Ara Maxima* itself; a chastity-testing stone from the temple of Pudicitia near-by, used, as in our legend, by the daughter of Regulus Volaterranus when she was accused of adultery; the idol of the Temple of Truth; the cover of a well of Cacus, which echoed the lowing of the cattle stolen from Hercules, so revealing the theft; a fountain; the cover of the above-mentioned fountain of Mercury, which purified merchants of the dis-

honesties they found necessary in their trade; or —
a most likely hypothesis — merely a drain-cover.[33]
If it is indeed a drain-covering, it may very possibly
have come from the early round temple mentioned
above, said to be dedicated to Hercules, which had
a drain in the middle of the floor. The *bocca* had in
any case appeared at Santa Maria in Cosmedin
before the time of the actual demolition of the
temple by Sixtus IV.[34]

Whatever may have been the real nature of the
stone, the chances are that it came from the immediate neighborhood of its present location, and that
neighborhood was certainly rich in associations sympathetic to the *bocca della verità* legend as we know
it. It was a place of oracles, a holy of holies for the
swearing of great oaths, where one must rid oneself
of the stain of perjury — a place where women
must tread softly, where unchastity was abhorred,
and, coming closer to our special interest, where the
very powers possessed by Virgil the magician were
attributes of the principal local deities.

It is, of course, impossible to say to what extent
dim memories of the nature and traditions of these
holy places may have remained among the folk.
The important thing is that information about
them did not altogether disappear, whether it survived in monastic libraries, in tales circulated by
pilgrims, or in purely local recollection.[35]

LUCAS VAN LEYDEN: LA BOCCA DELLA VERITÀ

(Courtesy of British Museum)

Such being the case, the odor of a very special sort of sanctity had never departed from the *Forum Boarium*, and as a consequence the *bocca della verità* was probably already clothed in an awe-inspiring mystery peculiarly appropriate to Virgilian legend when some whimsical fancy brought the two together.

The cults of ancient Rome are bewildering in their complexity, and modern knowledge of them cannot be anything but fragmentary. Yet mediaeval notions of those cults indicate that they survived after a fashion. Basing definite conclusions upon this kind of material is of course out of the question, but when the ancient legends reappear here and there in the Middle Ages and apparently fit together in such a way as to constitute a background for the legend of the *bocca della verità*, the natural thing to do is conjecturally to associate the background with the object, to link these once ardent and potent religious beliefs which refused to die with the oath-testing *bocca*.[36]

The stone with its curious legend has never ceased to call forth comment. The nature of the remarks made by travellers who have gazed upon it varies with each person, ranging from awed credulity to flippancy.

In the fifteenth century, John Capgrave, Austin friar of King's Lynn, went to Rome, and about

1450 wrote a description of that city, called *Ye Solace of Pilgrims*. He gave an account of Santa Maria in Cosmedin ("Santa Maria iuxta scolam grecorum"), in which he said:

"Be fore þe dore of þis cherch stant a grete round ston and þat is mad aftir þe figure of a mannes face. This ston calle þei þere *os iusti*. This ston was enchaunted sumtyme be swich craft þat what man cam to þis ston or woman and swor a trew oth in ony mater þat he wer charged of he schuld putte his hand in þe mouth of þis ston & pulle it oute esely. And if so were þat his oth were fals he schuld neuyr pulle oute his hand with oute grete hurt. Therfor was þis ston cleped *os iusti* þe rithful mouth." [37]

In Steffan Planck's 1485 edition of the *Mirabilia Urbis Romae, vel potius Historia et descriptio urbis Romae*, there is mentioned as being at Santa Maria in Cosmedin a round stone in the fashion of a countenance which is called *bucca veritatis*, at which men purify themselves. It lost its power through a woman.[38]

In neither of these early accounts is Virgil's name mentioned, but such is not the case with the German versions of the *Mirabilia*. In an early block-book edition of this pilgrim's manual, which may have appeared about 1475, the *bocca della verità* is said to have stood at Scola Graeca. Virgilius made it, and it lost its power when a wicked woman betrayed him.[39]

Arnold von Harff, of a noble family of Cologne, set out on an extended pilgrimage which took him through Rome in 1497. His description of the city, while accurate enough in its topography, is influenced by his knowledge of the *Mirabilia*, which he repeats almost word for word in his report of the *bocca*.[40]

A curious appearance of the stone is in a heavily jocose article on virginity published in Germany in 1615.[41]

Richard Lassels, in his widely known book of travel (1670), has a sage remark or two to make. He says:

Passing on, I came to an ancient *Church* called *Santa Maria in Cosmedin*, or in *Schola Graeca*, Where *St. Austin* before his conversion, taught *Rhetorick*. In the *portch of this Church* stands a great *round stone* cut into the face of a man, with a great *wide mouth*, commonly called, *La bocca della Verità, The mouth of Truth*; but this not being affirmed by *the Mouth of truth*, I dare not beleeve it. I rather beleeve it served in some old building for a gutter spout: I know, *truth* may speake lowd, and have a *wide mouth*; but he that takes every wide mouth for the mouth of *Truth*, is much mistaken. [42]

The Comte de Caylus is also moved to sober reflection:

At this church is the *bouche de Vérité*, which served the Romans for taking oaths. "They say too that they used it for testing virginity. If that were true, how many girls in France would be bitten!" [43]

Edward Wright, who published an account of his travels in 1730, has an ingenious explanation of the legend. He suggests that the stone owed its miraculous power to the priests, who remained hidden behind it and burned the fingers of the guilty with hot irons.[44]

The anonymous author of a work called *A True Description and Direction of what is most worthy to be seen in all Italy*, closes an account of the story with a brief "*Credat qui volet.*" [45]

The urbane De Blainville contributes the following comment anent the stone, which he calls the *Ara Maxima*:

> The *Italian* jealousy was the Invention of it. . . . The *Roman* Husbands have found Ways and Means to persuade their Wives, that if a Lady has forgot herself so far as to cuckold her Husband, and then should be bold enough to thrust her Hand into this Mouth, both Jaws would immediately join and chop it off. There is Invention for you, and Credulity at the same Time.[46]

As we pass to the nineteenth century we find the legend regarded differently. M. Vasi, in his *Itinéraire instructif de Rome*, reports on Santa Maria in Cosmedin:

> To-day it is commonly called *the mouth of truth*, because of a great piece of round marble placed in the portico and made in the shape of a mask of Pan: it has staring eyes and gaping mouth, and children are told

GEORG PENCZ: LA BOCCA DELLA VERITÀ

(Courtesy of British Museum)

that if they don't tell the truth they cannot withdraw their hand.[47]

— a version repeated by Erasmo Pistolesi in his description of Rome in 1846.[48]

So are the mighty fallen! The great stone, for centuries an object of concern to everyone who looked upon it, whether scoffer or worshipper, has become by 1800 a bugaboo to frighten children.[49]

VIII

CAESAR'S SEPULTURE

ONE of the chief sights of Rome which has excited wonder since the days of Caligula and has attracted every traveller's attention is the great obelisk standing before the Church of St. Peter. Its earliest history has not been determined, but it seems pretty certain that it was brought from Heliopolis in Egypt by Gaius Caligula and placed in the circus of Nero on the Vatican hill. The only inscription on the column was Caligula's dedication to his predecessors Augustus and Tiberius:

> Divo Caesari Divi Iulii F. Augusto Ti.
> Caesari Divi Augusti F. Augusto Sacrum.

The circus disappeared in the course of time, but the obelisk remained beside the old Church of St. Peter, the only obelisk in all Rome to stand during the centuries.

In 1586 Pope Sixtus V, beautifier of Christian Rome, caused this "Agulia di San Pietro" to be moved to the place in front of St. Peter's where it is standing to-day. The process of removal was a masterpiece of engineering on the part of the Pope's architect, Fontana, and excited the widest interest throughout all Christendom. At that time the great bronze ball on top of the column was removed and a cross placed in its stead. The ball may be seen today in the Palazzo dei Conservatori.[1]

It was inevitable that this huge stone, twenty-five metres high and quarried in one piece, should attract legends to itself during the Middle Ages. One legend was to the effect that it had witnessed the crucifixion of St. Peter — a story still more or less current.[2] Another and very persistent one, in existence as early as the beginning of the eleventh century, was that the metal ball on the point of the obelisk contained the ashes of a Roman ruler — nearly always Julius Caesar.[3] The precise reason for the rise of this tradition is unknown. The reference to "Iulii" in the inscription may have had something to do with it,[4] and a vague reminiscence of the memorial column to Caesar in the Forum may have also played its part.[5]

The fact that Fontana found the ball to be quite devoid of ashes had, very naturally, but little effect on the legend. Just as it had been believed up to the time of the removal of the obelisk, in spite of dissenting voices, so it continued to live well into the eighteenth century and is echoed even later.[6]

The earliest twelfth-century manuscripts of the *Mirabilia Urbis Romae* quote an inscription alleged to have been on the ball:

> Caesar tantus eras, quantus et orbis,
> Sed nunc in modico clauderis antro.[7]

A pilgrim-book of the following century adds these verses:

> Si lapis est unus, dic qua arte sit levatus,
> Si lapides plures, dic ubi congeries.[8]

By the fifteenth century the lines run:

> Caesar erat tantus quantus fuit ullus in orbe,
> Se nunc in modico clausit in antro suo
> Mira sepultura stat cesaris alta columpna
> Regia structura qua rite nouercat in aula
> Aurea concha patet qua cinis ipse latet
> Si lapis est unus dic qua fuit arte leuatus
> Et si sunt plures dic ubi iunctura inest

and are translated thus by John Capgrave:

> This man was swech þer is now non him lich.
> Now passed fro men and spered in his litil den
> A meruelous supultur a piler of hy figur.
> To a kyngis bildyng futt in halle stand þere no swech.
> The rounde balle we se in which his asches be
> If þis be but o ston be what craft myth it up gon
> If ioyntis ony ᵹe se telle us wher þat þei be.[9]

Amazement and some incredulity at the feat of transporting such a mammoth object and raising it in one single piece may be expected from the children of the Middle Ages, since even after Fontana's exploit, the obelisk is sometimes regarded askance. A young French nobleman visiting it in 1669 exclaims: "Its height is miraculous, but that it could be made of a single piece is inconceivable!" [10]

THE OBELISK WITH BALL BEFORE ITS REMOVAL

From B. Gamucci, *Le Antichita della citta di Roma,*
Venezia, 1565, p: 195

(*Courtesy of British Museum*)

Richard Lassels, finding difficulty in swallowing the story, says: "The whole *Guglia* is sayd to weigh 956148 pound weight. I wonder what scales they had to weigh it with."[11] It seems inevitable that the idea of magic sleight-of-hand should have suggested itself at some time or other; and when we find Helinandus attributing a version of the epitaph on the bronze ball, including the first couplet mentioned above, to Virgil, we may feel sure that it is only a matter of time before Virgil's whole hand will be in the pie.[12]

The next step is taken by Jean d'Outremeuse, who tells the following story about Julius Caesar and Virgil:

Strange and unnatural signs were seen at Rome which lasted for three days and nights. The senators came to Virgil and besought him to interpret them. Virgil said that these were omens foretelling that before a year was over Caesar would be killed in a temple and that other signs would appear three days before his death. When the event actually happened, the people wept for three days. And by the counsel of Virgil, they burned the body and placed the ashes in an apple which they set upon a column twenty feet high made by Caesar and put in the middle of Rome, and they fastened it over his image from which a thunderbolt had struck away the first letter of his name, wherefore Virgil had foretold Caesar's death.[13]

In Jean d'Outremeuse's *Chronique des Evesques de Liége*, Virgil's connection with Caesar's death is of a more intimate, if slightly different, character; the poet's friends kill the "Emperor" in return for his daughter's insult in exposing Virgil to derision, and as a result Virgil is universally detested thenceforth.[14]

It is not in France but in Spain, however, that the legend is treated most fully, in an amusing tale by that accomplished liar, Gutierre Diez de Games. This gay gentleman was squire to Pedro Niño, and in 1431 commenced a book in honor of his patron, entitled *El Victorial*, an *olla podrida* of history, extravagant tales, flights of oratory, and serious reflections on life. In a section devoted to the life of Julius Caesar, Virgil appears in a more active rôle than hitherto:

Before Julius Caesar dies, he says one day to the wise Virgil that two things in this world grieve him: that the names of great men die with them and that their sepultures perish too. Virgil suggests that Caesar substitute his name for the month of "Quintil" and as for the tomb, Virgil promises that he will attend to that too. Solomon, king of Judea, had had a marvellous stone carved as high as a tower, and had ordered his bones placed on it in a golden apple. It is lying in a field where Virgil finds it, when, mindful of his promise to Caesar, he goes to Jerusalem to buy it. In his purchase of it, Virgil outwits the Jews and by some sort of magic levitation transports it to Rome in nearly a single night. There it is placed in the market, and Caesar's bones are said to be in it. It is about twenty arms tall; it has four sides finely worked; it is smooth and tapering. It stands upon four brass figures on a base of a single stone, and from this descend three or four steps of the same stone, and from the top arises a great golden apple containing, they say, the ashes of Caesar.[15]

The story seems to have run its course with Gutierre's flights of fancy, but two faint echoes of it are sounded in France. The first of these is a fleeting reference by Rabelais in his account of a delicate operation performed upon Pantagruel:

In order to relieve Pantagruel of a stomach-ache, the doctors devised seventeen great copper apples, larger than the one in Rome on Virgil's needle, fashioned so that they could be opened and closed in the middle. Into the first entered one of his people carrying a lantern and a torch; in the others were more people with odd remedies, and all of these Pantagruel swallowed like little pills.[16]

There is not the slightest doubt that the Vatican obelisk, the only one standing in Rome in Rabelais's time, is the "aiguille de Virgille." [17]

The second reference to it is by a man who undoubtedly knew Rabelais, if not in France, then surely in Rome itself. Pierre Belon of Le Mans was in that day of eager pioneering spirits among the most inquisitive of them all as naturalist, doctor, traveller, and writer.[18] He enjoyed the favor of the great men of France, his patrons being such persons of consequence as René du Bellay and the Cardinal

de Tournon. When the latter was sent to Rome in
1549 to prepare the way for a conclave, he took
Belon with him. As Rabelais was there with Cardinal Jean du Bellay, the two men of science can
hardly have failed to meet and to compare notes
on the strange things of the world. It may have
been Rabelais himself, collector of tales as he was,
who told the story of Virgil's Needle to Belon on
some stroll about the Vatican hill; the memory of
it is crystallized in a book published by Belon in
Paris in 1553, entitled *De Admirabili Operum anti-
quorum et rerum suspiciendarum praestantia.*[19] In a
chapter called "De Obeliscis," Belon says:

> None of these obelisks which the Caesars had brought
> to Rome was quarried by them. They rather imported
> those which they came across already quarried in
> Egypt. One of the greatest of these remains whole and
> erect, but it is in no way remarkable, being smooth and
> without inscriptions save for that of Claudius Caesar.
> It is, however, the one that Caius Caesar imported,
> about which Pliny talks a great deal. Its width is thir-
> teen palms from one angle to the other. This obelisk is
> called to-day by the rude and inexpert herd Virgil's
> Needle, but erroneously.[20]

That this is the Vatican obelisk is apparent.
First, Belon says it is the only one of the greater
obelisks remaining erect. Secondly, it is bare of all
inscriptions save that of Caesar. Thirdly, in the
"many words which Pliny made" it is the only

obelisk in which both Claudius Caesar and Gaius Caesar are implicated — indeed, it is the only Roman obelisk about which Pliny can be said to have made "many words," the only one which he declares to have been imported by Gaius, and the only one of the three which he mentions (the obelisk of the Circus Maximus, that of the Campus Martius, and that of the Vatican) which is bare of hieroglyphics.[21]

Are we to see an inaccuracy in the learned doctor's assertion that to the ignorant the obelisk is known as "Virgil's Needle"? In view of his colleague Rabelais's technique, the reference in *Pantagruel* does not necessarily imply a familiarity with the legend on the part of his readers, and nowhere else have I been able to find any indication that the column was known among the folk otherwise than by the name of "Aguglia di San Pietro." The *vulgus rude* would appear to be strictly non-Roman, in any case, and for lack of better evidence one is tempted to see the fine French hand of Rabelais himself in the scornful remark of our scientist of Le Mans. The author of *Pantagruel* would hardly shrink from making his story just a little better by declaring that it was told him on the spot; and Belon, filled with the light of the Renaissance, would of course feel called upon to deplore and refute such an abominable superstition.[22]

IX

THE VIRGILIUS ROMANCE

MANY a knightly hero of Romance continued his glorious career long after the nobility had lost their exclusive title to the form of literature which his deeds of derring-do adorned. As the genre passed below stairs from great hall to scullery and market-place, the more lowly figure of Virgil the necromancer, which had played no part in the earlier romances, and had served a long apprenticeship in the later ones as a name to conjure with, came at last into its own in a romance devoted almost exclusively to his life in legend, from birth and *enfances* to his bizarre taking-off. It will be remembered that Jean d'Outremeuse devoted an inordinate amount of space in his chronicle to a romantic record of the magician. The final step was taken by an anonymous French writer of the sixteenth century in *Les faictz merveilleux de Virgille*, a complete and well-organized romance of the chapbook sort.

It has been supposed that this French text is the earliest form of the work, that the Dutch version is translated from it, and that the English romance in turn is a translation from the Dutch. There are

VIRGIL IN THE BASKET

From the Dutch Virgilius Romance

(Courtesy of British Museum)

two early undated French editions, one in octavo
printed by Jean Trepperel or Tréperel, the other in
quarto printed by Guillaume Nyverd. The place of
publication in both instances is Paris. The former,
regarded by Graesse as the first edition, appeared
at "rue 9 nostre dame a l'escu de France," an
address to which Trepperel moved in 1502. He
died in 1511, but his widow continued his business
until 1525, so that the date of publication may fall
at any time during these twenty-three years.
Guillaume Nyverd the elder printed between about
1500 and 1515. Only investigation by a typographical expert would settle which is the earlier
edition. The evidence which I have seen is not conclusive either way.[1]

The earliest Dutch text, *Virgilius, Van zijn
leuen, doot, ende vanden wonderlijcken wercken die
hi dede by nigromancien, ende by dat behulve des
duvels*, is also undated, but is ascribed variously to
the years 1518 and 1525 or later. It was printed at
Antwerp by Willem Vorstermann.[2]

The English version, called *Virgilius. This book
treath* [sic] *of the lyfe of Virgilius and of his deth and
many maruayles that he dyd in his lyfe tyme by
whychcraft and nygramansy thorowgh the helpe of the
deuyls of hell*, was printed, also without date, at
Antwerp by Jan van Doesborgh, perhaps about
1518.[3]

Detailed examination of these French, Dutch, and English versions indicates clearly that a relationship of some kind obtains among them. Since the date of each is conjectural, internal evidence must be resorted to in an effort to determine which is the earliest. In the absence of a critical text of any one of the three, however, this kind of evidence cannot be implicitly trusted.

One definite fact which emerges is that the English and Dutch versions are very closely related. In these, several episodes appear which are missing in the French, such as Virgil's learning magic through the help of a devil liberated from his prison under a board, Virgil's making *Salvatio Romae* and the moving horseman who polices the streets, and Virgil's attempted rejuvenation by causing his apprentice to chop him up and place the pieces in a barrel. We can go farther than this. In the prologue, the river Vesle, which runs by Rheims, is called in the French *Veille*, in the Dutch and English *Vellen*. In the French, Virgil goes to *Tollette* to learn necromancy, in the Dutch to *Toleten*, in the English to *Tolleten, Tolenten*. When the emperor besieges Virgil's castle, the magician protects it by a wall of air, called in French *laer*, in the Dutch *lucht*, and at first in the English *aeyr*; but a line or two later it appears as *light*, evidence that the translator of the English misread Dutch *lucht* as *licht*. In the basket episode, Virgil sends to interview the lady in the French *une vieille sorciere*; in the Dutch she is visited *met een touerersse*; but in the English we find that Virgil "made a crafti negromancy [*sic* in the Thoms reprint which I use; in the Bodleian text "a crafte in egromancy"] that told hir all his mynde." This I take to mean that the translator of the English did not understand the Dutch *touerersse*. Certainly he would not have misunderstood the French *sorciere*, if he had been using a French text. In addition to this evidence, the English and the Dutch agree in the vast majority of differences, whether omissions or additions, from the French text. Thus I feel justified in inferring that the English version is in the main a translation from the Dutch.

The question of priority between the French and the Dutch version is more difficult. In the Dutch, Virgil's father is "een ridder van zijnder moeder wegen die seer scoon was eñ cloeck ter wapenē," which would seem a clumsy paraphrase of the French "ung chevalier de part sa mere, moult preux et sain." The story of the devil imprisoned beneath a board is a good devil-story.[4] If the French writer were translating from the Dutch, why did he omit it? I assume that it was added by the Dutchman, rather than omitted by the Frenchman. The French mentions the precise distance to which the basket was raised, and is followed closely by the Dutch: "jusques au second estage de la tour. Et quant il fut ainsi que à dix piedz de la fenestre . . . ," the Dutch having: "tot der tweeder stadiē vāden torē. Eñ als hi op .x. voetē. . . ." The English does not give the details. The sultan's daughter, according to the French, "ne lavoit veu que de nuyt," according to the Dutch, "hadse hem niet ghesien dan by nachte," while the English differs in reading "thoughe he neuer sawe hyr." Thus again the Dutch seems to have been drawn from the French. The sultan tells his daughter to bring back fruit from Virgil's garden, "si sçauray par adventure de quel pays il est," "so sal ic bi auontuerē wel wetē vā wat lande dat he is." The English omits this passage. From my line-by-line and word-for-word comparison of the three texts I could easily add twoscore more of such instances. From them I should like to infer that the Dutch is a translation from the French; but there is another kind of evidence to consider.

When Virgil returns to Rome from Toledo, the French says that his mother greets him, and "il y avoit plus de douze ans quelle ne lavoit veu." The English has "she saw hym not afore by the space of xij years afore," and the Dutch *omits the passage*. Virgil solicits the lady at the beginning of the basket story, and she replies "quil y avoit grant dangier, et en la fin luy dist quelle navoit peur de luy octroyer sa voulenté." In the English: (since the reprint falsifies, I use the Bodleian text, [fo. B iv, r°] here) "it was great dannger so to do but at ȳ last she cōsented." In the Dutch: "seere sorchlijckē ware alsulcke dinghen te beginnē. Met ten lesten seyde si dattet wel soude zijn." Finally, in the account of the revenge, the French has: "Les riches y boutoient des torches et les pauvres des chandelles ou de lestran," while the English reads: "The pore men with candels and strawe, and the ryche men lyghted they there theyr torches" (fo. C i, v°), and the Dutch has: "Dye rijcke hielden toortsen eñ terstont werden si ontsteken, ende die arme toortsen oft stroo." All of this points to a direct relationship between the English and the French; certainly the Dutch could not have been the source of this material in the English version. Yet we have seen that the English translator must have had the Dutch version before him.

My guess is that the translator of the English version had access to the French romance as well as to the Dutch. The Dutch he used for, say, a first draft, later resorting to the French for passages that seemed doubtful to him in the Dutch. Both Vorstermann, printer of the Dutch romance, and Doesborgh, printer of the English, lived at Antwerp. I assume that the Dutch translator had a copy of the *Faictz merveilleux* at Antwerp, and when the English translation was made the same copy would have been accessible, there being at least a possibility that the two works were printed during the same year, 1518.

What effect does this conjectural relationship have upon the probable dates of publication of the three versions? Proctor's date (1518?) for the English version I regard with some confidence. If that be correct, then his date for the Dutch (also 1518?) might also be correct, for internal evidence points to a close relationship between these versions. The *Faictz merveilleux* would consequently be dated during, or more probably prior to, 1518. Certainly 1525 or later would be very late for the Dutch, unless it be a reprint, and I have been unable to perceive any evidence that it is. The state of the woodcuts in the Dutch and English editions might lend evidence of one kind or another. My inexpert comparison of them leads me nowhere. Proctor (p. 7) says "the Dutch edition of *Virgilius* printed by Vorstermann is illustrated with copies of the cuts in the English edition." If this be true, the "copies" are accurate almost beyond belief; but, assuming that they are copies, the question of date remains as before. So much for the relationship of the three versions. I now turn to a brief consideration of the contents of the romance.

I have listed in the table appended to Chapter I about a score of legends told in the *Faictz merveilleux*, of which some seven appear also in the chronicle of Jean d'Outremeuse, and a half-dozen in the *Image du Monde*. The legends as told in the latter are so brief that it is impossible to decide whether the French author used it; and the correspondences with those told by Jean d'Outremeuse are not very close. Yet a comparison of the spirit of the work of Jean d'Outremeuse with the spirit of *Les faictz merveilleux* induces me to believe that a relationship may exist. As I have already pointed out, Jean d'Outremeuse treats the materials of history with gay abandon. He seems more interested in amusing the reader than in edifying him. Unquestionably the same thing is true of the French author. Jean added several legends to the group, and so did the Frenchman. Jean is greatly preoccupied with magic appearances and disappearances, in Virgil's ability to get himself out of scrapes by conjuring armies into a state of impotence, and the like; so is the Frenchman. Jean uses his own imagination freely; so does the author of *Les faictz merveilleux*. Jean treats the legends at great length; the French writer is more brief. The very lengthy and elaborate death of Virgil which Jean narrates, with its stress on the religious element, does not appear at all in the French, where a more appropriate end for a magician, disappearance in a tempest at sea, is used. In general, a detailed comparison of the two gives me the distinct impression that the author of *Les faictz merveilleux* based his romance on the account by Jean d'Outremeuse.

In the French romance there are other circumstances which encourage this suspicion. The first few lines inform us that the city of Rheims was founded by Remus, when he quitted Rome so that his brother might rule alone and took with him his treasure to "Ardenne," on the "little river named Veille," — accurate enough in that Rheims is on the river Vesle, a tributary of the Aisne. When Remus went back to Rome for a visit, Romulus killed him in a fit of rage provoked when Remus drew invidious comparisons between Rheims and Rome. Jean d'Outremeuse tells a somewhat similar story. Because Romulus, the elder of the twins, desired to rule alone, he banished Remus and proclaimed that anyone who killed Remus should be rewarded with riches. When Remus heard this, he fled to the lands of the "duc de Galle," and went to Liége. There the duke "Ector," his brother, gave him the district of Champagne, and Remus founded a noble city which he called *Rains* after his name, and that city is "Rains en Champangne, qui fut parfaite l'an David III c et XXVIII, le quart jour de marche, qui fut ly an del origination de monde IIII m. IIII c et LII ans." And when the town was finished, Remus set out to request colonists from his brother; but a shepherd recognized him and killed him.[5]

Now Jean makes no connection whatever between the founding of Rheims and the deeds of Virgil. In the French romance, Virgil's father is a "chevalier des Ardennes," a liegeman of Remus's son, and thus the connection is established, a connection which seems fortuitous as the romance goes on, for Virgil does nothing at Rheims; in fact, he is born at Rome, and his life is passed there and at Naples, save for his years of study at Toledo. Making Virgil's father a knight of the Ardennes I regarded for some time as merely the caprice of the author; but even caprices have causes. My suggestion for the cause of this one is that in the biographies of Virgil current in the sixteenth century and now, Virgil's father is reported to have owned land in the neighborhood of Andes, not far from Mantua. It would be in perfect conformity with manuscript usage for a copyist to write the name of the district as *ādes*, a name which would have little meaning for one not familiar with the facts of Virgil's life. It appears to me that a Frenchman might expand *ādes* to the name of a district familiar to him, Ardennes, particularly if he suspected the omission of the nasal sign over the *e*, and thus turn Virgil's father into a native of what is now Northern France or Belgium.[6] Probably a chapbook about a man associated with Rheims would sell in France better than one about an Italian magician.

There is another clue in the Dutch or Flemish sound of the printer's name, Nyverd. Did Guillaume Nyverd move to Paris from the north before he succeeded to the printing business of Pierre Le Caron's widow, bringing with him a familiarity with the chronicle of Jean d'Outremeuse, a work full of Walloon terms? [7]

If there is some reason to suspect that *Les faictz merveilleux de Virgille* is based in part on the chronicle of Jean d'Outremeuse, there is further reason to suspect that the Dutch translator of the romance was also familiar with it. It will be recalled that the Dutch and English versions add to the French the legends about *Salvatio Romae* and about the mechanical horseman who policed the streets after curfew. Both of these are told by Jean d'Outremeuse also, though they may have been drawn from the *Gesta Romanorum*, from Neckam, or from various other sources. The fact which I regard as conclusive proof that the work of Jean d'Outremeuse was used in the making of the Dutch chapbook is that on the title-page and on fo. C i, v° appears a woodcut of the revenge which must have been devised by someone who knew the chronicle, for it portrays a woman sitting out of a window while the people gather to procure fire. Now the sole version of the revenge story in which the woman appears thus instead of standing or sitting on a column or the like, is that of Jean d'Outremeuse,[8] and thus the artist who made this woodcut, whether for Vorstermann or for Jan van Doesborgh, must have known the story in the chronicle of Jean d'Outremeuse.

The additions to the French romance in the Dutch and English versions are, with the exceptions just noted, of the nature of the devil literature of the Renaissance. Virgil's finding a devil under a board, releasing him, and being taught magic by him, can of course be matched in Enikel, *Der Wartburgkrieg*, *Reinfrit von Braunschweig*, and *Von Virgilio dem Zauberer*, though in these the devil is imprisoned in a bottle. In all of them Virgil beguiles the devil into returning to his prison after the books of magic have been delivered. It is in the death of the magician that the Dutch writer felt the need of change. In *Les faictz merveilleux* his disappearance in a tempest at sea is orthodox enough for magicians, but it is not spectacular, though for the purposes of a chapbook it is an improvement on Jean d'Outremeuse's long-drawn-out account, full of beautiful religious lessons, and probably borrowed from Solomonic tradition. According to the Dutch and English translations Virgil decided that he must find a means of prolonging his life. He showed a trusty servant how to make the ever-beating flail-men stop smiting their iron anvils so that he could enter and leave Virgil's castle at will, and then the magician ordered the servant to cut him up and put the pieces in a barrel of brine placed so that a lamp would drip into it. After nine days he said he should be rejuvenated, provided the lamp was kept filled and the barrel was left undisturbed. But after seven days the emperor became distressed at the disappearance of his favorite, and under threats of death forced the servant to turn the "vyce" and still the flail-men so that he could enter. When the servant's deed was discovered, the emperor in a rage slew him, and "then sawe the Emperoure and all folke a naked chylde, iij. tymes rennynge a boute the barell, saynge the words: 'cursed be the tyme that ye cam euer here;' and with those wordes vanyshed the chylde away, and was neuer sene ageyne: and thus abyd Virgilius in the barell, deed."

The sorcerer who attempts resuscitation or rejuvenation, either upon himself or upon other people, through hacking in pieces and treating the fragments with some liquid in a receptacle, is a

familiar character in story subsequent to the Virgilian romances.   Whether Virgil was the first
magician reported to have adopted this method of
regaining his youth is not definitely known, for this
type of story has not been studied, but I suspect
that he was.[9] The classical tale of Medea and the
daughters of Pelias may be the ultimate background of this type, but the very widely disseminated legend of St. Nicholas and the Three Clerks
should not be left out of account, as it has been a
commonplace of hagiographical literature from the
twelfth century to the present.   Three scholars, or
sometimes three children, as in the modern song,
are slaughtered by an innkeeper and their bodies
are chopped fine and placed in a barrel of brine; but
St. Nicholas, patron of clerks, appears at the inn
and resuscitates the victims.   In the modern song,
St. Nicholas revives them after seven years.[10]

Before glancing at the Scandinavian versions of
the romance, I should like to advert to an episode
which appears toward the end of the romance in its
French, Dutch, and English forms. It appears that
the emperor took a fancy to Naples, which, according to the Dutch and English translations, lay
in the fairest market-place about Rome — a misunderstanding of the French "et si estoit assise en
la meilleure marche de toute Rommanie" — and
therefore determined to take it from Virgil by

force. I quote from the English translation in the Thoms reprint:

And when Virgilius knewe that the Emperour beseged Napels, than made he all the fresshe water to be lyke rayne, in suche maner that the Emperours folke had neuer a drop of water and they of Napels had a noughe; and in the meane season reysed Virgilius his hoste, and cam towarde the Emperoure to Napels. But the Emperoure myght no lenger taray, for the horse and men dyed for faute of water, and so he loste a great parte of theym. Than the Emperoure seynge this, departed home ageyn to the cytie of Rome, all eschamed and dyscumfyt; and as he returned homewarde, in the waye, he met with Virgilius comynge with all his companye towarde Napels.

And when Virgilius sawe the Emperoure, he cam to him, and salued hym in this manere: "O noble Emperoure, howe fortuned this to you, that be so nooble a prynce as you be, to gyue up the seage of Napels, and to returne home agene to the cytie of Rome, all dyscumfit, without doynge any harme at all so schortly?"

Than wyste the Emperoure well that Virgilius mocked hym, and he was therwith very angery.

And than went Virgilius to Napels, and he caused the lordes of the towne to make a othe that they shulde beyre [in the French, *nentreroit*] no Romans within the forsayde towne.

What is one to surmise from the presence of this passage in the romance? In Chapter III, I have described the sieges of Naples by Roger II of Sicily during the fourth decade of the twelfth century. One of these was terminated because of a pestilence which broke out during the summer months among Roger's soldiery. In Chapter III also the chronicle of Alexander of Telese is referred to; in it Alexander remarks that Naples had never been subject to Rome. The inference is compelling: somehow the echoes of the historical siege of Naples were preserved until they reached the author of *Les faictz merveilleux de Virgille* or his unknown source for this passage. It should be noted that nowhere else in the Virgilian legends is a siege of Naples mentioned, so that apparently a line of tradition existed which I have been unable to find.

I now pass to a brief discussion of the German "Volksbuch" version of this romance, which is a palpable, if perhaps unintentional, hoax. Its initial appearance is in Karl Simrock's collection of "Volksbücher," along with other tales such as "Bruder Rausch" and "Der Schwanenritter." It is interesting to compare the language of this "folk" romance with that of Spazier's German translation of Thoms's reprint of the English original; after a sentence or two from each, it is obvious that Simrock's has no more "folk" in it than Spazier's; that Simrock's, too, is a translation from the English or the Dutch. Simrock has nothing to say about his version. The subtitle of his work implies that it is a genuine German *Volksbuch*. Yet

Görres, writing in 1807, says definitely that he knows only the Dutch version. That is, in 1807 no German *Volksbuch* of Virgilius was known. If one had turned up between 1807 and 1847, the year of Simrock's publication, it would have been hailed as a discovery of some importance. There is no evidence to indicate that a German Virgilius *Volksbuch* ever existed, with the exception of *Von Virgilio dem Zauberer*, which was discovered by Johannes Bolte in 1898, as has already been noted.[11]

The vogue of the romance was not restricted to France, Holland, and England, for in the seventeenth century the Dutch version was translated into Icelandic, presumably first in 1676. Ten manuscripts are known; none has been printed. Most of them state explicitly that they are translated from the Dutch. Perhaps the earliest is Reykjavik MS. Lbs. 661, *Lijf Saga Wirgelij utlögd ur Halendsku Ano 1676*, which represents a type to which several manuscripts belong,[12] although it would seem that the type represented by MS. Copenhagen University Library AM 600c is closer to the Dutch original, as the correspondences extend even to the chapter-headings, which are missing in the group above mentioned. AM 600c is entitled *Ein fogur historia af Virgilio, um hans lyf og dauda, og af hans undarlegum verkum, sem hann giorde fyrer galldra kunst og hialp Diofulsinns*.[13]

These manuscripts are probably responsible, rather than the earlier *Virgiless Rímur*, for the appearance in an eighteenth-century Icelandic manuscript of Virgil as the maker of a stone vase in which Nitida the Famous, virgin queen of France, sees the world reflected, and for the appearance in another Icelandic manuscript written about 1800 of Virgil as a king of France with a son named Hunnem and a daughter named Blómalin.   In each of these, Virgil is named casually and then dropped; in the latter, the story is concerned with the deeds of the two children, and Virgil appears no more.[14]

X

ICONOGRAPHY

SINCE in every age artists are wont to devote their talents to depicting literary subjects, it is only natural that the wide dissemination of the Virgilian legends was soon followed by artistic efforts on the part of painters and other craftsmen to illustrate them. We have already had occasion to observe that the story of Virgil in the basket was the most popular of all these tales; it follows that it was most frequently represented in art. Its corollary, Virgil's revenge, was treated often, as was Virgil's third legendary experience with women, the episode of the *bocca della verità*.[1]

During the fourteenth century several interesting illustrations were made. In the Église St.-Pierre at Caen, in Normandy, the capital of one of the pillars in the nave is adorned with scenes in bas-relief derived from bestiaries, from mediaeval romance, and from the stories of Virgil and Aristotle humiliated by women. Piously thrown stones are no doubt responsible for the disfigurement of the faces of the ladies and of Aristotle; but by a miracle Virgil's face, his eyes cast down in shame, escaped.[2]

VIRGIL IN THE BASKET, CAEN

(Photograph by Brossard d'Alban)

At Freiburg-im-Breisgau in the second quarter of the fourteenth century a tapestry was woven which depicts a whole series of hapless love adventures, among them the same pair as at Caen, and in addition the scene at the tower when Virgil and the lady — the latter looking fell and treacherous enough for anything — agree on the rendezvous. This tapestry is also of religious origin, coming from a Dominican monastery.[3]

Sermons in stone and in cloth were not the only contributions of the fourteenth century, for a manuscript of Jansen Enikel's *Weltchronik* now at Regensburg contains four illuminations on Virgilian subjects. We see Virgil breaking the glass from which the devils escape, Virgil in the basket with the crowd mocking him, the revenge, and a drunken man breaking the bronze statue containing the treasure.[4]

The variety of materials is increased further by fifteenth-century miniatures of Italian workmanship in ivory showing both the basket and revenge in one tablet.[5] The basket and revenge appear also in an Italian engraving of the same century now preserved in the collection of prints at Dresden;[6] and, curiously enough in view of that writer's expressed scepticism about Virgil's being a magician, in two manuscripts of Petrarch's *Trionfi* are illuminations of the triumphant chariot of Cupid being driven among some of the love-god's more illustrious victims — Samson being shorn, Aristotle being ridden, Virgil hanging in the basket.[7] The same scene is portrayed in oils on a circular wooden tray now at the Victoria and Albert Museum, London, and on marriage coffers at Trieste and Siena.[8] Carved, not painted, in wood were Virgil in the basket and Aristotle as a riding-horse on misereres in the choir of the cathedral at Rouen in 1457–69, but the former has been destroyed.[9] The ceiling of a hall in the Hôtel de Ville at Courtrai was decorated with the Virgil-basket story;[10] and, more interesting, an Italian engraving of the same century, now in the Dresden print collection, shows Virgil in the basket hanging from what looks like the Frangipani tower, with the Colosseum in the middle, and the revenge on the opposite side, the lady standing near a structure resembling the Arch of Titus.[11]

Again Virgil's suspension edified the religious in the abbey at Cadouin, where an entire pillar was given over to elaborate sculptures, now badly damaged, of the magician in the basket and several other figures, the pillar itself serving as the tower.[12] A pilaster of the tomb of Philippe de Commines, who died in 1509, of which fragments are to be seen at Paris in a courtyard of the École des Beaux-Arts, shows in bas-relief several luckless lovers,

THE APPOINTMENT
From a Tapestry at Freiburg-im-Breisgau
(*Courtesy of Augustinermuseum, Freiburg*)

among them Virgil hanging, not in a basket, but in
a sling attached to a rope. In Chapter V, I have
referred to several stories in which just such an
apparatus was substituted for the basket.[13] An
Italian engraving by Enea Vico after Perino del
Vaga dated 1542 shows only the revenge, with
the lady seated on the pedestal of a pyramid.[14]
The revenge is also the subject of a fragment of
a coffer in the Cabinet des Médailles et Antiques
at the Bibliothèque Nationale;[15] and it holds the
centre of interest in an engraving by Daniel Hopfer,
although the basket hangs in the background.[16]

In the work of other sixteenth-century artists
we pass to the richest period of illustration of the
legends. Albrecht Altdorfer, a Regensburg master
who died in 1538, depicted the revenge and the
bocca della verità; Lucas [Cranach] van Leyden,
who died in 1533, was unquestionably the greatest artist whose conceptions of the basket episode
and of the *bocca della verità* have survived; Georg
Pencz, who died in 1550, produced the basket and
revenge stories, and an elaborate illustration of
the adulterers' bridge as described by Hans Sachs.[17]

Of these, Lucas van Leyden's dated basket saw
service in another capacity, for it reappears on a
saltcellar along with other scenes symbolical of
the besetting weakness of wise men — Adam and
Eve, Sisera and Jael, Samson and Delilah, Aris-

totle and Phyllis, Solomon, and Virgil in the basket. Three examples of this piece of craftmanship I have seen.[18] The rather conservative treatment of the revenge by Georg Pencz was repeated without acknowledgment as an emblem in Theodor de Bry's *Emblemata nobilitati et vulgo scitu digna singulis historijs symbola adscripta*, with the initials "G P" removed and the whole reversed.[19]

It would be strange if the sixteenth-century art of the woodcut were not represented in the iconography of the Virgilian legends. *The lyfe of Virgilius* printed by Jan van Doesborgh about 1518 is richly adorned with woodcuts of which an idea can be derived from the one of Virgil in the basket here reproduced, from the Dutch version printed by Vorstermann. This cut reappears in *The Historie of Frier Rush*, printed a century later in London by E. Allde.[20] The most interesting of the other woodcuts are those of the revenge and of the *Salvatio Romae*. To illustrate the *bocca della verità* an old woodcut was thrown in which had already been used to illustrate a work on natural history, for it shows two snakes curled about one another.[21]

The cut for the basket story in *The Deceyte of Women*, reproduced here, is an entirely different piece of work. With interest in Virgilian legends high, it is strange that this cut was not used else-

THE MEETING

From a Tapestry at Freiburg-im-Breisgau

(*Courtesy of Augustinermuseum, Freiburg*)

where, but I have been unable to find a trace of it.[22]

Thus far I have been noticing only independent works of art devoted to the illustration of the legends. There is another and in some respects more interesting kind of representation in title-page borders. During the early sixteenth century the pictured story of Virgil's deception and revenge might be seen in the home of anyone who could afford to own a book.

In Basle, city of great printers, in or about the year 1516, the elder brother of Hans Holbein, Ambrosius, turned his hand to a title-page border, which is reproduced here opposite page 264. Across the top we see Delilah cutting Samson's hair; at the right, Solomon worships Ashtoreth, goddess of the Zidonians, at the behest of "his strange wives, which burnt incense and sacrificed unto their gods"; [23] below, Aristotle is ridden by Phyllis, and at the left hangs Virgil in the basket. Ambrosius Holbein's initials, reversed, are seen on the banner held by the false goddess; and the device of the printer, Pamphilus Gengenbach, consisting of his own coat-of-arms and that of the city of Basle, is in the lower corners. It is possible that some rather bungling assistant may have helped Ambrosius Holbein, as the execution of the cut is none too even.[24] It seems to have remained at Basle in the possession of Gengenbach during the rest of his stormy career, which closed in 1523.[25]

We do not know for what book this *Weibermacht* border was designed. It may have been a free-lance composition, for the hazards of love and the deceitfulness of women as themes were common enough in both literature and art. Once in the possession of a printer, a border might be used for almost any book, since the publishers of the time concerned themselves little with the appropriateness of illustrations, and in the interests of economy used their woodcuts over and over again. Even so lavish a printer as Jean de Tournes used the same title-page border for a Xenophon and for a book of French verse, and the somewhat free woodcuts of his *Metamorphoses* of Ovid (1557) for his edition of *Les Pseaumes mis en rime françoise par C. Marot et Theodore de Beze* (1563).[26] Thus we find another title-page border by Ambrosius Holbein showing Apollo and Mercury, Daphne and Apollo, Venus, Cupid on the one hand, and on the other an "Image of Court Life" in the form of allegorized figures of "Adulacio," Desperation, Old Age, Contumely, Opulence, and so on, which was cut originally for Erasmus's translation of Lucian, used a second time in Froben's edition (1519) of Maximus Tyrius's *Sermones e Graeca in Latinam Linguam versi Cosmo Pacio interprete*, and again in

VIRGIL BREAKS THE GLASS FULL OF DEVILS

VIRGIL IN THE BASKET

From Cod. perg. III, Fürstlich Thurn und Taxissches
Zentralarchiv, Regensburg

THE DRUNKEN MAN SMASHES THE STATUE

From Cod. perg. III, Fürstlich Thurn und Taxissches
Zentralarchiv, Regensburg

(Courtesy of Fürstlich Thurn und Taxissches Zentralarchiv)

the same year in *Novum Testamentum omne multo quam antehac diligentius ab Erasmo Roterodamo recognitum*.[27]

It is not out of the ordinary, then, to find that Gengenbach used the *Weibermacht* border for the title-page of Cunz Kistener's poem *Ein hübsch lesen und groß wunderzeichen von dem heiligen zwölffbotten sant Jacob, und zweien Jacobs brüdern*, Basle, 1516.[28] With equal incongruity, the border appears next in an edition of the Epodes of Horace, *Epodon liber*, published at Basle in 1517. In July of the same year Gengenbach uses it for his *Alda Guarini Veronensis*, and again in an unspecified month of that year in *Croacus. Elisii Calentii Amphraten. De Bello Ranarum. In quo Adolesccens* [sic] *iocatus est . . .*, an imitation of the pseudo-Homeric *Batrachomyomachia*. The next year it is in Martin Luther's *Sermo de Penitentia*, with Gengenbach's initials at the end. Here the two side-pieces of the border are interchanged, so that Virgil is on the right and Solomon on the left, a change explained by the fact that the parts of the border were cut and set up separately.[29]

Another and more appropriate use was in Gengenbach's own play, *Diß ist die gouchmat so gespilt ist worden durch etlich geschickt Burger einer loblichen stat Basel. Wider den Eebruch und die sünd der unküscheit*, 1521(?). The piece is a *Fast-*

nachtspiel much on the order of Thomas Murner's *Gäuchmat*, which appeared in 1519, and it has echoes of Hans Sachs's first work of this type, *Das Hofgesind Veneris*, first published in 1517. As the title suggests, it is a poem defending chastity, and was directed against another poem, now lost, celebrating the pleasures of love. The subjects of the woodcut and of the book are already close, and as reference is made in the poem to Virgil as an unfortunate lover, we seem to see good reason for the use of the border. It is a temptation to speculate upon the possibility of an earlier edition of the *gouchmat*, or at least upon an early project for such a poem. If Holbein made the border for any particular book, it may very possibly have been for just such a work as this.[30]

In 1526, Hans von Gülch, otherwise known as Johann Faber Emmeus Juliacensis, appears to have taken over Gengenbach's printing business. He used the border in which we are interested on the title-page of the first edition of the *Artis Veterinariae, sive mulomedicinae libri quatuor* by P. Vegetius Renatus, published at Basle in 1528. Only the sides and bottom of the border are used, the section showing Samson and Delilah being replaced by a strip with a purely decorative design. The shield at the lower left containing Gengenbach's coat-of-arms in the older works is blank,

DETAIL FROM PILASTER OF TOMB OF PHILIPPE
DE COMMINES

(Photograph by Giraudon)

but the one on the right still displays the Basle device.

Three years later Johann Faber went to Freiburg-im-Breisgau, taking the Holbein border with him, as it appears again in the form just described in an edition of *Die Epistel D. Erasmi von Rotterdam, wider etlich die sich fälschlich berümen Evangelisch sein . . .*, issued there in 1530, as well as in his edition published during the same year of Henricus Glareanus, *De Geographia liber unus*. I have been unable to trace any further use of the border.[31]

Another painter-engraver whose imagination was stirred by the contemplation of Virgil's troubles was Urs Graf, contemporary with the Holbeins and very nearly as important in the history of art at Basle. His influence, which was felt in many fields, was particularly great in the still youthful art of printing. In his designs and illustrations he introduced more than anyone else the style of the Italian Renaissance to the great printing houses of Basle. In 1519 he produced a title-page border, more ambitious than Ambrosius Holbein's, which was destined to carry the basket legend and its corollary far afield. It sets forth the Judgment of Paris, the deaths of Pyramus and Thisbe, the encounter between David and Goliath, and, in the upper corners, Virgil in the basket and the humiliation of the faithless lady. Urs Graf's signature is in the lower right-hand corner, and the date is cut on the base of the pillar at the right.[32]

As in the case of Ambrosius Holbein's border, we do not know the book for which this curious combination of illustrations was designed. Apparently it was not used at Basle, for its first appearance was at Paris in 1520, in an edition of Q. Asconius Paedianus, *In Orationes M. Tulii enarrationes . . .*, printed by Pierre Vidoue for Conrad Resch. This journey is not surprising, as the relationship between the printers of Basle and of Paris was close. Indeed, Conrad Resch was only one of several printers who hailed from Basle and had establishments at Paris; he himself kept his headquarters at Basle and had as his agent at Paris one Chrestien Wechel, at the sign "sub scuto Basiliensis." It was the fashion, set by Resch, for these printers to import woodcuts and engravings from their native city, and Urs Graf's handiwork was especially sought after; his borders were already known in Paris when Resch and Vidoue began to use the Virgil woodcut.[33]

The books in which these two collaborators used the border followed one another for a time in rapid succession. In July, 1521, it appeared in the *Dictionarium Graecum* by Joannes Crastonus, and in September in Joannes Eckius, *De Primatu Petri Adversus Ludderum*, a work in which it would be

Diſz iſt die gouch

mat/ſo geſpilt iſt worden durch etli=
ch geſchickt Burger einer loblichen
ſtat Baſel. Wider den Eebruch vnd
die ſünd der vnküſcheit.

Pamphilus Gengenbach

Durch bit ward ich gefochten an/
Ich ſolt diß faßnacht nit hinlan/
Solt machen yn ein nüwes ſpyl/
So ſetz doch wer des vnmüts vyl.
Hat ich mich daruff bald bedacht
Vnd diſe geüch zuſamen bracht
In den man nit allein kurtzwyl
findt/ſunder auch deß ernſtes vyl/
Der nun die geüch wirt träffen an
Die ſich die wyb ſtäts geüchen lan.

AMBROSIUS HOLBEIN'S TITLE-BORDER

(Courtesy of British Museum)

difficult to find any remarks related to the subjects treated in the border, as is the case also with Stunica's *Annotationes contra Des. Erasmum, in defensionem tralationis novi Testamenti*, printed by Vidoue for Resch in 1522.[34]

The border was now retired for seven years. In 1526 Wechel bought Resch's establishment, and at that time Vidoue must have taken exclusive possession of the woodcut, if he had not already done so, as he placed it with rather more appropriateness than usual on the title-page of the *Æneid* printed in 1529 for Jean Petit. He used it once more, apparently for the last time, in an edition of Étienne de l'Aigue's commentary on Pliny's Natural History, printed in 1530 for Poncet Le Preux and Galliot Du Pré.[35]

Meanwhile, the border had been admired, presumably, and Philippe Le Noir had a copy of it made, which he used in at least ten of his more prominent books published at Paris between 1523 and 1532. The first of these is an edition of the *Saincte Graal* printed in 1523; it is just possible that Le Noir chose the border because of the Ypocras story contained in it, which includes the pre-Virgilian basket in great detail. Next comes *Le vergier dhonneur*, by Octavien de Saint-Gelais and André de la Vigne, 1525(?), in which there is at least a fleeting reference to Virgil's magic powers. At approximately the same time the border appeared in an edition of *Les triumphes de messire Francoys Petraque* [*sic*], printed by Le Noir for Jean Petit, 1525(?). We have already observed that in some manuscripts of the *Trionfi* there is an illustration showing Virgil in the basket.[36]

An edition by Farget, dated 1525, of Bartholomaeus Anglicus, *Le Propriétaire des choses tresutile & profitable aux corps humains*, carries our border, for no particular reason; and the next appearance, equally unsuitable, is in *Le premier volume de Orose certain compilateur de tous les sages du monde* (*Sensuyt le second volume de Orose*), 1526, where, however, "les baingz de Virgille" are mentioned. Following this, it is on the title-page of Le Noir's edition of Antoine de la Salle, *La Salade*, which is dated March 13, 1527 [i. e., 1528], and of P. de Crescentiis [or Des Crescens], *Le Livre des prouffitz champestres et ruraulx . . .*, both in the edition dated February 15, 1529 [1530] and in that of 1532. In 1531 the border appeared twice, first in *La Bible des poetes de Ovide Metamorphose*, published in May, and then in September in *Bocace de la généalogie des dieux*. These, with the 1532 edition of Crescentiis, seem to conclude the career of Virgil on the title-page.

In the next chapter we shall glance briefly at the efforts made during the seventeenth century to

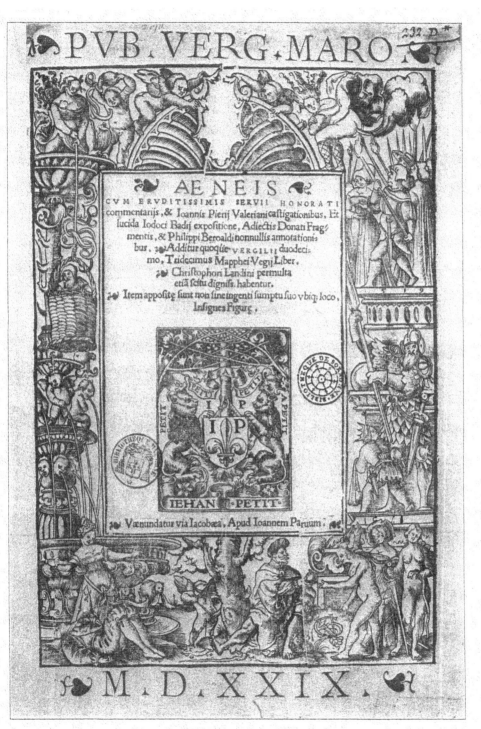

URS GRAF'S TITLE-BORDER
(Courtesy of Bibliothèque Mazarine. Photograph by Giraudon)

destroy belief in the Virgilian legends. It is interesting to note here that during the sixteenth century they were perpetuated by the very persons and often in the very works responsible in large degree for the most advanced thought of the Renaissance.[37]

SHADES OF SHADOWS

I. THE ANCIENTS AND THE MODERNS

THE scholars of the sixteenth and seventeenth centuries regarded the Virgilian legends with mixed feelings. Some perceived nothing incredible in them and accepted them without question; others considered them ridiculous, and attempted to discredit them by dwelling on their absurdity, not realizing that by devoting so much attention to them they were actually giving them new life; still others seem to have been unable to make up their minds definitely, and remained undecided which was the less heretical opinion.

Jean Bodin, writing in 1580 of his belief in sorcerers and witchcraft, is a little hesitant about accepting Virgil as a necromancer; he says merely that Virgil had the reputation of being a wizard — a cautious statement, at once true and non-committal. In the same spirit, Pierre Le Loyer reports that the peasants in the neighborhood of Pozzuoli call a "whispering cave" the echo of Virgil. He does not enlarge upon Virgil's magical powers, however. Tommaso Porcacchi, on the other hand, who wrote a life of the poet in 1581 for Annibale Caro's

great Italian translation of the *Aeneid*, thinks the
vulgar crowd entirely mistaken in believing that
Virgil made the Appian Way by enchantment, and
that because of love he was hung out of a window
— the same Virgil who was at Naples commonly
called a virgin. According to Blaise de Vigenère,
Virgil devised a secret alphabet, which he reproduces. But de Vigenère is not one of your easily
credulous persons. He inveighs against the ridiculous fables told of the poet, like those of the basket
and the revenge, and similar "reveries" for the
pastime of babes and ancient beldames.[1] Another
writer not entirely at one with himself on the subject is Alfonso Tostado. He is able to demonstrate
pretty clearly that St. Jerome was wrong in accepting the Fourth Eclogue as a prophecy of the coming
of Christ, but at the same time he describes Virgil
as a magician, and on the authority of Elinandus
repeats a number of the legends: "Virgil made
yet other things which seem almost incredible, but
nevertheless they exist to this day" — and then we
read again of the road through the rocks, of the
marvellous bridge, and of the medicinal baths.
Forthright in his condemnation of the "mere
fables" is Martino del Rìo, and since Theodoric of
Niems follows Petrarch, he too is sceptical, though
he leans toward a belief that Virgil had something
to do with buildings at Naples.[2]

An esteemed edition of Virgil's works by a Spanish Jesuit, Juan Luis de la Cerda (ca. 1560–1643), discusses Virgil's magical powers in some detail. He was an astrologer — so says Macrobius; and he was a most ingenious workman (*"ingeniosissimus rerum Artifex"*) according to St. Jerome and Elinandus; but he was undeservedly called a necromancer, for, to take the story of the magic meat-market as an example, such things could not be accomplished by the aid of necromancy.

Because Virgil was interested in natural philosophy he was held in his own time to be a great necromancer, says P. de l'Ancre, King's Counsellor, in his book discussing sorcery. De l'Ancre has learned of the Virgilian legends from Alexander Neckam, and repeats them. The drift of men's minds is shown by the introductory *Epistre au Roy*, in which are mentioned "Academiciens nouveaux" who maintain that there is no truth in what is said of sorcerers and sorcery, — that the whole business is founded on illusion.[3]

Gabriel Naudé's youthful *Apologie pour tous les grands personnages qui ont esté faussement soupçonnez de magie* (1625) was, then, a tract for the times. The future librarian of Cardinal Mazarin devotes a chapter to the vindication of Virgil. He selects Gervasius of Tilbury, who was copied, he says, by Elinandus, as the especial object of attack.

Gervasius, whom he regards as the originator of the legends, is disposed of easily as a liar. Those who, lacking Naudé's sagacity, blindly and stupidly echo Gervasius are roundly rebuked, Jean Bodin being one of them. Yet, as we have just seen, Bodin did not actually commit himself on the subject, although he was credulous about witchcraft in general and therefore suspect in all his ways to Naudé. With Scaliger, Naudé makes merry over talismans, and he collects a large number of the legends. While one cannot admire Naudé's logic in settling the matter by calling Gervasius a liar, it should be noted that his essay is the first critical study of Virgilian legends.[4]

Naudé did not long retain undisputed possession of the field, for shortly after 1625 Jacques Gaffarel wrote a treatise on talismans in which he took direct issue with him. The *Unheard-of Curiosities of the Talismanical Sculpture of the Persians*, as the title reads in the English translation, is a very learned work, full of material interesting from many points of view. The author knew that he was treading dangerous ground, and attempted to protect himself in the introduction:

And that thou mayst be fully acquainted with my purpose in this discourse, know, that I give no more credit to any of these Curiosities, then the Catholique and Apostolique Church permits; and that I have not published them, at least some of the most nice and ticklish, but after many Christians of my Profession.

Chapter VI is entitled

That according to the Opinion of the Eastern Men, Figures and Images may be so prepared, under certaine Constellations, as that they shall have the power, Naturally, and without the Aide of any *Demon*, or Divell to drive away Noysome Beasts, allay Winds, Thunder, and Tempests, and to cure diverse kinds of Diseases.

Gaffarel proceeds to develop his case methodically:

First then, it is Certain, and we cannot deny it, without denying the most Authentick Historiographers that are, that there have been seen, both in Our dayes, and in the daies of our Fathers, some of these *Talismans* . . . that have cured those, that have been bitten by Serpents, Scorpions, Mad Dogs, and divers other Mischances, that are but too frequent with us. The Ancient Arabians . . . give us many examples of this kind; which gave *Haly* occasion to conclude, that, *Utilem serpentis imaginem effici posse, quando Luna Serpentem Caelestem subit, aut faeliciter aspicit; Similiter Scorpionis effigiem efficacem, quando Scorpij signum ingreditur,* &c. Neither did he deliver this Doctrine, without having had Experence [*sic*] of the Effects: for he affirms, that himselfe, being in Ægypt, had in his hand one of these Images of a Scorpion, which did cure those that were stung by this Venomous Beast. . . . It will be objected, perhaps, that these *Arabians* are Trifling, Vaine Writers; and therefore that there is little Credit to be given to them. But I shall elsewhere undertake the Vindication of them from this Calumny; and shall at present, for the satisfaction of Self-willed men, forbear to cite them any further.

There follow lengthy dissertations upon various kinds of prophylactic talismans, with workable formulas for making them. Naturally, Gaffarel is aware that all this is directly contrary to Naudé's recent treatise; and in Chapter VII he turns upon Naudé to overwhelm him with arguments. If Naudé denies Virgil's magical powers, then he must deny the efficacy of the talismans which Virgil made. Moreover, Gervasius of Tilbury was a man of high position; he was Chancellor to the Emperor Otto. He could not afford to lie as Naudé maintains he did, for then some envious person would be sure to malign him. Nobody has maligned him; therefore he was telling the truth.

That Admirable Tower, or Steeple, which Necham [*sic*] reports to have been made by Virgil, with such wonderfull Art, as that the Tower, which was built all of stone, moved to and fro, when the Bell rung out; is not without Parallel: for at *Moustiers*, a City of *Provence*, the *Steeple*, whose stones are all mortaised one within another, hath in a manner the very same motion that the Bell hath in Ringing; and that is so strange a manner, as that sometimes those which are on the top of it, knowing nothing of it, when they perceive the Bells begin to ring, are very much affrighted: which, I confesse, happened once to my selfe. . . . I could in like manner make good the greatest part of those other Stories, which are reported of this Poet.

Perhaps close thought caused Gaffarel to feel that there might be a slip somewhere in his reasoning, for he concludes, somewhat lamely, "A man might . . . defend this Excellent Poet, against the Imputation of Magick, without denying . . . the Power of *Talismans.*" [5]

Gaffarel is more interested in the power of talismans than he is in Virgil; and he soon found that professing belief in the wrong kind of talismans was dangerous, although he might at the same time believe in the right sort, those used in the Church. On October 4, 1629, he was compelled to appear before the Sorbonne and retract the doctrines promulgated in *Curiositez Inouyes*. This we learn from a lengthy volume written by Charles Sorel to refute Gaffarel's ideas, *Des talismans ou figures faits sous certaines constellations pour faire aimer et respecter les hommes, les enrichir . . . avec des observations contre le livre des "Curiosités inouies" de M. I. Gaffarel*. But while Gaffarel could save his immortal soul by retracting the heresies into which he had lapsed, his book went marching on through the century. Sorel's defence of Naudé is interesting. Gervasius of Tilbury, he says, was indeed in high position, and therefore no one dared impeach his work. Anyhow, he was writing to amuse the idle hours of his sovereign, and therefore may well have permitted himself some license. If the things which

Gervasius says about Virgil were true, we might expect to find them in Pliny; but the writer of the *Natural History* says nothing about them, and Sorel for one would rather trust Pliny than Gervasius. Moreover, nobody bothered to contradict Gervasius, as everyone knew that what he wrote was the purest fiction. The climax of Sorel's argument comes when he reprints Gaffarel's retraction, which had been issued at Paris by Jean Guillemot in a little pamphlet. This, Sorel thought, might easily escape notice. Hence he resolves to make it accessible to all, so that everyone may realize that Gaffarel's book merits no confidence, since the author himself confessed his errors.[6]

The real issue in this battle of the books was not whether Virgil was a magician or Gervasius a liar, but whether belief in magic and the supernatural was tenable by men of intelligence. Virgil's name, and hence Gervasius's, enters the controversy only through the accident that his name had been linked with magic in the legends; and the occasional works in which one or both are mentioned in the course of the struggle do not fairly depict its progress.

Gaffarel found a defender in another cleric, Jacques d'Autun, who notices Virgil's reputation as a magician, and flays Naudé for his sweeping denial of charges of necromancy against great men.[7]

In a series of satirical essays Carlo Celano, a Jesuit canon, tells a fanciful tale of "Prince Virgil" and his unsuccessful suit before the emperor to have harmful plants removed from the neighborhood of his house near a grotto where Apollo prophesied. Several members of Prince Virgil's household, it seems, including Alexis, were made ill by the poisonous herbs.[8]

Presumably from Naudé the Abbé Bordelon learned of the Virgilian legends, and in the spirit of Naudé's *Apologie* he wrote a treatise *De l'astrologie judiciaire. Entretien curieux où l'on répond d'une manière aisée et agréable à tout ce qu'on peut dire en sa faveur*, in which he makes a valiant effort to expose the vulgar errors of the past concerning astrology. Much more amusing is the same author's imitation of *Don Quixote*, in which Monsieur Oufle becomes mentally deranged by reading too many books of magic and the like, and decides that he is a magician himself. The list of M. Oufle's books is a valuable as well as interesting one. His experiments in imitation of Virgil and other magicians are no more successful than Don Quixote's efforts to set right the wrongs of the world, and M. Oufle's end is as chastening to the reader as the end of the Knight of the Sorrowful Figure.[9]

Belief in magic, Virgilian or other, could not long withstand the laughter of the Abbé Bordelon and the weight of authority of the great *Dictionnaire historique et critique* by Pierre Bayle, where the article on Virgil follows Naudé closely and approvingly. Gaffarel's attempts to reply to Naudé are ridiculous, says Bayle. In general, he adopts Naudé's attitude consistently. But superstitition dies hard, if ever. In 1717 another treatise on talismans appeared, and although it was sceptical in tone, the Virgilian legends once more appear, this time from (of all sources!) Naudé, Bayle, and Bordelon's burlesque on M. Oufle.

By this time, however, the battle against belief in witchcraft was won among people of intellectual pretensions, and this curious phase of the struggle between the ancients and the moderns came to an end. Before turning to another class of persons who interested themselves in Virgilian legends during these centuries, I would note "Sir" John Hill's once more affirming that "Virgil was a great Natural Philosopher, as well as a Poet and a Farrier," in one of the most extraordinary products of eighteenth-century virtuosity. At about the same time, Voltaire expressed pained surprise that "to-day Virgil passes for a sorcerer at Naples: the Eighth Eclogue supplies the reason." [10]

Virgil was regarded as an authority by astrologers and alchemists. I presume that the author of the *Æneid* was meant, rather than that Virgil of

Cordova to whom is attributed an hermetic book in Arabic, translated into Latin perhaps in the fourteenth century, on astrology and necromancy, in which Virgil is "a master of that science called by us *refulgentia*, by others *nigromantia*." [11] In a Latin manuscript of the thirteenth century there is a Virgilian *cento* on astronomy, consisting of verses on snow, ice, the scorpion, and so on. In later manuscripts Virgil is said to have possessed the secret of the Philosopher's Stone; for example, to quote from a seventeenth-century English manuscript —

> A Treatise of the Philosopher's Stone.
> A Letter from Edward Kelly to his Son.

This is the worke that Virgill ye philosopher did give unto ye Emperour Maximianus for the haveinge of his daughter. And it is ye most trusst [*sic*] worke, both to the Sonne, and also to ye Moone: as he by his verses heereafter doth showe.

Of Mercury crude sixe parts: of Sol and Luna seven:
So thou Amalgame make: in gentle fire to ioyne:

Then grinde with common Salte: this Masse that thou hast made
Till it in Colour slacke: their brightness overshade:

With water then made hotte: mashe thou them in glasse:
till thou have Cleane substracte: the Salte out of ye Masse:

And that thou dost not tease: whilst water blacke doth seeme:
till it come forth againe as fresshe: *and* cleane as it went in:

Then Heaven lyke shines this Masse: such drye thou at the Sonne:
And put it in thy glasse: wherein noe moysture come:

Then poure on tentanous oyle: upon this shining Masse:
In gentle fire them boyle: And close thou fast thy glasse

And this being once conieald: as Virgills verse doth saye:
Alchimins Arte is assoylde: for him therefore thou praye.

finis.[12]

II. OBITER DICTA

For many centuries Italy in general and Rome in particular have been centres of interest to travellers. Whatever the main object of the visit, the curiosity of most strangers has been excited by the numerous monuments enduring in more or less dilapidated state from the days of Rome's supremacy. The traveller looked and marvelled. Scholarly Italians were not so easily content, and the sixteenth and seventeenth centuries saw the publication of many an erudite work devoted to matters of topographical interest. The conclusions reached in these have of course been critically examined and sifted, frequently by scholars, Italian and other, of our own day. From the literature of the travellers and the topographers a few allusions to Virgilian legends have been gleaned for the following pages, since they throw light upon the later life of the legends. I have had occasion in previous chapters to mention some works that fall within these two classes; to avoid needless repetition I refrain from systematic presentation of the material, and collect here only a few of the more interesting references.

In the twelfth century, when Rome was struggling to regain her ancient prestige, some practical-minded person, possibly a canon of the Church, compiled a guide-book for those who sought salvation through a pilgrimage to the Holy City. This booklet was perhaps a descendant of an eighth-century document or of an even earlier one, but it was augmented with bits of miscellaneous information and misinformation both ecclesiastical and classical. In this twelfth-century version of the *Mirabilia Urbis Romae* there are references to such legends as that of the *Salvatio Romae*, of the stone image that deceived Julian, and so on; but it is not until the fourteenth century that Virgil makes his appearance in the *Mirabilia*. In naming the hills of Rome, the compiler comes to the Viminal Hill, "where stands St. Agatha's church, and where Virgil, being taken by the Romans, escaped invisibly and went to Naples, whence it is said, *vado ad Napulim*" — an ingenious bit of etymologizing designed to account for the name *Balneapolis* attached to the eastern side of Trajan's Forum.

John Capgrave relies heavily upon the *Mirabilia* for information, and gets into difficulties. He laments that he "cannot discerne" the names of the hills of Rome because of

errours of writeres. . . . For þei write þat þere shuld be a hill in which þe romanes wold a slayn uirgill and fro

þat hiłł he went inuysible to naples summe men calle
þis hiłł uiuenalis & summe riualis.[13]

The *Mirabilia* was early translated into many
languages and suffered considerable changes in the
course of its career.   Omissions and additions
abound. Several versions figure among the earliest
incunabula, notably the German edition entitled
"In dem püchlein stet geschriben wie Rom gepaut
ward."   Here we find certain curious ruins accounted for in a manner interesting to us.

On the other side of the Colosseum [i. e., away from old
St. Clement's] is a high round wall where stood the
young woman who hung Virgil up before the window.
Because of her, Virgil put out all the fires of Rome and
none could kindle his fire save at the person of the
young lady.

Perhaps under the circumstances this legendary
young lady would have been only too glad to stand
on that particular high round wall, as it was
probably indeed the goal-shaped fountain emitting
streams of water from countless small apertures
along the shaft, known as the *Meta Sudans*. It was
built in the first century of our era, and by the time
of the *Mirabilia* here referred to, it was piled about
with the débris of centuries.[14]

In the Jubilee year 1450 a wealthy Florentine
merchant, Giovanni Rucellai, was moved to make
the pilgrimage to Rome and to write about it. In

enumerating the ruins of palaces which he saw he mentions "the palace where Virgil was held at the windows," and nearby "a little cupola where the lady who held him at the windows stood with the fire between her legs." In the light of later tradition, it seems clear that the palace in question was the ruins of the fortress-like tower, once belonging to the Frangipani family, which stood beside the triumphal arch of Titus at the entrance of the Forum Romanum. The *cupoletta* would then undoubtedly be the *Meta Sudans*.[15]

Two years later, Nikolaus Muffel, a distinguished young citizen of Nürnberg, went to Rome for the coronation of Frederick III. Among the curiosities of the Eternal City he mentions the arch of Titus and Vespasian commemorating the triumph over Jerusalem, and in front of it "the stone walled about with brick, upon which the emperor's sweetheart stood, and all Rome had to come to her, since a sorcerer had put out all fires and no stone had power to give fire. Nearby is the round *Spiegelpurck* [Colosseum]."[16]

Arnold von Harff, knight, set out from the Lower Rhine in 1496 on a trip to the Holy Land by way of Rome. Obviously he was armed with the German *Mirabilia*, for he alludes to Virgil's tower in very nearly the words quoted above, and in perfect good faith.[17]

THE *META SUDANS*, WITH THE ARCH OF TITUS AND THE FRANGIPANI TOWER

From Étienne du Pérac. I Vestige dell'antichita di Roma, Roma, 1680, plate xv

(Courtesy of British Museum)

The authority of the *Mirabilia Urbis Romae* did not long remain unquestioned, however, for soon learned men began to interest themselves in the topography of the Seven Hills, and great is their contempt for their predecessors' efforts. Fabricius, writing on Roman topography in 1550, warns against heeding the comments of the vulgar found in that anonymous book on the marvels of Rome. They even say that the brick pile in front of the Amphitheatre which was called the *Meta Sudans* was Virgil's tower! [18]

Although we now approach the time when popular imagination ceased to respond vigorously to the stimulus of the sorcerer's personality, his legend was far from forgotten. Virgil's tower was by this time a matter of everyday speech. A casual reference is made to it in a deed of sale in 1559 in order to identify a boundary line.[19]

In his monumental work on the antiquities of Rome, J. J. Boissard speaks with lofty scorn of the ridiculous beliefs held by the people concerning the tower near the arch of Titus. They call it "Virgil's little study" (*studiolo*), and they say that he was strung up in a basket by a certain meretricious woman, and for a whole day he was a spectacle for the mob. The infuriated Virgil called upon his magic art and extinguished the fires throughout the city, with the result that all lights had to be kindled from the girl's person. A picture has been made of this fable, he says, but the artist is unknown. It is most unlikely, he continues, that the great poet, who was called "Parthenias" for his chastity, could be the subject of such a story. It is more probable that the story was told about that other Virgil, the sorcerer of whose prodigies the Neapolitans tell, — for example, the tunnel made through Mount Posilippo, near which lies Virgil's tomb.[20]

Thirty years later, Schottus dismisses the matter briefly. The little square tower on the right-hand side of the "Arca di Noè" [the arch of Titus] is called the *Studiolo di Virgilio*, concerning whom the vulgar tell many lies. In the middle of the eighteenth century Giovanni Marangoni published a book on the Colosseum in which he spoke of the Frangipani palace as having fallen in the time of Gregory IX, but remarked that the lower part near the arch of Titus was still called vulgarly *di Virgilio*.[21]

It is difficult to say how truly popular these stories were; they were kept in existence by the demand for explanations of the monuments. Now it is safe to assume that native Italians living in Rome were not over-curious about the ruins which they saw daily, unless they had a special interest in them. For the uneducated, that special interest would be due most probably to the hordes of visitors, who needed guides and paid them in proportion to the curiosity awakened by them. One obvious topic of concern was Virgil, whose name at least any visitor would be sure to have heard, and whose legendary deeds of magic must have been known to large numbers, as we have already had opportunity to observe. Thus a guide could be sure of eliciting a look of recognition, and an ultimate gesture toward the pocket-book, whenever he mentioned the name of Virgil; and the legends, or such of them as could be attached to ruins in Rome, were assured of a prolongation of their existence. Some of the legends of this group are discussed in the following pages.

SEPTIZONIUM

On the Palatine across from the Circus Maximus stood the building called the Septizonium of Septimius Severus. No one knows for certain what the word *Septizonium* means. It has always been the subject of conjecture and ingenious theories of one sort and another. One of the many forms the word took during the Middle Ages was *Septodium*, which to the learned seemed at that time to indicate the academic trivium and quadrivium. The ruins, known sometimes as the "School of the Seven Wise Men," — *school* being a term then widely used for any ruin, — came also to be called "School of the

Liberal Arts." Since education could not exist without Virgil, and since Virgil was also a great sage, it was fitting that the Septizonium should acquire the title of "School of Virgil," and during the fifteenth and sixteenth centuries it was commonly so termed. Sketches made by visitors to Rome as well as documents relating to the demolition of the edifice by Sixtus V refer to the "Settizonii overo Scola di Vergilio," and it is spoken of in a fifteenth- or sixteenth-century poem as the academy which Virgil built.[22]

VIRGIL'S RESIDENCE

If in the vast mass of tradition that is Rome there is a place in the late Middle Ages and the centuries following them for Virgil the necromancer, we have reason to look for traces of the legend in the much smaller and less complex city of Naples, the poet's adopted home.

That he lived in or near the ancient city of Naples is of course a matter of historical fact. The exact location of his dwelling or dwellings is unknown, but recent studies have indicated that he probably lived on the Puteoli side of Naples until his privacy was invaded by the construction of the Via Puteolana, when he withdrew to Sorrento. He may have owned property also at the town of Nola nearby, and mediaeval tradition asserted that a house belonging to Virgil, with a remarkable or even magic garden, stood on Monte Vergine. The name of this mountain, which may be explained by the worship here of Vesta and Cybele, was used, at least during the late Middle Ages, interchangeably with the name *Mons Vergilianus*, thereby lending force to the tradition. Scholars have attempted to see an indication of Virgil's residence on Monte Vergine in the epithet "Parthenias" bestowed upon him by the Neapolitans, but the point is decidedly a moot one. In any case, whether or not he had property on Monte Vergine, it is not at all impossible that he may have lived on an estate bordering upon the site of the columbarium now known as Virgil's tomb.[23]

The tradition that Monte Vergiliano was named from Virgil's residence there was not a passing one. Before the middle of the twelfth century the name *Mons Vergilianus* seems to have been in use. About 1591 Tomaso Costo mentions it in his edition of Collenuccio's comprehensive work on Neapolitan history. At about the same time it is repeated in works on Monte Vergine by Vincenzo Verace and Costo. In 1624 it appears in *Napoli sacra*, by Cesare d'Engenio Caracciolo, and in 1663 in *Monte Vergine Sago*, by D. Amato Mastrullo. A century later the story is told again, but this time of the neighboring Monte Barbaro. The mountain was called Monte Vergiliano as late as the eighteenth century, but the usage by then was uncommon and needed explanation, as we see in Celano's work on Naples.

In the seventeenth century, guides about Naples were pointing out some old ruins at Pozzuoli as remains of Virgil's house, for reasons best known to themselves. Bourdin accepts the identification in all good faith, but Burnet rejects it as a very "dubious Tradition," as indeed it was.[24]

VIRGIL'S TOMB

On the side of Mount Posilippo at Naples, almost above the entrance of the tunnel called *Grotta Vecchia*, is a small round edifice shown as Virgil's tomb. The tradition is an ancient one and sufficiently honorable to make any flat denial of the identification unsound. It is certain that the poet intended to be buried at Naples, and Donatus says that his grave was at the second mile-post of the Via Puteolana, a point applicable, as nearly as we know, to this traditional spot. It is not impossible, however, that his tomb was upon a site now below sea-level, and that at the time the sea rose, to reverse the phraseology of the legend, his bones were removed — perhaps to the columbarium-like structure now known as his tomb. King Roger is reported to have taken Virgil's ashes to the Castel

Nuovo, from which presumably they disappeared in course of time.[25]

Virgil's grave, the boast of Naples as late as the fifth century, receives scant attention in the literature of the waning Middle Ages. Whatever reverence may have been accorded to Virgil's bones was apparently not bestowed upon his sepulchre until well into the period of the Renaissance, when Naples became a routine port of call for tourists. Whether or not the columbarium was considered to be Virgil's tomb at that time, we know that in the last part of the fifteenth century it was used as a tavern![26]

Very shortly after this, however, we find the columbarium in good standing as Virgil's tomb. Benedetto di Falco mentions it, asserting that here was ground sacred to the goddess Patulcis, in whom Virgil was interested. F. Leandro Alberti, writing about 1550, refuses to commit himself on the authenticity of the tomb. Georg Fabricius, visiting Naples in 1543, saw Virgil's tomb at Mount Posilippo. In 1554, clerics of Santa Maria di Piedigrotti, the owners of the ground on which the tomb stood, officially recognized — no doubt for the usual reason — the tradition by placing at its entrance an inscription commemorating the poet. Hieronnimus Turler wrote, about 1574, that Virgil's tomb may have been the one above the entrance to the grotto. By this time the Neapolitans were aware of the "tourist value" of the tomb, and had encouraged the growth of a laurel spreading over it. A myth was propagated to the effect that the laurel grew of itself and constantly renewed itself no matter how ruthlessly it was plucked. It is mentioned by Sandys in his *Travailes*, by James Howell fifty years later — who, however, calls it a bay tree — by Misson, in 1691, who remarks that "nothing has as yet been decided about the occult virtue causing this surprising effect," and by many others who find it a very pretty and gracious tribute of Nature to one of her great poets.

Another side of the picture is given by travellers who are shocked by the neglect into which the tomb fell. In 1632, J. J. Bouchard came from Paris to visit Naples. He says of the columbarium: "They assert that it is Virgil's tomb; but the monks who owned it were so neglectful, and the Neapolitans so incurious, that it is all cluttered up." We find what most travellers will agree is a familiar touch in John Raymond's account. He says that the tomb is on a high rock, "so that it is scarce to be seen by those that passe below, The Guides commonly shewing a false."

The canon Carlo Celano concurs in the opinion that the tomb is on Virgil's estate of Patulcis, and feels that he was actually buried here. Whether he was or not is a matter of indifference to John Owen, Rector of Paglesham, Essex, who cries out: "Grateful to me was the monument which bore so high a name. I embraced with credulous joy, in defiance of the cold and captious doubts of the antiquarian, a prejudice so dear to classical feelings." Equally unconcerned is Mme. Fiquet du Boccage, who announces that "we began [a picnic] by eating oysters upon the tomb of *Virgil*, which is so renowned, that people of the lower class have a persuasion that the ashes of a saint or a magician, are contained in it."

It is perhaps heretical to suggest that the most suitable note of all is struck by James Fenimore Cooper in the following reflection on the tomb: "The best reason for believing it to have been erected in honour of the Great Mantuan is, that if it be not his tomb, no one can say whose tomb it is." [27]

VIRGIL'S GHOST

A legend that developed in connection with Virgil's tomb was that from time to time his ghost was seen wandering about the neighborhood. The story was, however, either short-lived or else was considered not worth recording, for we have very few references to it. Capaccio speaks of it in his book on the antiquities of Pozzuoli in 1607, and in 1615 Sandys remarks in his *Travailes*:

It is fabled that the ghost of *Virgil* hath been here-about: whereof a Poet of these later times,

> True it is that this gentle ghost hath been
> Amongst these fragrant groves so often seen.
> O happy eyes, woods fortunate!
> What ere within your sacred confines grow!

A variant perhaps of this legend is that mentioned by Massmann, to the effect that Virgil's grave is supposed to be guarded by ghosts.[28]

GROTTA DI VIRGILIO

Immediately beside the monument known as Virgil's tomb is the lofty opening of a curious passageway cut perhaps in the time of Augustus or even earlier through Mount Posilippo to the Cumaean side. This, the *Grotta Vecchia*, has been replaced by a new passage opened in the last century, and is no longer used. Its former name was *Crypta Neapolitana*, or *Grotta di Virgilio*, and it was the famous tunnel believed to have been made overnight by Virgil through his magic powers. [29]

His name persisted here for centuries. Gervasius of Tilbury, as we have seen, reports the legend, and so does the author of the *Cronica di Partenope*. Petrarch denied Virgil's ability to make the passageway by conjuration; Fazio degli Uberti said that he himself had been inside it. When Octavien de Saint-Gelais accompanied Charles VIII on his

Italian campaign he recorded a visit which the king made to the mountain of the "*crote*" which Virgil pierced so subtly. Benedetto di Falco rises superior to superstition, saying that only the ignorant vulgar believe the legend. Turler, writing in 1574, reports that it is commonly supposed that anyone who commits murder in the grotto cannot leave it. In England the fame of the tunnel was spread by the English Faust Book of 1592, according to which Faust saw "the Tombe of Virgil; and the high way that hee cutte through that mighty hill of stone in one night, the whole length of an English mile," — an incident included in Marlowe's *Doctor Faustus*. But the English, too, become sceptical; for in his *Travailes* (1615) Sandys, remarking that although there is a report that Virgil made the grotto by "art magick," asks indignantly, "Who ever heard that *Virgil* was a magician?" Joseph Mormile, writing a description of Naples in 1625, solemnly denies the story, on the testimony of Petrarch, who was doubtless also Sandys's authority. The Jesuit Celano, who flourished in Italy toward the end of the century, credits the *Cronica di Partenope* with the continued life of the legend, and censures its author severely for his credulousness. In his *Remarks on Italy* Joseph Addison says that the people believe that Virgil made the Grotto, and adds mordantly that he is "in greater Repute among the

Neapolitans for having made the Grotto, than the
Æneid." In 1728 John Breval comments on the
local belief, and recalls that "*Naudeus* has been
at the Pains of collecting all their silly Traditions
concerning that great Poet." Equally scornful is
Keysler: "I heartily pity poor *Virgil*," he declares,
"who, without any fault of his, is thus classed
among magicians," and he goes on to speculate on
the causes of the belief. The abbé Coyer, who
visited Naples in 1763 or 1764, remarks, "Villani
asserts that it [the grotto] was the handiwork of
Virgil, who made it with the stroke of a wand,
and the people of Naples repeat this foolishness.
One had to live in the fourteenth century to write
thus."

An anecdote much in the spirit of the times is
told by Dr. John Moore (1787):

Mr. Addison tells us, that the common people of Naples,
in his time, believed that this passage through the mountain was the work of magic, and that Virgil was the magician. But this is the age of scepticism; and the common people, in imitation of people of fashion, begin to
harbour doubts concerning all their old established
opinions. A Neapolitan Valet-de place asked an English
gentleman lately, Whether Signior Virgilio, of whom he
had heard so much, had really, and bona fide, been a
magician or not? "A magician!" replied the Englishman; "ay, that he was, and a very great magician too."
"And do you," resumed the Valet, "believe it was he
who pierced this rock?" "As for this particular rock,"

answered the Master, "I will not swear to it from my own knowledge, because it was done before I was born; but I am ready to make oath, that I have known him pierce, and even melt, some very obdurate substances."

Giustiniani made a bibliography of historical works on Naples in 1793, including in it the *Cronica di Partenope*; but he resented the presence of the legends, and wrote that "they make us pity the credulity of those times."

Dr. Moore's story very well illustrates the way in which the legends were perpetuated. Travellers visiting Italy wanted to hear stories about Virgil, and if their guides could not produce them, then the travellers themselves told them to the guides; and so we have an endless chain of repetitions which does not necessarily depend upon purely local recollection as distinct from that of the travellers and their guides.[30]

VIRGIL'S CHAPEL

In 1675 an English gentleman named Clenche made the grand tour and on his way very naturally took in the sights of Naples. Close by Virgil's tomb he reports that "they show a little stone seat, enclos'd like a Closet, with an excellent Prospect, where he writ his Georgicks." This was probably a small chapel which formerly stood just below the tomb, and which was very likely the false tomb mentioned above, pointed out as Virgil's in order to save the guides a little extra scrambling.

That the poet put this little chapel to other uses than literary ones is told us in a Dutch travel-book of 1697. Several steps from the grave was an old building which the guide pointed out as the chapel where Virgil heard mass every day. Misson tells the same story in his *Nouveau Voyage d'Italie*, and it is repeated in a German travel-book of 1701. By the time Montesquieu reached Italy in 1728 the tale had suffered a slight change: "The doctors who show the rare sights of Naples show sometimes the spot where Cicero used to say Mass; at least, the prince de Beauvau told me that they had shown it to him." [31]

VIRGIL AND THE CASTEL DELL'OVO

After the fifteenth century the legend of Virgil as architect of the Castle of the Egg seems to have had at best a shadowy existence. Although it is reported by various Neapolitan writers, who assert that the vulgar believe it, I am inclined to suspect that their sole source of information was the *Cronica di Partenope*. In 1604, Capaccio remarks in his book on the history of Pozzuoli, that people tell ridiculous stories about Virgil and the "Lucullan Egg" [i. e., the Castle of the Egg, which occupies the hypothetical site of a palace of Lucullus]. At the end of the century, the canon Celano deplores the vulgar belief that Virgil made the castle, adding that Villani, the supposed author of the *Cronica,* wrote down this legend in his simplicity. Parrino chides the same credulous historian for having written that the castle was named from Virgil's enchanted egg, since it is clear that the name is derived from the shape of the island. Paoli, writing in 1768, says he does not know by what ancient authority Villani makes his assertion, and Lalande rejects the story as without foundation except in the brains of certain authors.[32]

PESQUIER

Virgil was supposed to have made a miraculous fishpond. This pond has not been localized, but it is not outside the range of possibility that the fishponds built presumably by Lucullus on the island where now stands the Castle of the Egg may have given rise to the legend. The ponds were known, and since Virgil made the castle, he would naturally have made its appurtenances.

These fishponds were used in legend. The story of Niccolò Pesce, which appears as early as 1188 in the *De nugis curialium* of Walter Mapes, and had a continued existence in Naples and elsewhere through at least the sixteenth century, includes as one of the exploits of the fish-child the discovery of an enormous treasure in the mysterious grottos under the Castel dell'Ovo. Since the *"pesquier"* of Virgil is spoken of by a Provençal poet, it is perhaps significant that one of the narrators of the Niccolò Pesce story was another Provençal poet, "nichola dabar," or Niccola da Bari, who lived in the thirteenth century.[33]

Another possibility is the amazing *Piscina Mirabilis*, which is an enormous underground vault near Naples. It may have been a storage place for the water supply of the fleet, but its mysterious dim corridors and arches lend themselves to less prosaic attributions. The Neapolitans of the Middle Ages felt its strangeness, as its name indicates, and their surmises might easily have led in Virgil's direction.

THE SCUOLA DI VIRGILIO AT NAPLES

Not far from Naples and close to the little town of Pozzuoli lie the ruins of an ancient amphitheatre. At some time as yet unidentified, the tradition of Virgil as a great scholar and teacher became attached to this spot, and the theatre acquired the title of the School of Virgil. By the sixteenth century this was the common nomenclature, and it is so recorded by the topographer Benedetto di Falco, as well as by Jérome Maurand, who sailed from Antibes to Constantinople in 1544 and paused at Pozzuoli on his way. A hundred years later J. J.

Bouchard saw the amphitheatre of Pozzuoli and was told that it was Virgil's school, where he taught magic. The tradition wandered into Germany and appeared in a so-called topographical study of Italy published in 1688. James Howell (1654) mentions the fact that Virgil esteemed Naples so highly that he lived there, writing and conducting a famous school.[34]

The amphitheatre appears gradually to have lost the title and another edifice to have taken it over at about this time. In any case, the term *Scuola de Virgilio* from now on applies exclusively to a cluster of ruins much nearer Naples, on the shore overlooking the reef of *la Gaiola*. Celano says in 1692 that the common people speak of these ruins as Virgil's school, believing implicitly an old tradition that here Virgil taught magic. From this time on there are constant references to it by travellers, and the name persists to this day. Günther reports that a crag standing close to the *Scuola* has assimilated the Virgilian aura and is called the *Scoglio di Virgilio*.

It is not displeasing that the last trace of the legend of Virgil the Sorcerer should ignore the formerly ubiquitous basket story in which he plays such a sorry rôle, and commemorate only the benevolent sage and teacher.[35]

I have not followed the legends into the nineteenth century, nor have I made any effort to exhaust the material in preceding centuries, since my purpose is to put before the reader enough examples to enable him to determine for himself what the typical developments in the earlier centuries were. The notes here collected suffice to show that the legends were kept in existence through the eagerness of visitors to come upon a familiar name, and the resultant willingness of guides, who became important when travel to Italy first assumed proportions comparable to those prevailing today — that is, in the sixteenth century — to entice extra emoluments from the ever-gaping pocketbooks of the travellers.

While nineteenth-century travel in Italy is here left out of account, there are a few collections of Virgilian legends which should be mentioned. All of them, I think, betray pretty clearly that they are the direct results of precisely the same conditions as those prevailing between guide and traveller in the preceding century. Sometimes the traveller — in nearly every case the collector is a foreigner — has himself complete faith that the stories told him come straight from the folk; sometimes he seems deliberately disingenuous. None is so disarmingly frank as Charles Godfrey Leland in his *Unpublished Legends of Virgil*:

The reader will bear in mind the following frank and full admission, of which all critics are invited to make the worst, that in many cases I had already narrated these Virgilian tales to my collector, as I did here — a course which it is simply impossible to avoid where one is collecting in a specialty.

In other words, he reaped as he sowed — a procedure which is obviously unsound for the scientific collection of tales. Leland's story-tellers knew that they should be paid liberally for the stories which they told him. Naturally, after he had himself told a group of the legends to them, they grasped the fact that he wanted more stories about a wizard named Virgil, and accordingly he got a concentration of all the wizard and witch stories known to the tellers, transferred, of course, to Virgil. By this method one could do a brisk business in collecting "Virgilian" legends almost anywhere in the world. Read the Virgilius Romance to a group of people anywhere, announce that five dollars will be paid for every story brought in, and — how rich will the harvest be! [36]

XII

POETA DOCTUS ET MAGUS

THAT Virgil was a profoundly learned poet is
obvious to any thinking person who has read
his works, and that he was so regarded within a few
centuries of his death is just as obvious from the
commentary of Servius and the *Saturnalia* of
Macrobius. Comparetti's study has demonstrated
that Virgil's reputation for learning continued un-
abated throughout the Middle Ages, a period when
many men reputed to have been of great learning
had a way of turning into magicians. Galen, Hippocrates, Aristotle, Pythagoras, Plato, Horace,
Gerbert, Albertus Magnus, St. Thomas Aquinas,
to mention no more, were thus suspected of dealing
in the art of magic. One is tempted to reason by
analogy that since all of these famous men and
more were dubbed magicians, it is easy enough to
see why Virgil joined their company, since in his
works, particularly in the Eighth Eclogue and in
the Sixth Book of the *Æneid*, he frequently mentions or discusses at length matters pertaining to
witchcraft, to augury, to magical rites, and to the
supernatural in general.[1]

This is a very seductive line of reasoning, and more often than not it has been followed by those who would understand why Virgil the Poet became to the later Middle Ages Virgil the Necromancer. The great difficulty with it is that it is so abstract that to all intents and purposes it is reasoning in a vacuum. After the fact, of course, it has a specious appearance of soundness; but if we turn on the one hand to the actual text of Virgil's writings, and on the other to the texts of the Virgilian legends, we find it virtually impossible to seize upon any given line in the works and say that it gave rise to such and such a legend. If a generalization is sound, its particulars must support it. Since we can discover no particulars whatever, — let alone sound ones, — we must abandon the attractive but hazy and illusory idea that the poet Virgil's lucubrations on magic had anything definite to do with his becoming a magician. After all, it is a fallacy more common to modern than to ancient or mediaeval literary criticism to apply inferences drawn from a man's writings to the man himself.

Virgil's works, then, yield no reliable clue to the reasons underlying the metamorphosis of poet to mage. There is another kind of venerable literature dealing with Virgil which should be scrutinized — the ancient biographies. Here we feel somewhat surer of our ground, for there actually are legends in most of the biographies, including the most authoritative and important of them all, that attributed to Donatus. Virgil's mother had a prodigious dream before his birth in a ditch, a life-tree developed with him, and so on. One legend easily leads to another — and so grew the legendary cycle which is the subject of these studies. But here again we cannot bridge the gap between the two sets of texts, for not a single one of the legends in the biographical works can be twisted into a form even remotely approaching the stories told by John of Salisbury and his successors.[2]

To me the insuperable obstacle to all such attempts is that, search as I would, I have been unable to find one fact in what Comparetti calls the literary tradition of Virgil which leads in any way to this group of legends devoted to Virgil's magical powers. All of this reasoning has been developed, I think, through the *post hoc, propter hoc* fallacy. The mediaeval attitude toward the author of the *Æneid* was fixed as early as St. Jerome, and it remained substantially the same until the twelfth century and after, when the tales of Virgil the necromancer got into circulation; and even this new material, it should be noted, had relatively little effect upon the classical tradition, which was too strong to be seriously affected, and endured through the Renaissance and down into modern times.[3]

If Virgil had not been a great and learned man, there would never have been any legends of his becoming a magician; but this is as far as one can go, I think, in relating the necromantic legends to the man Virgil. If, as Comparetti maintains, the legends grew naturally out of the conception of Virgil as a wise man, why is it that they do not appear until the middle of the twelfth century? The mediaeval conception of Virgil as a wise man was essentially a constant, from the times of Macrobius and St. Jerome, and nothing happened to it in the twelfth century to bring about the development of the legends. Comparetti bridges the gap between the literary and legendary reputation of Virgil by means of the poet's tomb at Naples:

Whatever doubts may be thrown on the grave which at the present day is pointed to as Vergil's, or that which in the Middle Ages may have passed for such, it is an historical fact admitting of no reasonable doubt that Vergil wished to be buried at Naples, and that he actually was buried there.   (C.-B. 276.)

It is true also that in the life attributed to Donatus we are informed that "ossa eius Neapolim translata sunt tumuloque condita, qui est via Puteolana intra lapidem secundum." *Ossa* here means "ashes"; but, as we have seen, the legends refer to actual bones, which could be carried about in a sack — an interesting, and, I think, significant difference, since I have been unable to find any

evidence whatever for Comparetti's conviction
that the whereabouts of Virgil's tomb was known
after the fifth century, when Sidonius Apollinaris
visited it. In fact, the Italian scholar frequently
goes farther than the known facts warrant in his
speculations on the origin of the legends:

Its origin [of the Virgilian legend] in Italy was entirely
the work of the lower classes, and had nothing to do
with poetry or literature; it was a popular superstition,
founded on local records connected with Vergil's long
stay in Naples and the celebrity of his tomb in that city.
(C.–B. 253.)
It was certainly not left to the Normans to point out to
the little republic of Parthenope, proud of its connection with ancient Rome, the existence of the grave of
Vergil on its classic soil.   (C.–B. 278.)

It is unfortunate that Comparetti did not produce
these local records dealing with Virgil's tomb at
Naples, and unfortunate that I have been unable to
find any trace of them, for upon them depends the
validity of the whole argument. I am sceptical
about the records, for if there had been such a
tradition as Comparetti here conjectures, surely
Alexander of Telese, interested as he was in Virgil's
relationship to Naples, would not have failed to
mention so impressive a landmark as Virgil's
tomb, if its location were known. Since the sentence in the Donatus biography, then, must be the
sole means of bridging the gap above referred to,

the chances of bridging it are forlorn, for that vague statement is so indefinite that modern scholars are unable to agree on what it means. If the resources of modern scholarship are insufficient, how could the Middle Ages know where the tomb was? It is true, of course, that a traditional connection of some sort could have been maintained with classical antiquity, or with the fifth century; but if it was maintained, why is there no evidence? There is none, and any effort to assert that there was such a tradition must be based upon documents supporting it.

The question that remained in my mind after reading Comparetti's great work was, "Why did the legends start, if they are a direct result of the literary tradition, which remained essentially static throughout the Middle Ages?" At some time or other, there were none of these necromantic legends; they must have begun sometime. When? Comparetti implies that the literary tradition and the popular legends coexisted for a time — how long he does not say, but the implication seems to be for a considerable time — before the popular legends became known:

The two met eventually, as they were bound to do, but the popular legend did not leave the home of its birth or acquire any celebrity by means of literature earlier than the twelfth century.   (C.–B. 142.)

That is, at some misty time before the twelfth century, the popular legends were formed, and they existed for an indefinite period among the Neapolitan folk, just happening to get written down in the middle of the twelfth century; there is no moment of formation, no impulse. In this same direction tends a gallant recent effort to push back the date of origin to the ninth century; but we shall need more than a line in a biography, of which the interpretation and connotation are none too clear, before John of Salisbury can be regarded as the second, rather than the first, writer to inform us of the legends.[4]

In Chapter III, I have set forth as clearly as I could my hypothesis of the origin of the legend concerning Virgil's bones. We cannot know which of all of the legends is the oldest, but this one occurs, along with that of the fly, in the oldest text which we have, the *Policraticus* of John of Salisbury. Once Virgil came to be regarded as a magician, we may perhaps be content, with Hasluck, to say simply that "progressive lying" is responsible for the rest. Where I have felt able to conjecture what specific reasons might underlie additional legends, I have done so. There is no reason to believe, however, that because an early legend may have been explained, all the others follow merely from that one. Other causes, naturally, might produce other legends, without reference to any other one of the lot.

I devoted part of Chapter XI to a brief survey of the continued life of the legends among travellers in Italy. Now we have no means of knowing so much about the early narrators of the Virgilian legends — that is, so much about their purpose in telling the legends; but if we consider the Table appended to Chapter I, a curious fact will be observed. So far as facts, not conjectures, are concerned, the legends first appeared in the *Policraticus*, a work written about 1159. Then, during the next one hundred and seventy years, they were told pretty much all over Europe, by Englishmen, Frenchmen, Germans, by a troubadour of Provence, in chronicles, encyclopædias, romances, and in two of the greatest collections of stories known in the Middle Ages; but *never once* are the legends told by Italians during this period of one hundred and seventy years. Then Cecco d'Ascoli, the *Cronica di Partenope*, Cino da Pistoia, and Antonio Pucci — to name no more — follow one another in rapid succession. This silence in Italy, and especially at Naples, where the legends presumably had their origin, I find most striking, and I feel that particular attention should be directed to it. It is one reason why I am unable to follow my distinguished predecessor in postulating for these tales a

long life among the Neapolitan folk. After 1326
the legends came to life, perhaps among the folk
at Naples, but certainly at Naples; but for the existence of the legends at Naples before this date,
the evidence is scarcely convincing; there is, in fact,
virtually none. It is true that, of the earlier con-
tributors, John of Salisbury, Conrad of Querfurt,
Gervasius of Tilbury, and Maître Gossouin, the
presumed author of the *Image du Monde*, travelled
in Italy and actually visited Naples or Sicily, or
both. We might not be far from the truth in sup-
posing that Guiraut de Calanso was also there, in
view of the large numbers of troubadours known
to have been welcomed at the court of Palermo.
About Neckam's presence or absence in Italy we
can decide nothing; and about the others among
the earlier narrators we are in a similar quandary.
If we fix our attention upon these four, we observe
in the first place that they were all foreigners, in
the second place that they were all clerics. Birds
of a feather flock together, and when the religious
joined company, the *lingua franca* was Latin. Now
of these four, all but John of Salisbury wrote down
their stories after 1194, when the invading forces of
Henry IV of Germany captured Naples; and John's
legends number but two, as we have seen. Building
conjectures upon conjectures is dizzy business, but
nevertheless I wonder whether the Virgilian legends

during this period were travellers' tales told by clerics with not a little malicious satisfaction at the ultimate downfall of the popular faith in the sage's power of protecting the city? Certainly, never was traveller in any century or any country more ebullient with enthusiasm, more curious, and, even among travellers, more gullible than Conrad of Querfurt. If it was a cleric who added the basket story to the legends, a cleric who was familiar with the Germanic punishment basket, we can imagine his satisfaction at succeeding in making Virgil out a kind of criminal, thus doing his bit in the praiseworthy and Christian task of removing Virgil from the ranks of the thaumaturges so as to leave that field the undisputed territory of the saints.

In all of the foregoing there has been no room for that other and greater magic of Virgil's perennially lovely verse. This phenomenon indeed surpasses all feats of mere thaumaturgy, and transports the thoughtful mind to the realms of the purest genius. This learned poet was in sober truth a mage; this

> Wielder of the stateliest measure
> ever moulded by the lips of man

wove in his verses spells more potent than all his legendary deeds of magic.

NOTES

ABBREVIATIONS

C.-B. . . . . E. F. M. Benecke's translation of Comparetti, Virgilio nel medio evo [from proofsheets of the second edition], London, 1895.

*Comp. . . . . Domenico Comparetti, Virgilio nel medio evo², 2 vv., Firenze, 1896.

Chauvin . . . . . . Victor Chauvin, Bibliographie des ouvrages arabes . . ., 12 vv., Liége, 1892–1922.

Graf . . . . Arturo Graf, Roma nella memoria e nelle immaginazioni del medio evo, 1 vol., Torino, 1923.

      A literal reprint of the first edition in two volumes, Torino, 1882–83. The chapter-numbers are the same in all editions. Chap. XVI, "Virgilio," occupies pp. 520–566 in the edition which I use. Chap. VI, "La potenza di Roma," pp. 143–179, is also frequently referred to in my notes.

Hwb. d. d. Abergl.   Handwörterbuch des deutschen Aberglaubens, ed. Hanns Bächtold-Stäubli, Berlin and Leipzig, 1927 — [not yet completed; I use through art. Frau].

Manitius . . . . . . Max Manitius, Geschichte der lateinischen Literatur des Mittelalters, 3 vv., München, 1911–31 [Handbuch der Altertumswissenschaft, edd. Iwan von Müller and Walter Otto, IX, ii, 1–3].

Thorndike, Magic² Lynn Thorndike, A History of Magic and Experimental Science in the Middle Ages², 2vv., New York, 1929.

   * See next page.

CONVERSION TABLE

For the convenience of readers who use the Italian second edition of Comparetti, I append a table which will enable them to convert my references, which are chiefly to Benecke's translation, to the proper pages of the original. This seems more practical than publishing here the full index to Comparetti's work which I have prepared for my own use.

Since the *Prefazione* is not included by Benecke, it must be read in the original.

C.–B.			Comparetti	
PART i			PART i	
Ch.	I	1– 14	Volume I	1– 20
	II	15– 23		20– 32
	III	24– 33		32– 44
	IV	34– 49		45– 65
	V	50– 74		66– 98
	VI	75– 95		99–128
	VII	96–103		129–138
	VIII	104–118		139–158
	IX	119–134		159–178
	X	135–155		179–207
	XI	156–165		207–220
	XII	166–182		220–243
	XIII	183–194		243–258
	XIV	195–209		259–278
	XV	210–231		278–307
	XVI	232–238		308–316
PART ii			PART ii	
Ch.	I	239–256	Volume II	1– 23
	II	257–263		23– 32
	III	264–289		33– 66
	IV	290–294		66– 72
	V	295–301		73– 80
	VI	302–308		81– 89
	VII	309–324		90–111
	VIII	325–339		111–131
	IX	340–357		132–156
	X	358–376		156–181
Texts of some of the legends (not reprinted by Benecke)				182–324

NOTES

CHAPTER I

1. A list of some of the general discussions published during the past century or so will illustrate the interest in Virgilian legends during that period. More important contributions are starred. *F. H. von der Hagen, Briefe in die Heimat, Breslau, 1819, III, 184 ff., IV, 118 ff.; F. L. F. von Dobeneck, Des deutschen Mittelalters Volksaberglauben und Heroensagen, Berlin, 1815, I, 188 ff.; Collin de Plancy, Dictionnaire infernal², Paris, 1826, IV, 538–540; *F. W. Genthe, Des Publius Virgilius Maro zehn Eclogen, mit einer Einleitung über Virgils Leben und Fortleben, Magdeburg, 1830, 44–97 (second ed., Leipzig, 1855, 47–85); Xavier Marmier, Études sur Goethe, Paris, 1835, 58–63; *La Chronique rimée de Philippe Mouskes, ed. Baron de Reiffenberg, Bruxelles, 1836–37, I, pp. clxxxi–clxxxiv, II, pp. v–vi, 817; San Marte [= Albert Schulz], Parcival, Rittergedicht von Wolfram von Eschenbach, Magdeburg, 1836, cols. 635–647; *Heinrich Adelbert von Keller, Li Romans des sept sages, Tübingen, 1836, cciii–ccxii; Carl F. H. Siebenhaar, De fabulis, quae media aetate de Publio Virgilio Marone circumferebantur, Berlin, 1837; *A. Loiseleur Deslongchamps, Essai sur les fables indiennes . . ., Paris, 1838, 150–154; *Francisque Michel, Quae vices quaeque mutationes et Virgilium ipsum et ejus carmina per mediam aetatem exceperint explanare tentavit . . ., Lutetiae Parisiorum, 1846; *F. H. von der Hagen, Gesammtabenteuer, 3 vv., Stuttgart and Tübingen, 1850, III, pp. cxxix–cxlvii; *Édélestand Du Méril, Mélanges archéologiques et littéraires, Paris, 1850, 424–478; *J. G. T. Grässe, Beiträge zur Literatur und Sage des Mittelalters, Dresden, 1850, 27–37; *G. Zappert, Virgil's Fortleben im Mittelalter, Denkschriften der k. Akademie der Wissenschaften, Phil.-Hist. Classe, II, Vienna (1851), 46–100; Thomas Wright, Narratives of Sorcery and Magic, London,

1851, I, 99–121; *Schwubbe, P. Virgilius per mediam aetatem gratia atque auctoritate florentissimus, Paderborn, 1852 [28 r Jahresbericht über das Gymnasium Theodorianum zu Paderborn . . .]; *Hans Ferdinand Massmann, Kaiserchronik, Quedlinburg and Leipzig, 1854, III, 426 ff. [very learned and still valuable]; *Karl Wilhelm Milberg, Memorabilia Virgiliana, Meissen, 1857 [Programm der Fürstenschule St. Afra], and *Mirabilia Virgiliana, Meissen, 1867 [same]; *K. L. Roth, Germania, IV (1859), 257–298; Domenico Comparetti, articles in Nuova antologia, I (1866), 1–55, IV (1867), 605–647; V (1867), 659–703; *same, Virgilio nel medio evo, 2 vv., Livorno, 1872, reprinted, Livorno, 1885? — cf. de Puymaigre, in La revue nouvelle d'Alsace et Lorraine, Vᵉ année, viᵉ vol. (1886), 241–250 [of the many reviews, only two contributed anything save praise: (1) by an anonymous reviewer in the Quarterly Review, CXXXIX (1875), 77–105, who notes the confusing method, and (2) by Gaston Paris in Revue critique d'histoire et de littérature, VIII (1874), premier semestre, 133–142, who says, in part (137): "Les faits, épars dans les ouvrages les plus divers de temps, de lieux et d'idiomes, sont recueillis avec une sûreté et une abondance auxquelles il est à peu près impossible à rien ajouter;" — a statement little calculated to encourage the future student! The whole review is still worth consulting]; this first edition, including the German translation in one vol. by H. Dütschke, Virgil im Mittelalter, Leipzig, 1875, is superseded by the second edition, 2 vv., Firenze, 1896, of which the English translation by E. F. M. Benecke (Vergil in the Middle Ages, 1 vol., London, 1895, 1908, and New York, 1929, this last with inadequate index) was made from proofsheets of the second Italian edition, and lacks the reprints of texts; the sole constructive review of the second edition is by V. Rossi, in Rassegna bibliografica della letteratura italiana, IV (1896), 174–181; *Wilhelm Viëtor, Der Ursprung der Virgilsage, Zeitschrift für romanische Philologie, I (1877), 165–178; E. Celesia, Storia della letteratura in Italia ne' secoli barbari, Genova, 1882, II, 91–107; *Arturo Graf, Roma nella memoria e nelle immaginazioni del medio evo, 2 vv., Torino, II (1883), chap. xvi, 196–258 [the most recent reprint, in 1 vol.,

Torino, 1923, which I use, discusses the legends pp. 520–566.
Graf's chief contribution is clarity]; Robert Dernedde, Über
die den altfranzösischen Dichtern bekannten epischen Stoffe
aus dem Altertum, Erlangen, 1887, 150–158; *J. S. Tunison,
Master Virgil, Cincinnati, 1888 [of some value independently
of Comparetti; at times follows him almost word for word];
*T. J. B. de Puymaigre, Folk-lore, Paris, 1885; *J. Stecher,
La légende de Virgile en Belgique, Bulletin de l'académie
royale de Belgique, 3ᵐᵉ série, XIX (1890), 585–632; P. Schwie-
ger, Der Zauberer Virgil, Berlin, 1897 [not a contribution;
reviews were uniformly unfavorable; e. g., Litterarisches Zen-
tralblatt for 1897, 1568–70; Berliner Philologische Wochen-
schrift for 1897, 1025–28; Romania, XXVI (1897), 621]; Victor
Chauvin, Bibliographie des ouvrages arabes . . ., Liége, 1892–
1912, VIII, 188 ff., No. 228 [rich bibliographical notes the use-
fulness of which is lessened because of cryptic abbreviations
which were to have been resolved in the bibliography, un-
finished at the time of the author's death]; *Karl Schambach,
Vergil ein Faust des Mittelalters, two parts, Nordhausen,
1904–05 [Königliches Gymnasium zu Nordhausen, Ostern,
1904–05, Wissenschaftliche Beigaben, Progr. nr. 290, 291;
a careful and illuminating study]; Kirby Flower Smith, The
Later Tradition of Vergil, Classical Weekly, IX (1916), 178–
182, 185–188; Marbury B. Ogle, same title, Classical Journal,
XXVI (1930), 63–73; E. W. Bowen, Vergil as a Magician,
Sewanee Review, VIII (1900), 297–305, E. Rodocanachi,
Études et fantaisies historiques, 2ᵉ série, Paris, 1919, 106–132,
and Domenico Tinozzi, Virgilio nella storia e nella leggenda,
Pescara, 1930 [Biblioteca dell' Istituto Fascista di Cultura di
Pescara], are too slight to be of any value. Master Vergil, an
Anthology of Poems on Vergil and Vergilian Themes, ed.
Elizabeth Nitchie, Boston, 1930, does not refer to the ma-
gician. Luigi Suttina, Virgilio nella leggenda e nella fantasia
del medio evo, in Supplemento al N. 49 de L'Illustrazione
Italiana del 7 dicembre, 1930, 47–50, is a pleasing popular
essay.

2. K. Schaarschmidt, Johannes Saresberiensis, Leipzig,
1862; articles by Reginald Lane Poole in Dictionary of Na-

tional Biography, XXIX, 439–446, in Illustrations of . . .
Medieval Thought ², London, 1920, 176–197, in English Historical Review, XXXV (1920), 321–342, and in Proceedings of
the British Academy, XI (1924); John Dickinson [translator
of Books Four, Five, Six, and parts of Seven and Eight, of]
The Statesman's Book of J. of S., New York, 1927; Helen
Waddell, J. of S., in Essays and Studies . . . of the English
Association, XIII (1928), 28–51; Lynn Thorndike, A History
of Magic and Experimental Science ², New York, 1929, 155–
170; Manitius, III, 253–264; Clement C. J. Webb, John of
Salisbury, London, 1932 [Great Medieval Churchmen Series].

3. Joannis Saresberiensis Policratici libri VIII, ed. C. C. J.
Webb, Oxford, 1909, lib. i, cap. 4 [vol. I, p. 26]: Fertur uates
Mantuanus interrogasse Marcellum, cum depopulationi
auium vehementius operam daret, an auem mallet instrui in
capturam auium, an muscam informari in exterminationem
muscarum. Cum uero quaestionem ad auunculum retulisset
Augustum, consilio eius praeelegit ut fieret musca, quae ab
Eneapoli muscas abigeret, et ciuitatem a peste insanabili li-
beraret. Optio quidem impleta est; unde liquet privatae
uoluptati cuiusuis praeferendam esse multorum uilitatem.

4. De uenatica, et auctoribus et speciebus eius, et exercitio
licito et illicito.

5. C.-B. 267; Graf, Roma . . . (1923), 551. Andrea Dandolo, Chronicon Venetum (1339. Muratori, Rerum italicarum scriptores, XII, Mediolani, 1728, 283) summarizes the
legends in Gervasius.

6. Policraticus, lib. ii, cap. 23 [vol. I, p. 132]: Restat tibi
illius Stoici tui quaestio, quem in Apulia diutius morantem
uidi, ut post multas uigilias, longa ieiunia, labores plurimos et
sudores, tanto infelicis et inutilis exilii questu, in Gallias Virgilii ossa potius quam sensum reportaret. Quaerebat et enim
Ludowicus ille, an posses aliquid facere eorum quae minime
facturus es. Cf. C.-B. 274–277.

7. Comparetti, Ricerche intorno al Libro di Sindibād,
Milano, 1869, translated by A. C. Coote, Researches Respect-
ing the Book of Sindibâd, London, 1882 [Folk-Lore Society];
H. L. D. Ward, A Catalogue of Romances . . . in the British

Museum, II, London, 1893, 228–234; Chauvin, Bibliographie des ouvrages arabes . . ., VIII, 1904, 30–31; Killis Campbell, The Seven Sages of Rome, Boston, 1907 [Albion Series]; Alfons Hilka, Johannis de Alta Silva Dolopathos . . ., Heidelberg, 1913 [Sammlung Mittellateinischer Texte 5]; Laura A. Hibbard, Mediaeval Romance in England, New York, 1924, 174–181; Manitius, III, 278–282. For the discovery of the trick referred to, Hilka's edition, pp. 16–17; for Lucinius's foreknowledge of his mother's death, pp. 18–19. Cf. C.-B. 233 ff., 248, 292. The Old French translation, Li romans di Dolopathos, by one Herbers, was edited by C. Brunet and A. de Montaiglon, Paris, 1856 [Bibliothèque Elzevirienne].

8. The Latin Poems commonly attributed to Walter Mapes, ed. Thomas Wright, London, 1841, 283. Another translation (p. 272) renders the one line "And Virgill then did shape the small bees of the aire," which in the best text reads ". . . video . . . formantem ereas muscas Virgilium." — Die Apokalypse des Golias, ed. Karl Strecker, Rome, 1928, p. 18 [= Texte zur Kulturgeschichte des Mittelalters V]. Cf. Manitius, III, 931. The poem is dated about 1180. C.-B. 267. Tunison 105.

9. Alexandri Neckam De naturis rerum libri duo, ed. Thomas Wright, London, 1863 [Rerum britannicarum medii aevi scriptores, XXXIV], lib. ii, cap. CLXXIV. Biographical details are prefixed by the editor. Comparetti's references to Neckam in this connection are on pp. 262 ff., 296, 314. By far the greater part of his works remains in manuscript. Recent discussions are C. H. Haskins, [Harvard] Studies in Classical Philology, XX (1909), 75–94 [= Studies in the History of Mediæval Science ², Cambridge [Mass.], 1927, 356–376]; M. Esposito, On some Unpublished Poems attributed to Alexander Neckam, English Historical Review, XXX (1915), 450–471; Thorndike, Magic ², II, 188–204; Manitius, III, 784–794; J. C. Russell, Alexander Neckam in England, English Historical Review, XLVII (1932), 260–268. The slenderness of our stock of facts is well illustrated by the opposing inferences by Comparetti and Thorndike on the same poem. The former [p. 263] interprets the satirical verses by Neckam in

De laudibus divinae sapientiae [pp. 447–448 of Wright's edi-
tion] as indicating that he never visited Italy; the latter [II,
189] says "Neckam visited Italy, as his humorous poem bid-
ding Rome good-bye attests. . . ." The verses read in part:

Romae quid facerem?   Mentiri nescio, libros
   Diligo, sed libras respuo; Roma, vale . . .
Respuo delicias tantas, tantosque tumultus;
   Cornutas frontes horreo; Roma vale . . .

In sum, the difference between the two opinions is that because
a man writes a poem about a given place he must have been
there or he must not have been there. Obviously neither is
necessarily the case, and the question remains as before.

Walter Burley's Liber de vita et moribus philosophorum is
edited by H. Knust, Tübingen, 1886 [Bibliothek des Litter-
rischen Vereins in Stuttgart, CLXXVII]; Virgil's deeds appear
in cap. CIV. See especially pp. 401 note 20, 404, 410, 413–
416 on the Continental vogue of Burley's work, and Hermann
Varnhagen, Fiori e vita di filosofi . . ., Erlangen, 1893, xii. A
Spanish translation of Burley which Knust apparently did not
mention is Hernando Diaz, La vida y excelentes dichos de los
mas sabios philosophos que vuo eneste mundo . . ., Toledo,
1527, reprinted by Cromberger at Seville in 1541.

10. Conrad's letter is printed by G. W. von Leibnitz, Scriptores rerum brunsvicensium, Hannover, II (1710), 695–698,
and is reprinted in part by Comparetti [2], II, 185–186. I use
the text in Monumenta germaniae historica, Scriptores, XXI,
Hannover, 1869, 192–196. For the date and other information,
see Franz X. von Wegele, Kanzler Konrad, gestorben 1202,
in Historisches Taschenbuch, VI. Folge, III. Jahrg. (1884),
31–71. If Conrad had lived in the sixteenth instead of the
twelfth century, his name would now be a byword. The
Cambridge Medieval History, V, 1929, chapter xiv, ignores
him. C.-B. 266, 269, 270$_{24}$, 272, 278, 342$_6$, 347, 375.   ·

11. Wolfram von Eschenbach, Parzival, ed. Ernst Martin,
Halle a. S., 1900 [Germanistische Handbibliothek IX, I],
Book XIII, 656, p. 233. Schambach, II, 41, offers the conjecture that the relationship between Virgil and Clinschor arose
from the close political connections between Sicily, Clinschor's

home, and Naples during the period of development of the
Virgilian legends.   C.–B. 294.

  12.   de Virgili,   [line 158
              com de la conca's saup cobrir;
                        e del vergier
                        e del pesquier
              e del foc que saup escantir.

The entire poem is edited by Wilhelm Keller in Romanische
Forschungen, XXII (1908), 99–238, "Das Sirventes 'Fadet
joglar' des Guiraut von Calanso." See especially pp. 132, 143,
206–209. The second line may refer to the basket episode (see
Chapter V). The third line alludes probably to Virgil's garden, the fourth is clear enough, as we shall see later, and the
last line seems to glance at Virgil's revenge for the basket episode, on which see Chapter VI. One manuscript (D) has the
reading *vengier* for *vergier* in line 160 — "revenge" instead of
"orchard." Cf. Joseph Anglade, Histoire sommaire de la
littérature méridionale au moyen-âge, Paris, 1921, 183$_4$. A
bibliography of works on Guiraut is supplied by Willy Ernst,
Die Lieder des . . . Guiraut von Calanso, Romanische Forschungen, XLIV (1930), 255–259. C.–B. 247$_{13}$, 291–292, 330,
350$_{25}$.

  13. Otia imperialia, ed. G. W. von Leibnitz, Scriptores rerum brunsvicensium, Hannover, 1707–11, I, 881–1006, Emen-
dationes, II, 751–784. The Virgilian legends are all in the
Tertia decisio, which was reprinted in part by Comparetti[2],
II, 187–191, and partly reprinted, textually improved, and
annotated by Felix Liebrecht, Des Gervasius von Tilbury Otia
imperialia in einer Auswahl . . ., Hannover, 1856. Gervasius
is discussed by Joseph Stevenson, Radulphi de Coggeshall
Chronicon anglicanum . . ., Excerpta ex Otiis imperialibus
Gervasii Tileburiensis, London, 1875 [Rerum brittanicarum
medii aevi scriptores], pp. xxiii–xxv; by William Stubbs, The
Historical Works of Gervase of Canterbury, London, 1879
[Rerum britt. med. aevi ss.], I, pp. xli-xliii; best of all, by
Reinhold Pauli, in Nachrichten von der K. Gesellschaft der
Wissenschaften . . . zu Göttingen (1882), 312–332. Cf. S. Kę-
trzyński, Ze studyów nad Gerwazym z Tilbury, Rozprawy

VIRGIL THE NECROMANCER

324

Akademii Umiejętności, Wydział Historyczno-Filozoficzny, Ser. II, tom. xxi, XLVI [Krakow, 1903], 152–189. C.-B. 257, 259 ff., 262, 280, 341 ff., 344, 370. The passage about the search for Virgil's bones is translated in full, C.-B. 273–274.

14. Leibnitz, I, 963; only last part quoted by Liebrecht, 14.

15. Liebrecht, p. 17, cap. xvi; Comp.² 191.

16. On Helinandus, see the article by Brial, Histoire littéraire de la France, XVIII, Paris, 1835, 87–103; L. Delisle, La Chronique d'Hélinand, moine de Froidmont, in Notices et documents publiés pour la Société de l'histoire de France à l'occasion du cinquantième anniversaire de sa fondation, Paris, 1884, 141–154, and F. Wulff and E. Walberg, Les Vers de la mort, par Hélinant moine de Froidmont, Paris, 1905, p. xxvii [Société des anciens textes français]. The Chronicon is printed by Migne, Patrologia Latina, vol. CCXII, cols. 771–1082. Since the legends are extant only in the work of Vincent, they will be analyzed in the discussion of that author, pp. 21 ff.

17. C. H. Haskins, Studies in the History of Mediæval Science², Cambridge [Mass.], 1927 [Harvard Historical Studies, XXVII], 286, and Studies in Mediæval Culture, Oxford, 1929, chapter vii, pp. 148–159. Cf. Lynn Thorndike, Magic², II, 307–337, and James Wood Brown, An Enquiry into the Life and Legend of Michael Scot, Edinburgh, 1907, on which see Haskins, Mediæval Science², 272.

18. On the Image du Monde, see L'Image du Monde de Maître Gossouin, ed. O. H. Prior, Lausanne, 1913. This is an edition of the prose version of 1245 and a discussion of the Image du Monde, including bibliography. The versions in verse are discussed by Carl Fant, L'Image du Monde, poème inédit du milieu du xiiie siècle . . ., in Upsala Universitets Årsskrift for 1886 [Filosofi, Språkvetenskap och historiska Vetenskaper], p. 6. Many manuscripts were made of both versions during the following centuries and also several early printed editions, mostly abridgments of the prose version, both in French and English. These are listed by O. H. Prior (Image . . . de Maître Gossouin) who has made also an edition of Caxton's Mirrour of the World, E. E. T. S., e. s. CX, London, 1913; Hermann Hesse, Studien über die zweite Re-

daktion des Image du Monde, Göttingen, 1932 (diss.) I have not seen. For identification of the French versions, cf. also Hugh William Davies, Catalogue of a Collection of Early French Books in the Library of C. Fairfax Murray, London, 1910, 2 vols., I, 342 ff., and Robert Proctor, Early Printed Books in the British Museum, London, 1898, II, 588. These printed versions played an important part in the continued life of the legends through the sixteenth century, and even later; a Hebraic version was printed as late as 1733.

On finding books of magic, see J. Klapper, Exempla aus Handschriften des Mittelalters, Heidelberg, 1913, No. 81, "De Iudaeo, qui prophetiam invenit in Tholeto." Cf. Moses Gaster in Monatsschrift für Geschichte und Wissenschaft des Judentums, XXIX (1880), 121 ff. [= Gaster's Studies and Texts in Folk-Lore . . ., London, 1925–28, II, 1187 ff.]; Hasluck, Christianity and Islam . . ., II, 472, note. Aristotle was said to have requested that his books be buried with him — Wilhelm Hertz, Gesammelte Abhandlungen, ed. Friedrich von der Leyen, Stuttgart and Berlin, 1905, 371.

19. Vincentii Burgundi Speculum quadruplex, 4 volumes, Duaci, 1624, I, Speculum naturale, lib. vii, cap. 87; IV, Speculum historiale, lib. vi, capp. 60, 61, 62. I use this edition of the Spec. hist., rather than that of 1473 preferred by Thorndike, because whatever its faults it is far more accessible than the incunabulum. Thorndike's chapter on Vincent, Magic [2], II, 457–476, is the most recent discussion. J. B. Bourgeat, Études sur V. de B., Paris, 1856, one of the chief accounts of Vincent, reaches conclusions to the effect that the Catholic church has always been very favorable to philosophy and the arts and sciences, and the Middle Ages may be cited in proof. The most usable recent general survey of Vincent is Pierre Feret, La Faculté théologique de Paris et ses docteurs les plus célèbres, 4 vv., Paris, 1894–97, II, (1895), 401–420, now supplemented by B. L. Ullman in Speculum, VIII (1933), 312–326. Worth consulting also are Desbarreaux-Bernard, Étude bibliographique sur . . . V. de B. . . ., Paris, 1872; A. Lecoy de la Marche, Le treizième siècle littéraire et scientifique, s. l., 1895 [Société de Saint-Augustin], 233–241; Émile Mâle, L'art re-

ligieux du XIII⁰ siècle en France[5], Paris, 1923, pp. 23–26.
The incunabula are listed by W. A. Copinger, Supplement to
Hain's Repertorium bibliographicum, London, 1902, II, ii,
pp. 186–192, Nos. 6241–6259. C.-B. 271, 293 f., 296, 306,
320 f., 323. One of a large number of transcriptions of Vincent
on Virgil is in the Annales Hannoniae of Jacques de Guyse
(d. 1399), ed. by the Marquis de Fortia d'Urban, 21 vv.,
Paris, 1826–38, III, 438–440; Vincent is copied word for word.
Another is in the Spiegel historiael of Rijmkronik by Jakob
van Maerlant, written 1393–1402, edd. M. de Vries and E.
Verwijs, Leyden, 1863 [Maatschappij der Nederlandsche Let-
terkunde], I, 257 (I. Partie, vi. Boek, 26. Deel). A third is in
the rare Mirouer historial, Lyon, Barthelemy Buyer, 1479
(at the Bibliothèque Nationale: Rés. G. 1098), fo. ccxliiii, with
additions to Vincent — Virgil's brazen image which quelled
Vesuvius by sounding a trumpet, the medicinal baths which he
made in "Patrolana," later destroyed and abandoned "when
the study of medicine came to Salerno." C.-B. 254, 293 f.
Virgil founded Brescia, according to a thirteenth-century
manuscript — C.-B. 323₄₃.

Felix Faber of Ulm took issue with Vincent's denial that
Virgil made a bell-tower, citing St. Jerome as an authority
that bells did exist in ancient times. — Fratris Felici Fabri
Evagatorium in terrae sanctae . . . peregrinationem, ed. Con-
radus D. Hassler, Stuttgart, 1849, III, 421, sec. 217a [Bib-
liothek des litterarischen Vereins in Stuttgart IV]. The part
of this work translated by Vincenzo Lazzari which is referred
to by V. Rossi (Rassegna bibliografica della letteratura italiana, IV [1896], 176) I have not seen.

20. Li Haut Livre du Graal Perlesvaus, edd. William A.
Nitze and T. Atkinson Jenkins, Chicago, 1932, I, ll. 5788 ff.,
p. 250 (Modern Philology Monographs). I have to thank
Professor Nitze for answering inquiries concerning this
passage.

21. Jansen Enikels Werke, ed. Philipp Strauch, Hannover
and Leipzig, 1900 (Monumenta Germaniae historica, Scriptorum qui vernacula lingua usi sunt III). The legends occupy
ll. 23695–24224, as follows: introductory remarks and glass

full of devils, 23695–23764; chastity-working statue, 23765–23778; basket episode, 23779–23950; revenge, 23951–24138; founding of Naples, 24139–24156; statue with treasure, 24157–24224. The legends alone are printed also by F. H. von der Hagen, Gesammtabenteuer, Stuttgart and Tübingen, 1850, II, 509–527; by H. F. Massmann, Kaiserchronik, Quedlinburg and Leipzig, 1854, III (still valuable for its wealth of comparative notes); and by Comparetti[2], II, 222–236. C.–B. 303–317 ff., 331, 365$_{13}$. Cf. Marta Maria Helff, Studien zur Kaiserchronik, Leipzig and Berlin, 1930 [Beiträge zur Kulturgeschichte des Mittelalters XLI].

22. Die Roman von Escanor von Gerard von Amiens, ed. H. Michelant, Tübingen, 1886 (Bibliothek des litterarischen Vereins in Stuttgart, CLXXVIII). For the date see J. D. Bruce, The Evolution of Arthurian Romance, 2 vv., Göttingen, 1923 (Hesperia. Ergänzungsreihe, VIII, IX), II, 275, 276, especially note 25 (second ed. 1930, same). For the Provençal poem, see the edition by Antoine Thomas, Les Proverbes de Guilhem de Cerveira, in Romania, XV (1886), 25–108, esp. p. 95, stanzas 95 f.

23. Cléomadès, ed. A. van Hasselt, Bruxelles, 1865, ll. 1649–1835. Mirror, ll. 1690–1698; fire, 1707–22; statues of the seasons, 1723–1812. Worth consulting, though not in connection with the Virgilian legends, are the following articles by H. S. V. Jones: Publications of the Modern Language Association, XX (1905), 346–359, XXIII (1908), 557–598; Journal of English and Germanic Philology, VI (1906–07), 221–243. Comp.[2] reprints pertinent parts, II, 202–206. C.–B. 302 ff., 306, 359$_2$. There seems to be some relationship between the legends as they appear in Cléomadès and in some of the Old French versions of the Roman des Sept Sages. For bibliographical information see post, p. 329, note 31, on the Middle English Seven Sages. These thirteenth-century texts have the following readings for the archer's inscription: Cléomadès, Qui me ferra, je trairai ja; Sept Sages, ed. Plomp, same; ed. Le Roux de Lincy, Qui me ferra, je tresrai jà; ed. Keller, Ki me ferra, je trairai ia; ed. Gaston Paris, se nul me fiert je trairay toste. The order of the legends in these texts is as follows:

Cléomadès	ed. Plomp	ed. Le Roux	ed. Keller	ed. G. Paris
1. mirror	1. archer and fire	1. archer and fire	1. archer and fire	1. archer and fire
2. archer and fire	2. two statues toss ball to one another	2. mirror	2. two statues throw ball to one another on Saturdays	2. two statues throw ball to one another on Saturdays
3. four statues who toss ball to mark change of seasons	3. mirror		3. mirror	3. mirror

This information is not sufficient to justify an inference regarding relative dates of composition of the texts or influences; but it does seem sufficient to indicate that one of three things must have taken place; (1) that Adenès li Rois knew something of some text or other of Sept Sages; (2) that the writer of some text of Sept Sages knew something of Cléomadès; (3) that both Adenès li Rois and the writer of some text of Sept Sages knew something of a common source, now lost, in which the Virgilian legends occurred. I omit Sept Sages from the text here because the date of the earliest manuscripts is not defined more closely than "thirteenth century."

24. Der Wartburgkrieg, ed. Karl Simrock, Stuttgart and Augsburg, 1858. The allusions occupy parts of section VI, called by the editor "Zabulons Buch," especially strophes 156, 159, 160–162 (fly). For the date, not earlier than 1287, see page 322.

Adolf E. Strack, Zur Geschichte des Gedichts vom Wartburgkrieg, Berlin, 1883. C.-B. 316 ff.

25. Quoted by Edmund Stengel, Mitteilungen aus französischen Handschriften . . ., Halle a. S., 1873, 14, from ms. B. N. fonds fr. 19525; cf. Henri Omont, Catalogue général des mss. français, ancien St. Germain français, III (Paris, 1900), 341. C.-B. 315.

26. Reinfrit von Braunschweig, ed. Karl Bartsch, Tübingen, 1871 [Bibliothek des litterarischen Vereins in Stuttgart, CIX]. The date is about 1300 (p. 810). The basket incident is alluded to in ll. 15175–15179; the finding of the book, in

ll. 21023–21054 and 21530 ff. C.–B. 316 ff., 331₉. The rela-
tionship between Wartburgkrieg and Reinfrit is examined by
Paul Gereke, Beiträge zur Geschichte der deutschen Sprache,
XXIII (1898), 358–483.

27.　　　　Si Aristoteles fuste en vie,
　　　　　E Virgile qe savoit l'art,
　　　　Les valurs ne dirraient mie
　　　　　Del prodhome la disme part.

T. Wright, Political Songs of England . . ., London, 1839, 245.

28. I quote from An Alphabet of Tales: an English Fifteenth-century translation of the Alphabetum Narrationum
. . ., 2 vv., London, 1904–05 [Early English Text Society,
original series, CXXVI, CXXVII], II, 517, No. dcclxxiv. The
shift from Virgi*n*ius to Virgi*l*ius, which is plainly what happened, is clearer in the Latin texts, where the *l* in Virgil's name
is not doubled. The late Professor T. F. Crane first pointed
this out in The Academy for Feb. 22, 1890, No. 929, pp. 134–
135. See particularly J. A. Herbert in The Library, new
series, VI (1905), 94–101.

29. Le Romans de la Dame à la Lycorne et du biau Chevalier au Lyon . . ., ed. Friedrich Gennrich, Dresden, 1908,
ll. 3882 ff. [Gesellschaft für Romanische Literatur, XVIII].
Cf. p. 55, and J. D. Bruce in Modern Philology, X (1913),
511–526. This particular invention of Virgil's never reappears
again, to my knowledge.

30. The manuscript, L II 14, University Library, Turin,
is best summarized by Edmund Stengel, Mittheilungen aus
französischen Handschriften der Turiner Universitäts-Bibliothek, Halle a. S., 1873, 14 ff. The pertinent section is
printed in Comp.² II, 212–221, but the title used, Li Roumans
de Vespasien, is misleading, as Stengel pointed out. The Virgilian material has nothing to do with the romance. C.–B.
314.

31. Killis Campbell, The Seven Sages of Rome, Boston,
1907 [Albion Series]. On the Middle and later English versions, see pp. xxxvi–lxvi; on Virgilius, xciv–xcvii. Ever-burning fire, ll. 2159–2195; figures of brass, ll. 2197–2206; image
with mirror, ll. 2207–2336. Campbell, lix, conjectures that the

lost Middle English original was written about 1275. The French originals are discussed, pp. xxvii–ix, xxxii–xxxv. Campbell echoes (xxvii) the conjecture of Gaston Paris, La littérature française au moyen-âge[2], Paris, 1890, 247, that the oldest version may have been written about 1155. The oldest French manuscripts are of the thirteenth century, but I have not attempted to insert them in chronological order because the dates are not sufficiently definite. The thirteenth-century text published as an appendix by H. P. B. Plomp, De Middelnederlandsche bewerking van het Gedicht van den VII Vroeden van binnen Rome, Utrecht, 1899, recounts "Virgilius" in substantially the same way as do the Middle English versions, and such is the case also with those published by Gaston Paris, Deux rédactions du roman des Sept Sages de Rome, Paris, 1876 [Société des anciens textes français], 40–44, by Le Roux de Lincy, Le Roman des Sept Sages de Rome, Paris, 1838 [with A. Deslongchamps, Essai sur les fables indiennes], 50–54, though the ball-throwing statues are omitted, and by Heinrich Adelbert von Keller, Li romans des Sept Sages, Tübingen, 1836, 153. If the existence of the Seven Sages in the middle of the twelfth century could be established our conception of the early history of the Virgilian legends would have to be revised. A none too reliable bit of evidence against such an early date is supplied by our table of the legends, where we see that Adenès li Rois, writing about 1285, is the first to recount stories similar to those in the Seven Sages versions of Virgilius. If the Seven Sages had been in existence as early as the middle of the twelfth century we might expect to see its influence before 1285. It will be observed that the Dolopathos portrayal of Virgil is very different, and therefore does not affect the present question. There is a convenient bibliography on the Seven Sages in Laura A. Hibbard, Mediæval Romance in England, New York, 1924, 181–183. C.-B. 234, 302 ff., 306, 359_2, 371_2. The tremendous vogue of the Seven Sages may be imagined in some degree from the existence of "at least forty different versions ... preserved in upwards of two hundred manuscripts and nearly two hundred and fifty editions." — Campbell, xvii.

These tales found their way, along with the rest of an early version of the Seven Sages into the Scala Celi, a collection of exempla arranged alphabetically under rubrics by Joannes Gobi the younger probably between 1323 and 1330. Under the rubric Femina ["Femina est omnis malitiae inventiva"] the Historia de septem sapientibus is entered. See J.-Th. Welter, L'exemplum, 319–325, esp. 319$_{73}$ for references on Joannes Gobi the younger (Dominican d. 1350), and 325$_{73}$ for indications on the score of MSS. and the five editions of Scala Celi before 1500; and cf. H. L. D. Ward, A Catalogue of Romances . . . II, 1893, 201; Alfons Hilka's ed. of Hist. septem sapientum in Beiträge zur Sprach- und Völkerkunde, Festschrift für Alfred Hillebrandt, Halle a/S., 1913, 54–80; A. H. Krappe in Archivum Romanicum, XVI [1932], 271–282.

32. Il Commento di Cecco d'Ascoli all' Alcabizzo, ed. Giuseppe Boffito, Firenze, 1905, 43 [Pubblicazioni dell' Osservatorio del Collegio alla Querce, No. 1]. Cf. Thorndike, Magic ^{2}, II, 948–968, chap. LXXI; L'Acerba, con prefazione, note e bibliografia di Pasquale Rosario, Lanciano, 1916 [Scritti Nostri 58]. I have not seen the unpublished dissertation of John P. Rice, A Critical Edition of the Bestiary and Lapidary of the Acerba of Cecco d'Ascoli, Yale University, 1909.

33. Le Roman de Renart le Contrefait, edd. G. Raynaud and H. Lemaître, 2 vv., Paris, 1914. Virgil as physician, I, l. 5015; as author, 19587; "Maro," II, p. 227; best of poets, taught to children, "certain chroniclers," II, p. 228; prophet of Christ, II, p. 230; legends in later part, II, ll. 29351–29662; death and burial, description of person, II, ll. 34289–34308. C.-B. 302 ff., 304, 308, 321, 331. Comparetti ^{2}, II, 207–211, reprints the latter part from Édélestand Du Méril, Mélanges archéologiques et littéraires, Paris, 1850, 440–444. For the dates, see I, pp. v–vi, II, p. 204. The article by Raynaud, Romania, XXXVII (1908), 245–283, summarized in the introduction to the edition, is nevertheless worth consulting.

34. The Virgilian parts of the Cronica were printed by Pasquale Villari, Annali delle università toscane, VIII (1866), parte prima, 162–172, and reprinted by Comp.^{2}, II, 246–257.

See Bartolommeo Capasso, Le fonti della storia delle provincie napolitane dal 568 al 1500, con note ... del D^r. E. Oreste Mastrojanni, Napoli, 1902, 131–137, and Ferdinando Galiani, Del dialetto napoletano, ed. Fausto Nicolini, Naples, 1923, 99–112 [Biblioteca Napoletana di storia letteratura ed arte, VI]. C.-B. 267, 271, 274, 281$_{61}$, 285, 340, 344–345, 348$_{22}$, 356.

35. Guido Zaccagnini, Le Rime di Cino da Pistoia, Geneva, 1925 [Biblioteca dell' Archivum Romanicum, serie I, vol. iv], p. 261, No. clxxxvii, "Deh, quando rivedrò 'l dolce paese." Cf. the notes, pp. 262–263; Luigi Chiappelli, Nuove ricerche su C. da P., Pistoia, 1911 ["Estratto dal Bollettino storico pistoiese, anni XII–XIII"]; Luigi di Benedetto, Studi sulle Rime di C. da P., Chieti, 1923; Gennaro M. Monti, C. da P. giurista, Città di Castello, 1924 [Biblioteca di Coltura Letteraria, I], with bibliography, pp. 16–31; Benedetto Croce, Napoli nelle descrizione dei poeti, in Napoli nobilissima, II (1893), 175–176; C.-B. 346.

36. Wilhelm Dick, Die Gesta Romanorum nach der Innsbrucker Handschrift vom Jahre 1342, Erlangen and Leipzig, 1890 [Erlanger Beiträge zur englischen Philologie, VII]; S. J. H. Herrtage, The Early English Versions of the Gesta Romanorum, London, 1879 [Early English Text Society, Extra Series XXXIII]; G. Brunet, Le Violier des Histoires Romaines, Paris, 1858; Hermann Oesterley, Gesta Romanorum, Berlin, 1872. The numbers of the chapters are as follows: Salvatio Romae, Dick 82, "De ymagine et pomo" [I reproduce the titles from Dick]; law-enforcing image, Dick 143; Herrtage 10, Brunet 55, Oesterley 57 [misnumbered 37], "De Tyto et Virgilio et statua et Foca"; magic cloth, ascribed to Virgil only by Dick 147, but mentioned by Brunet 85, Oesterley 89, "De Ionatha qui habuit iii^a iocalia a patre Dario pre aliis fratribus"; magic mirror, ascribed to Virgil only by Dick 167, but mentioned by Herrtage 1, Brunet 93, Oesterley 102; Merchant of Venice story, Oesterley, pp. 187–192, 237–239, Dick [without Virgil], No. 168, "De Lucii filia et milite" — cf. A Catalogue of Romances ... in the British Museum, II, 231, No. 4 (in a ms. of the Dolopathos), III, 205, No. 48,

Thomas Wright, Political Songs of England . . ., London, 1839, 387 [Camden Society], and C.-B. 322.

In addition to the introduction and notes in Oesterley's monumental edition see J. A. Herbert, A Catalogue of Romances . . . in the British Museum, III, London, 1910, pp. 183–271. M. Krepinsky, Quelques remarques relatives à l'histoire des Gesta Romanorum, in Le Moyen Age, 2ᵉ série, XV (1911), 307–318, 346–367, speculates interestingly but hardly convincingly; e. g., he follows Oesterley, pp. 257 ff., in conjecturing that the original date may be as early as 1326; but Oesterley was admittedly guessing as to the contents of a manuscript since published by Salomon Herzstein, Tractatus de diversis historiis Romanorum et quibusdam aliis, verfasst in Bologna im Jahre 1326, Erlangen, 1893 [Erlanger Beiträge zur englischen Philologie, XIV], and the evidence is negative. Using more reliable evidence, J.-Th. Welter, L'exemplum dans la littérature religieuse et didactique du moyen âge, Paris, 1927 [Bibliothèque d'histoire ecclésiastique de France], 369–375, decides that the collection originated in England "dans la seconde moitié de la quatrième décade du XIVᵉ siècle" (371). It is easy to see how the author learned of the Virgilian legends, for he used among his sources John of Salisbury, Gervasius of Tilbury, a Latin version of the Seven Sages, Neckam, and Vincent of Beauvais (Welter, 372₇₄). See 373₇₅ on translations and printed editions. "Aucune production du Moyen Age, la Légende dorée à part, n'a eu à enregistrer un pareil succès." (373–374.) C.-B. 254, 302₅, 304₉, 307₁₇, 313.

37. Juan Ruiz, El libro de buen amor, ed. Jean Ducamin, Toulouse, 1901 [Bibliothèque Méridionale, 1ʳᵉ série, t. vi], pp. 48–49, st. 261–269. Ed. also by Cejador y Frauca in Clásicos Castellanos, 2 vv., Madrid, 1913, and by Alfonso Reyes, Madrid, 1917 [Biblioteca Calleja, segunda serie]. Cf. Julio Puyol y Alonso, El Arcipreste de Hita, Madrid, 1906; José María Aguado, Glosario sobre Juan Ruiz . . ., Madrid, 1929; Henry B. Richardson, An Etymological Vocabulary to the Libro de Buen Amor of Juan Ruiz . . ., New Haven, 1930 [Yale Romanic Studies, II]; A. F. Whittem, Modern Language

Notes, XLVI (1931), 363–367. C.-B. 331. I have to thank my friend Dr. Charles Fraker for assistance at this point. So far as I know the circular stairway beset with knives is original with Juan Ruiz, and unique, as is many another curious item in his book. Perhaps the shining copper bottom of the Tiber is explained by Jean d'Outremeuse when he says that Virgil made copper conduits to Rome for wine and oil; or, better still, both may be explained by Al-Idrisi's remark that a river at Rome was revetted with plates of copper. — L'Italia descritta nel "Libro del Re Ruggero" compilato da Edrisi, edd. M. Amari and C. Schiaparelli, Roma, 1883, 87; on the matter see Graf, Roma . . . (1923), 115 ff. Al-Idrisi was geographer to Roger II of Sicily and was thus close to the beginnings of the legends; on him see George Sarton, Introduction to the History of Science, II (Washington, 1931), 410–412.

38. The poem was first printed by Karl Bartsch, Germania, IV (1859), 237–239, and was reprinted by Comp.[2] II, 241–245. Cf. Karl Bartsch, Meisterlieder der Kolmarer Handschrift, Stuttgart, 1862 [Bibl. des Litt. Ver. in Stuttg., LVIII], 107, and Ignaz V. Zingerle, Bericht über die Wiltener Meistersängerhandschrift, Sitzb. der K. Akad. der Wiss., Vienna, Philosophisch-historische Classe, XXXVII (1861), 398.

39. The list of legends was drawn up in prose. In verse Pucci refers to the basket incident. Both selections were first published by A. d'Ancona, Una poesia ed una prosa di Antonio Pucci, Il Propugnatore, II (1869), parte seconda, 397–438, III (1870), parte prima, 35–53. The prose is reprinted Comp.[2] II, 258–259; the verse, II, 124 [= C.-B. 334–335]. Cf. Ferruccio Ferri, La poesia popolare in Antonio Pucci, Bologna, 1909. Kenneth McKenzie's edition of Le Noie, Princeton and Paris, 1931 [Elliott Monographs 26], contains a bibliography, pp. 83–101. C.-B. 291, 334–335, 347.

40. Chronique du Bertrand du Guesclin, par Cuvellier, trouvère du XIVe siècle, ed. E. Charrière, Paris, 1839, I, p. 325, ll. 9127–9141 (from Robert Dernedde, Über die den altfranzösischen Dichtern bekannten epischen Stoffe . . ., Erlangen, 1887, 152–153, 156).

41. Petrarch's Itinerarium Syriacum, ed. G. Lumbroso,

Atti della Reale Accademia dei Lincei, 4ª serie: Rendiconti, IV
(1888), 390–423 = G. Lumbroso, Memorie italiane del buon
tempo antico, Torino, 1889, 16–49. C.-B. 313, 335, 341, 343,
349. The best discussions of Petrarch's attitude toward Virgil
are chapter III of Pierre de Nolhac's Pétrarque et l'hu-
manisme, Paris, 1907, I, 123–161 [Bibliothèque Littéraire de
la Renaissance]; Duane R. Stuart, The Sources and the Extent of Petrarch's Knowledge of the Life of Vergil, Classical
Philology, XII (1917), 365–404; Vladimiro Zabughin, Vergilio
nel Rinascimento italiano . . ., I, 21–39. The Commentum
super libros Eneydos Virgilii by Cionus de Magnalis remains
unpublished. For the manuscripts see Zabughin, I, 47 ff., 94.

Benvenuti de Rambaldis de Imola, Comentum super Dantis
Aldigherij Comœdiam, ed. J. P. Lacaita, 5 vv., Florentiae,
1887, III, 86–87; cf. Paget Toynbee in Furnivall Miscellany,
Oxford, 1901, 436–461, and Zabughin, I, 44–47. Francesco
d'Ovidio, Benvenuto da Imola e la leggenda Virgiliana, Atti
della Reale Accademia di archeologia, lettere e belle arti,
nuova serie, IV (1916), parte prima, 85–122 [Società Reale di
Napoli] has an eminently sane treatment of Dante's knowledge of the legends; cf. Zabughin, I, 3–21, and Comparetti in
Atene e Roma, V (1924), 149–164 (published when the author
was 89). Both Petrarch's and Benvenuto's allusions to Virgil's
magic art are dated approximately 1360.

42. Published by I. V. Zingerle in Germania, V (1860),
368–371; reprinted, Comp.² II, 237–240. C.-B. 318, 354.
This poem appears in the same manuscript — the "Wiltener
Meistersängerhandschrift" — as the anonymous verses on the
bocca della verità, on which see above. On Heinrich see Karl
J. Schröer, Die Dichtungen Heinrichs von Mügeln, Sitzungs-
berichte der K. Akademie der Wiss., Vienna, Philosophisch-
historische Classe, LV (1867), 451–520.

43. Gaetano Milanesi, Il Comento di G. Boccaccio sopra la
Commedia, con le annotazioni di A. M. Salvini, 2 vv., Firenze,
1863, I, 121–122. Cf. Paget Toynbee, Modern Language Review, II (1907), 111, F. d'Ovidio, Atti della Reale Accademia
di Napoli, IV (1916), 86–87, and Zabughin, I, 39–43. C.-B.
273, 346.

44. Le songe du vergier qui parle de la disputacion du clerc et du cheualier [Lyon], Jacques Maillet, 1491–2, chap. CLXXXV; [Paris, 1500?] J. Petit, chap. CLXXXVI; Somnium viridarii . . ., Paris, Jacob Pouchin for Galiot Du Pré (1516), Liber secundus, chap. CCCLVI, and frequently reprinted. See on the date (1374–76) Gustav Brunet, Manuel du libraire . . ., V (1864), 439, and Robert Proctor, Index to Early Printed Books in the British Museum . . ., II, 586.

45. The Complete Works of John Gower, ed. G. C. Macaulay, 4 vv., Oxford, 1899–1902 [vols. II and III of this edition were published also by the Early English Text Society, extra series LXXXI, LXXXII, London, 1900–01, as The English Works of John Gower]. For the automata protecting Rome, see Mirour de l'omme, ll. 14725–14748, vol. I, p. 171; for the mirror, Confessio amantis, Book V, ll. 2031–2234, and for the lists, Confessio amantis, Book VI, ll. 90–99 and [the one quoted in part] Confessio amantis, Book VIII, ll. 2666–2719. This last is particularly interesting, as Gower may have seen just such a procession in illuminated manuscripts of the Trionfi of Petrarch. See post p. 427. C.–B. 304 $_{10}$, 331$_{19}$. The Mirour de l'omme is dated about 1375, and the English poem about 1390. Cf. Macaulay's edition, I, xiii, II, xxi.

46. The Processus Beliali exists in a large number of manuscripts, and the editio princeps is in German, printed by Albrecht Pfister perhaps as early as 1464, an edition which I have not seen. The early printers produced it in Latin, French, and Dutch as well. The work is long and involved, and as a result hurried bibliographers have misunderstood it. The best source of general information is D. Heubach, Der Belial kolorierte Federzeichnungen aus einen Handschrift des XV Jahrhunderts, Strassburg, 1927. Graesse, Trésor de livres rares . . . VI, ii (1867), 129, lists other editions, but Heubach's work should be compared, as Graesse occasionally goes astray, as does A. Claudin, Histoire de l'imprimerie en France au XVe et au XVIe siècle, Paris, 1904, III, 180 ff., in his analysis, and C. de Douhet, Dictionnaire des mystères, Paris, 1854, cols. 838–839 [J. P. Migne, Nouvelle encyclopédie théologique . . . XLIII]. The work seems to have been called indifferently

Processus Beliali or Consolatio peccatorum; sometimes both titles are used. The references to Virgil will be found as follows in editions which I have seen: (German) s. l., 1472 [G. Zeiner] fo. 19 r°, fo. 24 r°; Augsburg, 1473 [J. Bämler] fo. 21 v°, fo. 26 v°; Strassburg, s. a. [J. Prüsz] fo. xxii v°, fo. xxviii r°; (Dutch) Haarlem, 1484, fo. b 5 r°, fo. b 8 v°; (French) [Lyon], 1482, fo. c i r°, fo. c 5 v°; Paris, s. d., fo. c i r°, fo. c i v°; (Latin) [Augsburg], 1492, fo. [9 v°], fo. [12 r°]. The work was very popular, and was edited by such prominent humanists as Albrecht von Eyb and Jacob Ayrer (Historischer Prozessus Juris, Nürnberg, 1597). Cf. Copinger, A Supplement to Hain's Repertorium bibliographicum, two parts, Part II, vol. ii, London, 1895–1902, pp. 120–124, Nos. 5785–5821, and D. Reichling, Appendices ad Hainii-Copingeri R. b., fasc. iii, Monacii, 1907, p. 199, fasc. vi [1910], p. 169. In his note on the Virgilian legends Strauch (ed. of Enikel's Weltchronik) refers to a manuscript of this work; cf. Die Deutschen Handschriften der K. Hof- und Staatsbibliothek zu München, Erster Theil, München, 1866, p. 50.

47. Ly Myreur des Histors, chronique de Jean des Preis dit d'Outremeuse, edd. A. Borgnet and S. Bormans, 7 vv., Bruxelles, 1864–1887 [Collection de chroniques belges]. For the several Virgils, in the order used in the text, see (1) I, 183–184; (2) I, 197–435, II, 34–243, IV, 55–70, all passim; (3) I, 184–185; (4) I, 184, 196; (5) II, 234. There is also a Virgilia, sister of (2), I, 192. For specific references to the various adventures of our subject, (2), see the (unnumbered seventh) volume devoted to the introduction and very full index, p. 514. On Jean see, in addition to the introduction, Godefroid Kurth, Étude critique sur J. d' O., Mémoires de l'Académie royale de Belgique, Classe des lettres et . . . des beaux-arts, Collection in-8°, deuxième série VII (1910). C.-B. 358–363. Apparently Jean knew the works of Gervasius of Tilbury, Vincent of Beauvais, and some version of the Image du Monde.

48. Le croniche di Giovanni Sercambi, ed. Salvatore Bongi, 3 vv., Lucca, 1892 [Fonti per la storia d'Italia. Scrittore. Secolo XIV–XV. Vols. 19, 20, 21], III, 258–260, No. 301. First printed by M. Pierantoni, Novella inedita di G. S. tratta

da un ms. della pubblica libreria di Lucca, Lucca, 1865. Also printed in Scelta di curiosità letterarie, ed. A. d'Ancona, CXIX, Pisa, 1871, p. 265, and in the edition of the Novelle by R. Rénier, Torino, 1889, No. 31. C.-B. 332.

49. The Life and Acts of the Great Tamerlane . . ., ed., trans. Clements R. Markham, London, 1859, 8 (cf. 35) [Hakluyt Society]. C.-B. 323$_{42}$.

50. Dirc Potter, Der Minnen loep, ed. P. Leendertz, 3 vv., Leiden, 1845–47 [Vereeniging . . . der Oude Nederlandsche Letterkunde. Werken. Tweede Jaargang, eerste Aflevering, 1845; Derde J., eerste Afl., 1846; Vierde J., eerste Afl., 1847] Book I (1845), ll. 2515–2758, pp. 94–103. For later discussions of Potter's work see Jan te Winkel, Geschiedenis der Nederlandsche Letterkunde, Haarlem, 1887, I, 497–513 (fuller than same author's remarks in Paul's Grundriss . . .², Strassburg, 1901–09, II, i, 450, or in De Ontwikkelingsgang der Nederlandsche Letterkunde, Haarlem, 1908, I, 103–104), and Jan ten Brink, Middeleeuwsche Liefdesgeschiedenissen, Nederland (1888) tweede Deel, 357–404.

51. "Aliprandina," o "Cronica de Mantua" dalle origini della città fino all' anno 1414, di Bonamente Aliprandi, ed. Orsini Begani, Città di Castello, 1910 [L. A. Muratori, Rerum Italicarum Scriptores², vol. XXIV, parte xiii]. The date cannot be definitely set as 1414. Begani edited the oldest manuscript, which is from either the first or the second half of the fifteenth century; see introduction, pp. xviii, xx, xxi for date and for comment on the older edition in Muratori. C.-B. 142, 321$_{28}$, 332, 351 ff.

52. L. G. Lemcke, Bruchstücke aus den noch ungedruckten Theilen des Vitorial von Gutierre Diez de Games, Marburg, 1865, 17–18; cf. p. 9. See James Fitzmaurice-Kelley, A New History of Spanish Literature, London, 1926, 105–106. The Unconquered Knight, A Chronicle . . . by . . . Gutierre Diaz de Gamez (1431–49), translated and selected from [a French translation of] El Vitorial by Joan Evans, London, 1928 [Broadway Medieval Library], does not include the passage on the obelisk. C.-B. 323–324.

53. John Lydgate, The Fall of Princes, ed. Henry Bergen,

3 vv., London, 1924 [Early English Text Society, extra series, CXXI–CXXIII], vol. I, p. 376, ll. 4495–4501. The poem was finished during the fourth decade of the fifteenth century; see I, pp. ix–x.

54. Alfonso Martínez de Toledo, Corvacho, ó Reprobación del amor mundano, ed. D. Cristóbal Pérez Pastor, Madrid, 1901 [Sociedad de bibliófilos españoles], pp. 49–50. Seven printed editions are listed between 1495 and 1547. Cf. J. Fitz-maurice-Kelley, A New History of Spanish Literature, ed. Julia Fitzmaurice-Kelley, Oxford, 1926, 107–108. C.-B. 331_{19}.

55. Martin Le Franc, Le champion des dames (Lyon? 1485? —the best edition) Book ii, fo. g iii v°; also printed at Paris, 1530, fo. ciiii (104) v° — fo. cv r°. Gaston Paris, Romania, XVI (1887), 383: "Martin Le Franc . . . avec Charles d'Orléans et Villon, c'est assurément le poète le plus remarquable du XVe siècle. . . ." For the date see 395–396, and compare A. Piaget, Martin Le Franc, Prévot de Lausanne, Lausanne, 1888, 18. C.-B. 331_{19}.

56. The goodli history of the moste noble and beautyfull Ladye Lucres of Scene in Tuskane, and of her lover Eurialus . . . (1550?), fo. B iii v°; Aeneae Sylvii opera omnia, Basel, 1571, 627 B 12. On the author see Cecelia M. Ady, Pius II, the Humanist Pope, London, 1913. C.-B. 333.

57. Felicis Malleoli, vulgo Hemmerlin: De Nobilitate et Rusticitate dialogus . . . [Strassburg, 1490?], chapter II, ff. viii, v°, ix, r°, and ix, v°. On Hemmerlin see Balthasar Rever, Felix Hemmerlin von Zürich neu nach den Quellen bearbeitet, Zürich, 1846, esp. 197 and 199, and Albert Schneider, Der Züricher Canonicus und Cantor Magister Felix Hemmerlin an der Universität Bologna . . ., Zürich, 1888. C.-B. 318, 353.

58. John Capgrave, Ye Solace of Pilgrims, ed. C. A. Mills, Oxford, 1911, 27 (= fo. 364, r° and v°) [British-American Archaeological Society of Rome].

59. The Rudimentum was first printed at Lübeck in 1475. The material on Virgil appears on folios cclxxviiii, v°, and cclxxxvi, r° of vol. II. This edition is studied by Theodor Schwarz, Über den Verfasser und die Quellen des Rudimentum novitiorum, [Dissertation] Rostock, 1888. This Latin ex-

pansion of the account of a trip to the Holy Land made by one
Burchard or Brocard, called "of Mount Sion," a Dominican
monk (see vol. XII of Palestine Pilgrims' Texts Society, London, 1895), was made by an anonymous writer, perhaps of
Lübeck, about 1473. It was translated into French by another
unknown and published at Paris in 1488 as La mer des histoires. After having been reprinted several times, this edition
was in turn augmented by an unknown hand to include historical material since 1488, and republished in 1536 with the
same title, La mer des histoires; this edition was reprinted at
least four times, the latest which I have seen being that of
Paris [1550?], printed by A. Langellier. All editions which I
have seen, Latin or French, are in two volumes. The attribution of the republished editions of 1536 and following to
J. Colonna is false, and arose through a misapprehension that
Colonna's ms. Mar historiarum was involved. This puzzle
was solved by V. Leclerc in vol. XXI of the Histoire littéraire
de la France, Paris, 1847, 180–215, esp. 206, but still causes
confusion, e. g., in the British Museum Catalogue and in A
Short-Title Catalogue of Books in France in the British Museum, London, 1924, pp. 83, 387. In the colophons of the two
volumes of the 1536 edition it appears that the work was also
known as La fleur des histoires; and in the preface, vol. I, fo.
ii v°, we are told that the translator of the 1488 French edition
was "ung natif du pays de Beauuoisin. Et pour decorer une
chose si riche ay [that is, the 1536 adapter] faict rafreschir et
ampliffier les chapitres daucunes substances que y estoient de-
faillantes. . . ." On the whole matter see Leo Baer, Die illu-
strierten Historienbücher des 15. Jahrhunderts, Strassburg,
1903, 93–117. In the 1488 translation, the Virgilian material
appears on fo. lxiii r° and v° of vol. II; in the rearrangement of
1536, on fo. ccxxx v° of vol. I. The fact that "Vigilius papa"
is mentioned, Latin ed. of 1475, vol. II, fo. cccxlix r°, illustrates how Jean d'Outremeuse probably came to write of Virgilius papa; cf. note 47, p. 337.

60. Voua [sc. Nuova?] canzon de femena tristitia . . ., Gabriel Petri, Venice? 1486? [British Museum pressmark IA.
19959] fo. [ii r° and v°]:

Dissa una che uergilio hauia in balia
Vieni sta sera dentro ne la cesta
E tieroti a la camera mia
E lui uentro: & lei molto presta
Lo tiro suso insino ameza uia . . .

61. Hartmann Schedel, Liber chronicarum, Nürnberg, 1493, fo. xcii v° and index. Cf. C. Ephrussi, Étude sur le L. c., Paris, 1894.

62. Stephen Hawes, Pastime of Pleasure, ed. William E. Mead, London, 1928 [Early English Text Society, CLXXIII], ll. 3626–3727. Cf. p. lxxix. C.–B. 331_{19}.

63. Le premier (second) volume de Orose, 3 vv., Paris, A. Vérard, 1509, "De Campaigne," fo. xix r°. Cf. the translator's note, fo. xiiii r°.

64. I reprint this in an appendix.

65. The earliest appearance of the Romance which I know is the chap-book-like "Romance de don Virgilios glosado, con otro dos romances del amor," 1524. Cf. R. Menéndez Pidal, Cancionero de Romances, Madrid, 1914, p. xxix; the Romance is reprinted at fo. 189, v°, as frequently elsewhere, e. g., in Sammlung der besten alten Spanischen Historischen, Ritter- und Maurischen Romanzen, ed. Ch. B. Depping, Altenburg and Leipzig, 1817, No. 43, pp. 303 f.; the earlier texts which I have seen are in the Cancionero de romances en que estan recopilados la mayor parte de los romances, Anvers, 1555, and Lisboa, 1581, in both of which this Romance appears at fo. 200. It is also reprinted in B. C. Aribau, Biblioteca de Autores Españoles, Madrid, 1849, X, 151 ff., in the Primavera y Flor de Romances . . ., edd. F. J. Wolf and Don C. Hoffmann, Berlin, 1856, II, No. 111, pp. 11 f., and elsewhere. The Romance has travelled as far as Constantinople, presumably carried there by Jews expelled from Spain in 1492; see Abraham Danon in Revue des études juives XXXII (1895) and XXXIII (1896), esp. the latter, p. 268, where Virgil has become "Duvergini"; and cf. R. Menéndez Pidal, El Romancero, Madrid (1928), 110 ff., 144 f. C.–B. 368.

The plot is so slight that it is not easy to point to a definite source, but I am inclined to suspect that the story of Bernad de Cabrera in Sicily told in El Corvacho by Alfonso Martínez de Toledo (Madrid, 1901, 53 f., cap. xvii, "Cómo los letrados pierden el saber por amor" [Sociedad de Bibliófilos Españoles]) may be the original of it. Like Virgil, Bernad wrongs a lady and is put in prison. He is caught when he falls into a net outside the lady's window. "E quando fué dentro en la red, cerraronla e cortaron las cuerdas los que estaban dalto en la ventana, e asy quedó ally colgado fasta otro dia en la tarde que le leuaron de ally syn comer nin beuer. E todo el pueblo de la çibdad e de fuera della, sus amigos e enemigos, le vinieron a ver ally, adonde estava en jubon como Virgilio, colgado . . ." Thus Virgil is brought into relationship with Bernad's plight. Maybe the author of the Romance changed the name of the hero because he knew more interest would be taken if Virgil were a protagonist. But cf. Quarterly Review, CXXXIX (1875), 104.

66. C'est le secret de lhistoire naturelle contenant les merueilles *et* choses memorables du monde . . . Paris (1522?). There are later dated editions of 1527, 1534, and an undated one of about 1539. Cf. Geoffrey Atkinson, La littérature géographique française de la Renaissance . . ., Paris, 1927, 502–503.

67. Sebastian Franck, Chronica, Zeÿtbůch vnd geschÿchtbibel von anbegyn biß inn diß gegenwertig M.D.xxxj. jar, Strassburg. On Franck, see Carl Alfred Hase, Sebastian Franck von Wörd, Leipzig, 1869; Haggenmacher, Sebastian Franck, Zürich, 1886; Arnold Reimann, S. F. als Geschichtsphilosoph, Berlin, 1921 [Comenius-Schriften zur Geistesgeschichte I], bibliography, pp. 31–32; Hwb. d. d. Aberglaubens II, 1729–30.

68. Gratian Dupont, Les controverses des sexes masculin et femenin, Tholose, 1534, livre second, fo. xlix r°. There are also editions of 1536 and 1540. C.–B. 328₄.

69. The deceyte of women, to the instruction and ensample of all men, yonge and olde, newly corrected, London, n. d., Abraham Vele [about 1550?], reprinted by Friedrich Brie, Archiv für das Studium der Neueren Sprachen . . . CLVI (1929), 16–52, as my friend V. B. Heltzel informs me. This

collection of twenty-two tales would seem to be a reprint, as the title indicates, but no earlier copy is known. I use the unique copy in the British Museum [pressmark: C. 20. c. 31 (1).]. The unique copy of a later edition (1561?) is at the Huntington Library; see A. W. Pollard, G. R. Redgrave, et al., A Short-title Catalogue of Books Printed in England . . . 1475–1640, London, 1926 [Bibliographical Society], Nos. 6451, 6452, in which the date is put at (1560?). Cf. A. F. Johnson, One Hundred Titlepages, 1500–1800, London, 1928, p. 80.

70. Sebastiani Corradi Commentarius, in quo P. Virgilij Maronis liber primus Aeneidos explicatur. Florentiae, excudebat Laurentius Torrentinus, 1555, pp. 16 ff.

CHAPTER II

1. The ideas underlying the use of talismans during the Middle Ages are well set forth in Thorndike, Magic[2]. A useful introduction to the voluminous literature of the sixteenth and seventeenth centuries is provided by Martin F. Blumler, A History of Amulets (Halle, 1710), English translation by S. H., Gent., 2 vv., Edinburgh (privately printed by E. and G. Goldsmid), 1887, I, 6–8 [Collectanea Adamantaea 18]; it may be supplemented by the learned notes in the translation of Jacques Gaffarel's earlier work, Curiositez inoyes [*sic*], hoc est: Curiositates inauditae de figuris Persarum talismanicis, latine opera M. Gr. Michaelis, Hamburg and Amsterdam, 1676. Francis Barrett, The Magus, London, 1801, is a wild but interesting compilation. Later works of some value are Moritz Steinschneider, Zur pseudepigraphischen Literatur insbesondere der geheimen Wissenschaften des Mittelalters . . . [Veitel Heine Ephraim'sche Lehranstalt. Wissenschaftliche Blätter. Erste Sammlung, Berlin, 1862, no. 3]; Émile Gilbert, Essai historique sur les talismans, Paris, 1881; L. Finot, Les lapidaires indiens, Paris, 1896 [Bibl. des Hautes Études]; Ludwig Blau, Das altjüdische Zauberwesen, Strassburg, 1898; F. Leigh Gardner, A Catalogue Raisonné of Works on the Occult Sciences, 3 vv., London, 1911–23, II (privately

printed); Joan Evans, Magical Jewels of the Middle Ages and the Renaissance, Oxford, 1922; J. H. F. Kohlbrugge, Tier- und Menschenantlitz als Abwehrzauber, Bonn, 1926; Siegfried Seligmann, Die magischen Heil- und Schutzmittel aus der unbelebten Natur. . . . Eine Geschichte des Amulettwesens, Stuttgart, 1927 [very learned. Note on pp. vi–vii the statement of the publishers, Messrs. Strecker and Schröder, that the remainder of the author's collectanea will be published by subscription]. More popular, but occasionally including valuable references, are: the two works of [Sir] E. A. Wallis Budge, Egyptian Magic, London, 1899, 24–64, and Amulets and Superstitions, Oxford, 1930; W. and K. Pavit, The Book of Talismans, Amulets, and Zodiacal Gems, London, 1914; G. F. Kunz, The Magic of Jewels and Charms, Philadelphia, 1915; R. Grötzinger, Das Geheimnis der Amulette und Talismane, Leipzig, 1919; the same author's Talismanische Dämonologie and Talismanische Astrologie, both Leipzig, 1920; R. H. Laarss, Talismanische Magie, Leipzig, 1920 (second ed., Leipzig, 1926); H. Stanley Redgrove, Bygone Beliefs, London, 1920, 57–86; J. Chalon, Fétiches, idoles, et amulettes, 2 vv., Namur, n. d. (1920–22?); "Sepharial," The Book of Charms and Talismans, London, n. d. (1923) — a practical manual for preparing talismans; Hwb. d. d. Aberglaubens I, 374–383, s.v. Amulett. The best general introduction to this, as to other matters related to mediaeval science, is Thorndike, Magic [2], passim. See also chapter III of George Lyman Kittredge's Witchcraft in Old and New England, Cambridge [Mass.], 1928, 73–103, rich notes 411–436. Menéndez y Pelayo, Historia de los heterodoxos españoles, Madrid, 1888, I, 576, alludes to a catalogue listing 7700 works on talismans by Jews and Moors.

2. Comp.[2] II, 195; L'Image du Monde de Maître Gossouin, ed. Prior, 184.

3. The three passages in the Historia naturalis are as follows (Teubner text, ed. C. Mayhoff, Leipzig, 1906 ff.):

X. 28. (40.) et [invocant] Elei Myacoren deum muscarum multitudine pestilentiam adferente, quae protinus intereum quam litatum est ei deo.

X. 29. (41.) Romae in aedem Herculis in foro Boario nec musċae nec canes intrant.

XXI. 14. (46.) Aliud in Creta miraculum mellis: mons est Carina VIIII passuum ambitu, intra quod spatium muscae non reperiuntur, natumque ibi mel nusquam attingunt.

4. C. Iulii Solini Collectanea rerum memorabilium. Iterum recensuit Th. Mommsen, Berlin, 1895, I, 11 (p. 4); Pausanias's Description of Greece, ed., trans. [Sir] James G. Frazer, 6 vv., London, 1898, I, p. 256 [= Book V, ch. 14, 2, of Pausanias]; see the note, vol. III, pp. 558–559, and for additional material, Ernst Maass, Fliegen- und Mottenfeste, Zeitschrift für Volkskunde, N. F. I (1929), 149–156, and Hwb. d. d. Aberglaubens II, 1621–30. Karl Knortz, Die Insekten in Sage, Sitte und Literatur, Annaberg, 1910, has nothing pertinent to this discussion. On Solinus in the Middle Ages, see C. H. Haskins, Harvard Studies in Classical Philology, XX (1909), 91[8].

5. Another personage associated with flies is Baalzebub (II Kings i), 'lord of flies,' whose oracle was impiously consulted by Ahaziah; but the function of Baalzebub is too vague to permit comparison with the fly-talisman. George Barton, in An Encyclopædia of Religion and Ethics, ed. James Hastings, II, 298 f. (Edinburgh, 1909) refers to passages in the Talmud which are more or less similar. "The Schunamite woman perceived that Elisha was a man of God, because no fly crossed his table." (Bᵉrākhŏth 10 b.) "This estimate goes back to the Mishna, for in Aboth, 5 [8], we read: 'A fly, being an impure thing, was never seen in the slaughter-house of the temple.'" Cf. also Wolf Baudissins's article in the Herzog-Hauck Real-Encyclopädie für protestantische Theologie und Kirche [3], II (Leipzig, 1897), 515. These passages allude to flies as something devilish and therefore offensive to sanctity, as coming from Satan himself, a belief implicitly concurred in (not humorously!) by Mr. Montague Summers in this twentieth century: ". . . when the demon, under whatsoever disguise or name he might be adored, had received those divine honours . . . he withdraws his emissaries the tormenting flies who are often his imps in the form of insects." — The Vampire, His Kith and Kin, New York, 1929, 198.

6. The Πάτρια Κωνσταντινυπόλεως is edited by Theodor Preger in Scriptores Originum Constantinopolitanarum, 2 fasciculi, Leipzig, 1901–07, 136 ff. (Teubner series), who warns against the corrupt texts of the earlier editions (1) by Immanuel Bekker, Georgii Codini Excerpta de Antiquitatibus Constantinopolitanis, Bonn, 1843 [Corpus scriptorum historiae Byzantinae], (2) in Migne's Patrologia Graeca, CLVII. See Preger's remarks in the apparatus to his edition, in Beiträge zur Textgeschichte der Πάτρια Κωνσταντινουπόλεως [Gymnasialprogramm], München, 1895, and in his articles in Byzantinische Zeitschrift X (1901), 455–476, XIII (1904), 370–388.

7. The life of Apollonius by Philostratus does not include an account of the manufacture of these talismans; and since much of the literature on Apollonius is based exclusively on Philostratus, they are seldom noticed elsewhere (Philostratus, The Life of A. of T., translated by F. C. Conybeare, 2 vv., London and New York, 1912 [Loeb Classical Library]); e. g., J. Jessen, A. von T. und sein Biograph . . ., Hamburg, 1885; George Wotherspoon, A. of T., Sage, Prophet, and Magician . . ., London, 1890; G. R. S. Mead, A. of T., the Philosopher-Reformer . . ., London and Benares, 1901 [Theosophical Publishing Society]; M. Wundt in Zeitschrift für Wissenschaftliche Theologie, XLIX (1906), 309 ff.; Thomas Whittaker, A. of T. . . ., London, 1906; F. W. G. Campbell, A. of T. . . ., London, 1908; O. Weinreich, Antike Heilungswunder, Giessen, 1909 [Religionsgeschichtliche Versuche und Vorarbeiten, VIII, 1], 162 ff. The reputation of Apollonius is discussed by M. Steinschneider, A. von T. (oder Belinas) bei den Arabern, in Zeitschrift der deutschen Morgenländischen Gesellschaft, XLV (1891), 439–446. Richard Gottheil, in the same journal, XLVI (1892), reports his appearance in a Syriac manuscript of 1712. References are collected by Wilhelm Hertz, Gesammelte Abhandlungen, ed. F. von der Leyen, Stuttgart and Berlin, 1905, 45₃. Apollonius is of interest in hermetic literature; see Julius Ruska, Tabula Smaragdina, Heidelberg, 1926 [Heidelberger Akten der Von-Portheim-Stiftung, Heft 16], esp. pp. 56, 78, 106–110, 125, 136; with this work compare the

remarks of Martin Plessner in Islam, XVI (1927), 77–113. A comprehensive study of the reputation of Apollonius is needed.

Since the text of Πάτρια Κπόλεως is of some interest, I quote the pertinent sentences from the edition by Preger, iii, 24, p. 221 (appears only in a manuscript of the thirteenth century): Παρέλυσε δὲ ἀβούλως καὶ τὸν κωνωπίωνα, ὃς ἦν ἐστηλωμένος καὶ ἐστοιχειωμένος παρὰ ᾿Απολλωνίου, ὡς μὴ ᾖ ἐν τῇ πόλει μήτε μυῖα μήτε κώνωψ μήτε ψύλλα μήτε κόρις. From the same section, but part of the accepted text: Παρέλυσε δὲ καὶ τὸν Κωνωπίωνα, ὅσπερ ἦν ἐστηλωμένος μετὰ μυιῶν καὶ κωνώπων καὶ ἐμπίδων καὶ φύλλων καὶ κορίδων. Preger's note on Κωνωπίωνα: "Statua hominis (aut genii cuiusdam Mithriaci?) fuisse videtur cui vulgus propter culices aliasque bestiolas additas hoc nomen indidit." iii, 200, p. 278: ᾿Αλλὰ καὶ Κωνωπίων ἐστοιχειώθη καὶ ἵστατο ἐστηλωμένος ἐπάνω τῆς ἀψίδος τοῦ Ταύρου τῆς δυτικῆς· χαλκοῦς δὲ ἦν ὁ κώνωψ καὶ μυῖα καὶ κόρις· καὶ ἐξ αὐτῶν τῇ πόλει οὐκ ἐπεφοίτων. ῾Ο δὲ Βασίλειος ὁ βασιλεὺς ἔκλασεν αὐτόν. The variant readings betray the uncertainty of the scribes. On p. 319 the editor glosses Κωνωπίων "genus instrumenti ad arcendos culices," thus indicating that he accepts the usual meaning, mosquito-bar. A detailed study might show whether Apollonius was originally supposed to have made a mosquito-bar, whether this mosquito-bar is a rationalization of an earlier mosquito- or gnat-talisman, or, finally, whether a human figure with various insects on it was meant.

The sixth-century Byzantine chronicler Joannes Malalas also knew of a talisman against gnats [πρὸς τοὺς κώνωπας] made by Apollonius; see his Chronographia, ed. L. Dindorff, Bonn, 1831, X, 343, p. 264 [Corpus scriptorum historiae Byzantinae], of which an eighth-century Latin translation is reported by Mommsen in Byzantinische Zeitschrift, IV (1895), 487–488. On Malalas, see A. Rueger, Studien zu Malalas . . ., Bad Kissingen, 1895; H. Bourier, Ueber die Quellen der ersten vierzehn Bücher des Johannes Malalas, 2 parts, Augsburg, 1899–1900 [Erster Teil = Münchener Dissertation; Zweiter Teil = Programm des Gymnasiums zu St. Stephen für 1899/

1900]; Edmund S. Bouchier, Syria as a Roman Province, Oxford, 1916, 58–60. For a fly-talisman which attracted flies and held them until they died or were killed, see L'Abrégé des Merveilles, trans. Carra de Vaux, Paris, 1898, 285. St. Nicholas kept the flies out of his church at Liége — Aegidii Aureaevallensis Gesta Episcoporum Leodiensium, ed. Johann Heller, Hannover, 1880, lib. ii, c. 73 = pp. 69 ff. [Monumenta Germaniae Historica, Scriptores, XXV]; cf. Analecta Bollandiana XX (1901), 429–431.

8. The idea (without the material on Apollonius) was first suggested by Wilhelm Viëtor in Zeitschrift für romanische Philologie, I (1877), 176, repeated by him in Academy, XXXVI (1889), 10, and was arrived at independently by Frederick W. Hasluck, Letters on Religion and Folklore, London, 1926, 96, 130, who, not knowing Viëtor's article, remarks: "May be the idea is new: one would think Comparetti would have to notice it else." The Italian scholar, however, familiar though he was with Viëtor's article, ignored the suggestion. Fly in C.–B.: 259, 262, 263, 265₅, 266, 267, 282, 293, 346, 347, 353, 364, 373; compare Moses Gaster, Monatsschrift für Geschichte und Wissenschaft des Judentums, XXIX (1880), 123. Alexander Neckam thought that Virgil played the rôle of the shepherd in the Culex poem. — De naturis rerum, ed. Wright, 190 (chap. 109); C.–B. 148.

9. The name of Pope Vigilius appears in the Πάτρια Κπόλεως, ed. Preger, on p. 183, some seven hundred lines away from the reference to the talismans of Apollonius — physically not very far. Too late to be useful as evidence here, but none the less interesting, is the occurrence together in a fourteenth-century Greek manuscript of the names of Apollonius of Tyana and Virgil "the philosopher"; see the description of the manuscript in Catalogus codicum Graecorum Bibliothecae Ambrosianae, edd. A. Martini and D. Bassi, 2 vv., Milan, 1906, I, p. 134 (ms. 134, fo. 232). Compare the review by F. Boll, Byzantinische Zeitschrift, XVII (1908), 549.

10. Fly-scarabs are pictured by W. M. Flinders Petrie, Amulets illustrated by the Egyptian Collection in University

College, London, London, 1914, p. 12, no. 19, and by the same
author in Buttons and Design Scarabs . . ., London, 1925
[British School of Archæology in Egypt, twenty-fourth year],
plate XIV, Nos. 927 and 937. It has been conjectured that the
original fly of the Virgilian legend was "qualche fibula d'oro
antica" (no historical one cited), or that it arose from an
architectural detail on a gateway of Naples — Galiani, Del
dialetto napoletano, ed. F. Nicolini, 1923, 106$_2$. On possible
relationships between images and legends, see Salomon Reinach, De l'influence des images sur la formation des mythes, in
Cultes, Mythes, et Religions, IV (Paris, 1912), 94–108.

11. The lapidaries of incised gems have not been studied
extensively as such. L. Pannier, Les Lapidaires français du
Moyen Age . . ., Paris, 1882 [Bibliothèque de l'Ecole des
Hautes Etudes, LII], proposed (p. 14) to devote a special work
to them, but died before he could carry out his design. M.
Steinschneider's articles are valuable, especially Arabische
Lapidarien, in Zeitschrift der deutschen Morgenländischen
Gesellschaft, XLIX (1895), 244–279, and Lapidarien, ein cul-
turgeschichtlicher Versuch, in Semitic Studies in Memory of
. . . Alexander Kohut, Berlin, 1897, 42–72. F. de Mély and
C. E. Ruelle, Les Lapidaires de l'antiquité et du Moyen Age,
3 vv., Paris, 1896–1902, stop with the Greeks. Joan Evans,
Magical Jewels of the Middle Ages and Renaissance particularly in England, Oxford, 1922, is excellent within the
limitations of the title, and especially so for the present purpose is chapter V, Mediaeval Astrology: Lapidaries of Engraved Gems, pp. 95–109. P. Studer and Joan Evans, Anglo-
Norman Lapidaries, Paris, 1924, is also useful. Cf. note 1,
chap. II above. Vincent of Beauvais's discussion of gems will
be found in Book IX of the Speculum naturale (Douay, 1624).

12. Evliyá Efendi, Narrative of Travels in Europe, Asia,
and Africa, in the Seventeenth Century, translated from the
Turkish by Joseph von Hammer, 2 vv., London, 1834–50
[Oriental Translation Fund], I, part i, p. 17. See also R. M.
Dawkins, Ancient Statues in Mediaeval Constantinople, Folk
Lore, XXXV (1924), 209–248, 380. Another image too late
to affect the origin of Virgil's fly is the one of gold attributed

to Albertus Magnus in Pauli Antonii de Tarsia Historiarum Cupersanensium libri III, in J. G. Graevius and Peter Burmann, Thesaurus antiquitatum et historiarum Italiae, Campaniae, Neapolis, et Magnae Graeciae, IX, pars v (Lugduni Batavorum, 1723), 26. On Albertus Magnus see the article in Hwb. d. d. Aberglaubens I, 241–243.

13. On the story of the Devil in the Flask there is an excellent brief discussion in Bolte and Polívka, Anmerkungen zu den Kinder- und Hausmärchen der Brüder Grimm, II, 415–419, No. 99; cf. Moses Gaster, in Monatsschrift für Geschichte und Wissenschaft des Judentums, XXIX (1880), 121–131, 422–442 (the first of these is reprinted in Gaster's Studies and Texts in Folklore, Magic, Mediaeval Romance . . ., 3 vv., London, 1925–28, II, 1208–18); Chauvin, Bibliographie, VI, p. 23, No. 195; Hwb. d. d. Aberglaubens II, 1573; Schambach, Virgil ein Faust des Mittelalters, I, 19. C.–B. 316–318.

The magnetic mountain, it will be recalled, is the scene of the devilish operations of Virgil in Reinfrit von Braunschweig and some of the others. This mountain, probably the result of a fusion of stories about lodestones and why Chinese junks were built without nails of iron, appeared first in occidental fiction in Herzog Ernst (ca. 1180); it is discussed best by Arturo Graf in Miti, leggende e superstizioni del medio evo, 2 vv., Turin, 1892–93, II, 363–393. Cf. René Basset in Revue des traditions populaires, IX (1894), 377–380, and Chauvin, Bibliographie . . . V, 202–203, No. 117, VII, 86_1. It is interesting to note that the story of the magnetic mountain also appears later in the Thousand and One Nights dissociated from that of the demon in the bottle.

14. Wilhelm Viëtor first made the conjecture about macellum: Marcellum, in Zeitschrift für romanische Philologie, I (1877), 176, and Academy, XXXVI (1889), 10. It occurred independently to Frederick W. Hasluck, Letters on Religion and Folklore, London, 1926, 96, 208. Moses Gaster, Monatsschrift für Geschichte und Wissenschaft des Judentums, XXIX (1880), 123 (= Gaster's Studies and Texts in Folklore, Magic, Mediaeval Romance . . ., 3 vv., London, 1925–28, II, 1208 ff.), regards the fly-less slaughter-house in the

temple at Jerusalem as the origin of the macellum: Aboth de R. Nathan, c. 35, Joma f. 21 a, which is in the Annotated Edition of the Authorized Daily Prayer Book of the United Hebrew Congregations of the British Empire, trans. and edited by S. Singer and I. Abrahams, London, 1914, p. 200, "No woman miscarried from the scent of the holy flesh; the holy flesh never became putrid; no fly was seen in the slaughter house. . . ." Cf. note 5, above. A text-book of general knowledge, written in Latin for children, contains the only genuine parallel which I have found to Virgil's meat-market. Johann Christoph Wagenseil, Pera librorum juvenilium; qua, ingenuos, viamque ad eruditionem et bonam mentem affectantes adolescentes donat, 6 vv. in 5, Altdorff, 1695, Loculamentum secundum. Synopsis Geographiae, p. 316 reads: "Ajunt, in hujus urbis [Prague] macello, etiam aestate, cum maxime calet, nullam muscam carnes sectari, arcente eas, Musca quadam, ad coelestium astrorum singulares influxus, ex materie ignota, efficta; qua, illius artifex, supremum, quod meruerat, supplicium, effugit." Whence this plum of knowledge came to nourish childish minds in quest of learning I know not. C.-B. 259 f., 262, 293.

15. C.-B. 293-373. F. Galiani, Del dialetto napoletano, ed. F. Nicolini (1923), 108$_1$. Nicolini's conjecture is supported by the statement in a printed version of the Cronica di Partenope (Croniche de la Inclyta Cita de Napole . . ., Napoli, 1526, fo. ix r°) to the effect that the leech — no frog is mentioned — was thrown, not into just any well, but into the Pozzo bianco, the well which Nicolini suspects of being the starting-point of the legend. Moreover, this conjecture had already been made by Domenico Antonio Parrino, Napoli città nobilissima, Napoli, 1700, 369, who speaks of an alley named Pozzo bianco, "per un pozzo di marmo con alcune mignatte, ò sanguisughe scolpite, che diede luogo alla favola, che per incanto di Virgilio non possino entrare ne'formali detti animali."

16. On these serpents in general: C.-B. 259, 262, 264-265. Comparetti (262) interprets Gervasius: "the serpents were confined by Vergil beneath a statue (*sigillum*) near the Porta Nolana." What Gervasius says is: "Est et in eadem porta

dominica Nolam, Campaniae civitatem olim inclytam, respiciens, in cuius ingressu est via lapidibus artificiose constructa, sub huius viae sigillo conclusit Virgilius omne genus reptilis nocui. . . ." I find no authority for interpreting sigillum as = statue; it seems to mean "seal" in mediaeval Latin; the form for "statue" in classical Latin is the plural, sigilla. Moreover, the Cronica di Partenope has "et a la ditta via pose uno sigillo lo ditto Virgilio. . . ." In Italian sigillo appears to mean only "seal." Hence, with some hesitation, I am inclined to believe that Virgil was said to have shut up the serpents under a seal, rather than under a statue. The Solomonic tradition seems capable of accounting for the seal simply enough. Gaster, Monatsschrift f. Gesch. u. Wiss. des Judentums, XXIX (1880), 125, interprets as "seal." Comparetti's interpretation is the easier of the two, because if a statue is admitted, then one is free to imagine the kind of statue, which would obviously be some figuration of a snake. Most medicine-men, from Aesculapius and Moses to St. Patrick and St. Columba, are likely to be preoccupied with snakes and how to control them. Many religions have employed the serpent as a symbol of one idea or another, and such symbolism is reflected in the sculpture of all periods. Hence we may be sure that in the Middle Ages there was no lack of opportunity to explain sculptured serpents as talismans. If they were so explained, then the construction of any one could be transferred to Virgil; but the texts of the legends do not seem to uphold such a theory, and therefore it is not clear what, if anything, the golden serpent which restrained plagues of them in Paris at the Pont-neuf has to do with Virgil's ban — Gregory of Tours, Historia Francorum, VIII, 33 [Monumenta Germaniae Historica, Scriptores rerum Merovingicarum, Hannover, 1885, I, p. 349]. Nicephoros Callistos Xanthopoullos, a fourteenth-century Byzantine chronicler, in Ecclesiasticae historiae libri xviii, iii, 18 (Migne's Patrologia Graeca, CXLV, col. 919 B), says that Apollonius of Tyana put to flight serpents and scorpions by devilish tricks and incantations. Were these incantations perhaps supposed to resemble those employed in the application of Solomon's seal? Snakes and other noxious beasts were kept out of Alexandria by carved images placed in the walls by a wise woman, according to the fifteenth-century Nobili fatti di Alessandro Magno, ed. Giusto Grion, Bologna, 1872, 31; cf. clxix [Collezione di opere inedite o rare . . .] — Rossi, Rassegna Bibliografica . . ., IV (1896), 177; these were in all probability astrological talismans, and the Virgilian marvels may well be their source. On various ways and means of banning snakes, sometimes by means of talismans, see Frazer's note on Pausanias, X, 17, 12 (vol. V, pp. 325–326), and The Golden Bough[3], Spirits of the Corn and of the Wild, II, 274–284; Otto Weinreich, Antike Heilungswunder, Giessen, 1909 [Religionsgeschichtliche Versuche und Vorarbeiten, VIII, 1], 162–170, and index s.v. Schlange; Hugo Gressmann, Der Zauberstab des Mose und die eherne Schlange, Zeitschrift des Vereins für Volkskunde, XXIII (1913), 18–34. Although Virgil apparently was credited with using a seal, it is not difficult to pass from banning snakes by means of incantations to banning them by means of a talisman constructed with the aid of incantations. The prevailing method of interpreting ancient objects during the later Middle Ages is well illustrated by the properties ascribed to ancient intagliated gems in Cethel aut veterum Judaeorum Physiologorum de lapidibus sententias, ed. by J. B. Pitra in Spicilegium Solesmense . . ., III, Paris, 1855, pp. 336 ff., especially in IX: "Quando inveneris in lapide hominem qui una manu tenet figuram diaboli, quas cornuta et alata describitur, et altera manu serpentem, et sub pedibus leonem, et super has figuras stent sol et luna, hic lapis poni debet in plumbo, et habet virtutem cogendi daemones, ut dent responsa interrogantibus," — a consummation greatly to be wished by the magician! — and in XVIII: "Quando invenitur in lapide homo alas habens in pedibus et baculum in manibus, hic valet ad gratiam." In the last the figure is of course that of Mercury, unrecognized. See Thorndike, Magic[2], II, chap. LIII, who reports a twelfth-century manuscript, and cf. the index s.v. snake.

17. C. Iulii Solini Collectanea rerum memorabilium, ed. Mommsen, Berlin, 1895, 2, 39, p. 41. C.-B. 265. Cf. C.-B. 341, where Italian *cicala* is mistranslated "grasshopper."

18. Pliny, Historia naturalis, XXVIII, 11 (49) = ed. Janus, Teubner series, Leipzig, 1880, vol. IV, p. 189. Cf. Pausanias, V, 27,3, and Frazer's note, vol. III, p. 649, but especially the article by Stadler in Pauly-Wissowa's Real-Encyclopädie der classischen Altertumswissenschaft, XVI, Stuttgart, 1913, coll. 1879–82. Professor Taylor refers me also to M. A. van Andel's article on Hippomanes in Nederlandsche Tijdschrift voor Geneeskunde, Jaargang 1922, Eerste Helft, No. 13, pp. 1280–1284.

19. Malalas's Chronographia, ed. Dindorff, X, 343, p. 264. J. Marquart, Osteuropäische und ostasiatische Streifzüge, Leipzig, 1903, 207 ff., 222 (note on Apollonius 236), reports Harun ibn Yahya. Cf. the excellent article by R. M. Dawkins on ancient statues in mediaeval Constantinople in Folk-Lore, XXXV (1924), 209–248, 380. I have not seen the article by A. J. Kirpičnikov on the same subject in Odessaer Jahrbuch, IV, Byz. Abteil. 2 (1894), 23–47. For Nicephoros Callistos Xanthopoullos's reference to the horse, see Migne's Patrologia Graeca, CXLV, col. 919 B. L'Abrégé des Merveilles, trans. Carra de Vaux, Paris, 1898, 272, alludes to the image of a horse which strengthened all horses within the circle of its magic influence.

20. The legend was at one time related of a statue actually existing at Naples, and after that statue was destroyed, it was transferred to another, the head of which is still on view in the National Museum at Naples. The new legend, repeated by many later writers, started in a baseless conjecture by one Tarcagnota in 1566. See F. Galiani, Del Dialetto Napoletano, ed. F. Nicolini, 1923, 109$_1$. C.–B. 259, 262, 268, 346–347, 355, 364. The fifteenth-century interpolation in the biography of Virgil attributed to Donatus, in which Virgil is reputed to have cured by means of medicine and mathematics many and various maladies incident to horses, is derived from the legend of the bronze horse-talisman, rather than the reverse. Viëtor, Academy, XXXVI (1889), 10, by implication inverts the relationship.

21. H. F. Massmann, Kaiserchronik, Quedlinburg and Leipzig, 1854, III, 442, cites an allusion to the legend—Naples

will sink if the egg on which it stands is broken. For the text, see Lieder Saal; das ist, Sammelung altteutscher Gedichte, hsg. von Joseph Maria Christoph, Reichsfreiherr von Lassberg, 4 vv., St. Gallen, 1846, III, 561–564.

22. C.-B 269₂₁. See C.-B. 347 for a possible allusion to the egg by Andrea Orcagna (d. 1368).

23. Croniche de la Inclyta Cita de Napole Emendatissime. Con li Bagni de Puzolo *ed* Ischia. Nouamente Ristampata. Con la Tauola. Pauia, 1526, fo. lxxi v°. The Virgilian legends appear in this work on ff. viii v°–xiv. I have not seen the first edition, s.d. This, the second, was reprinted at Naples in 1680? and in Raccolta di varii libri d'historie del regno di Napoli . . ., Napoli, 1680. For the date of the fourth part of the Cronica di Partenope, see B. Capasso, Le fonti della storia delle provincie napolitane dal 568 al 1500, con note . . . del Dr. E. Oreste Mastrojanni, Napoli, 1902, 131–137.

24. Professor T. Atkinson Jenkins kindly translates "entretalhiet" as "carved."

25. Bernard de Montfaucon, Les monumens de la monarchie françoise, Paris, 1729–33, II, 329. To this bit we may add the famous inscription, also historical, formerly on the arch which led from Santa Lucia to the bridge of the castle. According to Capasso's correction of the badly-garbled lines, it reads as follows:
OVUM (IN) VITRO NOVO NON SIC TURBABOR (AB) OVO. DORICA CASTRA CLUENS TUTOR, TEMERARE TIMETO. See Antonio Columbo, Napoli Nobilissima, VII (1898), 44. Cf. C.-B. 269, and F. W. Hasluck, Letters on Religion and Folklore, London, 1926, 96–98.

The building, to this day called Castello dell' Ovo, played an important rôle in the government and defence of Naples, but the egg appears to have had no historical existence, although, as might be expected, the actual castle and the fabulous egg frequently appear together. It is true, e. g., that Ambrogio Visconti escaped from the castle in 1370, or so the Cronicon Siculum avers; but that he broke the egg at his departure is another matter (cf. above, p. 90). Antonio Columbo discusses the history of the castle and some of the legendary material in

Napoli Nobilissima, VI (1897), 9–12, 141–143; VII (1898), 42–46, 178–181, 190–192. Cf. Schipa in the same journal, II (1893), 129–130, and F. d'Ovidio, Atti della R. Acc. di Napoli, n.s. IV (1916), 93.

26. M. P. Nilsson, Das Ei im Totenkult der Alten, Archiv für Religionswissenschaft, XI (1907–08), 530–546. J. J. Bachofen, Versuch über die Gräbersymbolik der Alten², Basel, 1925, 1–300, provides the most extensive study of the symbolism of the egg in ancient times. He notes (p. 50) that some of the eggs found in tombs are provided with holes, apparently for suspension. An interesting but probably adventitious parallel to the pillars or columns reported by Jean d'Outremeuse, Hemmerlin, and the Romance is provided by Bachofen (pp. 122–124 and 221 ff.) when he cites sepulchral monuments involving an egg on a *stele*, and eggs on platforms at the Circus. Bachofen's inferences concerning the original purpose of the egg are of no assistance in solving the present problem. It has been conjectured that the famous egg of Leda, suspended in ribbons from the roof of a Spartan temple, and supposed to be the egg from which the swan's maiden hatched forth Castor and Pollux, was an ostrich egg. Cf. James Marshall, Society of Biblical Archæology, Proceedings, XIV (1891–92), 6–7, and Berthold Laufer, Open Court, XL (1926), 258. On the folklore of eggs in general (ostrich eggs are not mentioned), see Hwb. d. d. Aberglaubens II, s.v. Ei.

27. W. Robertson Smith, Lectures on the Religion of the Semites, Edinburgh, 1889, 169 = 185 in third ed., London, 1927.

28. Richard Hakluyt. The Principal Navigations . . . of the English Nation, I, ii, 153 (Hakluyt Society, Glasgow, 1903–04, Extra Series, V, p. 211).

29. The Works of Sir Thomas Browne, ed. Charles Sayle, Edinburgh, 1927 (1903–07), 3 vv., III, 542. A similar observation is made by Andre Brüe about 1700: A New General Collection of Voyages and Travels . . ., London, 1745, II, 144.

30. Martin Sarmiento, Costumbres, etiquetas, ceremonias, . . . supersticiones y vulgaridades que se practican en diferentes partes de España . . . (1730), reprinted by José M.

Sbarbi in El Refranero General Español, 10 vv., Madrid, 1874–78, VII. Pedro de Loriano, Historia del Santo Cristo de Burgos, 1740, well illustrates how folklore can be made. Apparently the eggs were no longer suspended when he wrote, but lay at the feet of a figure of Christ, the reason being to mask the loss of one of the toes, cut off by a French bishop as he kissed the feet. The toe was used in France to work miracles. Cf. Notes and Queries (Tenth series), II (1904), 474 and III (1905), 192.

31. Henry F. Tozer, Researches in the Highlands of Turkey . . ., 2 vv., London, 1869, I, 79. Similarly, Frederick G. Burnaby, On Horseback through Asia Minor, 2 vv., London, 1877, I, 316: "I was struck by seeing a large ostrich egg suspended from the ceiling by a silver chain. On my asking the Turk who showed me over the building why this egg was hung there, he replied, 'Effendi, the ostrich always looks at the eggs which she lays; if one of them is bad she breaks it. This egg is suspended as a warning to men that, if they are bad, God will break them in the same way as the ostrich does her eggs.'"

32. Alfred J. Butler, The Ancient Coptic Churches of Egypt, 2 vv., Oxford, 1844, I, 55, II, 77–79. See also I, 163, 240, 281, 313, 343. In George P. Badger's The Nestorians and their Rituals, 2 vv., London, 1852, II, 20–21, is a drawing of a church at Mosul showing suspended ostrich eggs; and Martin S. Briggs, Muhammadan Architecture, London, 1924, shows at p. 139, fig. 146, ostrich eggs suspended in a sanctuary of a mosque at Cairo; cf. 226, and figs. 237–238. Other instances, with varying accounts of the purpose of suspending the ostrich egg, are reported by W. Denton, The Ancient Church in Egypt, London, 1883, 20; by A. de Vlieger, The Origin and Early History of the Coptic Church, Lausanne, 1900, 72 ("Ostrich-eggs . . . remind the congregation of the eye of God which watches the believers, as the ostrich watches her eggs whilst they are being hatched by the hot sand."); by George F. Abbott, Tale of a Tour in Macedonia, London, 1903, 316 ("Symbols of devotional concentration of thought . . . the young of the bird in question are hatched by the mother's eye affectionately fixed upon the eggs."); and by Sir J. Gardner

Wilkinson, Manners and Customs of the Ancient Egyptians, ed. Samuel Birch, 3 vv., London, 1878, II, 91 (chapter VIII).

33. F. W. Hasluck, Christianity and Islam under the Sultans, 2 vv., Oxford, 1929, I, 232. Hasluck's inferences about the evil eye, all the more interesting because arrived at independently, are supported by Siegfried Seligmann, Der Böse Blick und Verwandtes, 2 vv., Berlin, 1910, II, 133, and, for ancient times, by Bachofen, Gräbersymbolik², 133–136. Hasluck's highly diverting surmises in Letters on Religion and Folklore, London, 1926, 97–98, based merely on reading Comparetti and on familiarity with the Near East, are responsible for my efforts to ascertain whether Virgil's egg can be explained satisfactorily as an ostrich egg.

34. Hasluck and Butler, as above.

35. In Germania, V (1860), 483, Felix Liebrecht recorded his belief that Virgil's egg (as described in the first part of the Cronica di Partenope) is of the sort studied by Bachofen, but he later changed his mind after investigating foundation sacrifices (Germania, X [1865], 408), and propounded the theory just outlined in the text, using chiefly the version in the Image du Monde. The Hwb. d. d. Aberglaubens II, col. 617 (1929–30) follows Liebrecht and cites further occurrences. On human sacrifices at foundations, see A. H. Krappe, Balor with the Evil Eye [New York], 1927 (Institut des Etudes Françaises), 165₁, and the (unpublished) Harvard dissertation by John A. Walz, The Foundation Sacrifice and Kindred Rites (1898). Comparetti (C.-B. 269, 303, 342, 345, 353) assumes that the egg developed from the palladium mentioned by Conrad von Querfurt, but gives no evidence.

CHAPTER III

1. This passage is translated in full, C.-B. 273–274. I do not feel that Liebrecht's quotation from Alexander ab Alexandro (Des Gervasius . . . Otia imperialia, 159–160) supplies the source for this passage. Solomon's connection with the "notory art" perhaps is the key.

2. Andrea Dandolo, Chronicon Venetum, in Muratori,

Rerum italicarum scriptores XII (Mediolani, 1728), 283. This chronicle has not yet appeared in the new edition of Muratori.

3. The version of Gervasius is repeated, perhaps as Comparetti thinks by way of the Cronica di Partenope, in Ioannis Scoppae Parthenopei in diversos auctores collectanea ab ipso revisa . . ., Napoli, 1534. This work I know only through Comparetti. C.–B. 267, 274, 343. Apparently through a typographical error the author's Christian name is changed to Andrea, C.–B. 274.

It is possible that the version of Virgil's death in a tempest along with three companions, as it appears in Les faictz merveilleux de Virgille (Comp.² II, 299–300), is an echo of the storms caused by disturbing Virgil's bones; but in view of the numerous disappearances of magicians in tempests, I see no reason for arguing for a relationship.

4. Muratori, Rerum italicarum scriptores, Milan, 1723–51, V, 637–644; the De rebus gestis Rogerii Siciliae Regis libri quatuor also appears in Cronisti e scrittori della dominazione normanna nel regno di Puglia e Sicilia, ed. Giuseppe del Re, Napoli, 1845, 81–156 [Cronisti e scrittori Napolitani editi e inediti, I]. Jean de Meung had at least part of this idea when he said that "Naples fu donnée à Virgile," (Roman de la Rose, ed. E. Langlois, Paris, 1914–24, l. 19517 [Société des anciens textes français]). In this connection I have found K. L. Roth's article Über den Zauberer Virgilius, Germania, IV (1859), 257–298, most valuable. On the rôle of the Normans, see Erich Caspar, Roger II (1101–1154) und die Gründung der normannisch-sicilischen Monarchie, Innsbruck, 1904; Ferdinand Chalandon, Histoire de la domination normande en Italie et en Sicile (1009–1194), 2 vv., Paris, 1907, and his chapter in the Cambridge Medieval History, V (1926), 167–207, with bibliography, 855–859; Charles H. Haskins, The Normans in European History, Boston and New York, 1916.

5. De rebus gestis Rogerii . . ., ed. del Re, I, ch. xii.

6. De rebus gestis Rogerii . . ., III, xx; cf. Caspar, Roger II . . ., 153 f.

7. Falconis Beneventani Chronicon, Muratori, Rerum

italicarum scriptores, V (1724), 120: "Rex [i. e., Roger II] autem, Pisanorum exercitum reverti compraehendens, iterum Neapolim obsedit, cumque die quodam in festivitate Nativitatis Sanctae Mariae, Rex ipse navale bellum cum Neapolitanis incipere vellet, en subito tempestas affuit, & omnes naves illas divisit; ita quòd in profundum mergi putarent, & sic ad portum Puteolanum revertuntur. Tunc Rex videns neque mari, neque terra, contra civitatem agere, navigia illa reverti praecepit, & ipse Salernum repedavit, deinde Siciliam ingressus est." Cf. Caspar, 154, and Chalandon, II, 42. The chronicler's attributing this miracle by implication to the Virgin does not necessarily exclude other explanations.

8. Chalandon, Histoire de la domination normande . . ., II, 97.

9. Charles H. Haskins, Studies in the History of Mediaeval Science[2], Cambridge [Mass.], 1927, 155. Cf. 242 ff., and the same author's Studies in Mediaeval Culture, Oxford, 1929, 124 ff.

10. Michele Amari, Biblioteca Arabo-Siculo (ossia raccolta di testi arabici che toccano la geografia, la storia, la biografia e la bibliografia della Sicilia . . .), versione italiana, three parts, Torino, Roma, 1880–89, I, pp. 10 ff., Dal Kitab 'al masalik . . . ["Book of Roads and Provinces"], per 'Abu 'al quasim Muhammad 'ibn Hawqal. Cf. Amari's Storia dei Musulmani di Sicilia, 3 vv. in 4 parts, Firenze, 1854–72, II, 301 (the second edition by Giorgio Levi della Vida and Carlo Alfonso Nallino, Catania, 1930 —, is announced for completion in 1932) and George Sarton, Introduction to the History of Science, Washington, 1927, I, 674. The suggestion of a relationship between Virgil's bones in Naples and Aristotle's in Palermo comes from F. W. Hasluck, Letters on Religion and Folklore, London, 1926, 91, 97. Cf. Transferences from Christianity to Islam and Vice Versa, part I, vol. I, of Hasluck's Christianity and Islam . . ., 2 vv., Oxford, 1929. That Aristotle's supposed relics should be revered is not surprising — his grave was holy elsewhere (Wilhelm Hertz, Gesammelte Abhandlungen, ed. F. von der Leyen, Stuttgart and Berlin, 1905, 400 ff.) — in view of the respect for the relics of heroes in classical antiquity.

The bones of Pelops were believed effective against pestilence (Pausanias, V, 13, 6; cf. Otto Weinreich, Antike Heilungswunder, Giessen, 1909 [Religionsgeschichtliche Versuche . . ., VIII, 1] 135, and Friedrich Pfister, Der Reliquienkult im Altertum, 2 vv. paged continuously, Giessen, 1909–12 [same series, V]), as were those of Hector, Hesiod, Palinurus and others (Pfister, Reliquienkult, 440, 441, 516–517); those of Orestes brought victory to the Spartans (Pfister, 439). When the relics of Alcmene were moved, unfruitfulness and inundations at Thebes followed until the relics were restored to their rightful place (Pfister, 443, 516); water rose when the bones of Orpheus were disturbed (Pfister, 521); and meddling with the earth of Antaeus's grave-mound resulted in rainstorms until it was replaced (Pomponius Mela, Chorographia, ed. G. Parthey, Berlin, 1867, iii, 106). Plato's tomb was and is venerated in Asia Minor (Hasluck, Christianity and Islam . . ., 363–369).

The relics of Christian heroes — i. e., of saints — were similarly respected. In times of flood the waters left untouched the burial-place of St. Vedastus (P. Toldo, Studien zur vergleichenden Literaturgeschichte, VI [1906], 316). A letter written by Christ prevented Edessa's falling into the hands of the Persians in A.D. 544 (Ernst Lucius, Die Anfänge des Heiligenkults, Tübingen, 1904, 246). It was believed in 415 that removal of the body of St. Stephen the protomartyr would result in a revolt of the people of Jerusalem. When his coffin was opened, an earthquake occurred (Charles Mommert, Saint Étienne et ses sanctuaires à Jérusalem, Jerusalem [Leipzig], 1912, 59, 82–101; the story is told in Migne, Patrologia latina, XLI, col. 815). So long as the head of Bran the Blessed was properly buried, no invader could enter Britain (Alfred Nutt, Folk-Lore Record, V [1882], 7, 14). On the exposure of six holy corpses, heavy floods ensued at Milan in 1517 (G. A. Prato, Archivio storico italiano, III [1842], 408 ff.).

11. Cf. here Alexander of Telese (ed. del Re), III, chap. XIX: Erat autem civitas ipsa antiquissima, quam Aeneas, cum illuc navigio transvectus applicuisset, primus fertur condidisse, cujus quoque magnitudo praegrandis erat, quae a

parte meridiana non solum murorum altitudine, verum etiam
Tyrrheno mari munitur. A caeteris vero partibus excelsis
moenibus roboratur. Quam ob rem adeo ipsa inexpugnabilis
constat, ut nisi famis, periculo coartata nullatenus compre-
hendi queat. Nempe hujusmodi urbis dominus, olim Octa-
viano Augusto annuente, Virgilius maximus poetarum exstitit,
in qua etiam ipse volumen secum ingens hexametris compo-
suit versibus. C.-B. 282-287. The idea that Naples was especially protected was not new. The Vita Sancti Athanasii
(Bollandist Acta Sanctorum, July, IV, 78 f.) of the last of the
ninth or beginning of the tenth century says that the city had
been saved by divine interposition when it was besieged by the
Saracens in 961; the people were indifferent to the danger, saying, "Quare fatigamus, quare in vanum laboramus, ad anti-
quos fugiamus patronos, ad amicos scilicet Domini nostri
Jesu Christi Januarium et Agrippinum, et illorum quaerea-
mus exilium."

12. Chalandon, in Cambridge Medieval History, V (1926),
202.

13. C.-B. 269. On public talismans — objects in which the
safety of the state is bound up — see the note on Pausanias
8,47,5 in [Sir] James G. Frazer's edition (London, 1898, 6 vv.),
IV, pp. 433-434; Chauvin, VIII, p. 191; R. M. Dawkins,
Folk Lore, XXXV (1924), 209 ff.; Friedrich Pfister, Der Reliquienkult im Altertum, Giessen, 1909-12, 512-513.

14. Graf, Roma nella memoria . . . (1923), 520₂. Margaret
Bryant says in the article on the Virgil legend in the Encyclopædia Britannica [11] (1911), vol. 28, p. 116, that St. Virgilius,
Bishop of Salzburg, "may have been the real eponym of the
legend." F. J. Hosford, Classical Journal, VI (1910–11), 7,
writes, "A curious body of Virgilian myths sprang up in the
later Middle Ages, significant for an utter dissociation with
the Virgil of Roman days, which proves the widespread veneration of his name, even among the ignorant."

15. See Ulysse Chevalier, Répertoire des sources historiques
du moyen âge², Paris, 1907, Bio-bibliographie, pp. 4695 f.
On St. Virgil of Salzburg, Giuseppe Boffito, in Miscellanea
di studi critici in onore di Arturo Graf, Bergamo, 1903, 592 f.;

W. Wattenbach, Deutschlands Geschichtsquellen . . .⁷, Stuttgart and Berlin, 1904, I, 136–138; Analecta Bollandiana, XIV (1895), 340, XX (1901), 177–181; the [Bollandist] Bibliotheca hagiographica latina, Brussels, 1898–1901, Nos. 8680–86; the Cambridge Medieval History, III, 512–513; John S. Ryan, Early Irish Missionaries on the Continent and St. Virgil of Salzburg, Dublin, 1924 [The Sheaf Mission Series, No. 5]; Francis S. Betten, St. Boniface and St. Virgil, St. Anselm's Priory [Washington, 1927] [Benedictine Historical Monographs, II]. On St. Virgil of Arles, H. Gaidoz, Mélusine, V (1890–91), 84; the [Bollandist] Bibliotheca hagiographica latina, 1898–1901, No. 8679.

On Virgilius Maro, grammarian of Toulouse, Desazars de Montgailhard in Revue des Pyrenées, XIV (1902), 1–22, 144–160; D. Tardi, Les Epitomae de Virgile de Toulouse, essai de traduction critique avec une bibliographie . . ., Paris, 1928 (dissertation, Université de Paris).

On "a certain fool named Virgilius" (apparently a versifier who took the name of the poet) see Magni Felicis Ennodii opera, ed. F. Vogel, Berlin, 1885 [Monumenta Germaniae Historica, Auctorum antiquissimorum, VII].

16. C.–B. 99, 101, 237, 310, 360, 372.

CHAPTER IV

1. Edmund Stengel, Mitteilungen aus französischen Handschriften der Turiner Universitäts-Bibliothek, Halle a.S., 1873, 14 f. Cf. C.–B. 315.

2. Arturo Graf, Roma nella memoria . . ., Torino, 1923, 148–167 (chapter VI). Cf. C.–B. 294, 298 ff., 303 ff., 314, 343; Carlo Cecchelli's article in Italien, Monatsschrift für Kultur, Kunst, und Literatur, II (1929), 307–310 (illustrated); A. H. Krappe, in Archivum Romanicum, XVI (1932), 271–278; A Catalogue of Romances . . . in the British Museum, III, 122, No. 30, 230, No. 8.

3. Willelmi Malmesbiriensis monachi de gestis regum anglorum, ed. W. Stubbs, 2 vv., London, 1887, lib. II, sec. 169 [Rerum Britannicarum medii aevi scriptores]. A very similar story is told in Alberici Monachi Trium Fontium

Chronicon, ed. G. G. Leibnitz, Leipzig, 1698, part 2, pp. 37 ff. sub anno 999. C.-B. 306 f. Cf. Raphael Meyer, Gerbertsagnet, København, 1902; A Catalogue of Romances . . . in the British Museum, III, 191, No. 6; Kittredge, Witchcraft in Old and New England, 545_{12}; the full note on Gerbert in Arthur Dickson's Valentine and Orson, New York, 1929, 206_{115}; A. H. Krappe, Archivum Romanicum, XVI (1932), 271; Marjorie Williamson, Modern Philology, XXX (1932), 5 ff.

4. Scoppa also mentions it. C.-B. 262, 268.

5. James Douglas Bruce, Human Automata in Classical Tradition and Mediaeval Romance, Modern Philology, X (1912–13), 511–526. I have found the following also of value on the subject: Robert Dernedde, Über die den altfranzösischen Dichtern bekannten epischen Stoffe aus dem Altertum, Erlangen, 1887; Otto Söhring, Werke bildender Kunst in altfranzösischen Epen, Romanische Forschungen, XII (1900), 580–598; Adolf Hertel, Verzauberte Örtlichkeiten und Gegenstände in der altfranzösischen erzählenden Dichtung, Hannover, 1908 [Göttingen dissertation]; Edmond Faral, Recherches sur les sources latines des contes et romans courtois du moyen âge, Paris, 1913, 307–388, especially 328–335; Marguerite Hallauer, Das wunderbare Element in den Chansons de Geste, Basel, 1918, 11–13 [dissertation]; M. B. Ogle, Modern Language Notes, XXXV (1920), 129–136; Laura A. Hibbard, Mediaeval Romance in England, New York, 1924, 180_{12}, 192_{20}; John R. Reinhard, Publications of the Modern Language Association, XXXVIII (1923), 436_{41}; Arthur Dickson, Valentine and Orson, New York, 1929, 196_{80}.

6. Karls des Grossen Reise nach Jerusalem und Constantinopel, ed. Eduard Koschwitz[5], Leipzig, 1907, ll. 352 ff.; Eneas, ed. J. J. Salverda da Grave, Halle, 1891, ll. 7691 ff. [Bibliotheca Normannica, IV]; Thomas's Tristan, ed. Joseph Bédier, 2 vv., Paris, 1902–05, I, 309 ff. [Société des anciens textes français]; Roman d'Alexandre, ed. H. Michelant, Stuttgart, 1843, 343 [Bibliothek des litterarischen Vereins in Stuttgart, XIII]; Huon de Bordeaux, edd. F. Guessard and C. Grandmaison, Paris, 1865, ll. 4562 ff. Cf. Bruce, Modern Philology, X (1912–13), 515–523.

7. The Journey of William of Rubruck to the Eastern Parts of the World, 1253–55, as narrated by himself, translated and edited by Woodville Rockhill, London, 1900, 207 f. [Hakluyt Society].

8. Baron Carra de Vaux, L'Abrégé des Merveilles, traduit de l'Arabe. . ., Paris, 1898, 179, 245, 356. Cf. the review by G. Maspéro, Journal des savants for 1899, 69–86, 154–172, the article in the same volume by Marcellin Berthelot, 248–253, 271–277, and George Sarton, Introduction to the History of Science, Washington, 1927, I, 638.

9. Constantini Porphyrogeneti Imperatoris De ceremoniis aulae Byzantinae libri duo Graece et Latine e recensione Io. Iac. Reisckii . . ., 2 vv., Bonn, 1829–30, Bk. II, cap. 15 [vol. I, p. 569]. On this kind of thing in the Middle Ages, cf. vol. II, pp. 642 ff., and, for discussions of this passage, Jules Labarte, Le palais impérial de Constantinople, Paris, 1861, 85; Jean Ebersolt, Le grand palais de Constantinople . . ., Paris, 1910; Charles Diehl, Manuel d'art byzantin[2], Paris, 1925–26, 420 f.; and, for other occurrences of the same type, Faral, Recherches sur les sources latines . . ., Paris, 1913, 323–335, especially 334[1].

10. Heronis Alexandrini opera quae supersunt omnia, ed. Wilhelm Schmidt, 5 vv., Leipzig, 1899–1914, I: Pneumatica et Automata. The best general account is that in the Pauly-Wissowa Real-Encyclopädie der classischen Altertumswissenschaft, Stuttgart, 1912, s.v. Heron, cols. 992 ff. Cf. Eugène A. A. de Rochas d'Aiglun, La science des philosophes et l'art des thaumaturges dans l'antiquité, Paris, 1882; Conrad W. Cooke, Automata, Old and New, London, 1893 [Opuscula of The Sette of Odd Volumes, XXIX]; Les Mécaniques ou l'Élévateur de Héron d'Alexandrie . . . sur la version Arabe de Qostà ibn Luqâ . . . traduite en français par M. le Baron Carra de Vaux, Paris, 1894 [Extrait du Journal Asiatique, IXe série, I (1893), 386–472, II (1893), 152–269, 420–514] (date shortly before A.D. 1445); Albert Neuburger, Die Technik des Altertums, Leipzig, 1909, 206–236 (cf. bibliography, p. 235), translated by Henry L. Brose as The Technical Arts and Sciences of the Ancients, London, 1930 — but "those readers

who wish to pursue the facts to their sources are referred to the German original." — Translator's preface, v; the discussion of Hero in Thorndike, Magic[2], I, 188–193, and in George Sarton, Introduction to the History of Science, Washington, 1927, I, 208–211 [Carnegie Institution of Washington, Publication No. 376]. An instance of Hero's influence early in the thirteenth century is The Treatise of Al-Jazari on Automata, discussed by Ananda K. Coomaraswamy, Museum of Fine Arts Bulletin No. 6, Boston, 1924; on this, cf. Paul Wittek, in Der Islam, XIX (1931), 177–178. A relationship between the theorems of Hero and the automata of romance was perceived by Faral, Recherches sur les sources latines . . ., Paris, 1913, 334[1]; Norman M. Penzer, The Ocean of Story, 10 vv., London, 1924–28, III, 56–59; and A. Chapuis and E. Gélis, Le monde des automates, 2 vv., Paris, 1928, I, 35–41. Of these, the first two merely refer in notes, and the third is inaccurate and refers only in passing to the matters here considered.

11. Heronis Alexandrini Pneumatica et Automata, ed. W. Schmidt, theorems xv, xvi, pp. 91–97.

12. Ed. Schmidt, pp. 187–191.

13. Ed. Schmidt, p. 97.

14. Ed. Schmidt, pp. 265–275 (water-pressure forces oil in through a hidden pipe, or a float resting on the surface of the oil turns a cog-wheel as the oil-level sinks. This cog-wheel pushes the wick up as it is burned down).

15. Ed. Schmidt, pp. 413–453.

16. Hero's explanation occupies pp. 417–453 in Schmidt's edition. It appears to me that if we combine the "taboo" idea in Hero with the storm, we have a possible explanation of the experience of Yvain in Chrétien's romance. The knight, it will be remembered, picks up a basin at a fountain and throws water on a stone. (In René I's Livre du cuer d'amours espris, edd. O. Smital and E. Winkler, Vienna, 1927, II, 20 = Oeuvres complètes du roi René, 4 vv., ed. M. le Comte de Quatrebarbes, Angers, 1846, III, pp. 22–23, the invention of this fountain is ascribed to Virgil). The consequences are hardly more remarkable than the antics of the contraptions in Hero's automatic theatre. On the storm that follows see George L.

Hamilton, Storm-making Springs . . ., Romanic Review, II
(1911), 355–375, V (1914), 213–237, and, for another explanation of Yvain's trial, Charles B. Lewis, Classical Mythology
and Arthurian Romance, London (etc.), 1932 [St. Andrews
University Publications, No. XXXII]. Had Chrétien seen or
heard of such apparatus? Yvain's lifting the basin and the
prompt results which followed might be so explained, and this
particular bit of faëry would then become an unreal world in a
different sense — the world of automata, where time and
space and other human limitations may be set aside at will.
We might continue further, and inquire whether the storm
consequent upon lifting or disturbing Virgil's bones was due
to the same causes.

17. Thorndike, Magic², I, 190₁.

18. On Leon, not to be confused with Emperor Leon VI,
see George Sarton, Introduction to the History of Science,
I, 554 f.; cf. I, 116; II, 22, 510.

19. Michele Amari, Storia dei Musulmani di Sicilia, 3 vv.,
Firenze, 1854–68, III, 684–686. On water-clocks, see A.
Chapuis and E. Gélis, Le monde des automates, 2 vv., Paris,
1928, I, 32 ff.

20. Cf. George Sarton, Introduction to the History of
Science, I, 705.

21. Some of the stories are summarized, with notes, by
Chauvin, Bibliographie des ouvrages arabes . . ., III, No. 143,
p. 138; V, No. 30, p. 30 (cf. p. 294); V, No. 117, p. 200; V, No.
16, p. 33; V, No. 388, p. 40; V, No. 130, pp. 221–231.

22. Or does he mean hidden pipes for conducting air? The
passage is: "Item, Virgile fist I tieste qui parloit et respondoit
à ly de tout chu qu'ilh ly demandoit que ilh avenoit par toute
le monde, car ilh mist dedens des espirs priveis." The head informs Virgil of misconduct among the Roman matrons.

23. Arthur Dickson, Valentine and Orson, New York,
1929, 191–216, with rich notes, to which might be added
Adolf Furtwängler, Die antiken Gemmen, 3 vv., Leipzig and
Berlin, 1900, III, 245–252, 451; Salomon Reinach, La tête
magique des Templiers, in Cultes, Mythes et Religions², IV,
Paris, 1912, 252–266; Zeitschrift des Vereins für Volkskunde,

XXIII (1913), 109; Alexander H. Krappe's article in Le Moyen Age, XXXVI (1926), 85–92. C.-B. 307 f., 343, 347, 360.

24. Dickson, Valentine and Orson, 201.

25. Karl and Wilhelm Krafft, Briefe und Dokumente aus der Reformation im 16. Jahrhundert, Elberfeld (1875), 106 ff., 111–112.

26. W. Niemann, Sprechende Figuren, ein Beitrag zur Vorgeschichte des Phonographen, in Geschichtsblätter für Technik, VII (1920), 2–30, and Chapuis and Gélis, Le monde des automates, 2 vv., Paris, 1928, I, 199–213, Machines et têtes parlantes, and II, 335, to which I owe the reference to Niemann's article.

27. On these mirrors, C.-B. 298, 303 ff., 322, 343, 348_{19}, 370. Cf. Hasluck, Letters on Religion and Folklore, London, 1926, 193. For collections of materials on mirrors, see Chauvin, Bibliographie des ouvrages arabes . . ., VIII, p. 191, VI, p. 91, and Killis Campbell, The Seven Sages of Rome (Boston and New York, 1907), p. xcvi.

28. L'Abrégé des Merveilles, Paris, 1898, 80 f., 175, 201, 234, 238, 250, 275, 281 f., 286, 293. Cf. Berthelot, Journal des Savants for 1899, 245. On the lighthouse at Alexandria, see George Sarton, Introduction to the History of Science, Washington, 1927, I, 161; cf. 276–277, 721. For its effect on the popular mind, see Ibn Khordâdhbeh, Kitâb al-Masâlik wa'l-mamâlik, Liber viarum et regnorum, ed. M. J. De Goeje, Lugduni Batavorum, 1889, 8 [Bibliotheca geographorum arabicorum. Pars VIᵃ], and The Bondage and Travels of Johann Schiltberger . . ., trans. J. Buchan Telfer, London, 1879, 62–64 [Hakluyt Society].

CHAPTER V

1. On the basket story, see C.-B. 326–336, 355, 361 ff. (where the word *cesta* is consistently mistranslated "box" or "chest"); Tunison, Master Virgil, 148–150; Graf, Roma nella memoria . . ., Torino, 1923, 560; Fr. Moth, Aristotelessagnet eller elskovs magt, København, 1916, 161–178. I borrow here

from my note, The Basket Incident in Floire and Blanceflor, in Neuphilologische Mitteilungen, XXVIII (1927), 69–75.

2. Katha Sarit Sagara, trans. C. H. Tawney, 2 vv., Calcutta, 1884–87, II, 96; ed. Norman M. Penzer, 10 vv., London, 1924–28, V, 147. For the date, see Penzer, I, xxxiii.

3. The Book of the Thousand Nights and a Night, trans. . . . R. F. Burton, ed. Leonard C. Smithers, 12 vv., London, 1894, VIII, pp. 136 ff. Tausend und eine Nacht, Arabische Erzählungen . . ., von Max Habicht, F. H. von der Hagen und Karl Schall, Breslau, 1825–45, XIII, 25–31, Nights 551–552. For bibliographical material and references to later occurrences, see Chauvin, Bibliographie des ouvrages arabes . . ., V, No. 142, p. 241, La corbeille ou mariage d'al Ma'moûne.

4. G. Huet, Romania, XXXV (1906), 97; Antti Aarne, Folklore Fellows Communications 14, Hamina, 1914, p. 11; Enno Littmann, Tausendundeine Nacht in der Arabischen Literatur, 1923 [Philosophie und Geschichte 2].

5. Tausend und ein Tag, Morgenländische Erzählungen . . . Übersetzt von F. H. von der Hagen, 11 vv., Prenzlau, 1827–28, IX, 232–319, Days 571–591. For summary, with references, see Chauvin, Bibliographie des ouvrages arabes . . ., V, No. 143, pp. 242–244, La corbeille. Cf. IV, pp. 124–126, for a discussion of the collection, and Neuphilologische Mitteilungen, XXVIII (1927), 74$_1$.

6. Katha Sarit Sagara, ed. Penzer, V, 24; VI, 172 = ed. Tawney, II, 16; II, 234. In Gueulette's Mille et un quarts d'heure, trans. Thomas Flloyd, London, 1759, 357–358, is a story of an unwelcome lover forced to leave the lady's apartment by a rope, from which he falls into a net prepared for him. Another parallel, though one not much more convincing, is presented in The Bāgh o Bahār, or the Garden and the Spring . . ., by Emir Khusru of Delhi, trans. E. B. Eastwick, Hertford, 1852, 71–118 (cf. introduction, p. viii). Here the transportation to the Otherworld is provided, not by a basket, but by a throne. Other editions: The Tale of the Four Durwesh, trans. L. F. Smith, Calcutta, 1845, 72–121; Bāgh o Bahār, trans. Duncan Forbes, London (1857), 93–150, a reprint of Smith's translation with additional notes; Bāg o

Bahār . . ., trans. Garcin de Tassy, Paris, 1878, 29–47; another reprint of Smith's translation, Lucknow, 1895, 90–142.

7. O. M. Johnston, The Origin of the Legend of Floire et Blancheflor, Matzke Memorial Volume, Stanford University Press, 1911 [Leland Stanford Junior University Publications]; Laura A. Hibbard, Mediaeval Romance in England, New York, 1924, 190 ff.; Neuphilologische Mitteilungen, XXVIII (1927), 69 ff.

8. For the classification, see Gaston Paris in Romania, XXVIII (1899), 441. The Old French versions are edited by Édélestand Du Méril, Paris, 1856, the Middle English by A. B. Taylor, Oxford, 1927, the Icelandic by Eugen Kölbing, Halle, 1896, and the Danish by J. P. Jakobsen et al., København, 1925 [Danske Folkebøger, VII].

9. Du Méril's ed., ll. 1994–2155, pp. 80–88.

10. The Jātaka, or Stories of the Buddha's former Births, translated from the Pāli by various hands under the editorship of E. B. Cowell. Vol. I, trans. R. Chalmers, Cambridge, 1895, No. 62, pp. 151–155, "Aṇḍabhūta-Jātaka." Cf. p. viii.

11. On these, see Gaston Paris as above, V. Crescini, Il Cantare di Fiorio e Biancifiore, 2 vv., Bologna, 1889–99, I, 413 ff. (where the Greek romance also is quoted), Du Méril, as above, introd., p. xlv$_2$, and Boccaccio's Il Filocolo, ed. E. de Ferri, Torino, 1921, II, 143. Comparetti (C.-B. 329$_9$) would reject this parallel as impertinent: "Some . . . wish to connect this with the Nov. viii. 7 of the *Decameron* and with a passage in the *Filocopo* (p. 283, ed. Sansovino). But the parallel fails at the essential point." As far as Decameron viii, 7, Comparetti is certainly correct, in spite of the note by A. C. Lee, The Decameron: its Sources and Analogues, London, 1909, 259–261, on which see A. Borgeld's review of Lee, Museum, XVIII (1910), 380; but the text in Sansovino's edition (Venezia, 1612, 283), like that in de Ferri's as above, reads: "[Sadoc] avea comandato che per amore di lui a Biancofiore si presentasse [the basket of flowers in which Filocolo (= Floire) is concealed, and it] fu portato a pie d'ella torre; e quivi fatta chiamar Glorizia, la quale al servigio di Biancofiore dimorava, a lei face *la cesta collar suso a una finestra*."

(Italics mine.) Comparetti, of course, means by the "essential point" the fact that Virgil's basket never reaches the lady's window, of which more anon.

12. O. M. Johnston, in Matzke Memorial Volume, Stanford University Press, 1911. Joachim Reinhold, Revue de philologie française, XIX (1905), 170, attempts to derive the flower-basket from the wooden horse of Troy, since the horse was used to win a city and the basket was used to win a lady; but his efforts have not been well received. Reinhold's Floire et Blancheflor, étude de littérature comparée, Paris, 1906, should be consulted.

13. Johnston, as above, 134–137, and, on the development of the harem in story, F. W. Hasluck, Christianity and Islam . . ., Oxford, 1929, II, 741–750.

14. Heinrich Adelbert von Keller, Li Romans des Sept Sages, Tübingen, 1836, lxx–lxxiii. J. Alton, in his edition of Le Roman De Markes de Rome, Tübingen, 1889 [Bibliothek des litterarischen Vereins in Stuttgart, CLXXXVII], p. xiii, notices the manuscript — Bibliothèque Nationale F. F. M. 22548, LaVall. 13, formerly 4096 — briefly without mentioning this story. He attributes the manuscript to the end of the thirteenth century. Keller indicates that it must be dated after 1284, because the writer of this ms. must have seen another ms. which was written after that date (pp. xliii, lxiv). The language betrays that the author or scribe of this manuscript hailed from Picardy. Max Grünbaum, Neue Beiträge zur semitischen Sagenkunde, Leiden, 1893, 233 ff., lists other stories involving transportation of lovers to the towers of immured mistresses, though not by means of baskets.

15. The poem is edited by A. Tobler, Zeitschrift für romanische Philologie, IX (1885), 284 ff. Cf. C.-B. 335.

16. Lhystoire du Sainct Greaal . . ., Paris, Michel le Noir, 1514 (British Museum pressmark: C. 7. b. 4), fo. lxxiiii–fo. lxxx; the Vulgate version of the Arthurian Romances . . ., ed. H. Oskar Sommer, Washington, 1909, I, 173 ff. [The Carnegie Institution of Washington].

17. Here we have the connection established with another well-known legend, that of Hippocrates and his daughter, who

is enchanted in a castle and can be disenchanted only by a kiss. See G. Huet, La légende de la fille d'Hippocrate à Cos, in Bibliothèque de l'École des Chartes, LXXIX (1918), 45–59, and F. W. Hasluck, Christianity and Islam . . ., Oxford, 1929, 646–660. On the real Hippocrates of Cos, the "Father of Medicine," see George Sarton, Introduction to the History of Science, I, Washington, 1927, 96–102.

18. Felix Liebrecht recognized this in Germania, I (1856), 267. A mistaken remark of Legrand d'Aussy in his edition of Fabliaux ou Contes . . ., Paris, 1779, I, 212, third ed., Paris, 1829, I, 288, that the Hippocrates story appears in a manuscript of the prose Lancelot was corrected by Le Roux de Lincy in La revue française, XI (1839), 321–333.

19. Édélestand Du Méril, Mélanges archéologiques et littéraires, Paris, 1850, 430. I print here as of some interest the copy made for me by Mlle. N. Jourdan from ms. B. R. 6186, fo. 149, v°:

Legitur in gestibus Romanorum quod mirabilis prerogative specialis Virgilius, magice facultatis scientia circumspectus, Neronis tunc imperatoris romane urbis familiaris extitit; cujus filiam elegantis forme titulo resplendentem, sicut assolet, carnali concupiscentie stimulo precordialiter adamavit, qui, sine precibus inducens, ab ipsa diligentis instantie articulis impetravit ut prefata Neronis filia ei locum atque tempus prefigeret oportunum, in quo prefatus magister virginis prescripte amplo desiderio fungeretur. Cumque ferventi desiderio concitatus, tempore noctis ad ipsius virginis habitaculum accessisset, accidit quod ipsa virgo, muliebris astutie imbuta maliciis, nobilem magistrum suis vestimentis omnibus denudatam admitteret in cophino, ipsum in medio turris altissime usque ad effusionem solis detinuit in suspenso; [fo. 150] ita arte positus desistebat quod ascendere vel descendere sine mortis periculo non valeret. Cujus facti per civitatem romanam publica fama volans, fuit usque ad Imperatoris noticiam ventilata. Qui, ad iracundiam facto tam detestabili provocatus intra se, quod facti malicia mortis sententia(m) merebatur, secundum approbatas consuetudines temporis et Imperii, legaliter circumspexit. Qui licet in multis et experimentissimis esset culpis suis exigentib*us* affligend*us*, ab ip*so* Imperatore *gra*-*tiam* optinuit sp*e*c*i*alem, ut quo mortis gen*e*re mallet mori sibi eidem contulit eligend*um*. *Qui*, minus *grave* mortis p*e*riculum sibi eligendo assumens, in balneo tepentis aque sibi minui postulans [postulavit?]: q*uod* [sc. uim?] *secundum* sue elect*i*onis sententia*m* in balneo constitut*us* [esset?], magicis artibus suffragantib*us*, ap*ud* civitatem Neapolitana*m* e*st* translat*us*. U*bi*, ab angustia Neronis imperatoris lib*e*re conservat*us*, infra [intra?] civitatem Romana*m* duxit ignem talit*er* extingu*en*-dum, q*uod* n*isi* in inf*e*rioribus v*i*rginis Neroniane rep*e*riretur. N*u*llaten*us* val*e*ret ignis remedi*um* in civitate romana alit*er* obtineri. *Qui*, videns su*m*ma*m* maliciam super [fo. 150, v°] hoc iminere, verecu*n*diam filialem duxit gen*e*ralit*er* promulgandam ut ex co*mm*un*i*s nec*e*ssitatis redimeretur incursu, *et*, vocatis pop*u*lis univ*e*rsis, eisdem g*e*neralit*er* intimabat ut q*ui*lib*et* ad filiam imperatoris acced*e*ret, ignem in ej*us* inf*e*rioribus optenturas [obtenturus?]. Qui p*er* fallacia hominis incantantis ignem in ill*is* p*ar*tibus invenerunt. Cf. Catalogus codicum manuscriptorum bibliothecae regiae, Paris, 1745, pars tertia, tomus quartus, 212–213, and, for the contents of the rest of the manuscript, tomus secundus, 212. Just preceding this story is "Nonnulla de Christianis, Judaeis, Graecis, Aegyptis et Romanis" [fo. 141, v°], and immediately following it is "De aedificiis urbis Romae prologus: subjicitur termo sive carmen ad urbem Romam et responsio urbis Romae" [fo. 150, v°]. "Legitur in gestibus Romanorum" turns one's mind at once to the Gesta Romanorum, but that great collection had not yet been assembled. I am at a loss for the source of the passage. Earlier than this is Guiraut de Calanso's Fadet joglar; but does the allusion "Com de la conca's saup cobrir" refer to the basket-revenge incidents?

20. Ed. by Philip Strauch, Monumenta Germaniae Historica, Scriptores, Scriptores qui vernacula lingua usi sunt, III (1891), ll. 23765–23915; cf. p. lxxiii.

21. There is no reference to our story in Enikel's source for this section of his chronicle, De imagine mundi (ed. in Migne, Patrologia latina, clxxii, 239 ff.). Cf. Strauch, lxiv.

22. Lhystoire du Sainct Greaal . . ., Paris, Michel le Noir,

1514, ff. lxxiiii ff. Paulin Paris, Romans de la table ronde, Paris, 1868, I, 255. The latter does not name the ms. upon which he bases his translation, but by comparison of the material I decide that he used ms. 2455 of the Bibliothèque Nationale, Ystoire del Graal, thirteenth century (cf. Catalogue des mss. français, ancien fonds, Paris, 1868, I, 421), of which the Ypocras episode is printed by Eugène Hucher, Le Saint-Graal, Le Mans and Paris, 1878, III, 21–69, as a variant to the unnumbered Le Mans ms. (Hucher, II, 1) of the thirteenth century which he uses as text. My basis for this decision is the fact that ms. 2455 is the only one which I have seen which contains the story of the revenge of Ypocras as it appears in the translation by Paulin Paris. Ypocras gives a loathsome crippled beggar a magic herb with which he must touch the great physician's tormentor (cf. A. Hertel, Verzauberte Örtlichkeiten . . ., 45). As a result the beautiful French lady is seized with a love for the beggar which will not be denied, and makes a spectacle of herself before the court. Further, the ms. 2455 version is the only one I know which calls the vehicle at the tower a basket, as Paulin Paris does (Rom. de la table ronde, I, 254, *corbeille* [twice]; 255, *corbillon* [twice]; 257, *corbeille, corbeillon*; 258, *corbeille*; ms. 2455 as printed by Hucher, vol. III, 39, *corbaille*; 41, *corbillon*, but on 41, 42 it is also called *cofin*). For similar reasons I believe that Le Roux de Lincy also translates from ms. 2455, although he, too, fails to name his source. See his Essai historique et littéraire sur l'Abbaye de Fécamp, Rouen, 1840, 95–138. The Le Mans ms., British Museum mss. Additional 10292 (of which the Ypocras story is printed by Furnivall as a parallel text to Lonelich's translation of ca. 1450, Seynt Graal, Roxburghe Club, 1861–63, II, 19–43) and Royal 19. c. xii, and the Corpus Christi ms. (printed for the Roxburghe Club by Furnivall, and by the same editor for the Early English Text Society, Extra Series, XX, XXIV, XXVIII, XXX, 1874–1905) call it a *vessel* or *vaisselle*. British Museum ms. Royal 14. E. iii (early fourteenth century — see Catalogue of Romances in the British Museum, ed. Ward, London, 1883, I, 341) omits it. The English translation by Henry Lonelich or Lovelich, referred to above, contains the Ypocras incident, but omits the revenge. Evidently Furnivall believed that ms. Additional 10292 was Lonelich's source, as he prints portions of it as a parallel text to Lonelich's translation; but I suspect strongly that the version printed by Hucher as his main text ("Publié d'après un manuscrit du milieu du xiiie siècle, appartenant à la Bibliothèque de la ville du Mans" — Hucher, II, 1) is the more likely source.

23. Gesammtabenteuer, Stuttgart, 1850, III, cxliv.

24. Insolvent debtors were punished by having a basket thrown over them in Boeotia about the beginning of the Christian era — De moribus gentium, by Nicholas Damascenus, in Gronovius, Thesaurus antiquitatum Graecarum, VI, 3854; also in the Florilegium of Stobaeus, 293, 16, ed. T. Gaisford, Oxford, 1822, II, p. 227; and in Meier and Schomann, Der Attische Process, Halle, 1824, 512. The dates of Nicholas Damascenus are not certainly known, but it seems that he flourished in the time of Augustus and Herod. Here the disgrace by exhibition is certainly present; but I hesitate to relate it with the kind of basket punishment which we here consider, as neither suspension nor love-affair is present. Paul's escape from Damascus in a basket (II Corinthians xi, 33, Acts ix, 25) has no more to do with the case; and Socrates's entry in a basket in the Clouds of Aristophanes remains for me, as I believe it does for the commentators, something of a mystery, unless it is a burlesque of the philosopher's elevated language. Certainly no punishment, and no love affair, are present.

In chapter XII of the Germania of Tacitus is mentioned a punishment for cowards and for those committing crimes contrary to nature, by execution under a hurdle in a swamp. The passage reads: "ignavos, et imbelles, et corpore infames, coeno ac palude, injecta insuper crate, mergunt." Execution by this method seems to have continued late among the Germanic peoples, as we learn from Karl Müllenhoff's commentary on the Germania, Deutsche Altertumskunde, ed. Max Roediger, IV, Berlin, 1920, 243 ff. For other references see Francis B. Gummere, Founders of England, ed. F. P. Magoun, Jr., New York, 1930, 486. The *cratis* under which criminals were suffocated in the mud appears to have been a hurdle of basket-work, on which see F. A. van Scheltema, Die Altnordische Kunst, Berlin, 1923, 56–60, with references and illustrations. It is possible that in the passage in Tacitus the association between punishment for a crime and the instrument of basket-work is significant for the present topic; but the facts that no actual basket is employed and that the punishment seems in Tacitus to apply only to soldiers in the field make me hesitate to postulate a definite relationship. The survival of punishment by suffocation in swamps might lead one to believe that the punishment by means of a wickerwork hurdle, a simple enough development of which would be a basket, survived also; but the jump from Tacitus to the thirteenth century is a bit long to take with no positive evidence intervening.

25. S.v. *schupfe*. This description would apply in some respects to the punishment by the cucking-stool in England, on which I have a comparative study nearly completed. Jacob Grimm, Deutsche Rechtsaltertümer, edd. Andreas Heusler and Rudolf Hübner, Leipzig, 1899, reprinted 1922, II, 162, 323 ff., and the Deutsches Wörterbuch collect material which I have used extensively here. On the *Schupfstuhl, Schnellgalgen, Schandkorb, Pranger,* and similar punishments by exhibition in Germany, see the above and in addition A. Birlinger, Schwäbisch-Augsburgisches Wörterbuch, München, 1864, 404; J. L. Frisch, Teutsch-Lateinisches Wörterbuch, Berlin, 1741, I, 538; H. A. Gengler, Deutsche Stadtrechtsalterthümer, Erlangen, 1882, 126 ff.; von der Hagen, Gesammtabenteuer, III, cxliii f.; Matthias Lexer, Mittelhochdeutsches Wörterbuch, Leipzig, 1872–78, II, 826; E. Osenbrüggen, Studien zur deutschen und schweizerischen Rechtsgeschichte, Schaffhausen, 1868, 365; R. Quanter, Die Schand- und Ehrenstrafen in der deutschen Rechtspflege, Dresden, 1901, 114–116. General discussions are numerous, and vary greatly in value. The following I have found of use: Alsatia (1851), 37 f.; Anzeiger für Kunde des deutschen Mittelalters, n.f. X (1858), 341; Karl Ludwig von Bar, Handbuch des deutschen Strafrechts, Berlin, 1882, 103$_{423}$ (English translation, A History of Conti-

nental Criminal Law, Boston, 1916, 111 [Association of Ameri-
can Law Schools: Continental Legal History Series, VI]); H.
A. Berlepsch, Chronik vom Bäckergewerk, St. Gallen, n.d.,
106–111 [Chronik der Gewerke, VI]; 't Daghet in den Oosten,
XI (1895), 62; Hans Fehr, Das Recht im Bilde, München and
Leipzig, 1923, 109, 169–170, note 110, and plates 138 and 221;
F. Frensdorff, Die beiden ältesten Hansischen Recesse, Han-
sische Geschichtsblätter for 1871, 11–53 (especially valuable);
Otto von Gierke, Der Humor im deutschen Rechte, Leipzig,
1871, 52 ff., second ed. 1886, 69 ff.; Thüringen und der Harz,
ed. F. W. von Sydow, Sondershausen, 1844, VIII, 334–349;
K. D. Hüllmann, Städtewesen des Mittelalters, Bonn, 1829,
IV, 78–79, 277; J. A. Silbermann, Lokalgeschichte der Stadt
Strassburg, Strassburg, 1775, 172n.; G. L. von Maurer, Geschichte der Fronhöfe, Erlangen, 1862–63, IV, 269 ff., 378–379;
Montanus, Die deutschen Volksfeste, Iserlohn and Elberfeld,
1854, 82 ff.; A. Fr. Schott, Sammlungen zu den deutschen
Land- und Stadtrechten, Leipzig, 1772–75, 1–172; Paul Wigand, Wetzlar'sche Beiträge für Geschichte und Rechtsalterthümer, Wetzlar, 1840, I, 653; J. Verdam, Over eene middeleeuwsche Straf, in Handelingen en Mededeelingen van de
Maatschappij der Nederlandsche Letterkunde te Leiden over
het Jaar 1901–02, Leiden, 1902, Mededeelingen, 27–42; Karl
von Amira, Die germanischen Todesstrafen, München, 1922
[Abhandlungen der Bayerischen Akademie der Wissenschaften, Philosophisch-philologische und historische Klasse,
XXXI.Band, 3.Abhandlung].

26. Philippe A. Grandidier, Oeuvres historiques inédites,
Colmar, 1865, II, 208, but cf. Hegel, Chroniken der deutschen
Städte, IX, 928, and Frensdorff in Hansische Geschichtsblät-
ter for 1871, 11–53.

27. Livländisches Urkundenbuch, ed. Bunge, I, No. 77,
Art. 29. Frensdorff, 35, assigns this to the first quarter of the
thirteenth century.

28. Frensdorff, 33.

29. Strobel's Geschichte des Elsasses, ed. L. H. Engel-
hardt, Strassburg, 1851, I, 331, Art. 48; cf. p. 316.

30. Mecklenburgisches Urkundenbuch, Schwerin, 1866, IV, No. 2697; cf. Frensdorff, 32₅.

31. Quellen zur Geschichte der Stadt Köln, edd. L. Ennen and G. Eckertz, II, 556, No. 508. Cf. T. J. Lacomblet, Urkundenbuch für die Geschichte des Niederrheins, Düsseldorf, 1840–58, II, 591, and Frensdorff, 33.

32. Stadtbuch von Augsburg, ed. Christian Meyer, Augsburg, 1872, 52, 197; referred to also by M. von Freyberg, Sammlung teutscher Rechtsalterthümer, I, Heft 1, p. 121, and by C. G. Walch, Vermischte Beiträge zu dem deutschen Recht, Jena, 1854, part IV, p. 354. Cf. also C. G. Haltaus, Glossarium Germanicum medii aevi, Leipzig, 1758, s.v. *Korb, corbis,* and Nork [= Friedrich Korn], Sitten und Gebräuche der Deutschen, Stuttgart, 1849, 1138–40. Another inferential allusion is that in the chronicle of Ellenhard: "Anno Domini ut supra [i. e., 1298] Aug. 15 festo assumptionis beate Virginis hora matutina, cum iam quatuor essent lecte lectionis, ignis invaluit iuxta lacum, qui dicitur die Schuiphe . . ." — Monumenta Germaniae Historica, Scriptorum, XVII, ed. Pertz, Hannover, 1861, 139, lines 23–24.

33. Osenbrüggen, Studien zur deutschen . . . Rechtsgeschichte, Schaffhausen, 1868, 361–366, from Aegidius Tschudi, Chronicon Helveticum, Basel, 1734–36, I, 188. H. H. Bluntschli, Memorabilia Tigurina, oder Merkwürdigkeiten der Stadt Zürich³, Zürich, 1742, refers to this incident repeatedly: 66, 130, 285, 326, 406.

34. Regensburger Chronik, ed. K. T. Gemeiner, Regensburg, 1800, I, 463, sub anno 1306: ". . . den soll man von der Schuphen werfen in die Patzenhüll . . .;" I, 509, sub anno 1320: " . . . wenn ein Becke zu klein backe . . . er solle geschupft werden nach altem Recht . . .;" I, 519, sub anno 1321: "Diese Strafe wurde in vorhergegangenen Jahr an einem Becken in Beyseyn einer grossen zusehenden Menge vollzogen." In Holland, also, in the year 1315 "het in het water dompelen" was employed as a punishment for those who could not pay a fine assessed for blasphemy — P. C. Molhuysen, Aanteekeningen uit de Geschiedenis van het Strafregt, in Nijhoff's Bijdragen voor Vaderlandsche Geschiedenis en Oudheidkunde,

Nieuwe Reeks, daal 2, p. 81. For later examples, see pp. 82–84. Similarly, at Saarbrücken in 1321 perjury was punished by both fine and the plunge from the basket — Jacob Grimm, Weisthümer, Göttingen, 1840–78, II, 6.

35. Joseph Freiherr von Hormayr, Taschenbuch für die vaterländische Geschichte, N. F., V (1834), 233. Cf. also Nork in Scheible's Das Kloster, XII, 1139.

36. "Die pekchen sol man schuphen, als von altem fürstlichem recht, herchomen ist . . ." — Rerum Austriacarum Scriptores, ed. Rausch, Vindobona, 1744, III, 54, Jura municipalia ab Alberto II Aust. d. a. 1340. See also Karl Dietrich Hüllmann, Städtewesen des Mittelalters, Bonn, 1829, IV, 78.

37. H. A. Berlepsch, Chronik der Bäckergewerk, St. Gallen, n.d., 110$_2$. Cf. Johann Ehrenfried Böhme, Diplomatische Beiträge zur Untersuchung der Schlesischen Rechte und Geschichte, Berlin, 1770–75, II, theil 5, p. 24 [= Cap. III, Distinctio III of Codex Bregensis], but consult also Ernst T. Gaupp, Das Schlesische Landrecht, Leipzig, 1828, 12–48, 200, 292–295, 317–319, and F. Ortloff, Das Rechtsbuch nach Distinctionen nebst einem Eisenachischen Rechtsbuch, Jena, 1836, pp. xiv–xvi.

Various mediaeval cages and the like need not be considered here, as I find no record of their being used like the baskets here under inspection. Tamburlane's cage (Marlowe's Works, ed. Tucker Brooke, Oxford, 1910, pp. 47 ff., Act IV, sc. ii) is historical; cf. Jaique Dex, Metzer Chronik, ed. George Wolfram, Metz, 1906, 363. Not more closely related is Louis XI's famous cage, for which see Memoirs of Philippe de Commines, ed. Dupont, Book VI, xi = vol. II, pp. 264–265; E. Dupont, Les prisons du Mont Saint-Michel, Nantes, 1908, 20–30; J. Moisant, Le Prince Noir en Aquitaine, Paris, 1894, 84; Sir Walter Scott's Quentin Durward, London, Nimmo, 1894, I, 252–255, II, 192$_1$, 304, 313. Note also the "Kage de fort latiz de fuist et barrez et bien efforcez de fremet" in F. Palsgrave, Documents and Records illustrating the History of Scotland, London, 1837, I, 358–359. For a similar cage, see Alfred Beesley, History of Banbury, London [1841?], 223, and Ludovic Lalanne, Curiosités biographiques, Paris, 1846, 162–171.

Other examples of the basket punishment which I merely list here, as they are too late to add weight to my argument in the text, are J. A. Silbermann, Lokalgeschichte der Stadt Strassburg, Strassburg, 1775, 170 (1477), same in Jean Frederic Hermann, Notices historiques sur la ville de Strasbourg, Strassburg, 1819; Paul Wigand, Wetzlar'sche Beiträge, Wetzlar, 1840, I, 353 (1502); Thüringen und der Harz, ed. F. W. von Sydow, Sondershausen, 1844, VIII, 345 (1508), same in A. L. J. Michelsen, Rechtsdenkmale aus Thüringen, Jena, 1863, 423 f.; Lersner, Frankfurter Chronik, folio ed., Frankfurt, 1706, I, 514, chapter xxxvi (1571); Emil Herzog, Chronik der Kreisstadt Zwickau, Zwickau, 1845, II, 345, 348 (1588, 1591); A. Birlinger, Volksthümliches aus Schwaben, Freiburg i. B., 1861–62, II, 229–231, 458, 488–490 (1443); an anonymous writer in De Navorscher van 1852, Amsterdam, 1853, 185 (1485); J. B. Cannaert, Bijdragen tot de Kennis van het oude Strafregt in Vlaenderen, Gend, 1835, 520–525 (1511); Johann Kamprad, Chronik von Leisning, Leisning, 1753, 26, 436 (1530, 1593); Clemens Sender, Augsburger Chronik von 1535, a ms. quoted by Birlinger (just above), 403 (1535).

38. Codex juris Lubecensis anno 1240, ed. E. J. de Westphalen, Monumenta inedita rerum germanicarum, Leipzig, 1743, III, 639. J. H. Hach, Das alte Lübische Recht, Lübeck, 1839, codex 2, p. 252, ad ann. 1294.

In general, adultery was punished in early Germanic law by execution, by confiscation of goods, or by banishment. See Hans Bennecke, Die strafrechtliche Lehre vom Ehebruch in ihrer historisch-dogmatischen Entwickelung, Marburg, 1884; Eduard Rosenthal, Die Rechtsfolgen des Ehebruchs, Würzburg, 1880 [Jena dissertation]; F. Mitton, Les femmes et l'adultère de l'antiquité à nos jours . . ., Paris, 1911.

39. W. Moll, Kerkgeschiedenis van Nederland voor de Hervorming, Utrecht, 1869, 2de deel, 4de stuk, p. 12 (1399 and, at Haarlem, 1541; in this last instance "platste men . . . een overspeler in eene mand boven het Spaarne; hij hing der 'ten exempele' der aanschouwers, totdat hij het touw afsneed, in het water viel en zwemmende een heenkommen vond.")

40. Reinfrit von Braunschweig, ed. Karl Bartsch, Tübin-

gen, 1871, p. 443, ll. 15174–179 [Bibliothek des litterarischen Vereins in Stuttgart, CIX]. Heinrich von Meissen, "Frauenlob" (d. 1317), has a similar list of hapless lovers. See F. H. von der Hagen, Die Minnesinger, Leipzig, 1838–56, III, 355. On Heinrich see the references in Oskar Saechtig, Ueber die Bilder . . . Heinrichs von Meissen, Marburg, 1930 [dissertation].

41. Edd. G. Raynaud and H. Lemaître, 2 vv., Paris, 1914. MS. A, written 1319–22, does not contain the basket story (II, 304, and I, v–vi). Hence the date 1319 given for this basket story by Strauch in his ed. of Enikel, 463$_3$, is too early. For the story itself, see II, 71–72, ll. 29403–29492.

42. Kristoffer Nyrop, Elskeren i kurven på gammelfransk, Nordisk Tidskrift for Filologi, Ny Raekke, IV (1879–80), 272–281, printing from Copenhagen Royal Library ms. Thott 415.

43. The sole edition is that mentioned in Chapter I. The basket story is narrated in vol. I, pp. 226–239.

44. Virgilessrímur, ed. Finnur Jónsson in Rímnasafn, Samling af de ældste Islandske rimer, 14. Haefte, København, 1922, pp. 843–858. Cf. Eugen Kölbing, Beiträge zur vergleichenden Geschichte der romantischen Poesie und Prosa des Mittelalters, Breslau, 1876, 220 ff., and E. Mogk in Paul's Grundriss der Germanischen Philologie^2, Strassburg, 1901–09, II, 729.

45. See the excellent study by A. Borgeld, Aristoteles en Phyllis, Groningen, 1902, and add J. A. Herbert, Catalogue of Romances . . . in the British Museum, III (1910), p. 87, No. 53; Fr. Moth, Aristotelessagnet eller Elskovs Magt, København, 1916, who apparently did not know Borgeld's work; John L. Campion's ed. of the Middle High German versions, Modern Philology, XIII (1915–16), 347–360; J. R. Rahn, Anzeiger für schweizerisches Altertumskunde, III (1901), 58–65; Georg Polívka, Filosof jízdným koněm zeniným, in Národopisný věstník českoslovanský XVI [1923] 64–80; Katha Sarit Sagara, ed. Norman M. Penzer, London, 1924–28, II, 282, 285, 287–288, 291 f., 294–296, 299 f., VII, 230; Émile Mâle, L'art religieux du XIIIe siècle en France^6,

Paris, 1925, 337₁; Georges Huard in Mémoires de la Société des Antiquaires de Normandie, XXXV (1925–27), 4ᵉ Série, 5ᵉ Volume, deuxième fascicule, 291–292; Helga Kjellin, Aristoteles och Phyllis, ett moraliserande motiv i konsten, in Finn (1928), utgiven av Lukasgillet i Lund, Lund, 1928, 81–91, who does not mention Moth; Aarne-Thompson, The Types of the Folk-tale, Helsinki, 1928, No. 1501 [Folklore Fellows Communications 74]; Encyclopaedia Judaica, Berlin, 1929, III, 338–340; George Sarton in Isis, XIV (1930), 7–19; Raimond van Marle, Iconographie de l'art profane au Moyen-Age et à la Renaissance, II (La Haye, 1932), 492–494; George F. Black's ed. of The seuin Seages, by John Rolland, Edinburgh and London, 1932 [Scottish Text Society], pp. 395–397; Ovid turns up bridled and saddled in another poem by Rolland, The Court of Venus (1575), ed. Walter Gregor, Edinburgh and London, 1884 [Scottish Text Society] ll. 598 ff., p. 100. In 1519 Urs Graf drew the subject (Max J. Friedländer, Handzeichnungen deutscher Meister in der Herzogl. anhaltschen Behörden-Bibliothek zu Dessau, Stuttgart, 1914, plate lxiii) as did Hans Baldung Grien in 1513, and others (Eduard Fuchs and Albert Kind, Die Weiberherrschaft, 2 vv., München [1913], I, pp. 17, 35, 200 f.; II, pp. 584, 588, 598). Of some interest in connection with Aristotle's reputation, though it has nothing to do with the Phyllis story, is The Works of Aristotle the famous Philosopher, containing his complete Masterpiece and Family Physician; his experienced Midwife, his Book of Problems, and his Remarks on Physiognomy. Complete edition, with engravings, London, n.d., The Camden Publishing Company, pp. 474, which was purchased new in London in 1931. On *verso* of title-page: "The Midwife's Vademecum, containing Particular Directions for Midwives, Nurses, etc. Some Genuine Receipts for causing speedy Delivery. Approved Directions for Nurses." The work appears to be a practical manual, and sells for three shillings and sixpence. The earliest copy that I have seen was printed at London in 1750, but Arber's Term Catalogue, III, 156, lists one dated 1699.

46. Virgil is frequently mentioned in lists of humiliated or deceived lovers, such as a fourteenth-century paper manu-

script at Berne (cf. Li Livres dou Tresor par Brunetto Latini,
ed. P. Chabaille, Paris, 1863, xvi, and Catalogus codicum Ber-
nensium, ed. H. Hagen, Berne, 1874–75, 248, 293; C.-B. 328₂);
in a letter dated Oct. 15, 1371, in the Epistolario di Coluccio
Salutati, ed. F. Novati, Rome, 1891–1911, I, 150 (from Rossi,
Rassegna bibliografica della lett. ital., IV [1896], 177), cf.
Alfred von Martin, Coluccio Salutati und das humanistische
Lebensideal . . ., Leipzig and Berlin, 1916 [Beiträge zur Kulturgeschichte des Mittelalters und der Renaissance, XXIII];
Eustache Deschamps in a Ballade contre les femmes in Raynaud's ed. of Deschamps's Oeuvres, Paris, 1880–85, II, 36, No.
213, XI, 250 f. [Société des anciens textes français]; Guillaume
de Machaut in La fonteinne amoureuse in Hoeffner's ed. of
Machaut's Oeuvres, Paris, 1921, III, 207–208, ll. 1813 ff.
[Société des anciens textes français] (reference from Professor
Kittredge); Li Bastars di Buillon, ed. Auguste Scheler, Bruxelles, 1877, 209, ll. 5878–5890; John Gower, Confessio Amantis, VI, ll. 98–99, VIII, ll. 2714–17 = The Works of John Gower,
ed. C. G. Macaulay, Oxford, 1901, III, p. 169, p. 460; Pau de
Bellviure, Provençal poet writing about 1400, in D. Manuel
Milá y Fontanals, De los trovadores en España, Barcelona,
1861, 435₂ (omitted in the Obras completas of Milá y Fontanals, II, Barcelona, 1889; cf. Alfred Jeanroy in Annales du
Midi, XXVII [1916] 5). Mr. H. W. Davies refers me to Stephen Gaselee, Samuel Pepys's Spanish Books, in The Library,
fourth series, II (1922) 7₂ [= Supplement No. 2 (1921) to The
Bibliographical Society's Transactions, 11₂] where yet another
allusion is listed, and the idea is traced to Sts. Jerome and
Augustine.

47. Muratori, Rerum Italicarum scriptores², XXIV, parte
xiii, 1910. Comparetti² II, 260 ff., reprints from the older
edition of Muratori.

48. Le Croniche di Giovanni Sercambi, ed. Salvatore Bongi,
Lucca, 1892, III, 258–60, No. 301. Printed also in Scelta di
curiosità letterarie, ed. d'Ancona, CXIX, Pisa, 1871, p. 265, in
the edition of R. Rénier, Torino, 1889, No. 31, and in Novella
inedita di G. S. tratta da un ms. della pubblica libreria di
Lucca, ed. M. Pierantoni, Lucca, 1865.

49. Der Minnen loep, door Dirc Potter, ed. P. Leendertz, Leiden, 1845, I, 94–97, ll. 2515-33, 2547-98.

50. Since casual references to the basket story can show nothing save that the dissemination of it was very wide, I group several such allusions in a note.

El Cancionero de Juan Alfonso de Baena, ed. Francisque Michel, Leipzig, 1860, II, 87 (ca. 1424); Nicola Malpiglio, in a ms. written about 1440 (C.-B. 334); Martin Le Franc, Le Champion des Dames (ca. 1442), Lyons?, Guillaume le Roy, 1485?, fo. G iii verso, also printed at Paris in a poorer edition by Pierre Vidoue, 1530, fo. ciiii verso — cv recto; Aeneae Sylvii opera omnia, Basel, 1571, 627 B 12, De Euryalo et Lucretia (1444; cf. p. 50); Anonymi Chronique des Évesques de Liége, in J. R. Sinner, Catalogus codicum mss. bibliothecae bernensis, Berne, 1760, II, 149 (1455; this selection names the heroine as the daughter of Julius Caesar. This with other details makes it clear that Jean d'Outremeuse is the source); Hans Folz, Im Hanenkrat, in Heinrich Adelbert von Keller, Fastnachtspiele des 15. Jahrhunderts, Stuttgart, 1853 ⌊Bibliothek des litterarischen Vereins in Stuttgart, XXVIII–XXX], Nachlese, p. 314 (last quarter fifteenth century; other instances of Virgil's story in Keller's edition are: I, 263, No. 32, Ein Spil von Narren; II, 1039, Die X Alter Dyser Welt; II, 1471); Albrecht von Eyb, Margarita poetica (1472; E. Closson, Revue de l'université de Bruxelles, VIII [1903], 170, is wrong in inferring that von Eyb used Walter Burley's Liber de vita et moribus philosophorum as a source, as Burley does not include the story. See H. Knust's edition of Burley, Tübingen, 1886 [Bibliothek des litt. Vereins . . .], cap. CIV, p. 336); Sebastian Brant, Narrenschiff (1494; I use the reprint for the Gesellschaft der Bibliophilen, Basel, 1913, fo. ciii. This passage was not englished by Alexander Barclay; cf. A. Pompen, The English Versions of the Ship of Fools, London, 1925, 26 ff.); an unpublished Canzone morale in disprezzo d'amore (fifteenth century), C.-B. 333 (on the next page Comparetti prints a similar allusion from an undated Italian manuscript); Antonio Pucci, Contrasto delle donne, C.-B. 334; E. Celesia, Storia della letteratura in Italia ne' secoli barbari,

Genova, 1882, II, 104; Fernando de Rojas, La Celestina
(1500), ed. Julio Cejador y Frauca, Madrid, 1913, I, 245
[Clásicos Castellanos] (cf. the ed. of D. Marcelino Menéndez y
Pelayo, Vigo, 1899–1900, introduction); F. Castro Guisasola,
Observaciones sobra las fuentes literarias de "La Celestina,"
Madrid, 1924, 172 ff. [Anejos de la Revista de filología espa-
ñola, V], thinks Rojas got the story from Alfonso Martínez;
Stephen Hawes, Pastime of Pleasure (1509), ed. Wm. E. Mead,
London, 1928, ll. 3626 ff. [Early English Text Society,
CLXXIII]; Sebastian Franck, Chronica oder Zeytbuch, Strass-
burg, 1531, fo. 112 b; Cancionero de obras a burlas provo-
cantes a risa, ed. L. de Usoz y Rio, Madrid and London, 1841,
152 (1519); Pamphilus Gengenbach, Die Gouchmatt, ed. Karl
Goedeke, Hannover, 1856, ll. 931–933; cf. p. 617$_4$ (1519);
Thomas Murner, Die Gäuchmatt, ed. W. Uhl, Leipzig, 1896, ll.
4642–54; cf. ll. 5005–56 (1519); Cristóbal de Castillejos, Ser-
món de Amores (1542), in his Obras, ed. J. Domínguez Bor-
dona, Madrid, 1926, ll. 1424–46, pp. 103 f. [Clásicos Cas-
tellanos] (from J. M. Aguado, Glosario sobre Juan Ruiz, 630);
Diego Martínez, printed in El Cancionero de Juan Alfonso de
Baena, ed. F. Michel, Leipzig, 1860, II, 29 (first quarter sixteenth century); the anonymous Padiglione di Carlomagno,
C.-B. 333; an anonymous Sermon joyeux, imprimé nouvelle-
ment à Lyon en la maison de feu Barnabé Chaussard . . . , n.d.,
reprinted in Ancien théâtre français, ed. Viollet le Duc, Paris,
1854–57, II, 207–22 (from Deutsche Volkslieder aus Ober-
hessen, ed. Otto Böckel, Marburg, 1885, p. cxxxix). C.-B.
332$_{21}$ lists two other casual allusions by Francesco Berni and
Pietro Aretino.

5'1. Oeuvres complètes du roi René, ed. M. le Comte de
Quatrebarbes . . . , 4 vv., Angers, 1846, III, pp. 149–151; René
duc d'Anjou, Le livre du cuer d'amours espris, texte et miniatures publiés et commentés par O. Smital et E. Winkler, 3 vv.,
Vienne, 1927, II, pp. 127 ff. [Bibliothèque Nationale de
Vienne]. The third volume of remarkably beautiful reproductions of miniatures in color is worth seeing. The discovery of
the trophies of love is illustrated in ms. B. N. fonds fr. 24399,
fo. 105, r°, reproduced as Figure 12, volume I.

52. M. Casteleyn, Conste van Rhetoriken, Rotterdam, 1612, 122 (a reprint of the edition printed at Ghent, 1555). Professor Dr. E. Hoffmann-Krayer referred me to J. E. Gillet, Virgilius in de Mande, Volkskunde, XXIII (1912), 116 f., from which I derived references to Casteleyn, Houwaert, and Fokkens.

53. J. B. Houwaert, Den Handel der Amoureusheyt, begrepen in drij Boecken / indhoudende drij excellente / constighe / soetbloyende / Poetische spelen van sinnen / van Jupiter en Yo / met drij behaegelijke ende belachelijcke Dialogen . . ., Bruessels, Jan van Brecht, 1583; same author, Pegasides Pleyn, Leiden, 1611, pp. 182, 756; Delft, 1622, pp. 192, 768.

54. I use the reprint by P. H. van Moerkerken, Het Nederlandsch Kluchtspel in de 17de Eeuw, Sneek, 1898, 355–365, No. 49. The reference I found in A. Borgeld, Aristoteles en Phyllis, Groningen, 1902, 1$_1$.

55. Melchior Fokkens, Het Klucht van de verliefde Grysert, gespeelt op d'Amsterdamsche Schouwburg, 't Amsterdam, 1659.

56. This story is accessible to me only in the German translation of Johann Wilhelm Wolf, Niederländische Sagen, Leipzig, 1843, No. 407, Das erloschene Feuer zu Audenaerde, who says it was first printed as "mündlich, von J. Ketel im Feuilleton der Gazette von Audenaerde." Eugen Schmitz, Richard Strauss als Musikdramatiker, München, 1907, reprints from Wolf.

57. Feuersnot. Ein Singgedicht in einem Akt von Ernst von Wolzogen. Musik von Richard Strauss, Berlin, 1901, vollständiger Klavierauszug zu zwei Händen. For comments on the first performance, see Illustrierte Zeitung, No. 3048, p. 815 (Nov. 28, 1901). H. T. Finck, Richard Strauss, the Man and his Work, Boston, 1917, 227–234, discusses the opera entertainingly. The best treatment of the background is E. Closson, Les origines légendaires de Feuersnot, Revue de l'université de Bruxelles, VIII (1903), 161–179, 382–383. The author does not seem to know Comparetti's book.

58. Jean de Marconville, De la bonté et mauvaistié des femmes, I. Dallier, Paris, 1566, 74. Probably the eighteenth-

century paper ms. "Monologue de l'amoureux qui en poursui-
vant ses amours demoura trois heures pendu à une fenestre
pendu par les bras, et enfin se coucha dedans ung baing cuidant
se coucher en une couchette" should be listed here; cf. [Jules
Gay] Bibliographie des ouvrages relatifs à l'amour, aux
femmes, au mariage, et des livres facétieux[4], par M. le Cte.
d'I, Paris, 1894–1900, V, 115.

59. Charles Desmaze, M.-Q. de la Tour, peintre du Roi
Louis XV, Saint Quentin, 1853, 47–48, reprinted, Paris, 1854.
See the anonymous review in L'Athenéum Français for 1853,
p. 1078, which is wrong in inferring that the fabliau Le chevalier à la corbeille is the ultimate source of this tale, as will
appear later when that fabliau is discussed.

60. Reference from V. Rossi, Rassegna bibliografica della
letteratura italiana, IV (1896), 177. The play, I Vecchi scher-
niti per amore, is reported by Adolfo Bartoli, Scenari inediti
della Commedia dell' Arte, Firenze, 1880, p. xlvi [Raccolta di
Opere inedite o rare di ogni secolo della letteratura italiana].

61. Chants et chansons recueillis et classés par Achille
Millien, 3 vv., Paris, 1906–10 [Littérature orale et traditions
du Nivernais . . .], III, 100 ff., Le tailleur suspendu, III, 103,
Le cordonnier suspendu (with melodies). This I owe to William Powell Jones, The Pastourelle, Cambridge [Mass.], 129[4].

62. M. le Comte de Puymaigre, Chants populaires recueillis
dans le pays Messin, Paris, 1865, I, 151; second edition, Paris,
1881, I, 189, with notes, 193. The form in which the song appears is obviously the effort of a skilled versifier. Twelve-line
stanzas with a complicated rhyme-scheme do not savor of the
folk; but this cannot alter the fact that ancient tradition is
probably behind the song.

63. Gedenkbuch des Philippe de Vigneulles aus den Jahren
1471 bis 1522, ed. Heinrich Michelant, Stuttgart, 1852, 201
[Bibliothek des litterarischen Vereins in Stuttgart, XXIV].

64. Anatole France, L'île des pingouins, Book III, chapter VI.

65. Raccolta di novellieri italiani, Firenze, 1834, II, 1162–
68, also in Novelle di autori senesi, London, 1796, I, 257–259.
Cf. J. Ulrich, Ein Beitrag zur Geschichte der italienischen

Novella, in Festschrift der Universität Zürich zur Begrüssung
der 39. Versammlung deutscher Philologen und Schulmänner,
Zürich, 1887, p. 85 (Ulrich numbers this novella "G 28").

66. I have seen only the edition "di nuovo revista e cor-
retta" published at Trevigi, 1600. The reference I owe to V.
Rossi, Rassegna bibliografica . . ., IV (1896), 177. On Calmo,
see the same author's Le Lettere di M. Andrea Calmo, Torino, 1888, and Joseph S. Kennard, The Italian Theatre, 2 vv.,
New York, 1932, I, 173 f.

67. A. de Nino, Ovidio nella tradizioni populari di Sulmona,
Casalbordino, 1886, 38 ff. This district is in Austria, roughly
between Gratz and Marburg.

68. Felix Liebrecht, Zur Volkskunde, Heilbronn, 1879, 86,
from a history of the world by Dorotheos, Metropolitan of
Malvasia. Liebrecht used the Venice, 1763, edition; accessible to me is the one published at Venice in 1750, where the
tale is to be found on p. 364: Βιβλίον Ἱστορικὸν περιέχον ἐν
συνόψει διαφόρους καὶ ἀξιακούστους ἱστορίας . . . Συλλεχθὲν
. . . παρὰ τοῦ Ἱερωτάτου Μητροπολίτου Μονεμβασίας κυρίου
Δωροθέου.

69. Adolf Strauss, Die Bulgaren, Leipzig, 1898, 306; also
Lydia Shischmanoff, Légendes religieuses bulgares, Paris,
1896, 82, No. 42, but see the reviews in Revue des traditions
populaires, XII (1897), 503, and Volkskunde, XIII (1902),
155.

70. A. L. Stiefel, Quellen . . . des Hans Sachs, in Studien
zur vergleichenden Literaturgeschichte II (1902), 180 ff.
Sämmtliche Fabeln und Schwänke von Hans Sachs, edd. E.
Goetze and Carl Drescher, V, 146, No. 697 [Neudrucke deutscher Litteraturwerke des XVI. und XVII. Jahrhunderts, Nos.
207–211, Halle a.S., 1904], and II, 224, No. 264 [Neudrucke
. . ., Nos. 126–134, 1894]. I am inclined to give Franck a
little more of the credit than does Stiefel, because of the similarity of the moral in each.

71. Sämmtliche Fabeln . . ., edd. Goetze and Drescher, V,
322, No. 8 [Neudrucke . . ., Nos. 207–211, 1904].

72. Same volume as the preceding, p. 346, No. 815. An
earlier edition of Sachs gives this essay on penalties in a dif-

ferent form. It is even more realistic than the one here referred to. Again the poet seems to have forgotten previous
activity, for the version here analyzed is dated "Anno salutis
1552, am 19 tag Septembris," while the other (printed in
Hans Sachs, eine Auswahl für Freunde der alten vaterländ-
ischen Dichtkunst, 4 vv., Nürnberg, 1829 ff., IV, 3, No. 96b,
a reprint of the Nürnberg, 1558–79, edition in five volumes)
is dated "Anno salutis MD.LXIII am. 17. Junij."

73. The other two punishments in *Dreyerley straff* do not
concern us.

74. See K. F. W. Wander, Deutsche Sprichwörterlexikon,
Leipzig, 1867–80, II, col. 1538, s.v. Korb 27; the Deutsches
Wörterbuch s.v. Korb; Friedrich Seiler, Deutsche Sprich-
wörterkunde, München, 1922, 119 f.; Sartori, Sitte und
Brauch, Leipzig, 1914, III, 272; Osenbrüggen, Die deutschen
Rechtssprichwörter, in Öffentliche Vorträge gehalten in der
Schweiz, III, Heft ix, Basel, 1876; Archer Taylor, The Prov-
erb, Cambridge [Mass.], 1931, 197.

75. Sämmtliche Fabeln . . ., ed. Goetze, II, 554, No. 356
[Neudrucke . . ., Nos. 126–134, 1894]; also in the edition by
Adelbert von Keller and E. Goetze, Tübingen, 1892, pp. 21,
259 [Bibliothek des litterarischen Vereins in Stuttgart,
CXCV].

76. Some instances of skimmingtons are collected by Ruth
A. Firor, Folkways in Thomas Hardy, Philadelphia, 1931,
238–242.

77. This piece will be found in the Keller-Goetze edition,
Tübingen, 1892, p. 262. Cf. A. L. Stiefel, Hans Sachs-Forsch-
ungen, Nürnberg, 1894, 182. A brief reference to Virgil and
the basket is in K. A. Barack, Zimmerische Chronik², Freiburg i. B. and Tübingen, 1882, IV, 229 (first ed., IV, 327). The
date is 1554–67. One of the sources which the author says he
used is Aeneas Sylvius, whose use of our episode in 1444 I have
noticed above. Again, a paper ms. at Karlsruhe (No. 437),
dated "after 1559," refers to the episode — Wilhelm Meyer,
Nürnberger Faustgeschichten, 380 [Abhandlungen der Kö-
niglichen Bayerischen Akademie der Wissenschaften, philosophisch-philologische Classe, XX (1897)]; cf. Theodor Läng-

in, Deutsche Handschriften der Hof- und Landesbibliothek in Karlsruhe, Karlsruhe, 1894, 110, No. 287.

78. F. D. Gräter, Bragur, Leipzig, 1802, VII, 2, p. 93, which says that the song is derived from a fifteenth- or sixteenth-century ms.; Ludwig Uhland, Alte hoch- und niederdeutsche Volkslieder, Stuttgart and Tübingen, 1845, II, 745, No. 288, Der Schreiber im Korb; Arnim and Brentano, Des Knaben Wunderhorn, Heidelberg and Frankfurt, 1806–08, I, 53, Heinriche Konrade der Schreiber im Korb; Birlinger and Crecelius's edition of same, Wiesbaden, 1874, I, 49, notes I, 517 (cf. Karl Bode, Die Bearbeitung der Vorlagen in Des Knaben Wunderhorn, Berlin, 1909, 398 [Palaestra, LXXVI]); the Frankfurt Liederbuch of 1535, Grassliedlein, has a similar song, on which and for general discussion see L. Erk and F. H. Böhme, Deutscher Liederhort, Leipzig, 1893, I, 476–477, No. 144, Der Schreiber im Korb, taken in large part from Uhland's Schriften zur Geschichte der Dichtung und Sage, Stuttgart, 1869, IV, 253–254; cf. G. E. Benseler, Geschichte von Freiberg, Freiberg, 1846, I, 585, and Theatri Freibergensis Chronici, pars posterior, Beschreibung der alten löblichen Bergk Haupt Stadt Freyberg in Meissen, Ander Buch, von Andr. Mollero, Freybergk, 1653, p. 156: "Den 3. April [anno 1510] hat sich ein grosser Aufruhr unter der Clerisey und etlichen Bergleuten zu Freybergk wegen des Liedleins / Johannis im Korbe / erhoben / darüber so wol dieses als folgendes Jahr unterschiedene Todschläge geschehen / und der Lerm von der Obrigkeit kaum können gestillet werden." For other occurrences see, e. g., Otto Böckel, Handbuch des deutschen Volksliedes, Marburg, 1908, 346–347; Carl Köhler and John Meier, Volkslieder von der Mosel und Saar, Halle a.S., 1896, I, 206, No. 199, "Angeführt," with notes, p. 422.

79. Ulrich von Lichtensteins Frauendienst, ed. R. Bechstein, Leipzig, 1888, stanzas 1197 ff. (ii. Teil, p. 61); cf. p. xii, and stanza 1845, line 2, p. 320. On the use of the rope, see J. Bolte, Der Jungfrauen Narrenseil, Zeitschrift des Vereins für Volkskunde, XIX (1909), 56–57.

80. Arthur Kopp, Das Fuchsrittlied und seine Verzweigungen, Zeitschrift des Vereins für Volkskunde, XIV (1904),

64–65. Similar is Goethe's ballad Vom braun Annel: Ephemerides und Volkslieder, ed. E. Martin, Heilbronn, 1883, 46–47, also in Weimar edition of Goethe's works, XXXVIII, 252, No. 10; cf. Des Knaben Wunderhorn, edd. Birlinger and Crecelius, II, 119 f. That the song is genuinely popular is proved by K. Stückrath and J. Bolte in Zeitschrift des Vereins für Volkskunde, XXV (1915), 282, No. 1. Additional notes will be found in Sister Mary Coronata's Parallels to Goethe's "Elsässische Volkslieder," Journal of American Folk-Lore, XLIV (1931), 52. Yet another song belonging to this general cycle is in Curt Mündel, Elsässische Volkslieder, Strassburg, 1884, 103–104, No. 97.

81. Valentin Schumanns Nachtbüchlein (1559), ed. Johannes Bolte, Tübingen, 1893 [Bibliothek des litterarischen Vereins, CXCVII], 63–67, No. 20, Ein geschicht von einem jungen münch und eines bawren weib, notes 395–396, 416. It is the source of Jakob Ayrer's drama of 1598, Der Münch im Kesskorb (Jakob Ayrers Dramen, ed. Heinrich Adelbert von Keller, Stuttgart, 1865, V, 3093 ff.). Schumann's source in turn is Der münich im keskorb, by Hans Sachs (Sämmtliche Fabeln und Schwänke von H. S., edd. Goetze and Drescher, III, 91–93, No. 30 [Neudrucke . . ., 1900, Nos. 164–169].

82. The Historie of Frier Rush is to be found, e. g. in vol. I of W. J. Thoms's Early English Prose Romances, London, 1828, 1856, reprinted in one volume by Routledge, London, 1907. On the story, see F. W. Chandler, The Literature of Roguery, London, 1907, I, 56–62; H. Grimm, Deutsche Sagen, Berlin, 1891, 50–53; G. L. Kittredge, The Friar's Lantern and Friar Rush, Publications of the Modern Language Association, XV (1900), 415–417; Ellen Jørgensen, Djævelen i Vitskøl Kloster, Danske Studier for 1912–13, pp. 15–17; Robert Priebsch, Bruder Rausch, Zwickau, 1919 [Zwickauer Facsimile-drucke No. 28]; George L. Kittredge, Witchcraft in Old and New England, 1928, chapter XIII.

83. Karl Simrock, Ein kurzweilig Lesen von Till Eulenspiegel, "neunte Historie," p. 11 [Die Deutschen Volksbücher, Frankfurt a.M., 1834 ff.]; for Skelton, W. C. Hazlitt, Early Popular Poetry, London, 1895, IV, 127–128.

84. Emblemata nobilitati et vulgo scitu digna singulis historijs symbola adscripta . . . in aes incisa à Theodoro de Bry . . ., Francoforti ad Moenum, 1593, No. xii, p. 27. This reference I owe to Mr. Hugh W. Davies, the learned editor of the Murray Library Catalogues. A reprint of this edition was edited by Friedrich Warnecke, Berlin, 1894 (Paris, 1895).

85. Langbein's Sämmtliche Schriften, Stuttgart, 1835, III, 120, Der Korb. See H. Jess, A. F. Langbein und seine Verserzählungen, Berlin, 1902, 48 [Forschungen zur neueren Litteraturgeschichte, XXI].

86. F. J. Child, English and Scottish Popular Ballads, Boston and New York, 1882-98, V, No. 281. All versions there listed were collected during the nineteenth century. Certain of them were sung in America in the twentieth century; see British Ballads from Maine, edd. Phillips Barry et al., New Haven, 1929, 336-339.

87. Le chevalier à la corbeille, in Recueil général des fabliaux, edd. A. de Montaiglon and G. Raynaud, Paris, 1872-90, II, 183-192, No. 47; also printed separately by F. Michel, Gautier d'Aupais, Paris, 1835, 35-44. The action is closer to that in the ballad in the two other analogues listed by Child. To these may be added Rüdiger von Muner's Irregang und Girregar, in Gesammtabenteuer, ed. F. H. von der Hagen, Stuttgart and Tübingen, 1850, III, 36-82, No. 55. In his doctoral dissertation, Joseph Bédier declares that there is no relationship between the Chevalier à la corbeille and the Virgil-basket story, without adducing any evidence; see Les Fabliaux [5], Paris, 1925, 452. Indeed, there may be none, but a mere statement does not help to dispose of the matter. Possibly Gustav Gröber was on the right track when he suggested a relationship between this fabliau and the basket journey in Floire and Blanceflor (Grundriss der romanischen Philologie, Strassburg, 1888-1902, I, 619). For the passage in John Rolland's The Court of Venus, see the edition of Walter Gregor, Edinburgh and London, 1884 [Scottish Text Society], Book iii, ll. 586 ff., pp. 99-100. Cf. also Rolland's version of The seuin Seages (1578), ed. George F. Black, Edinburgh and London, 1932 [Scottish Text Society], ll. 2637 ff., p. 88.

88. Ernst Schulz, Englische Schwankbücher bis 1607, Berlin, 1912, 123, notes 215 ff. [Palaestra, CXVII]. The Whole Life and Death of Long Meg of Westminster, a chapbook popular for three centuries, of which the earliest edition is dated 1582 (reprinted repeatedly during the seventeenth and eighteenth centuries; most recently by Charles Hindley, The Old Book Collector's Miscellany, London, 1872, II, and by John Ashton, Chap-Books of the Eighteenth Century, London, 1882, 323–336), tells of Meg's beating a miller and pulling him up in a sack, to leave him suspended. In The Widdowes Teares (1612) George Chapman alludes directly to Virgil in the basket (Works, ed. Pearson, London, 1773, vol. III, pp. 7, 20, Act I).

89. The Works of Thomas Deloney, ed. Francis O. Mann, Oxford, 1912, 549. Thomas of Reading is also reprinted in Thoms, Early English Prose Romances. The jig only is quoted by Charles Read Baskervill, The Elizabethan Jig, Chicago, 1929, 202.

90. Hazlitt-Dodsley, A Select Collection of Old English Plays, London, 1875, X, 469 ff. C. R. Baskervill, The Elizabethan Jig, Chicago, 1929, 333, asserts that this incident is "drawn from the folk book *Vergilius*." I am very doubtful of this, as the step is long; moreover, the similarity with the trick in Harlequins Hochzeit (J. Bolte, Die Singspiele der englischen Komödianten . . ., Hamburg and Leipzig, 1893 [Theatergeschichtliche Forschungen, VII], 156), in which Harlequin tries to enter his lady-love's window and is left hanging when the ladder is removed, is not close. Stories were told all over Europe from the Middle Ages on concerning lovers and others hidden in tubs, vats, chests, or anything else handy in a moment of emergency; but they cannot in general be regarded as true analogues of the basket tale because of their wide divagations from the type as I understand it. On the general theme, see J. Bolte and G. Polívka, Anmerkungen zu den Kinder- und Hausmärchen der Brüder Grimm, Leipzig, 1913 ff., II, 373 ff.; Luzel, Soniou Breiz-Izel, Paris, 1890, II, 199; W. Stehmann, Die mittelhochdeutsche Novelle vom Studentenabenteuer, Berlin, 1909 [Palaestra, LXVII], 114 ff.; A. C. Lee, The Decameron, London, 1909, 152 ff.

91. The Dramatic Works of John Lacy, Comedian, Edinburgh and London, 1875, pp. 71, 75, 112 (IV, i, V, i). R. Ohnsorg, John Lacy's "Dumb Lady," Mrs. Susanna Centlivre's "Love's Contrivance" und Henry Fielding's "Mock Doctor" in ihrem Verhältniss zu einander und zu ihrer gemeinschaftlichen Quellen, Hamburg, 1900, and A. Warnicke, Das Verhältniss von John Lacy's "The Dumb Lady" zu Molière's "Le médecin malgré lui" und "L'amour médecin," Halle, 1903, know nothing as to the source of Softhead's elevation. On the Miller's Tale see Aarne-Thompson, Types of the Folk-tale, Helsinki, 1928, No. 1361 [Folklore Fellows Communications 74].

92. I use the London (1750?) issue, which was reprinted a half-dozen times in the next three-quarters of a century. The ballad with a similar title [Roxburghe Ballads, III, 406, British Museum], London (1710?), does not include this episode. John Ashton, Chap-Books of the Eighteenth Century, London, 1882, 258–262, includes a brief analysis.

93. The History of Thomas of Reading, London, n.d., p. 12 [British Museum pressmark: 1079. i. 15 (4)]. It is omitted from Ashton's List of Chap-Books published in Aldermary and Bow Churchyards, pp. 483–486. The corresponding woodcut will be found on p. 8 (misnumbered 3) of the (1750?) edition of Simple Simon's Misfortunes [British Museum pressmark: 1079. i. 15 (9)]. It is reproduced by Ashton, p. 259.

CHAPTER VI

1. On the revenge, see C.-B. 327, 329–330, 350 f.; Tunison, 138 f., 149 f.; Graf, Roma ... (1923), 560 f. The following, for which complete references will be found through the index, narrate the revenge story: Image du Monde (ca. 1245), Enikel (ca. 1280), "Nero's Daughter" (thirteenth century), Renart le Contrefait (1328–42), Juan Ruiz (ca. 1343), Pucci (ca. 1350), Coluccio Salutati (1371), Bertrand du Guesclin (by Cuvelier; fourteenth century), Jean d'Outremeuse (ca. 1400), Sercambi (1400), Dirc Potter (shortly after 1412), Aliprandi (ca. 1414), Alfonso Martínez (1438), Anonymi Chronique des evesques de Liège (1455; from Jean d'Outremeuse), the Ger-

man Mirabilia urbis Romae (1471–84), Albrecht von Eyb
(1472), Stephen Hawes (1509), Sebastian Franck (1531), Les
faictz merveilleux de Virgille (first quarter sixteenth century),
Von Virgilio dem Zauberer (ca. 1520?), The Deceyte of
Women (ca. 1550?), Hans Sachs (ca. 1550–63), Theodor de
Bry (1597). A parody on the revenge, with the sexes re-
versed and no mention of Virgil, is to be found in Die X alter
dyser welt, printed at Basel in 1587 (Heinrich Adelbert von
Keller, Fastnachtspiele aus dem fünfzehnten Jahrhundert,
Stuttgart, 1853, 100, No. 119 [Bibliothek des litt. Vereins in
Stuttgart, XXVIII]. The revenge story is also told with
Pietro Barliario, a legendary figure of perhaps the seventeenth
century, as the magician. See the long note in Comp.², II,
126₄, omitted in Benecke's translation, and add A. d'Ancona,
Saggio di una Bibliografia ragionata della Poesia popolare
Italiana, in Bausteine zur romanischen Philologie, Festgabe
für Adolfo Mussafia, Halle a.S., 1905, 140–142, and Giovanni
Pansa, Miti, leggende e superstizioni dell' Abruzzi, Sulmona,
1924–27, II, 278–284. Comparetti seems to ignore the content of d'Ancona's remarks in Varietà storiche e letterarie,
prima serie, Milano, 1883, 15–38, although he lists his work in
the note above mentioned.

2. "Utique, ait magus [Heliodorus, in answer to the emperor's inquiry]. Et si quidem me adversus iniuriam istam
publice vindicaveritis, faciam ex ea ignis erumpat; alioqui
enim ignem visuri non estis." — The Bollandist Acta Sanctorum, February, III, 225 (Amsterdam, 1658). Cf. Liebrecht
in Germania, III (1856), 267, and J. Scheible, Das Kloster,
Stuttgart, 1847, V, 372 f. Comparetti cites two parallels collected by Liebrecht, but while we have a magician extinguishing fires and rekindling them only after his enemy has accomplished a humiliating act, the similarity stops there, as the
acts are not the same, and neither woman nor love is concerned. G. W. Freytag, Arabum proverbia, Bonn, 1839, II,
445, No. 124, "Occurit podici caniculae," tells it thus: "Nar-
rant, regem quendam Edessae extinctis ignibus imperasse,
ut homines ignem ad podicum caniculae mortuae accenderent.
Hanc autem ob causam homines emigrasse." A somewhat

similar episode is recounted in Journal Asiatique, 4ᵉ série, XIX (1852), 85; cf. Liebrecht in Germania, X (1865), 414, and René Basset in Revue des traditions populaires, XII (1897), 185. A vague parallel is in Isaiah, iii, 16–17.

3. Felix Liebrecht, Zur Volkskunde, Heilbronn, 1879, 86 f.

4. V. Jagić, Aus dem südslavischen Märchenschatz, in Archiv für slavische Philologie, I (1876), 287, No. 213, "Der Meister und der Geselle." The notes by Reinhold Köhler are reprinted in the latter's Kleinere Schriften, ed. Johannes Bolte, Weimar, 1898, I, 417. Through the kindness of Professor Walter Anderson, of Dorpat, Esthonia, I learn of another variant which appears in a collection of folk-tales about Avicenna printed in the nineteenth century at Kazan. Avicenna is a magician who becomes incensed at an old woman who thwarts him. He extinguishes all fires, and they may be rekindled only as in the Virgilian legend. — N. Katanov, Materialy k izučeniju kazanso-tatarskago narěčija [Materialien zum Studium des kasan-tatarischen Dialekts], II, in Učonyja Zapiski Imperatorskago Karzanskago Universiteta, LXVI (1899), kn. 5/6, pp. 14–28, No. 7. For the text, see same journal, LXV (1898), kn. 7/8, pp. 47–61, with transcription, pp. 61–73, from Abû 'Alî Sînâ qₙysasy, ed. Abdu-l-Kajum Nasyrov, University of Kazan, 1881, 82–95. On Avicenna, see George Sarton, Introduction to the History of Science, I (1927), 709–713.

5. A. A. Macdonnell, The Brhad-Devata, A Summary of the Deities and Myths of the Rig-Veda, Cambridge [Mass.], 1904, II, 170–171, verses 14–22 [Harvard Oriental Series, ed. C. R. Lanman, VI]. Cf. E. Sieg, Die Sagenstoffe des Rgveda, Stuttgart, 1902, I, 67 f., with variant readings, and, for a discussion of the whole matter, 64 ff. Other commentators listed by Macdonnell throw little light on this passage. See the learned note by Hanns Oertel, Altindische Parallelen zu abendländischen Erzählungsmotiven, in Studien zur vergleichenden Literaturgeschichte, VIII (1908), 113. The passage which he cites from Roger of Hoveden's Chronicle, ed. W. Stubbs, London, 1871, IV, 171, I cannot admit as genuinely parallel: "Miraculum. Item in Lincolniaesiria para-

verat quaedam mulier pastam, quam deferens ad furnum post horam nonam sabbati, misit eam in furnum calidissimum, et cum eam extraheret, invenit crudam; et iterum misit eam in furnum valde calidum, et in crastino, et in die Lunae, cum aestimaret se invenisse panes coctos, invenit pastam crudam."

6. P. Saintyves (pseudonym for Émile Nourry), Le feu qui descend du ciel et le renouvelle ment du feu sacré, in Revue des traditions populaires, XXVII (1912), 449–473, XXVIII (1913), 1–18 [= Essais de folklore biblique, Paris, 1922, 1–58, which I use; the passage summarized appears on pp. 10 f.].

7. I summarize here in part from the special study of Georges Dumézil, Le crime des Lemniennes, Paris, 1924, 13–21; cf. especially p. 27, and Saintyves, Essais . . ., 31. See in addition the large collection of materials in [Sir] James G. Frazer, Balder the Beautiful, London, 1913, I, chap. IV, "The Fire-Festivals of Europe," 106–327, esp. 126 ff., 341 ff. [= The Golden Bough,³ Part VII], and in Hwb. d. d. Abergl. s.vv. Fackel, Feuer, Feuerweihe. A. H. Krappe, The Science of Folk-Lore, London, 1930, 281, indicates that he interprets the Virgilian story as I do; presumably F. H. von der Hagen did also many years ago (Gesammtabenteuer, III, p. cxlii₂, Stuttgart and Tübingen, 1850). H. Freudenthal, Das Feuer im deutschen Glauben, Leipzig, 1931, I have not seen.

8. Ly Myreur des Histors, I, 252. The words are: "Là prist de feu qui le voloit avoir, dont le peuple at fait si grant fieste en disant que oncques à teile lieu ne vinrent prendre le feu." On Gregory IX's decretal, see Hwb. d. d. Abergl., s.v. Fackel; Saintyves, Essais . . ., 15; Frazer, Balder the Beautiful, I, 126 f.

9. In Raoul de Cambrai, edd. Paul Meyer and A. Longnon, Paris, 1882, ll. 6859 f. [Société des anciens textes français], and in Orson de Beauvais, ed. Gaston Paris, Paris, 1889, ll. 580 ff. [Société des anciens textes français], herbs are used to inspire love in the objects of the lovers' affections — Adolf Hertel, Verzauberte Örtlichkeiten . . . in der altfranzösischen erzählenden Dichtung, Hannover, 1908 [diss. Göttingen], 45.

10. In the versions edited by de Lincy, p. 24, and by Plomp, p. 24 (see note 31, Chapter I).

CHAPTER VII

1. This, the earliest version of the Virgil-bocca story, was first printed by Karl Bartsch in Germania, IV (1859), 237–239. It was reprinted by Comp.[2] II, 241–245. On the bocca, see C.-B. 337 ff., 363, 365; Tunison, 144–146; Schambach, Vergil ein Faust des Mittelalters, I, 30, II, 26; Graf, Roma . . . (1923), 478, 554. Special studies: Novelle del "Mambriano" del Cieco da Ferrara [= Giuseppe Gioachino Belli] esposte ed illustrate da Giuseppe Rua, Torino, 1888, 79–82; Ersilia Caetani-Lovatelli, La Bocca della Verità in Roma e la sua leggenda nell' età di mezzo, in Miscellanea archeologica, Roma, 1891, 269–282 (reprinted from Nuova antologia, terza serie, XXXIII [1891], 152–159, which I use); Johann Jakob Meyer, Isoldes Gottesurteil in seiner erotischen Bedeutung, Berlin, 1914 [Neue Studien zur Geschichte des menschlichen Geschlechtslebens, II], esp. 93 ff.; Alexander H. Krappe, La leggenda della "bocca della verità," in Nuovi studi medievali, II (1925), 1–6. The best collection of references is in Johannes Bolte's edition of Pauli's Schimpf und Ernst, 2 vv., Berlin, 1924, No. 206, p. 309.

2. On the equivocal oath as a type of story, see G. Rua's edition of the Mambriano of Cieco da Ferrara, as above; Gertrude Schoepperle, Tristan and Isolt, Frankfurt and London, 1913, 223 ff. [Ottendorfer Memorial Series of Germanic Monographs 3]; Johann Jakob Meyer, Isoldes Gottesurteil . . ., 93 ff. [see the convenient table, p. 216. I have found Meyer's full analyses very helpful]; Wilhelm Golther's review of the two preceding in Deutsche Literaturzeitung, XXXV (1914), 669–674; Bolte's Pauli, as above, II, 309, second part of note. To illustrate: waters of Styx recoil before swearer of truthful oath, rise if oath is untruthful (Erwin Rohde, Der griechische Roman . . . [3], Leipzig, 1914, 515 ff.); ordeal of fire (The Jātaka or Stories of the Buddha's former Births, ed. E. B. Cowell, I, trans. Robert Chalmers, Cambridge, 1895, 154, No. 63, and the Thomas Tristan, ed. Joseph Bédier, 2 vv., Paris, 1902–05, I, 203 ff., chap. XXIV [Société des anciens textes français]); oath taken on sacred relics or magic stone (Tavola

ritonda version of Tristan, ed. F. L. Polidori, Bologna, 1864–
66, I, 237–240, reprinted by Bédier as above, I, 213–216, and
analyzed by Meyer, 106; see Meyer, 109, for a close Arabian
parallel); barley-seeds hop if oath is false (B. Jülg, Mongo-
lische Märchen, Innsbruck, 1868, 250; cf. Meyer, 205); water
of fountain retains or releases hand of swearer (Joannes de
Bromyard, Summa praedicantium, Venezia, 1586, prima pars,
p. 45, s.v. Adulterium, cap. XVIII; cf. Acta Sanctorum, May
11 [= vol. II for May, p. 645A], and Bolte's Pauli as above,
II, 314, on No. 224); St. Gangolph thwarts truth-telling idol by
giving woman a bit of his clothing to wear (second half of
thirteenth century; Raymond Feraudi de Thoard, Die Vita
Sancti Honorati . . ., ed. Bernhard Munke [Beihefte zur Zeitschrift für romanische Philologie, XXXII, 1911]; cf. Wilhelm
Schäfer, Das Verhältnis von Raimon Ferauts Gedicht La vida
de Sant Honorat zu der Vita Sancti Honorati [diss.], Halle
a. S., 1911, 2, 25 ff.); if oath on stone be false, lion nearby de-
vours swearer (second half fifteenth century; Cieco da Ferrara, ed. Rua, as above, 73 ff.); mountain swallows up perjurers (1899; Leo Reinisch, Die Somali-Sprache, Wien, 1900,
I, 57 [Kaiserliche Akad. der Wiss., Südarabische Expedi-
tion]); chain in mosque clamps on hand of perjurer (ca. 1908;
Johannes Hertel in Zeitschrift des Vereins für Volkskunde,
XVIII [1908], 66, 160, 379 ff.); perjurers die on swearing
falsely at mountain (René Basset, Mille et un contes, Paris,
1926, II, 3–5). For chastity-tests in general, see J. Bédier,
Les Fabliaux[4], Paris, 1925, 120; Tom Peete Cross, Modern
Philology, X (1912–13), 289–299; J. D. Bruce, Evolution of
Arthurian Romance, I, 34, 301, and Penzer, Ocean of Story,
s.v. Act of Truth. Cf. Numbers, v, 27–28.

3. É. Du Méril, Mélanges archéologiques . . ., Paris, 1850,
444.

4. Felix Hemmerlin, Opuscula [Strassburg, 1497], fol. dd
iiia. I have not seen the edition of 1498. A sixteenth-century
German song mentions the bocca and adds that a horn
sprouted on the forehead of an adulterous wife's husband until
the test was carried out. The ruse was accomplished and the
image broke into pieces — Liederbuch aus dem sechzehnten

Jahrhundert, edd. Karl Goedeke and Julius Tittmann, Leipzig, 1867, 355, "Von einer Kaiserin." Johannes Bolte, Zeitschrift des Vereins für Volkskunde, XIX (1909), 66, regards this as an elaboration of the poet's own. For another version of the same, see Otto Stückrath, in the same journal, XXII (1912), 278–284. Both of these would seem to be derived pretty directly from the fourteenth-century anonymous German song already summarized.

5. Bolte's edition of Pauli, Berlin, 1924, I, No. 206, "Ein Keiserin stiess ir Hand in das Maul Vergilii," pp. 130 f., with full notes which should be consulted, II, p. 309. This might possibly be a condensation of the anonymous fourteenth-century poem, with the sprouting horn omitted. Pauli obviously gives merely an outline for expansion in delivery. For the two renditions by Hans Sachs, see his Sämmtliche Fabeln und Schwänke, II, 504, No. 342, "Die Kaiserin mit dem Leben," and IV, 275, No. 421, same title [Neudrucke . . ., Nos. 126–134, 193–199]. Sachs borrows in both instances from Pauli. Cf. C.-B. 339$_{46}$. Matthias Abele, Metamorphosis telae judiciariae, Das ist, Seltzame Gerichtshändel[8] . . ., Nürnberg, 1712, II, Casus XXXVI [misnumbered XXXIV], pp. 97 f., repeats the story without naming Virgil. I have not seen the edition of 1651–54 mentioned in Bolte's edition of Pauli, II, p. 243, and in note to No. 206. Giovanni Sercambi also tells the story without naming Virgil — Novelle inedite di G. S., ed. R. Rénier, Firenze, 1889, No. 29, pp. 113 f., "De falso pergiuro" [Biblioteca di testi inediti o rari, IV]. The reference I take from V. Rossi, Rassegna bibliografica della lett. ital. IV (1896), 174 ff. The adulterers' bridge is twice described by Sachs, in 1530 and in 1545: (1) "König Artus mit der ehbrecher-brugk" (Hans Sachs, ed. Adelbert von Keller, II, Tübingen, 1870, 262 ff. [Bibliothek des litt. Vereins, CIII]; (2) "De eprecher prueck," in vol. XXI of the same series, p. 362. These exerted some influence in Germany; see Martin Montanus's Schwankbücher, ed. J. Bolte, Tübingen, 1899, Cap. 112, pp. 420 ff., "Von König Artus, wie er durch Virgilium die ehebrecherbrücke zurichten liess." [Bib. des litt. Ver., CXVII.]

6. Resemblances are at times very nearly verbatim; e. g.

Fourteenth-century song	Von Virgilio dem Zauberer
Virgilius die künste sîn	Virgilius der het sein kunst allein
ze Rôme an einem pild wol liez	vnd die zu rom gar wol erschein
werden schîn.	
daz ez sî prâcht vor männiclîch	das es die fraw zu schanden
ze schanden	pracht
ir êr die hiet si gern zerprochen,	Die fraw die het do gerne zerpro-
sô forcht si niur daz pild liez ez	chen
nicht ungerochn	ir ee sie forcht es würd an ir gero-
	chen
Mit einem ritter daz geschach:	Allzuhandt nun do geschach
alsâ zehant man an dem keiser	an dem keyser man wachsen sach
wachsen sach	Ein horn auf dem seynen haubt
ûz sînem houbt ein horn, daz	
muot in sêre.	
der keiser sprach "ich wil niht	Der keiser sprach ich wil nicht
langer pîten	peyten
Er sprach ze sîner frowen pald	Er sprach zu ir mit grosser
"nu sage mir,	schwer
du hâst mich mit eim andern	So sag du mir pey deinem leben
übergeben.	du hast mich mit eim anderen
ei du poese vâlentinn,	uber geben
daz horn an mînem houbt trag	Du pose schnode valentein
ich von dîner minn,	
daz gilt dir hiut din êr und ouch	das horn an dem haupte mein
daz leben."	Das trag ich von deiner valschen
	myn
	das kost dir do das leben dein
	Dein er vnd auch dein gut
si sprach "dâ für sô wil ich swern	Sie sprach do für so wil ich
wol tûsent eide und wil michs mit	schweren
dem rechten wern,	vnd wil mich mit dem rechten
	weren
dô si den eit aldâ geswuor,	Vnd do die fraw den aydt ge-
alsâ zehant daz pilt ze tüsent	schwur
stücken fuor:	das pildt zu tausent stücken fur
ez peiz nicht mer, der kunst was	Es paiß fürpaß kainen mit
im zerunnen.	synnen
	der kunst begundt ym zu rinnen.

I quote from Karl Bartsch, Germania, IV (1859), 237–239, for the earliest version, and from the unique copy in the University Library at Munich of Von Virgilio dem Zauberer. These parallels could be extended considerably. I cite only enough to show clearly that some relationship exists.

7. Die Kaiserchronik eines Regensburger Geistlichen, ed. Edward Schröder, Hannover, 1895, ll. 10638 ff., pp. 276 ff. [Deutsche Chroniken . . ., I, Monumenta Germaniae Historica, Scriptorum qui vernacula lingua usi sunt, I]; ed. H. F. Massmann, 3 vv., Quedlinburg and Leipzig, 1849–54, II, ll. 10649 ff., pp. 98 ff.

8. The manuscript is British Museum Add. 14641, ed. as Julianos der Abtrünnige, Syrische Erzählungen, by Johann Georg Ernst Hoffmann, Leiden, 1880, Kiel, 1888. This edition I have not seen. The quotation in the text is from Julian the Apostate . . ., trans. Sir Hermann Gollancz, London, 1928, 256, which is based on Hoffmann's text. This passage agrees with the translation by Theodor Nöldeke in Zeitschrift der deutschen Morgenländischen Gesellschaft, XXVIII (1874), 660. Cf. Graf, Roma . . . (1923), 474 ff.

9. Dirc Potter, Der Minnen loep, Book II, ll. 3207–89. Cf. S. J. Warren, D. P. en een Boeddhistische Loep der Minne, Tijdschrift voor Nederlandsche Taal- en Letterkunde, V (1885), 129–137, who says (132), as would seem indeed probable, that Potter found at Rome a local legend attached to an old stone.

10. Juan de Timoneda, Patrañuelo, Paris, 1847, Patraña, IV [Tesoro de novelistas Españoles]. Giuseppe Rua (Novelle del "Mambriano" del Cieco da Ferrara . . ., 82) thinks that this idea of the lion may be drawn from the presence of a lion in the Mambriano version. Straparola has a story almost identical, but the instrument here, as in the various versions of the Romance, is a serpent — Giovan Francesco Straparola, Le piacevoli notte, ed. G. Rua, 2 vv., Bari, 1927, notte IV, 2 [Scrittori d'Italia].

11. For oaths on stones in general, see An Encyclopaedia of Religion and Ethics, ed. James Hastings, New York, 1918–27, s.vv. oath, stone; James Endell Tyler, Oaths, their Origin,

Nature, and History ², London, 1835; [Sir] James G. Frazer, The Magic Art, London, 1911, I, 160 ff. [= The Golden Bough³, Part I]; Hwb. d. d. Abergl., s.v. Eid. For oaths on holed stones, see Hastings' Encyclopaedia of Religion and Ethics, XI, 865 f., 874; Transactions of the Society of Antiquaries of Scotland, III (1831), 119 ff.; James Fergusson, Rude Stone Monuments, London, 1872, 255 ff.; Examples of Printed Folk-Lore concerning the Orkney and Shetland Islands, edd. G. F. Black and Northcote W. Thomas, London, 1903, pp. 2, 212 f. [Folk-Lore Society. County Folk-Lore, III]; Proceedings of the Orkney Antiquarian Society, IV (1925-26), 15-19. Patrick W. Joyce, A Social History of Ancient Ireland, London, 1903, I, 277 ff., tells of a speaking stone in County Waterford: "On one occasion a wicked woman perjured herself in its presence, appealing to it to witness her truthfulness when she was really lying, whereupon it split in two, and never spoke again." Giraldus Cambrensis knew of a similar one in Wales.

12. Pausanias, i.28.5, i.3.1, with Frazer's notes; Tyler, Oaths . . .², 129; Georg Wissowa, Religion und Kultus der Römer², München, 1912, 118 [Handbuch der Altertumswissenschaft, V. Abt., 4. Teil].

13. On the Forum Boarium, see the notable work of S. B. Platner and T. Ashby, Topographical Dictionary of Ancient Rome, Oxford, 1929, 223 ff. This work contains excellent bibliographical material and classical references throughout.

14. Platner and Ashby, 253 f.; Otto Richter, Topographie der Stadt Rom², München, 1901, 187 [Handbuch der Altertumswissenschaft, II. Abt., 3. Teil, Bd. III].

15. F. Pfister, Der Reliquienkult im Altertum, Giessen, 1909-12, 150.

16. Georg Wissowa, Religion und Kultus der Römer², 272-279. Cf. Bachofen, Gräbersymbolik², 65. Is the vague recollection of this hostility of Hercules to women responsible for a woman's destroying the efficacy of the stone later?

17. W. H. Roscher, Ausführliches Lexikon der griechischen und römischen Mythologie, I, ii, Leipzig, 1886-90, s.v. Her-

cules, cols. 2256 ff., 2261 ff., 2296; I, 1884–90, s.v. Bona Dea, col. 789.

18. Platner and Ashby, Topographical Dictionary, 253 f.; R. Lanciani, Storia degli Scavi di Roma, 4 vv., Roma, 1902, I, 84, III, 42; F. de' Ficoroni, Le vestigie e rarità di Roma antica . . ., 2 parts, Roma, 1744, I, 17.

19. Platner and Ashby, 257 f.

20. Platner and Ashby, 257 f.; G. Lugli, Il culto ed i santuari di Ercoli Invitto in Roma, Associazione Archeologica Romana, 1915, p. 114. De Rossi made an exhaustive study of the Hercules temple: L'Ara Massima ed il tempio di Ercole nel Foro Boario, in Monumenti, Annali, e Bullettini dell' Istituto di Corrispondenza Archeologica, 1854, 28–38. Cf. also J. J. Boissardus, Romanae Urbis Topographiae, 6 parts in 2 vv., Franckfurt, 1597–1602, I, pt. 4, 27; on the bronze Hercules, see A. Michaelis, Storia della Collezione Capitolina . . ., in Römische Mitteilungen des Deutschen Archäologischen Instituts, VI (1891), 15 f.

21. W. Altmann, Italische Rundbauten, Berlin, 1906, 22 ff. Altmann makes no definite assertion, but the bulk of evidence, architectural and otherwise, which he offers in support of such a theory is impressive.

22. Altmann, Italische Rundbauten, 22.

23. C. L. Urlichs, Codex Topographicus Urbis Romae, Wurzburg, 1871, 112. This passage refers to the Church of Santa Maria del Sole, and not to that of Santo Stefano Rotondo Celiomontano, as was formerly thought. Cf. Christian Huelsen, Le Chiese di Roma nel Medio Evo, Firenze, 1927, p. 484, No. 92. The actual temple of Faunus lay on the island in the Tiber. Cf. Pauly-Wissowa, Real-Encyclopädie der classischen Altertumswissenschaft, Stuttgart, VI (1909), col. 2070. It is not amiss to note that this temple of Faunus was built out of fines collected from three pecuarii convicted of cheating! Cf. Platner and Ashby, Topographical Dictionary, 205–206.

24. On the Faunus cult cf. Ludwig Preller, Römische Mythologie[3], ed. Heinrich Jordan, 2 vv., Berlin, 1881–83, I,

379 ff.; Pauly-Wissowa, Real-Encyclopädie, VI, cols. 2054–2073.

25. Urlichs, Codex, 111. The Church of Santa Maria in Fontana is unknown. Huelsen, Chiese, p. 517, No. 56*, thinks that the author must have meant the little Church of S. Laurentii in Fontana on the Via Urbana. I wonder if it could not be the small Ionic temple in the Forum Boarium known now as Santa Maria Egiziaca, which may have been the temple of Mater Matuta (cf. Altmann, 32) but has been known as that of Fortuna Virilis. In a print-shop's catalogue of 1572, this church is called the "Tempio della Fontana virile detto santa Maria Egiptiaca" (Roma prima di Sisto V., ed. Francesco Ehrle, Roma, 1908, 55). This church is nearer the "templum Fauni" than is S. Laurentius.

26. The Fasti of Ovid, V, verses 673–692, ed. Sir J. G. Frazer, 5 vv., London, 1929, I, 294. Cf. also Frazer's notes on this passage, IV, 115; Christian Huelsen, La Pianta di Roma dell' Anonimo Einsidlense, Roma, 1907, 42; Altmann, Rundbauten, 21 f.; Platner and Ashby, Top. Dict., 27, 70, 339; Richter, Topographie, 180; Mirabilia Urbis Romae, ed. F. M. Nichols, London, 1889, 110.

27. Urlichs, Codex, 111.

28. Christian Huelsen, Il foro boario e le sue adiacenze nell' antichità, in Dizzertazione dell' Accademia Pontificia, Serie II, t. VI (1896), 269; Platner and Ashby, Top. Dict., 433 f.; Richter, Topographie, 190; Altmann, Rundbauten, 32, thinks that it may have been merely an annex to the temple of Fortuna, near the small Ionic church of Santa Maria Egiziaca. G. Wissowa (Gesammelte Abhandlungen, München, 1904, pp. 254–260) considers that an image of Fortune in the temple of Fortuna was erroneously thought by Livy and others to be that of Pudicitia, and that the temple of Pudicitia Patricia never actually existed. Cf. also Frazer, Fasti, IV, 294–295; Edmund Warcupp, Italy, in its original Glory . . ., London, 1660, 184.

29. On Santa Maria in Cosmedin and Pudicitia Patricia see, for example, Giacomo Pinarola, Trattato delle cose più memorabile di Roma, 2 vv., Roma, 1700, I, 340; Mariano Vasi,

Itinerario istruttivo di Roma, 2 vv., Roma, 1814, II, 332–334; G. M. Crescimbeni, Istoria della Basilica di Santa Maria in Cosmedin, Roma, 1715, 2; Edward Wright, Some Observations made in Traveling through France, Italy . . ., in the years 1720, 1721, 1722, 2 vv., London, 1730, I, 253–254; F. de' Ficoroni, Le Vestigie, I, 22; l'abbé Jérôme Richard, Description historique et critique de l'Italie[2], 6 vv., Paris, 1770, V, 509–511; R. Venuti, Descrizione Topografica delle Antichità di Roma, 2 pts., Roma, 1803, II, 49 f. M. Armellini, Chiese di Roma, Roma, 1887, 391, points out the error of such a theory. On this church as Ara Maxima, see M. A. Piganiol, in Mélanges d'archéologie et d'histoire de l'École française de Rome, 1909, 107–117, and G. Lugli, La Zona Archeologica di Roma, Roma, 1924, 256 f. Cf. also G. Fabricius, Roma . . ., Basle, 1551, 84, Crescimbeni, L'istoria, 31, and G. A. Vasi, Indice istorico del gran prospetto di Roma, Roma, 1765, 236.

30. They may have been ruins of the Statio Annonae, or of a temple of Hercules Pompeianus. Cf. Platner and Ashby, Top. Dict., 255 f.; Christian Huelsen, Chiese, 327 f., No. 33; Piganiol, 111; Richter, Topographie, 186, 189 f. In a recent study of the architecture and history of the church, subsequent upon restorations there, G. B. Giovenale returns to an older theory that Santa Maria was built upon a temple of Ceres, Liber and Libera as well as upon the Statio Annonae (La Basilica di S. Maria in Cosmedin, Associazione Artistica fra i cultori di architettura in Roma, Roma, 1927 [Monografie sulle chiese di Roma, II].

31. On the presence of the stone at Santa Maria, see P. d'Avity, The Estates, Empires, and Principallities of the World . . ., trans. Edw. Grimstone, London, 1615, 396; Topographical Study in Rome in a series of views by Étienne du Pérac, ed. T. Ashby for the Roxburghe Club, London, 1916, Plate 23, opp. p. 73; Martin Heemskerk's sketch in Coll. Berlin Grosse Sammlung, Stuttgart, I, 84, No. 209 (cf. Giovenale, Basilica, 53); C. de Fabriczy, Il libro di schizzi d'un pittore olandese nel Museo di Stuttgart, in Archivio storico dell' Arte, VI (1893), 118; Hernando de Salazar, Las yglesias & indulgencias de Roma, Medina, 1551, tenth church following

the principal churches (cf. Schudt, Le Guide . . ., 30); Mira-
bilia Urbis Romae, ed. Steffan Planck, 1485, fo. 37 (Hain
*11190; German blockbook Mirabilia, ed. R. Ehwald, 1905
[Weimar Gesellschaft der Bibliophilen]; John Capgrave, Ye
Solace of Pilgrims, ed. C. A. Mills, Oxford, 1911, 167 [British
Archeological Journal of Rome]; Crescimbeni, Istoria . . ., 27;
Giovenale, La Basilica, Plate XXVII, c. Cf. also Crescimbeni,
Stato . . . della Basilica di Santa Maria in Cosmedin nel
MDCCXIX, Roma, 1719, 10 f.

32. An interesting study of the bocca was made by Crescim-
beni, Istoria . . ., 27 ff., and another in our own time by Ersilia
Caetani-Lovatelli, as above. Cf. also Enrico Stevenson, Sco-
perte a S. Maria in Cosmedin, in Römische Quartalschrifte für
Christliche Alterthumskunde und für Kirchengeschichte, VII
(1893), 11. A scientific description of the bocca is made by F.
Matz, Antike Bildwerke in Rom, ed. F. von Duhn, 3 vv.,
Leipzig, 1881–82, III, 82, No. 3617; F. von der Hagen, Briefe
in die Heimat . . ., IV, 105 ff.; Helbig, in Bollettino dell'
Istituto di Corrispondenza archeologica for 1871, 22.

33. On the bocca as Jupiter Ammon, see Nicolas de Bralion, Les curiositez de l'une et de l'autre Rome, 3 vv., Paris,
1655–59, II, 200 f.; Edward Wright, Some Observations . . .,
I, 253 f. An inscription formerly above the stone stated that it
came from the temple of Jove Ammon so called by Hercules
near the Ara Maxima. Cf. Giovenale, La Basilica . . ., 69₅₆.
Massmann points out that the temple of Jupiter Pluvius was
called Virgil's house (Kaiserchronik, III, 449). On the bocca
as Pallore, see Venuti, Descrizione . . ., II, 49 f.; Ficoroni
(Vestigie . . ., 26 ff.) suggests that it was the image of the
Nile, the Egyptian Jove, becoming in Rome the Terrore. On
the bocca as some other god, see Fynes Moryson, An Itinerary, containing his Ten Yeeres Travel through Germany, . . .
Italy . . ., London, 1617, 133; Venuti, as above; M. Vasi,
Itinéraire instructif de Rome . . ., ed. A. Nibby, 2 vv., Rome,
1824, II, 381 f. Cf. Crescimbeni, Istoria . . ., 53 f., and
F. Matz, Antike Bildwerke . . ., as above. On the bocca as
an unidentified oracle, see J. Clenche, A Tour in France and
Italy, London, 1676, 61; Bernard de Montfaucon, Diarium

Italicum, Paris, 1702, 186 f. On the bocca as Ara Maxima, see O. Panciroli, I Tesori nascosti nell' alma città di Roma, Roma, 1600, 575; F. Pietro Martire Felini da Cremona [= A. Palladio], Trattato nuovo dell' alma città di Rome, Roma, 1610, 75; the priest Giorgio Porzio, Specchio overo Compendio dell' Antichità di Roma, 2 pts., Roma, 1625, I, 79; Bralion, as above ("ensuitte de ce que leur Hercule y eut iuré fidelité a Evander, Prince du Pays, ou depuis Rome fut bastie"); G. P. Rossini, Il Mercurio errante delle grandezze di Rome, Roma, 1693, 20. Rogissart and Havart, in their extremely popular travel book, Les Délices de l'Italie, 6 vv., Leyden, 1709, III, 3, assert that although it was long held that the stone was from the Ara Maxima, today we have recovered from that error. The error is, however, repeated by De Blainville, Travels through Holland . . ., Italy, 3 vv., London, 1743–45, II, 516. On the bocca as a chastity-testing stone from the temple of Pudicitia, see J. J. Boissardus, Romanae Urbis Topographia, I, part I, 24. Cf. Crescimbeni, Istoria . . ., 28. On the bocca as an idol of the Temple of Truth, see G. B. Arata, La Bocca della Verità, mentioned by Crescimbeni, Istoria . . ., 37. Philip Skippon, in speaking of the tradition about the stone (An Account of a Journey made thro' . . . Italy, in A. and J. Churchill's Collection of Voyages and Travels, London, 1732, VI, 659. Skippon was in Italy in 1663), explains it by saying that "At Schola Graeca, it is said S. Augustine read, and this place was dedicated to Veritas." The legend that St. Augustine taught or preached in Santa Maria in Cosmedin is a very usual one and is repeated by nearly all the travelers whose accounts of the church have come down to us. Cf. Crescimbeni, Istoria . . ., 19. On the bocca as the cover of the well of Cacus, see Crescimbeni, Stato . . . di Santa Maria in Cosmedin, 196 f., who quotes a manuscript of G. A. Brusi, dealing with the churches of Rome, but says "Ma quest parere quanto vaglia, lo giudichino i Lettori." Cf. B. Marliani, Topographia Antiquae Romae, Lyon, 1534, 185. On the bocca as a fountain, see Giovanni Marangoni, Delle cose gentilesche, e profane trasportate ad uso, e adornamento delle chiese, Roma, 1744, 59 f. On the bocca as Mercury's fountain, see Leopoldo de Feis, in Cronachetta Mensuale, Aprile, 1885, 53–64, also his articles in Bullettino dell' Istituto di Corrispondenza Archeologica, Marzo, 1885, 49, and Giornale Ligustico di Archeologia, Storia, e Letteratura, 1887, fasc. XI–XII, 184–194. Cf. M. Armellini, Le Chiese di Roma . . ., Roma, 1887, 395, and Cara Berkeley, Some Roman Monuments in the Light of History, 2 vv., London, 1927, I, 131. On the bocca as a drain-cover, see Felini da Cremona, as above; Mirabilia Urbis Romae [from the Italian of G. Franzini], Roma, 1618, 81; G. Porzio, as above; Philip Skippon, as above; Richard Lassels, Voyage of Italy, ed. S. W[ilson], 2 parts, Paris, 1670, pt. 2, 82; A Tour in France and Italy, made by an English Gentleman, 1675, in Thomas Osborne's Collection of Voyages and Travels, 2 vv., London, 1745, I, 410 ff.; A New and complete Collection of Voyages and Travels . . ., London, for J. Coote, 1760, 169; Ferdinand Gregorovius, Geschichte der Stadt Rom im Mittelalter, 2 vv., Dresden, n. d., I, 1226. Cf. Crescimbeni, Stato . . ., 10 f.

34. Giovenale (Basilica . . ., 375 ff.) says that the stone was found in the Hercules temple at the time of its demolition (between 1471 and 1485) but refers also to Muffel's account of the same stone, which was written in 1452. Earlier writers have associated the Hercules temple with the stone; see, for instance, the compilation of F. Schottus, Itinerarii Italiae Rerumque Romanorum libri tres, Antwerpia, 1600, 200, and the abbé Richard, as above.

35. Cf. Graf, Roma . . . (1923), 42 ff. Some of the early writers on Rome who attempted to reconstruct the truth about the antiquities of this neighborhood from old learned sources are B. Rucellai (1449–1514), De urbe Roma, published by Beccucci, Firenze, 1770, cols. 170, 299; Flavius Blondus, De Roma triumphante . . ., 2 pt., Paris, 1533, fo. 25, v°; Francesco degli Albertini, Mirabilia Rome, Lyon, 1510, fos. [Mi, v° and Miii, r°]; B. Marliani, Topographia . . ., 141, 149, 185; Andrea Fulvio, Le antichità della città di Roma, Roma, 1543, fol. 128, v°; G. Fabricius, Roma Antiquitatum Liber Duo, Basiliae, 1560, 39; L. Mauro, Le Antichita della Citta di Roma, Venezia, 1558, 44; B. Gamucci, Le Antichità della città di Roma, Venezia, 1565, 73 ff.; Boissardus, Antiquitatum

libri . . ., I, 24–28. For a more complete bibliography on students of Roman topography, see Le Guide di Roma, Materialien zu einer Geschichte der römischen Topographie, ed. Ludwig Schudt, Wien and Augsburg, 1930 [Quellenschriften zur Geschichte der Barockkunst in Rom].

36. A recent attempt to ascertain the origin of the bocca is Professor A. H. Krappe's La leggenda della "bocca della verità," in Nuovi studi medievali, II (1925), 1–6, who decides that the bocca was originally a man-eating lion-totem in Asia Minor, the evidence being (1) the Syrian legend of Julian and the widow, and (2) Salomon Reinach's Les carnassiers androphages dans l'art gallo-romain, in Cultes, mythes et religions[2], Paris, 1908, I, 279–298, reprinted from Revue celtique, XXV (1904–05), 208–224. As for (1), we have already seen that in the Syrian story there is neither lion nor bocca; hence the principal link in Professor Krappe's chain of argument breaks. When we examine Reinach's study, the other links give way, too, for the French scholar infers that the subjects of his study, two bronze figures of wolves — not lions — devouring corpses, are of Celtic origin; he does not attribute them to Asia Minor (Cultes, mythes . . ., I, 298 f.). Moreover, the "carnassiers" are shown with human bodies, legs, and occasionally hands dangling from their mouths, as if being devoured (see the illustrations, Cultes, mythes . . ., I, pp. 279–281, 287–289). The fact that an ancient Lydian king cut his wife in pieces and devoured her, only to be discovered when a feminine hand was seen projecting from his mouth (293 f.), has as little to do with the bocca as the tenth- or eleventh-century bas-relief of Scy-les-Metz (289) showing an animal with a human hand protruding from its mouth. If such were the originals of the bocca, one wonders why the hand projects from instead of reposing inside the mouth, as it certainly did in the bocca.

In representations of the bocca, chiefly by seventeenth-century artists, the fact that a lion is shown is due to the resemblance of the actual stone to a lion with mane. William Bromley (Several Years' Travels through . . . Italy, London, 1702, 173), who saw the bocca at Santa Maria in 1695, says it is the face of "a lyon."

In view of the Julian story one is inclined to link the bocca also with the oracular pagan idol (cf. Arthur Dickson, Valentine and Orson, New York, 1929, 191 ff., 200 ff.), and hence with other automata; but because of the age-old custom of placing the hand on stones or other objects when oaths are taken, a custom seemingly followed in the use of the bocca, I am inclined to dismiss these possibilities.

37. [John Capgrave], Ye Solace of Pilgrims, ed. C. A. Mills, Oxford, 1911, fo. 414, r° (pp. 167 f.) [British and American Archaeological Society of Rome].

38. Fo. 37. Hain *11190. For other editions of this version of the Mirabilia in which the bocca is mentioned, see Hain *11189–*11207; Copinger's Supplement, I, 4053–54; Graesse, Trésor . . ., IV, 535 f. This passage is found also in the form of the Mirabilia called "Indulgentiē Ecclesiarum Urbis Romae," for example in that printed by M. Silber als Franck in Rome, 1513 and 1519. Cf. also Mirabilia Urbis Romę noua recognita . . . per Antoninum Pontum, Roma, 1524, Antonio Blado de Asula [fo. xliii, v°].

39. Mirabilia Urbis Romae, ed. R. Ehwald, 1905 [Weimar Gesellschaft der Bibliophilen]. For the other editions of this version, see Hain, Nos. 11208–11219; Copinger's Supplement, pt. II, vol. I, 4055–57; Graesse, Trésor . . ., IV, 535–536. Cf. also the edition of Stefan Planck's 1489 German Mirabilia by Christian Huelsen, Berlin, 1925 [Wiegendruckgesellschaft].

40. Arnold von Harff, Pilgerfahrt von Cöln durch Italien . . . in den Jahren, 1496–99, ed. E. von Groote, Cöln, 1860, 25.

41. Facetiae Facetiarum; hoc est, Joco-Seriorum Fasciculus, exhibens varia variorum auctorum scripta . . ., Frankfurt am Main, 1615, 405–406.

42. Richard Lassels, The Voyage of Italy . . ., Paris, 1670, Pt. II, 82.

43. Comte de Caylus, Voyage d'Italie, 1714–15, Paris, 1914, 184–185.

44. Edward Wright, Some Observations . . ., I, 253–254.

45. Harleian Miscellany, V (1744), 1 ff.

46. De Blainville, Travels through Holland . . . Italy . . ., 3 vv., London, 1743–45, II, 516.

47. Vasi, Itinéraire . . ., II, 381 f.

48. Erasmo Pistolesi, Descrizione de Roma e suoi contorni
. . ., Roma, 1846, 466.

49. Some others who have mentioned the bocca della verità,
often speculating upon its origin but adding little of significance, are Giovanni Rucellai, in Il Giubileo dell' anno 1450
secondo una relazione di Giovanni Rucellai, Archivio della
Società Romana di storia patria, IV (1881), 580; [Anon.] Voyage de Provence et d'Italie, MS. Bib. Nat. Paris, fonds français 5550 (16th century), fo. 16, v°; G. Franzini, Le cose maravigliose de l'alma città di Rome, Venezia, 1565, 40; [Anon.]
Itinerarium Italiae totius . . . editum studio et industria
trium nobilissimorum Germaniae Adolescentum . . ., Coloniae Agrippinae, 1602, 138; J. W. Neumair von Ramssla,
Reise durch Welschland und Hispanien . . . genommen aus
Herrn Johann Wilhelms Neumair von Ramssla daselbsten
Itinerario Europaeo, Leipzig, 1622, 168; Joannes Henricus a
Pflaumern, Mercurius Italicus, Augustae Vindelicorum, 1625,
223; Joseph Furtenbach, Neues Itinerarium Italiae, Ulm,
1627, 124–125; Martin Zeiller, Itinerarium Italiae Nov-
Antiquae . . ., Franckfurt, 1640, 152; [Anon.] Voyage d'Italie,
MS. Bib. Nat. Paris fonds français 13375 [by a young noble-
man who went to Italy in 1669], 67; J. Clenche, A Tour in
France and Italy . . ., London, 1676, 61; Claude Jordan, Voy-
ages historiques de l'Europe, 8 vv., Amsterdam, 1692, III, 28;
William Bromley, Remarks on the Grand Tour of France and
Italy, London, 1692, 227; De Regnard and Dufresny, a com-
edy acted in 1695 in which a bocca plays an admonitory part:
Maurice Drack, Le Théâtre de la Foire, Première série, de
1658–1720, Paris, 1889, 153–157; [Anon.] A new Account of
Italy . . ., London, 1701, 111 [almost the exact words used by
Claude Jordan]; Joachim Christoph Nemeitz, Nachlese besonderer Nachrichten von Italien . . ., Leipzig, 1726, 199;
Guyot de Merville, Voyage historique d'Italie, 2 vv., La Haye,
1729, II, 56 [another paraphrase of Claude Jordan]; P. L.
Berkenmayer, Le Curieux Antiquaire, Leyden, 1729, 294
[also a repetition of Jordan]; Johann Georg Keysler, Travels
through Germany . . . Italy . . ., 4 vv., London, 1756–57 [an

English translation of his book first printed at Hanover in 1740], II, 107–108; l'abbé Richard, Description historique et critique de l'Italie . . .², Paris, 1770, V, 511 ff.; [Anon.] A Ramble through Holland, France, and Italy, 2 vv., London, 1793, 148–149; F. von Stolberg, Reise in Deutschland, der Schweiz, Italien, und Sicilien, 4 vv., Königsberg and Leipzig, 1794, III, 136; Ludwig H. Friedlaender, Ansichten von Italien, 2 vv., Leipzig, 1819, II, 66; Edward Burton, A description of the antiquities and other curiosities of Rome, Oxford, 1821, 490; M. H. Beyle [= Stendhal], Promenades dans Rome, 2 vv., Bruxelles, 1830, II, 214. This list could be increased indefinitely, from the earliest mention of the stone down to the present day, as the mystery of the mask has never ceased to engage human curiosity.

CHAPTER VIII

1. Important studies on this obelisk are those of Sarah Morehouse Beach, The "Julius Caesar obelisk" in the English Faust Book and elsewhere, Modern Language Notes, XXXV (1920), 27–31; Sir E. A. Wallace Budge, Cleopatra's Needles and other Egyptian Obelisks, London, 1926, 255 ff.; and especially R. Clédina, Rabelais et l'aiguille de Virgile à Rome, in Revue du seizième siècle, XVI (1929), 122–132. On its early history see Budge, as above; Franz von Reber, Die Ruinen Roms, Leipzig, 1863, who thinks that it was quarried after the Romans conquered Egypt, on the basis of a disputed reading of a passage of Pliny (H. N., XXXVI, 11. 75), saying that the obelisk was "fractus in mollitione" (broken in moving) or, as Reber thinks, "factus imitatione" (made in imitation [of older ones]), an opinion in which O. Marucchi, Gli obelischi egiziani di Roma², Roma, 1898, 149 f., concurs. Cara Berkeley, Some Roman Monuments in the Light of History, 2 vv., London, 1927, II, 232, asserts that it was made by Nectanebo in the fourth century B.C., and that Ptolemy Philadelphus (284–246 B.C.) erected it in Alexandria. Cf. also Otto Richter, Topographie der Stadt Rom², München, 1901, 377 [Bd. III, Abt. II, Zweite Hälfte of I. Müller's Handbuch

der Altertumswissenschaft], and Platner and Ashby, 370 f. On Nero's circus, see Christian Huelsen, Il Circo di Nerone al Vaticano secondo la descrizione inedita nel codice Ambrosiano di Giacomo Grimaldi, in Miscellanea Ceriani, Milano, 1910, 255 ff. On the removal of the obelisk, see Domenico Fontana's own account, Della Trasportatione dell' Obelisco Vaticano e delle fabriche di nostro signore Papa Sisto V., Roma, 1590; cf. also J. A. von Hübner, Sixte-Quint, 3 vv., Paris, 1870, II, 75–151. For a profusion of writings subsequent upon Fontana's feat, see Le Guide di Roma, ed. Ludwig Schudt, 482–486.

2. Cf. Hartmann Grisar, History of Rome in the Middle Ages, ed. Luigi Cappadelta, 3 vv., London, 1911–12, I, 292.

3. Platner and Ashby, as above; Heinrich Jordan, Topographie der Stadt Rom im Altertum, 2 vv., Berlin, 1871–85, I, pt. 2, 657; Ferdinand Gregorovius, Geschichte der Stadt Rom im Mittelalter, 8 vv., Stuttgart, 1859–72, III, 556–558, Urlichs, Codex, 221; R. A. Lanciani, The Ruins and Excavations of Ancient Rome, London, 1897, 552; the same author's Storia degli Scavi di Roma, Roma, 1902, II, 92. Graf, Roma . . . (1923), 226 ff., discusses the legend at some length.

4. This theory is mentioned as early as 1589 by Michele Mercati, Degli Obelischi di Roma, Roma, 1589, 2–3. Cf. also Graesse, Beiträge, 15₈, and Graf, Roma . . . (1923), 230. The passage in the Mirabilia Urbis Romae relative to the obelisk (Urlichs, Codex, 105) seems to indicate a connection between the inscription and the legend: "Et haec memoria [of Caesar] sacrata fuit suo more, sicut adhuc apparet et legitur." Pero Tafur, Travels and Adventures, 1435–39, trans. M. Letts, London, 1926, 37, says that there are "a few ancient letters carved in the stone which now cannot well be read, but in fact they record that the body of Julius Caesar was buried there." The name of the obelisk, "aguglia," which is obviously derived ultimately from the Latin acus, needle, was once supposed to be a corruption of "Iulia," i. e., the Columna Iulia. Cf. F. Pigafetta, Discorso d'intorno all' historia della Agulia, et alla ragione di moverla, Roma, 1586, 1; Nicolas Bralion, Les curiositez de l'une et de l'autre Rome, 3 vv., Paris, 1655–

59, I, 291 f.; Graf, Roma . . . (1923), 229 f. In the Libro Imperiale (ca. 1313) the suggestion is made that the presence of Caesar's arms with his eagle caused the obelisk, which was made by one Lugolo, to be called "Aquila," hence Tuscan "aguglia," and so "guillia"! Cf. Graf, Roma . . . (1923), 185₁₃, 225, and Gregorovius, Stadt Rom . . ., III, 556 f.

5. Mentioned by Suetonius, De Vita Caesarum, Divus Iulius, Cap. 85, in Opera Omnia, ed. M. Ihm, Lipsiae, 1908, I, 44 [Teubner Series]. Cf. Graf, Roma . . . (1923), 227 f.

6. See, for example, the Bull of Leo IX, Urlichs, Codex, 221; Mirabilia Urbis Romae, Urlichs, Codex, 105, 132, and the early printed editions of the Mirabilia in Latin, such as those of Adam Rot, 1473 (Hain 11175); Joh. de Reno, 1475?; Gerardus Lisa de Flandria, 1475 (Hain 11188); Freitag, 1492 (Hain 11178); Pieter van Os, 1495; S. Planck, 1495?; Martinus de Amsterdam and Joh. Besicken, 1500; J. Besicken, 1510?; M. Silber als Franck, 1512, 1515?, 1519?, 1520; for other editions of this early form of the Mirabilia which contain this passage, cf. Hain, Nos. 11174–11184; Copinger, Supplement, Nos. 4045–4052; Reichling, Appendices to Hain-Copinger, Fasc. 3 (1907), p. 107, Fasc. 4 (1908), p. 48, Fasc. 5 (1909), pp. 49 f., 194; Graesse, Trésor . . ., IV, 535–536. See also F. M. Nichols, The Marvels of Rome, London, 1889, 104. Others who have mentioned the legend are Gregorius, De Mirabilibus Urbis Romae, ed. G. McN. Rushforth, Journal of Roman Studies, IX (1919), 56 f.; Fazio degli Uberti, Dittamondo, in Urlichs, Codex, 246; Petrarch, Letter VI, 2, to Johannes Columna, in Urlichs, Codex, 183; Pero Tafur, Travels . . ., 37; Giovanni Rucellai, Il Giubileo . . ., 572; John Capgrave, Ye Solace of Pilgrims, 23 f.; Arnold von Harff, Pilgerfahrt . . ., 24; Cronica llamada: il triumpho de los nueue mas preciados varones de la fama, trans. from French by Antonio Rodriguez Portugal, Lisbon, 1530, fo. cxxix, v°; Flavius Blondus, Roma ristaurata, Venezia, 1543, fo. 10, r°; William Thomas, The Historie of Italie, London, 1549, fo. 33, v°; "Shakerlay Inglese," Guida Romana, in Le Cose maravigliose della città di Roma, Roma, A. Blado, 1562 (other editions, Venezia, 1544, 1565); J. du Bellay, Songe, Sonnet III, in Le Premier Livre des Antiquitez de

Rome, Paris, 1558, fo. 10, v°; G. Franzini, Le cose maravigliose de l'alma città di Rome, Venezia, 1565, 39; Andrea Palladio, L'Antichita di Roma, Venezia, 1575, fo. 11, v°; André Thevet, La Cosmographie universelle, 2 vv., Paris, 1575, I, fo. 34, r°; Jacques de Villamont, Voyages, Paris, 1595, fo. 29, r°; J. Rigaud, Recueil des choses rares d'Italie, Aix, 1601, fo. 54, r°; Giorgio Porzio, Specchio overo Compendio dell' Antichità di Roma, 2 pt., Roma, 1625, II, 154; John Evelyn, Diary, ed. Wheatley, 2 vv., London, 1906, I, 139; J. Raymond, An Itinerary contayning a Voyage made through Italy, London, 1648, 85; Edmund Warcupp, Italy . . ., 180; Germain Audebert, Venetiae, Roma, Parthenope, Hanoviae, 1703, 156; De Blainville, Travels . . ., II, 448; Étienne de Jouy, L'Hermite en Italie, 4 vv., Paris, 1824–25, III, 48. Learned writers in the sixteenth century who protested against such a belief include Lucius Faunus, De antiquitatibus urbis Romae . . ., Venezia, 1548, fo. 124, v°, and L. Mauro, Le Antichità de la città di Roma, Venezia, 1556, 112 f.

7. Urlichs, Codex, 105.

8. Cf. Gregorius, De Mirabilibus . . ., 56–57. An account of Caesar's death, foretold by his astronomer, follows the description of the obelisk. Cf. also Urlichs, Codex, 132.

9. Capgrave, Ye Solace of Pilgrims, 23 f. For variants of these verses, cf. Graf, Roma . . . (1923), 231$_{97}$. The original couplet was probably from an epitaph of either the emperor Henry III (d. 1056) or Lothair (d. 1137). Cf. Graf, Roma . . . (1923), 232 f.

10. Bibliothèque Nationale, Paris, MS. fonds français 13375, p. 63.

11. Richard Lassels, The Voyage of Italy . . ., 2 pt., Paris, 1670, II, 27 f.

12. Helinandus, Sermo V in Epiphania Domini 11, in J. P. Migne, Patrologia Latina, CCXII, col. 522. Cf. C.–B. 323.

13. Jean d'Outremeuse, Ly Myreur des Histors, I, 235, 243 f. For the thunderbolt see also Sicardi Cremonensis Episcopi Chronicon, in Migne, Patrologia Latina, CCXII, col. 444. There seems to be some confusion in Jean's account between the obelisk and the memorial column to Caesar in the

Forum. As for Caesar's image above the ball, I have already
mentioned the tradition that his eagle stood on the Vatican
obelisk (cf. above, note 4). In a drawing made by Giuliano
da San Gallo (1443–1517; cf. G. K. Nagler, Neues allgemeines
Künstler-Lexicon, München, 1832, V, 148 ff.), the ball on the
obelisk is shown topped by the Roman eagle. Cf. Christian
Huelsen, La Roma Antica di Ciriaco d'Ancona, Roma, 1907,
32. On the eagle as a symbol of Roman power cf. Graf, Roma
. . . (1923), 713–715. The statement that Caesar had ordered
the obelisk made is echoed in Marlowe's Doctor Faustus, ed.
A. W. Ward and C. B. Wheeler, Oxford, 1915, 29, and in the
English Faust Book, ed. H. Logeman, Amsterdam, 1900, 56,
where Caesar is asserted to have brought the obelisk from
Africa. Cf. Beach, as above. The vagueness in regard to the
measurements is quite typical of the early accounts of the
obelisk. Cf. Graf, Roma . . . (1923), 230.

14. Jean d'Outremeuse, Ly Myreur des Histors, I, Append.,
601, Stanzas LV and LVI.

15. L. G. Lemcke, Bruchstücke aus den noch ungedruckten
Theilen des Vitorial von Gutierre Diez de Games, Marburg,
1865, 17 f. Cf. Gutierre Diez de Games, Le Victorial, edd. le
comte A. de Circourt and le comte de Puymaigre, Paris, 1867,
542 f. The description of the obelisk seems to be to a certain
extent a reconstruction of past glories. The steps were no
longer in existence by the fifteenth century, nor does it seem
likely that any brass figures were adorning the base of the
column at the time Gutierre wrote of it. The lions which deco-
rate the obelisk to-day were placed there by Fontana. We
know that it rested from the beginning upon four simple
supports, as Pliny mentions them in the Historia Naturalis,
XVI, 40 (76) (ed. C. Mayhoff, Teubner Series, V, 331 f.).
Abulfeda (1253–1331) speaks of four supports of bronze
(Géographie, ed. J. T. Reinaud, 2 vv., Paris, 1848, II, 281),
attributing his description to Edrisi [= Al-Idrisi, ca. 1099–
1154; cf. above, p. 334]. The tradition that these feet were
once concealed by bronze lions or that the obelisk was
supported by them was, however, very strong. Alexander
Neckam reports their existence in his De laudibus divinae

sapientiae, Distinctio V, verse 320 (ed. T. Wright, 1863, 447
[Rerum Britannicarum Scriptores]), as do Gregorius (Mirabilibus . . ., 56 f.) and — probably by imitation — Ranulf
Higden (Polycronicon, ed. C. Babington, 2 vv., London, 1865,
I, 224 f. [Rerum Britannicarum Scriptores]). If Petrarch is to
be credited, the lions were there when he visited Rome in
1337 (lib. VI, Epist. 2 of the Epistolae, ed. Giuseppe Fracas-
setti, 3 vv., Firenze, 1859–63, I, 313. Petrarch's letter was
probably written in 1338. Cf. Francisci Petrarchae Epistolae
Selectae, ed. A. F. Johnson, Oxford, 1923, 41 and 219). At
some time after this date the lions disappeared, as they are
not mentioned by any of the early sixteenth-century works on
Rome. A drawing made by Étienne du Pérac showing a restoration of the Vatican district portrays the obelisk without
lions (Topographical Study in Rome in a series of views by
Étienne du Pérac, ed. T. Ashby for the Roxburghe Club, London, 1916, Plate II). Mercati (Degli obelischi . . ., 24) surmises that the lions vanished during the last sack of Rome, in
1527, when the Vatican region was brutally pillaged by the
army of Charles of Bourbon (cf. R. Lanciani, The Destruction
of Ancient Rome, New York, 1899, 214–226), but it seems
much more probable that they had not survived the century
following Petrarch's statement. A drawing made by Ciriaco
d'Ancona about the year 1450 shows the obelisk resting upon
four feet, without any trace of other supports or decorations
(Christian Huelsen, La Roma Antica di Ciriaco d'Ancona,
Plate XI. For a clearer drawing of the feet, see the sketch of
Giuliano da San Gallo mentioned above, note 13. It is reproduced on p. 32 of Huelsen, La Roma Antica. . . . Cf. also C.
Huelsen, Ricostruzioni di Roma nel Quattrocento, in Rivista
di Roma, Aug. 10, 1907, 494). It is not impossible that the
lions were seized upon by the condottieri who ravaged the
papal territory during the time of Pope Eugenius IV (1431–
47). Cf. William Miller, Mediaeval Rome from Hildebrand
to Clement VII (1073–1600), London, 1901, 172 [Story of the
Nations]. That their memory was still green, however, seems
to be evidenced in another drawing by Ciriaco (Plate VIII) in
which he set forth his conception of an ancient Roman street,

The column in the middle of it, which Huelsen thinks to be a variation of the Vatican obelisk (p. 29), not only has a male figure seated on the ball, holding a sphere and an eagle, but also is resting solidly upon two or three lions. (On the eagle, see above, note 4, and for the sphere as a symbol of Roman power see Graf, Roma . . . [1923], 719 f.). Du Bellay's reference to the lions (Songe, as above) is at first puzzling, but can probably be explained as a borrowing from Petrarch, of whose works he was an avid reader. Cf. Clédina, 126 f.

16. Pantagruel, in Oeuvres de François Rabelais, edition directed by Abel Lefranc, Paris, 1912 —, IV (1922), chap. XXXIII, 340. Pantagruel was published in 1532. Cf. III, introd., p. i. See Clédina, as above.

17. Clédina's article establishes this point.

18. On Belon's colorful career, cf. Paul Delaunay, L'aventureuse existence de Pierre Belon du Mans, Paris, 1926; also, Ludovic Legré, La botanique en Provence au XVIe siècle, the volume entitled "Louis Anguillara, Pierre Belon . . .," Marseille, 1901, 35 ff.

19. Two editions of this work appeared in the same year in Paris, one by Cavellat (which I use) and the other by Prévost. The work was reprinted in 1699 in the Thesaurus Graecarum Antiquitatum of J. Gronovius, VIII, Lugduni Batavorum, pp. 2529 ff. Cf. Delaunay, 163.

20. Fo. 8, v° (= p. 2555 of the 1699 edition).

21. Cf. Pliny, Historia Naturalis, XXXVI, 9 (14), ed. Carolus Mayhoff, Lipsiæ, 1897, V, 331–332 [Teubner Series]. Cf. also XVI, 40 (76), vol. III, p. 52, and XXXVI, 11 (15), vol. V, pp. 333 f., the last of these a passage quoted by Belon, fo. 8, r°. Fontana, 16, says that Pliny was right in asserting that the obelisk had been broken in moving. Cf. also Platner and Ashby, 366, article on "Obeliscus Augusti, Gnomon," and 367, article on "Obeliscus Augusti in Circo Maximo."

22. As a corollary to Virgil's obelisk, it is pertinent to mention the columns of porphyry which he made and endowed with magic properties in the Insulae Baleares. These columns, according to a fifteenth-century History of the Pisans, fell into the hands of the Pisans, who were forced to surrender

them to the Florentines, but sent them to Florence only after burning off their lustre — this, presumably, to destroy their supernatural qualities. Cf. J. R. Sinner, Catalogus Codicum MSS. Bibliothecae Bernensis, 3 vv., Berne, 1760–72, 115, 135 f. and C.-B. 365$_{13}$.

CHAPTER IX

1. The Nyverd text was reprinted by "Philomneste junior" (Gustave Brunet), Genève, 1867. There is another reprint by Techener, Paris, 1831, and yet another in the same year by Picard. Comparetti^2, II, 282 ff., reprints the Techener text. Since it is the most widely accessible, I follow Comparetti's reprint in spite of changes of spelling and some few errors. There is no really adequate edition of any version of the Romance.

On Trepperel's dates, see Philippe Renouard, Les imprimeurs parisiens, Paris, 1898, 354; cf. A. Claudin, Histoire de l'imprimerie en France au XVe et au XVIe siècle, 4 vv., Paris, 1900–14, II (1901), 94, 162, and Philippe Renouard, Les marques typographiques parisiennes des XVe et XVIe siècles, Paris, 1926, 344 [Revue des bibliothèques, Supplément 13]. On Guillaume Nyverd the elder, see Renouard, Marques typographiques . . ., 268 f., and the same author's Les imprimeurs parisiens, 283.

For later editions of this Romance, see J. G. T. Graesse, Trésor de livres rares . . ., Dresden, 1859–69, II, 547 f.; J.-C. Brunet, Manuel du libraire . . ., Paris, 1864, II, 1167; the edition of the Romance by Gustave Brunet above referred to; A Short-title Catalogue of Books printed in France . . . in the British Museum, ed. Henry Thomas, London, 1924, s.v. Virgil; Catalogue de la bibliothèque de Rothschild, ed. E. Picot, Paris, 1884–1920, II, 178 f.

2. I suspect that the copy at the British Museum, dated in the catalogue 1518?, is unique (pressmark now 1073. h. 44). I use a photostat of this copy. In the Nederlandsche Bibliographie van 1500 tot 1540, edd. Wouter Nijhoff and M. E. Kronenberg, 's-Gravenhage, 1923, 760 f., No. 2145, it is dated

1525?, with note "Mogelijk iets later gedrukt." It was reprinted in 1552, suppressed in 1570, and again reprinted frequently. Cf. Jan te Winkel in Paul's Grundriss der germanischen Philologie², II (Strassburg, 1902), 490. A later edition in
the British Museum (pressmark: 12403. aa. 15) presents an
interesting array of dates which tell their own story. The title-
page reads as follows: "Een schoone / Ende vermaeckelijcke
Historie, van / Virgilius leven, doodt, ende van zijn / wonder-
lijcke wercken, die hy dede door / Nigromantien, ende door de
hulpe / des Duyvels. / [woodcut of Virgil in the basket]
t'Amstelredam, / Gedruckt by Ot. Barents Smient, Boeck-
drucker woonend tusschen / bey de Regeliers Poorten, inde
nieuwe Druckerije 1672." Above the colophon, fo. [c iv, v°]:
"Dit Boecxken ist ghevisenteert ende geapprobeert / van een
geleerden Man, van C. M. daer toe ghe = / commiteert.
Ende is toe-ghelaten te moghen Prin / ten. Datum tot Brus-
sel den sesten Juiij, [sic!] Anno / M.D.LJJ." Colophon: "'t
Amstelredam, / gedrudckt by Ot. Barentß Smient, Boec-
drucker. . . . Anno 1656."

3. The unique perfect copy of this work, formerly in the
Britwell collection, is now in the J. P. Morgan Library. The
larger Bodleian copy (Douce 40) lacks only the title-page —
of which the verso is blank — bearing a woodcut of the revenge which is repeated at fo. c i, r°. The Bodleian Library
graciously permitted me to have a photostat of their copy.
On this text, see the masterly study by Robert Proctor, Jan
van Doesborgh, Printer at Antwerp, An Essay in Bibliography, London, 1894, 27 ff., 55 [Illustrated Monographs of
the Bibliographical Society II]. Doesborgh's version was reprinted, perhaps by Copland, about 1562. Cf. Stationers'
Register I, 176; Arundel Esdaile, A List of English Tales and
Prose Romances . . ., London, 1912, I, 136; A Short-title
Catalogue of Books printed in England . . ., edd. A. W. Pollard and G. R. Redgrave, London, 1926, 578, Nos. 24828-
24829. No critical edition has appeared, although modern
reprints are numerous, e. g., by E. V. Utterson, London, 1812;
by W. J. Thoms in Early English Prose Romances, London,
1828, frequently reprinted (I use a recent reprint in slightly

bowdlerized form by George Routledge and Sons, London, n. d. [Early Novelists Series], which omits the prologue, for which I use a photostat of the Bodleian original); by W. Clouston, in Popular Tales and Fictions, 2 vv., London, 1887, I, 178 ff.; by Henry Morley, The Early Prose Romances, Carisbrooke, 1890 [Carisbrooke Library]; by W. Carew Hazlitt, Tales and Legends of National Origin, London, 1892, 34 ff. — although the Romance is *not* native to England.

4. On this type, see Aarne-Thompson, The Types of the Folk-tale, Nos. 330 B, 331 [Folklore Fellows Communications 74].

5. Jean d'Outremeuse, Ly myreur des histors, I, 54. Perhaps this episode is derived by Jean or by the author of Les faictz merveilleux in part from Li Romanz d'Athis et Prophilias, ed. Alfons Hilka, Dresden, 1912, I, 2 ff., ll. 33–132 [Gesellschaft für Romanische Literatur 29], where the Romulus-Remus story serves as an introduction, though not in precisely the same way as in Les faictz merveilleux.

6. The best discussion of Andes as Virgil's birth-place is by Bruno Nardi, The Youth of Virgil, translated by Belle Kennard Rand, Cambridge [Mass.], 1930, 113 ff. The use of the adjectival form *Andensis* in oblique cases, e. g. *in pago Andensi* [which could be written $\bar{a}d\bar{e}si$] — cf. Nardi, 115_3 — would enhance the possibility of the misreading which I suggest. See also Vitae Vergilianae, ed. J. Brummer, Leipzig, 1912, 1, 40, 48, 54, 56, 62 [Bibliotheca Teubneriana], for occurrences of forms of the name in biographies.

7. The name Nyverd may be a Dutch place-name. Nyvaert was the appellation of a stretch of water near Utrecht in the fifteenth century (H. A. Poelman, Bronne tot de Geschiedenis van den Oostzeehandel, 's-Gravenhage, 1917, 459 [Rijks Geschiedkundige Publicatien 35]), and Nyverdal is a town in modern Holland some fifteen miles northeast of Deventer.

8. In Ly myreur des histors, I, 252, Virgil directs: "Promiers, vos mettereis Phebilhe en la thour halt à la fenestre, à laqueile ma figure fut sachié à la corbilhe . . . si c'on veirat tout son eistre et la feniestre qui oevre sens braire. . . ."

9. The type is not recognized as such in Aarne-Thompson, The Types of the Folk-tale, Helsinki, 1928 [Folklore Fellows Communications 74], but that it is quite clearly a distinct type is easily seen from the discussions, with rich references, in Anmerkungen zu den Kinder- und Hausmärchen der Brüder Grimm, 5 vv., edd. Johannes Bolte and Georg Polívka, Leipzig, 1913–32, II, 162 ff., No. 81, "Bruder Lustig," and II, 394 ff., "Das Wasser des Lebens." Cf. [Sir] James G. Frazer, Spirits of the Corn and of the Wild, London, 1912, I, 14, II, 263 ff. [= The Golden Bough³, Part V], and Adonis, Attis, Osiris, London, 1927, I, 181 [= The Golden Bough³, Part IV]; Joseph Loth, Les Mabinogion², Paris, 1913, I, 129, 143, and Alfred Nutt, Mabinogion Studies, Folklore Record, V (1882); Reinhold Köhler, Kleinere Schriften, ed. Johannes Bolte, 3 vv., Weimar, 1898, I, 140, 585; Moses Gaster, Monatsschrift für Geschichte und Wissenschaft des Judentums, XXVIII (1880), 128 [reprinted in same author's Studies and Texts in Folklore . . ., 3 vv., London, 1925–28, II, 1215]. This is not the "maiden melted young" type of story (Aarne-Thompson, No. 753, where the reference to Bolte-Polívka should be III, 198).

10. The story was first told by Wace, later by St. Bonaventura. See on this Auguste Marguillier, Saint Nicolas, Paris (1917. L'art et les saints), and for the modern song, p. 36. On St. Nicholas, see Analecta Bollandiana, XVIII (1899), 188 f.; Bibliographia hagiographica latina (1899), Nos. 6104–6221; Gustav Anrich, Hagios Nikolaos, 2 vv., Leipzig and Berlin, 1913–17, esp. 411₂ (on St. Nicholas in the Greek Church; a work on a similar scale on St. Nicholas in the Western Church is needed); Jean Bodel, Le Jeu de Saint Nicolas, ed. Alfred Jeanroy, Paris, 1925, with bibliography, pp. xiii-xix [Les classiques français du moyen âge]; Paul Aebischer, Le miracle des trois clercs ressuscités par saint Nicolas, in Archivum Romanicum, XV (1931), 386–399. On the iconography of the legend, see this last and Émile Mâle, L'art religieux du XIIIᵉ siècle en France⁵, Paris, 1923, 289 f., where the argument that the story arose from the misinterpretation of pictures representing St. Nicholas saving three soldiers from exe-

cution is cloudy and unconvincing; before the story of the dis-
section of the three victims could be attached to any pictorial
representation it had to be in circulation, surely.

An interesting later development of the legend of Virgil's
attempt at rejuvenation is the legend first told apparently by
Alarcón in 1600, in La cueva de Salamanca, and frequently
retold later, of the magician Enrique de Villena, whose dates
are 1384–1434. He had his servant cut him up, put the pieces
in a bottle and bury it. When it was found after eight months
through a forced confession, the bottle contained an eight-
months' child. See on this Samuel M. Waxman, Chapters on
Magic in Spanish Literature, Revue hispanique, XXXVIII
(1916), 325–463, esp. 408 ff., 418 ff. If there has been a transfer from Virgil to Villena here, as Waxman suspects, the reasons for it may be that Villena made the first translation of
Virgil into a vulgar tongue, and thus got his name associated
with that of the Roman poet-magician, and that Villena also
wrote a treatise on the Evil Eye, thus giving some basis for the
legends of his power as a sorcerer (for the Tratado del Aoja-
miento, see Revue hispanique, XLI [1917], 182 ff.)

11. Die deutschen Volksbücher, gesammelt und in ihrer
ursprünglichen Echtheit wiederhergestellt von Karl Simrock,
Frankfurt a. M., 1847, VI, 325 ff. Even if Simrock meant
"Germanic" by "deutsch" here, thus producing the usual
misunderstanding, the rest of the title is disingenuous as applied to the Virgilius Romance. More candid is F. H. von der
Hagen, who admits that he translates from the Dutch in his
Erzählungen und Mährchen², Prenzlau, 1838, I, 155 ff. J.
Scheible, Das Kloster, Stuttgart, 1846, II, 129 ff., reprints
this last. For the Spazier translation, see Alt Englische Sagen
und Mährchen nach alten Volksbüchern, herausgegeben von
W. J. Thoms; Deutsch von Richard O. Spazier, Braunschweig,
1830, I, 73 ff. For the statement by J. Görres, see his Die
teutschen Volksbücher, Heidelberg, 1807, 225.

Comparetti (C.–B. 364₉) was misled by Simrock, for he remarks that no ancient versions of Simrock "seem to be
known." I may as well note here another bit of deception,
perpetrated by an anonymous author and printed by David

Nutt. The Wonderful History of Virgilius the Sorcerer of Rome, Englished for the first Time, London, 1893; some copies have a frontispiece drawing of a magician by Aubrey Beardsley. On p. 17 the author acknowledges indebtedness as follows: "the translator of a German text desires to offer most grateful thanks and acknowledgment to Professor Comparetti." By a curious chance, he translates from Simrock's translation. It is hard to see how candor in such a matter would interfere with the sale of the booklet.

12. Others are MSS. Reykjavik IB 130, "Lijf säga þess nafn-fræga Wirgelij ut lögd ur Hollenzku Male"; IB 271, "Lyf Saga þess Nafn fræga Virgelij ür Hollensku útlogd"; Viðb. 23, "Lif saga þess Nafn fræga Virgelij ur Hollensku ut lógd"; MS. Royal Library, Copenhagen, Kallske Samling 614, "Lyfsaga Vergilii Ðess, . . . utlogd ur hollendska"; MS. British Museum Add. 4859, "Hier byriast Lijfs saga þess nafn-fræga Virgelij. Utløgð ur Hollendsku maale"; MS. British Museum Add. 11141, very close to Add. 4859, on which see H. L. D. Ward, A Catalogue of Romances . . . in the British Museum, I (1883), 196 f. (this MS. was formerly No. 2 in the Banks Collection).

13. On MSS. Am. 600c and 600b, which are virtually duplicates, see Katalog over den Arnamagnæanske Håndskriftsamling, I, København, 1889, p. 768, Nos. 1515, 1516, and cf. Jón Thorkelsson, Om Digtningen på Island i det 15. og 16. Århundrede, København, 1888, 180, the same reference being valid for MS. Holm 16 at Stockholm, which belongs also in this group. I have seen all of these MSS. save those at Reykjavik; for information on these I am indebted to Landbók-avörður Dr. Guðmundr Finnbogason, of the Landsbókasafn Íslands, Reykjavik.

14. Nitidae Frægu saga, MS. British Museum Add. 4860; cf. H. L. D. Ward, A Catalogue of Romances . . ., I, 686, 707, 846; the story was retold in rímur in MS. Add. 24973; cf. Ward, A Catalogue . . ., 872 f.

Virgil as king of France — not a great step from Virgil as son of a "chevalier des Ardennes" — is in Reykjavik MS. IB 362; the first few lines read: "Fordum Daga Riede einn

Kongur firer Frakk lande ad Nafne Virgelijus. Han atte sier einn son sem hiet Hunnem og Dottur er Hiet Blomalin. Ðaug olust upp bæde. So var hann settur ij skola ad læra allar þær lister sem einn mann matte Pryda og Hun med sama hætte. So var hun ij einn Kastala med 70 þernum sem attu ad þiona henne. Kastalenn uar miog Rambigge legur allu[r] med gim steinum so þad lyste af honum eins a nott sem Diege.'' Mr. Pjetur Sigurðsson writes me under date Jan. 26, 1928: ''This particular writer is very unskilled and untrained and his spelling is confused and very awkward and gives no evidence about the origin and age of this (very mediocre) romance.'' In a letter dated June 28, 1928, Mr. Sigurðsson says that the manuscript as a whole was written in the neighborhood of 1800, and ventures the opinion that these tales of Virgil probably never had oral life.

CHAPTER X

1. C.-B. 335, 339 (no illustrations). The best discussion of the iconography of Virgilian legend is Eugène Müntz, La légende du sorcier Virgile dans l'art des XIVᵉ, XVᵉ et XVIᵉ siècles, in Monatsberichte für Kunstwissenschaft und Kunsthandel II (1902), 85–91 (with five plates and three illustrations in the text). F. Moth, Aristotelessagnet eller Elskovs Magt, København, 1916, devotes chap. XI, pp. 179–192, to ''Ride- og Kurvemotivet i billedlige Fremstillinger''; he does not know Müntz's article. Émile Mâle, L'art religieux du XIIIᵉ siècle en France⁶, Paris, 1925, 338, alludes to the basket sculpture at Caen. Raimond van Marle, Iconographie de l'art profane au Moyen-Age et à la Renaissance, II (La Haye, 1932), 495–496, reached me too late to be of assistance in the preparation of this chapter. His discussion is independent of those by Müntz and Moth.

2. On the sculptures at Caen see Georges Huard, La Paroisse et l'Église Saint-Pierre de Caen . . ., Caen, 1925–27, 288–294 [Mémoires de la Société des Antiquaires de Normandie, XXXV (1925–27), 4ᵉ Série, 5ᵉ Volume, premier (deuxième) fascicule], far superior on this subject to Eugène de Robillard de Beaurepaire, Caen illustré . . ., Caen, 1896,

179, or to the special study by Armand Gasté, Un chapiteau de l'Église S.-P. de Caen, Caen, 1887 [Études Normandes]. A photograph of the sculpture is reproduced above, p. 254.

3. Professor Taylor Starck informed me of this tapestry. Dr. Majer-Kym of the Augustinermuseum at Freiburg kindly points out that it is fully described by Hermann Schweitzer, Die Bilderteppiche und Stickereien in der städtischen Altertümersammlung zu Freiburg im Breisgau, in Schauinsland, Zeitschrift des Breisgauvereins, XXXI (1904). (Reproduced above, pp. 256, 258.) The basket episode is illustrated in Swiss embroidery, dated 1522, now in the Museum at Zurich. It is reproduced by Raimond van Marle, Iconographie de l'art profane au Moyen-Age et à la Renaissance, II (La Haye, 1932), 463.

4. The manuscript is numbered Cod. perg. III in the Fürstlich Thurn und Taxissches Zentralarchiv. It is described by Philipp Strauch in his edition of Enikel's Weltchronik, Hannover, 1900, p. vi [Monumenta Germaniae Historica], with references to other illuminations. The illustrations appear in this manuscript as follows: Virgil breaking glass, fo. 135 r°; Virgil in the basket, fo. 136 r°; revenge, fo. 137 r°; drunken man breaking statue, fo. 137 v°. (First two and last reproduced above, p. 260.)

Another manuscript illustration is the crude sketch of the revenge in the Stockholm MS. (Cod. Holm perg. 22) of the Virgiless rímur; cf. Moth, Aristotelessagnet . . ., 177.

5. Bernard de Montfaucon, L'Antiquité expliquée . . ., Paris, 1719, II, pt. ii, 356, reproduced by Müntz, pl. 19, and by Moth, p. 189. Cf. Raymond Koechlin, Les ivoires gothiques français, 3 vv., Paris, 1924, II, 412, note on No. 1150, where other reproductions are recorded.

6. Reproduced by Müntz, pl. 20, and by Paolo d'Ancona, L'uomo e le sue opere nelle figurazione italiane del medioevo, Firenze, 1923, pl. LXX.

7. These are in two MSS. of the Trionfi, dated 1450–60, at Florence, Laurentian Library cod. Strozz. 174 and Riccardi Library cod. 1129. Both are reproduced by d'Ancona, L'uomo e le sue opere . . ., pll. LXIX a and LXIX b, and by Luigi

Suttina in the Virgilian memorial supplement to l'Illustrazione Italiana, No. 49, Dec. 7, 1930, pp. 48–49. The latter is reproduced by Müntz, p. 87.

8. In 1931 the tray was in room 103 of the Department of Paintings. Its museum number is 398–1890. Müntz, 87, calls it a "plateau d'accouchée." The coffer at Siena, painted by an unknown artist, is reproduced by Emil Jacobsen, Sodoma und das Cinquecento in Siena, Strassburg, 1910, pl. XLIX, 1; cf. pp. 118 f. [Zur Kunstgeschichte des Auslandes 74], and by Müntz, pl. 21. The latter mentions the coffer at Trieste on p. 87. Le Prince d'Essling and Eugène Müntz, Pétrarque: ses études d'art . . ., Paris, 1902, 159, reproduce a similar scene; see chapters IV, V, and VI, "l'Illustration des Triomphes." V. Zabughin, Vergilio nel Rinascimento Italiano, II, 434$_{156}$, has cryptic references to these last.

9. Cf. Müntz, 88, and Huard, as above, 292$_{26}$.

10. Fifteenth century. This I have not seen. Cf. E. Closson, Revue de l'Université de Bruxelles, III (1902–03), 175.

11. Reproduced by Müntz, pl. 20, and by d'Ancona, as above, pl. LXX. Cf. Graesse, Beiträge zur Literatur und Sage des Mittelalters, Dresden, 1850, 35 f.

12. Reproduced by Müntz, 88, and by Moth, 183, from F. de Guilhermy in Annales archéologiques, VI (1847), 153.

13. P. 139, above. Cf. Müntz, 89, Moth, 186. The latter reproduces several sections of the pilaster after Guilhermy, as above. Cf. Huard, 292 $_{26}$, and p. 262, above.

14. This I have not seen. Cf. Müntz, 88, and M. le Comte d'I *** [Jules Gay], Iconographie des estampes à sujets galants . . ., Genève, 1868, col. 733. The same authority reports an engraving by Andrea Andreani after Malpicci which I have been unable to see, col. 501. Müntz, 89, refers to a bronze plaquette in the Dreyfus collection, which has been dispersed.

15. Müntz, 89, gives the number as 677; it is now in the Salon du Grand Camée and is numbered 579.

16. Müntz, 91. The British Museum has this in two states. Cf. M. le Comte d'I ***, Iconographie . . ., col. 368, and Paul Kristeller, Kupferstich und Holzschnitt[4], Berlin, 1922, 249 f.

17. Altdorfer's revenge is reproduced by E. W. Bredt,

Albrecht Altdorfer, München, 1919, 82, and by Eduard Fuchs and Albert Kind, Die Weiberherrschaft, I, 225. On Altdorfer see Kristeller[4], 238 ff.

Lucas van Leyden's basket dated 1525 has been very frequently reproduced, e. g. by Müntz, pl. 22, while both illustrations of the basket are reproduced by Max J. Friedländer, Lucas van Leyden, Leipzig [1924] (Meister der Graphik, XIII), pll. LXII, LXXIX. N. Beets, Lucas de Leyde, Bruxelles and Paris, 1913 [Collection des Grands Artists des Pays-Bas], reproduces the dated basket and the bocca della verità. On Lucas van Leyden see in addition to these works Rosy Kahn, Die Graphik des Lucas van Leyden, Strassburg, 1918, and Kristeller[4], 312 ff. (All three are reproduced above, pp. 184, 186, 222.)

Georg Pencz's graceful basket and revenge are reproduced by Müntz, pl. 23, the adulterers' bridge by Heinrich Röttinger, Die Holzschnitte des Georg Pencz, Leipzig, 1913; see the bibliographical list, p. 5[1], and Kristeller[4], 245 ff. Johannes Bolte (Martin Montanus' Schwankbücher [Bibliothek des litterarischen Vereins in Stuttgart, CXVII], 631) reports two other adulterers' bridges, by Virgil Solis and Joost Amman; cf. Kristeller[4], 252 ff. (Pencz's basket is reproduced above, p. 188; his bocca, p. 226.)

18. Cf. Müntz, 89. One is No. 323 in the Louvre collection; see Léon De Laborde, Notice des émaux du Musée du Louvre, Paris, 1852–53, I, 218 f. Two are at the Victoria and Albert Museum, London, numbered respectively 551–1883, and C. 2453–1910. They are made by, or after, the school of Pierre Reymond, in the middle of the sixteenth century.

19. Francoforti ad Moenum, 1593; reprinted by Friedrich Warnecke, Berlin, 1894. This is No. xii, "Virgilij Magi Amasium."

20. The Historie of Frier Rush, London, 1620. The unique copy of this edition is numbered C. 34. 5 at the British Museum. The cut is on fo. E ii, v°. Cf. Robert Priebsch, Bruder Rausch, Zwickau, 1919, 69 f. [Zwickauer Facsimiledruck 28]. (The basket from the Dutch romance is reproduced above, p. 236.)

21. Since Robert Proctor has listed these woodcuts, with descriptions, in his monograph on Jan van Doesborgh, London, 1894 [Bibliographical Society, Illustrated Monographs, II], I do not itemize the series.

22. I would note here three other illustrations which I have not seen. Müntz, 91, refers to a painting by Jan Steen (1626–79) from which two engravings were made; these have presumably disappeared (cf. Closson in Revue de l'université de Bruxelles, VIII [1903], 383). The same author refers to a Flemish tapestry (91). In Les faictz merveilleux de Virgille, ed. Philomneste junior [= Gustave Brunet], Genève, 1867, 60, an engraving by Dolendo of Virgil in the basket is mentioned. On the brothers Dolendo see Ulrich Thieme and Felix Becker, Allgemeines Lexikon der Bildenden Künstler, Leipzig, 1907 —. G. M. Crescimbeni, L'istoria della Basilica . . . di S. Maria in Cosmedin, Roma, 1715, 28, notes a picture of the bocca della verità in a house at Rome near the Ponte Rotto. Cf. C.-B. 339₄₆.

23. I. Kings, xi, 4 ff. For studies of Ambrosius Holbein, see A. F. G. A. Woltmann, Holbein und seine Zeit², 2 vv., Leipzig, 1874; W. Hes, Ambrosius Holbein, Strassburg, 1911 [Studien zur deutschen Kunstgeschichte, 145]; Hans Koegler, Ergänzungen zum Holzschnittwerk des Hans und Ambrosius Holbein, in Jahrbuch der Kgl. preussischen Kunstsammlungen, Beiheft to vol. XXVIII (1907), 85 ff.

On this title-border in particular, see Woltmann, II, 206, No. 6, I, 209; Koegler, No. 8; Hes, pp. 39–40; J. Passavant, Le peintre-graveur, 6 vv., Leipzig, 1860–64, H. Holbein, 158; P. Heitz and C. Chr. Bernoulli, Die Basler Büchermarken bis zum Anfang des 17. Jahrhunderts, Strassburg, 1895, p. 23, No. 26. The border is reproduced above, p. 264.

24. Hes, 40; cf. Campbell Dodgson, Catalogue of Early German and Flemish Woodcuts, 2 vv., London, 1903–11, I, 253.

25. For the life of this poet-printer, see Karl Goedeke, Pamphilus Gengenbach, Hanover, 1856; S. Singer, Die Werke des Pamphilus Gengenbach, in Zeitschrift für Deutsches Altertum, XLV (1901), 153–177; Carl Lendi, Der Dichter Pamphi-

lus Gengenbach . . ., Berne, 1926; a brief notice in C. W. Heckethorn, Printers of Basle in the XV and XVI Centuries, London, 1897.

26. A. F. Johnson, One Hundred Titlepages, 1500–1800, London, 1928, p. ix; Robert Brun, Le livre illustré en France au XVIᵉ siècle, Paris, 1930, 256.

27. Erasmus's translation of Lucian was printed by Froben at Basle in 1518; cf. Woltmann, I, 205, II, 207–208, No. 8. The title-page of the 1519 Novum Testamentum is reproduced by Hes, pl. XI.

28. 1516 is the date assigned by M. Holzmann and H. Bohatta, Deutsches Anonymen-Lexikon, Weimar, 1902–11, II (1905), 49 f. The title-page is reproduced by Heitz and Bernoulli, 23, No. 26, and by Heckethorn, 69. On the poem see Karl Euling, Die Jakobsbrüder von Kunz Kistener, Breslau, 1899 [Germanistische Abhandlungen, XVI].

29. On the Epodon liber title-page, see Koegler, No. 8; Hes, p. 39; Heitz and Bernoulli, p. 22. That of Alda Guarini Veronensis is reproduced by Hes, pl. VIII; cf. Woltmann, II, 207. On Croacus . . ., see Graesse, Trésor . . ., VI, ii, 272, and on Luther's sermon Woltmann, II, 207, who says that the top and bottom strips of the border were used alone in a Fabelsammlung, Basle, 1518.

30. On Gengenbach's Gouchmat see Woltmann, I, 209. Goedeke (117 ff.) reprinted it and estimated its date as 1516. J. Bächtold, Geschichte der deutschen Literatur in der Schweiz, Frauenfeld, 1919, 278 ff., also discusses the date, and from internal evidence places it ca. 1520–24. W. Creizenach, Geschichte des neueren Dramas², III, ii, ed. A. Hamel, Halle a. S., 1923, 239 n., regards Bächtold's date as the latest possible. Lendi, 39 ff., judges from internal evidence and from woodcuts that it was not published before 1521.

On Murner's Gäuchmat see Woltmann, I, 210, Wilhelm Uhl, Die Gäuchmatt . . ., Leipzig, 1896, and Eduard Fuchs, Zur Geschichte der Gäuchmatt Thomas Murners, Braune's Beiträge zur Deutschen Sprache und Literatur, XLVIII (1923), 86–92. Cf. Lendi, 43 f., for Das Hofgesind Veneris.

31. On von Gülch-Faber see Heitz and Bernoulli, p. xxix; on Renatus see G. W. Panzer, Annales typographici, 11 vv., Nürnberg, 1793–1803, VI (1798), 266, and Graesse, Trésor ..., II (1861), 15; on Die Epistel D. Erasmi ..., Goedeke, 503.

Joseph Bédier, Les fabliaux⁴, Paris, 1925, 447, mentions the use of a frontispiece border showing on the left side Virgil in the basket, and at the bottom Aristotle saddled and ridden, while on the right is a scene which he cannot identify. This he says appeared in an edition of Henricus "Glarealus" [i. e., Glareanus], De Geographia, printed at Freiburg-im-Breisgau in 1522. I find no such edition listed. Graesse, III (1862), 93, reports that the first edition was printed at Basle in 1526 by Johann Faber. I have examined those published by Faber at Basle in 1527, at Freiburg-im-Breisgau in 1533, 1539, and 1543, and no such border appears; but, as Mr. H. W. Davies recalled, it does appear in the edition of 1530 printed at Freiburg. There are two copies of this at the Bibliothèque Nationale: G. 3491 and V. 7457.

32. On Urs Graf and his work see Emil Major, Urs Graf, Strassburg, 1907 [Studien zur Deutschen Kunstgeschichte 77], esp. 16 ff., 38, 138, 183; E. His, Beschreibendes Verzeichniss des Werks von Urs Graf, in Jahrbücher für Kunstwissenschaft, VI (1873), 143 ff., esp. No. 318; Hans Koegler, Beiträge zum Holzschnittwerk des Urs Graf, in Anzeiger für schweizerische Altertumskunde, N. F. IX (1906), 43 ff., 56, 132 ff., 213 ff. The border is reproduced above, p. 266.

33. See A. F. Johnson, Basle Ornaments on Paris Books, 1519–36, Transactions of the Bibliographical Society (1927), 355–360; Brun, 172; P. Renouard, Les imprimeurs parisiens, Paris, 1898, 317 f.

Resch himself had used one of Graf's borders in G. Brixius, Anti-Morus (1519) — Johnson, 356. Gilles de Gourmont had also used one in Edward Lee's Apologia (1519) — Brun, 247.

I wish to acknowledge gratefully Mr. A. F. Johnson's kind assistance in connection with various points on the Urs Graf border.

34. On the title-page of the Dictionarium Graecum, see

Johnson, 357; it is reproduced by A. F. Butsch, Die Bücher-ornamentik der Hoch- und Spätrenaissance, 2 vv., Leipzig and München, 1881, I, pl. 99. The place of sale is "Sub Crate in Via ad divum Iacobum," the shop of the first Jean Kerver, who died in the following year (Renouard, Imprimeurs parisiens, 199 f.). Butsch errs in attributing the publication to "Johann Badius," an error repeated by Koegler, 56. On Eckius's tract against Luther see Johnson, 357, and Brun, 192; on the work by Stunica, His, No. 318, pp. 7 and 182. The third part of this book is adorned by another of Graf's borders.

35. Cf. Renouard, 317 f., and Johnson, 359. The title-page of the Aeneid, here reproduced, is mentioned by A. Bernard, Geofroy Tory . . ., Paris, 1857, 119 ff., by Müntz, 85 f., and by H. W. Davies, A Catalogue of a Collection of Early French Books in the Library of C. Fairfax Murray, 2 vv., London, 1910, No. 303. On the commentary on Pliny see Koegler, 56, and Johnson, 357.

36. The authorship of this copy of Urs Graf's border is a moot point. The Lorraine cross with which it is marked in the lower centre gave rise to the opinion that it was the work of Geofroy Tory, an important artist and publisher of the time upon whose engravings this cross is often seen; cf. Bernard, 119 ff., 238, Butsch, 72, and Johnson, 357. Brun, pp. 50 ff., discusses the problem, inferring that it is not by Tory but by an unknown worker in some Paris atelier. He suggests that the cross may indicate either that the chef d'atelier made it or that some publisher or printer owned it. It is certain that in style the woodcut differs markedly from Tory's other work, and is much inferior to it. On the edition of the Sainct Greaal see Bernard, 119, and Johnson, 357. On Le vergier dhonneur, see Brun, 297–298, and Müntz, 85 f. Graesse, Trésor . . ., VI, 223, says that it is after 1521. Brunet, Manuel . . ., V, col. 45, mentions this edition but does not date it. The date 1520? is given in A Short-title Catalogue of French Books . . . in the British Museum, ed. Henry Thomas, London, 1924, 391, but Mr. A. F. Johnson of the British Museum now considers the date to be rather 1525. Brun's date, 1520–41, is over-cautious,

as the condition of the woodcut indicates that it was used after the 1523 Sainct Greaal.

37. On the Bartholomaeus Anglicus title-page, see Johnson, 357; on the Orosius, Butsch, I, 72; on La Salade, Brun, 245, and Davies, No. 303; on Crescentiis, Brun, 179 (I have not seen the edition of 1532); on Ovid's Metamorphoses, Brun, 275; on Boccaccio, Brun, 158.

Müntz, 90, mentions an appearance of the border in an edition of Livy's Decades printed in 1553 by J. Petit. Jean Petit I died about 1530 and his son Jean died in 1543 or 1544 (Renouard, Imprimeurs . . ., 291 ff.). The 1552 edition of Livy published by A. Petit does not have our woodcut, and I have not been able to find it on any other. It may be in a 1527 edition of the Decades published by Vidoue for J. Petit, which I have been unable to see.

CHAPTER XI

1. Jean Bodin, De la demonomanie des sorciers, de nouveau reveu et corrigé . . ., Anvers, 1593, book II, chap. ii, p. 131. C.-B. 370$_{23}$. Pierre Le Loyer, iiii. Livres des spectres ou apparitions et visions . . ., Angers, 1586, 150. C.-B. 369$_{21}$. Annibale Caro, L'Eneide di Virgilio . . ., Venezia, 1750, 8. The first edition, which I have not seen, is dated 1581. Blaise de Vigenère, Traicté des chiffres ou secrètes manières d'escrire, Paris, 1586, 329.

2. Alphonsi Tostati opera omnia quotquot in scripturae sacrae expositionem . . ., ex editione Ramerii Provosii, Venetiis, 13 vv. in 12, 1596, I, fo. 16, v°, "Comentarium in epistolam D. Hieronymi ad Paulinum," chap. VI.

Martino del Rìo, Disquisitionum magicarum libri sex, 3 vv., Lovanii, 1599–1600, II, 125, frequently reprinted during the seventeenth century. Théodorici à Niems, pontificii quondam scribae, deinde episcopi Verdensis, Historiarum sui temporis libri iiii. quorum tres priores de schismate universali . . ., Argentorati, 1608, lib. II, cap. XXII, pp. 100, 103 f.

3. P. Virgilii Maronis Bucolica et Georgica [et Aeneis], argumentis, explicationibus, notis illustrata, auctore Joanne

Ludovico de la Cerda Tolitano Societatis Jesu . . ., 2 vv., Matriti, 1608–17, I, fo. c 1, v°. Other editions repeat this passage, e. g., Lugduni (1612–19), 3 vv., I, fo. a 6, r° (best edition); Coloniae Agrippinae, 1628, 2 vv., I, fo. c 1, v°; same, 3 vv., 1647, fo. a 6, r°.

P. de l'Ancre, L'incredulité et mescreance du sortilege plainement convaincue, Paris, 1622, 280 f. The "Epistre au Roy," p. 4. Cf. C.-B. 280, 370$_{23}$.

4. Gabriel Naudé, Apologie pour tous les grands personnages . . ., Paris, 1625, "Du Poete Virgile," 605–634. This work was reprinted frequently, e. g., La Haye, 1653, 1679, Paris, 1669, Amsterdam, 1712. It appeared in English in 1657 and in German in 1704. A study of this interesting figure is needed, as the following are scattered and are not exhaustive: Alfred Franklin, Histoire de la Bibliothèque Mazarine, Paris, 1860; Jacques Denis, Sceptiques ou libertins de la première moitié du XVIIe siècle: Gassendi, Gabriel Naudé . . ., Caen, 1884 [Mémoires de l'Académie nationale des Sciences, Arts et Belles-Lettres de Caen]; J. -J. Bouchard, Deux lettres inédites à Gabriel Naudé, Paris, 1892; Gaston Lavalley, Études historiques et littéraires . . ., un courtisan de lettres, Gabriel Naudé . . ., Paris [1905]; Joseph W. Courtney, Gabriel Naudé, M.D., Preëminent Savant, Bibliophile, Philanthropist, in Annals of Medical History, VI (1924), 303–311. A fair estimate of Naudé may be derived from Naudæana et Patiniana; ou singularitez remarquables prises des conversations de Mess. Naudé et Patin^2, ed. A. Lancelot, 1703 (published by Bayle). C.-B. 219$_{14}$, 265$_5$, 369 f.

5. I quote from the English translation by Edmund Chilmead, London, 1650, introduction, A vi, v°; chap. VI, title, p. 145; chap. VI, art. 3, p. 152; on Virgil, chap. VII, art. 13, pp. 235 f.; conclusion, p. 239. The earliest edition of the original that I know was published at Rouen in 1632 (Curiositez Inouyes . . .). Reprints appeared (at Paris?) in 1637 and 1650. The work is most frequently found now in Curiositez inoyes, hoc est, Curiositates inauditae de figuris Persarum talismanicis, latine opera M. Gr. Michaelis, Hamburg and Amsterdam, 1676.

6. The title-page of this work bears the attribution "par le sieur de l'Isle," a pseudonym for Charles Sorel. Pp. 145–336 are devoted to the criticism of Gaffarel. The passage above summarized appears on pp. 273 ff.; Gaffarel's retraction on pp. 336–337, concluding "Huic rei ut sit manifesta fides nomen cum Chirographo apposui 4. die Octobris 1629. *I. Gaffarelus.*"

7. Jacques d'Autun, L'incredulité scavante, et la credulité ignorante: Au sujet des magiciens et des sorciers. Avecque Le Response à un Livre intitulé Apologie pour tous les Grands Personnages, qui ont esté faussement soupçonnés de Magie, Lyon, 1671, 868; cf. 1027 ff. Similarly, Baudelot de Dairval, in De l'utilité des voyages, et de l'avantage que la recherche des antiquitez procure aux scavans, 2 vv., Paris, 1686, who does not mention Virgil as a magician, believes that the true knowledge of talismans is natural and does not overstep the rules of philosophy; it is not necessary to turn to the abominations of magic in order to produce effects which philosophy teaches. — II, 390. On witchcraft in the seventeenth century, see G. L. Kittredge, Witchcraft in Old and New England, Cambridge [Mass.], 1929.

8. Carlo Celano, Degli Avanzi delle Poste, Venezia, 1677, 187 f. Cf. Celano's Notizie della citta di Napoli, Napoli, 1792, V, 223–228, for a notice of his life; Teresa Navarra, Un oscuro imitatore di Lope de Vega: Carlo Celano, Bari, 1919; Benedetto Croce, in Napoli Nobilissima, II (1893), 65–70. This "Alexis" is no doubt the darling of the Second Eclogue.

9. L. Bordelon, De l'astrologie judiciaire . . ., Paris, 1689, 65 f.; the same author's L'histoire des imaginations extravagantes de Monsieur Oufle causées par la lecture des livres qui traitent de la magie, du grimoire, des démoniaques, sorciers, loups-garoux, incubes, succubes & du sabbat des fées, ogres, esprits folets, genies, phantômes & autre revenans; des songes de la pierre philosophale, de l'astrologie judiciaire, des horoscopes, talismans, jours heureux & malheureux, eclypses, cometes & almanaches; enfin de toutes les sortes d'apparitions, de divinations, de sortilèges, d'enchantemens, & d'autres

superstitieuses pratiques. Le tout enrichi de figures & accompagné d'un très grand nombre de nottes [sic] curieuses, qui rapportent fidellement les endroits des livres qui ont causés ces imaginations extravagantes, ou qui peuvent servir pour les combattre, 2 vv., Amsterdam, 1710, I, 230, 232 f.; II, 141. For the list of books read by M. Oufle, see I, 12 ff.

10. In Bayle's Dictionnaire the article on Virgil, repeated in later editions, appears in that of Rotterdam, 1697, at pp. 2970 ff., that on Virgil's magic at pp. 2974 ff.

The 1717 treatise on talismans is Petrus Fridericus Arpe, De prodigiosis naturae et artis operibus, talismanes et amuleta dictis cum recensione scriptorum hujus argumenti, Hamburgi, 1717, 23 ff.

John Hill, Lucina sine Concubitu. A Letter Humbly addressed to the Royal Society, in which is proved, by most Incontestable Evidence, drawn from Reason and Practice, that a Woman may conceive, and be brought to bed, without any Commerce with Man, London, 1750, 149 f. (frequently reprinted during the next twenty years).

Voltaire's Essai sur les Moeurs (1756) and Un Chrétien contre six Juifs (1776), in his Oeuvres complètes, ed. M. Beuchot, 72 vv., Paris, 1829–40, XXV, 158, and XLVIII, 499 f.

11. See Samuel M. Waxman in Revue hispanique, XXXVIII (1916), 352 f., and C.-B. 319 f.

12. The cento is "Astronomicae artis liber, ex scriptis Virgilii compositus," in MS. British Museum Arundel 268, f. 92 b; cf. A Catalogue of Manuscripts in the British Museum, new series, I, part i, The Arundel Manuscripts, London, 1834, 266.

At the Bodleian, in MS. Digby 164, fo. 25 b–26 b (beginning fifteenth century) is "Ramus secretissimi lapidis per Virgilium a natura expletum"; and in MS. Museae 63, fo. 90 v°–92 v° (Dr. H. H. E. Craster kindly dates it in the third quarter of the sixteenth century), is "Virgilius de Lapide Veridico," a series of recipes.

In MS. B. M. Sloane 2327, fo. 12 b ff. (fifteenth century), is a "Liber Virgilii de lapide philosophico." This brief list could be expanded indefinitely; for an essay on Scot's alchemy, see C. H. Haskins, Mediaeval Culture[2], Oxford, 1929, 148–159.

The word for chemist in Welsh, fferyll, may be due to this same conception of Virgil; cf. Greek φαρμακός.

13. The passage in the Mirabilia concerning the Balneapolis can be found in The Marvels of Rome, ed. and trans. F. M. Nichols, London, 1889, 17. In the Latin form it is in C. L. Urlichs, Codex Topographicus Urbis Romae, Wurzburg, 1871, 128. For Capgrave's version, see Ye Solace of Pilgrims, fo. 360, v° [= p. 16]. For access to the voluminous literature of the Mirabilia, see Julius Schlosser, Die Kunstliteratur . . ., Wien, 1924, 45, 193, and Ludwig Schudt, Le Guide di Roma, Wien, 1930, 19$_1$.

14. "Zu der andern seitten der spiegelpurg do ist ain hoch sibel gemeur do stund die junkfraw die Virgilium het gehenget für das venster von iren wegen erlescht Virgilius als feur zü rom es mocht do niemant kain feur an zunden dan an der junkfraw scham." — From the edition of Hanns Awrl, printed "an sant Michel abent," 1481. Cf. R. Ehwald's reproduction of the earliest printed edition, a block-book of about 1475, for the Weimar Gesellschaft der Bibliophilen, 1905, and Christian Huelsen's edition of Stephan Planck's Mirabilia Romae of 1489, Berlin, 1925.

On the Meta Sudans, see G. Lugli, La Zona archeologica di Roma, Roma, 1924, 116, and R. A. Lanciani, The Ruins and Excavations of Ancient Rome, London, 1897, 193. On the identification of it in connection with Virgil, see below, p. 440, and cf. C.-B. 348.

15. "Il palazzo dove Virgilio fu tenuto alle finestre. . . . Una cupoletta dove stette quella donna chel tenne alle finestre col fuocho tral le gambe." — Giovanni Rucellai, Il Giubileo dell' anno 1450, ed. Giuseppe Marcotti, in Archivio della Società Romana di storia patria, IV (1881), 577. On the Rucellai family, see Giuseppe Marcotti, Un mercanto fiorentino e la sua famiglia nel secolo X, Firenze, 1881. On the identification of the palace as the Frangipani tower, see Ferdinand Gregorovius, Geschichte der Stadt Rom im Mittelalter, I, 1226. This tower, called the Cancellaria, from the office of Pietro Frangipani, once Chancellor of Rome, or the Cartularia, from the presence there of the papal archives, was built in the

eighth century. It was partially destroyed by Brancaleone in the thirteenth century and almost completely so in the nineteenth; see G. B. de Rossi, in Notizie degli Scavi, Decembre, 1883, 493 ff.; Louis Duchesne, Le Liber Pontificalis, Paris, 1884, I, 386₇ [Bibliothèque de l'École Française, III, 2me série]; G. Lugli, La Zona Archeologica . . ., 115; S. B. Platner and Thomas Ashby, A Topographical Dictionary of Ancient Rome, Oxford, 1929, 304. H. Jordan, Topographie der Stadt Rom im Altertum, Berlin, 1871–85, II, 506, thought that the Cartularia and the Frangipani tower were distinct but closely adjoining one another. E. Stevenson, in Bollettino della Commissione archeologica, 1888, 269–298, says — erroneously, I believe — that the "palace" of which Rucellai speaks was the ruins of the Septizonium, which is at some distance from the Colosseum. Cf. above, p. 285, and C.-B. 348.

16. "Vor dem eussersten schwipogen, der Tytus und Vespasianus zu eren gemacht ist darynn die uberwindung Jerusalem stet, do ist der stein gemauert von zigeln, darauf des keysers pull stand und all Rom mussten von ir holen, dan ein zaubrer alle feur erlescht het und kein stein kraft het feur zu geben. Item darnach ist der Simbel Spiegelpurck." — Nikolaus Muffel, Beschreibung der Stadt Rom, ed. W. Vogt, Tübingen, 1876, 57 [Bibliothek des litterarischen Vereins in Stuttgart, CXXVIII]. Vogt thinks that the "keysers pull" is from L. ampulla; as Graf, Roma . . . (1923), 54₆₄, says, the word is clearly that represented by modern German Buhle.

17. "Item voert zo der ander sijden der spiegelborch, dae steyt eyn slecht gemuyrs daer off die vrauwe gestanden is die Virgilium bedroegen hatte, dar umb he all die vuyr dede lesschen die bynnen Rom waeren ind moysten weder komen an desen steyn dae dese vrauwe off stoynt ind ontfengen der vuyr an deser vrauwen schemden." — Ritter Arnold von Harff, Pilgerfahrt . . . in den Jahren 1496–99, ed. E. von Groote, Köln, 1860, 25.

18. "De mirabilibus Romae non nominati auctoris libellis, in vulgi manibus est, ad deci piĕdos (ut apparet) illiteratos & superstitiosos homines confictus. In cognoscenda Urbe sermo vulgi audiendus non est. Molem latericiam ante Amphi-

theatrum, quae Meta Sudans dicta fuit, aiunt fuisse turrim Virgilij." — Georgius Fabricius, Roma . . . Eiusdem itinerum liber unus . . ., Basiliae, 1551, 19.

19. R. Lanciani, Storia degli scavi di Roma, 4 vv., Roma, 1902–12, II, 41 f.

20. J. J. Boissardus, Antiquitatum Romanarum libri, 2 vv., Frankfurt, 1597–1602, I, 56.

21. A. Scoto, Itinerario d'Italia . . ., Padova, 1629, part II, fo. 57, v°. Giovanni Marangoni, Delle memorie sacre e profane dell' Anfiteatro Flavio di Roma . . ., Roma, 1746, 51.

22. For the origin of the name Scuola di Virgilio, see Christian Huelsen's article on the Septizonium in Zeitschrift der Geschichte des Architectur, V (1911), 21. Instances of the use of the term may be found also in C. Huelsen, Das Septizonium des Severus, 46. Berlin. Winckelmanns-program (1886), 5, 8, 10 [Berliner Archäologische Gesellschaft]; Forma Urbis Romae Regionum XIV, ed. H. Jordan, Berlin, 1874, 39, cols. 1 and 2; A. Bertolotti, Artisti Lombardi, 2 vv., Milano, 1881, I, 79, 90; E. Stevenson, Il settizonio severiano e la distribuzione dei suoi avanzi sotto Sisto V, in Bollettino dellacommissione archeologica, 1888, p. 272. See also Bartoli, I Documenti per la storia del Settizonio Severiano e i disegni inediti de Marten van Heemskerck, in Bollettino d'Arte (Ministero della Pubblica Istruzione), Roma, 1909, serie 1, 253–269, and particularly for structural details, Theodor Dombart, Das Palatinische Septizonium zu Rom, München, 1922. Further bibliography on the Septizonium is found in Platner and Ashby, Topographical Dictionary, 475. For the use of the term Schola Septem Sapientium, see John Capgrave, Ye Solace of Pilgrims, 44. On the poem mentioning Virgil's Academy, see C.–B. 348 f.

The literature of travel in Italy is most easily accessible through the following works: L. Friedländer, Reisen in Italien in den letzten drei Jahrhunderten, in Deutsche Rundschau, VII (1876), 233–251; L. Hautecoeur, Rome et la Renaissance de l'Antiquité à la fin du XVIIIe siècle, in Bibliothèque des Écoles Françaises d'Athènes et de Rome, CV, Paris, 1912; H. Neville Maugham, The Book of Italian Travel, New York,

1903; Jules Bertaut, L'Italie vue par les Français, Paris, 1913 [Annales politiques et littéraires]; William E. Mead, The Grand Tour in the Eighteenth Century, Boston and New York, 1914; L. Rava, Roma negli scrittori stranieri, in Nuova Antologia, LXI (1926), 3ª serie, 407 ff.; E. Bourgeois and L. André, Les sources de l'histoire de France (1610–1715), Géographie et Histoires générales, Paris, 1913, 1923, 1926; Geoffroy Atkinson, La littérature géographique française de la Renaissance, répertoire bibliographique . . ., Paris, 1927 (travels among non-European peoples).

23. On the question of Virgil's residence, see Gaetano Amalfi, Montevergine, in Napoli Nobilissima, V (1896), 97 ff.; Enrico Cocchia, L'elemento tosco nella Campania, in Atti della Reale Accademia di archeologia, lettere e belle arti, nuova serie, IV (1916), parte prima, 264 f.; A. G. Amatucci, in Rassegna italica di lingue e lettere classiche, I (1919), 151; Giorgio Pasquali, Virgilio e Montevergine, in Atene e Roma, XXII (1919), 215–227; A. G. Amatucci, Virgilio e Montevergine, in Atene e Roma, XXIII (1920), 221–225; and especially Norman W. Dewitt, Virgil at Naples, in Classical Philology, XVII (1922), 104–110. C.–B. 278 ff.

24. On "Monte Vergiliano" see M. Pandolfo Collenuccio, Del Compendio Dell' Istoria del Regno di Napoli . . ., ed. T. Costo, Venezia, 1613, 12 [Costo's edition appeared first in 1591. Cf. the edition by Alfredo Saviotti, Bari, 1929, 328₃]; Vincenzo Verace, La vera istoria dell' Origine e delle cose notabile di Montevergine, Napoli, 1585, 33; Tomaso Costo, Istoria dell' Origine del Sagratissimo luogo di Montevergine, Venezia, 1591, fos. 6, r°, 9, v°; Cesare d'Engenio Caracciolo, Napoli sacra, Napoli, 1624, 305; D. Amato Mastrullo, Monte Vergine Sago, Napoli, 1663, 2; Carlo Celano, Notitie . . . di Napoli . . ., 6 vv., Napoli, 1692, Giornata III, p. 175; A Ramble through Holland, France, and Italy, 2 vv., London, 1793, 170. On Virgil's house at Pozzuoli, see Gilbert Burnet, Some Letters: Containing an account of what seemed most remarkable in Switzerland, Italy, &c., Rotterdam, 1686, 216; [C. Bourdin], Voyage d'Italie . . ., Paderborn, 1699, 224.

25. Discussions of the question of Virgil's grave are by O.

Lehmann, Virgil's Grab, in Europa, 1885, N. 2, 55 ff.; R. T. Günther, Pausilypon, the Imperial Villa near Naples . . . with observations on the Tomb of Virgil . . ., Oxford, 1913, 201 ff., who argues for the submerged site of the tomb of Virgil, an argument furthered by F. W. Kelsey, The Tomb of Virgil, in Art and Archaeology, VII [July–August, 1918], 264 ff.; Enrico Cocchia, La Tomba di Virgilio, in Archivio storico per le provincie napoletane, XIII (1888), Fasc. 3 and 4, pp. 511–568, 631–744, reprinted in L'Italia meridionale e la Campania, Naples, 1902, 135–249, and, with additions, in Μουσείον, IV (1927–28), 67–81, 129–140, who stoutly defends the theory that the columbarium is actually Virgil's tomb, continuing his argument in L'elemento tosco nella Campania, in Atti della Reale Accademia di archeologia, lettere e belle arti, nuova serie, IV (1916), parte prima, 253–265 [Società Reale di Napoli]. Cf. also Francesco d'Ovidio, Benvenuto da Imola e la leggenda Virgiliana, in Atti dell' Accademia di archeologia, lettere e belle arti, nuova serie, IV (1916), 85 ff. [Società Reale di Napoli], and Norman W. Dewitt, Virgil at Naples, in Classical Philology, XVII (1922), 104–110. Cf. C.-B. 275 ff.

26. Cf. Napoli Nobilissima, III (1894), 30 f. One Pietro di Steffano is reported to have said that in 1560 the urn enclosing Virgil's ashes was still in the columbarium, but such a statement is hardly credible. Cf. Johann Georg Keysler, Neueste Reisen durch . . . Italien, Hanover, 1740, English translation in 1756, 4 vv., London, II, 432 f.

27. Early references to Virgil's tomb are by Benedetto Falco, Descrizione dei luoghi antichi di Napoli, Napoli, 1535?, fo. B iiii, v°; F. Leandro Alberti, Descrittioni di tutta l'Italia . . ., Bologna, 1550, fo. 162 b; Georg. Fabricius, Itinerum. Liber unus, quo haec continentur. Iter Romanum primum. Iter Neapolitanum . . ., Basel, 1551, 24; Hieronnimus Turlerus, De Peregrinatione et agro Napolitano, Strassburg, 1574, 92 f.; G. Sandys, Travailes . . ., London, 1615, 206; Lucien Marcheix, Un Parisien à Rome et à Naples en 1632. D'Après un manuscrit inédit de J.-J. Bouchard, Paris, 1897, 104; John Raymond, An Itinerary Containing a Voyage made through Italy . . ., London, 1648, 145; James Howell, Parthenopoeia

..., London, 1654, 125; Maximilien Misson, Nouveau Voyage d'Italie, La Haye, 1691, 317; Carlo Celano, Notitie ... di Napoli ..., 6 vv., Napoli, 1692, Giornata IX, 54 f.; John Owen, Travels into different Parts of Europe in the years 1791 and 1792 ..., London, 1796, II, 130; Mme. Fiquet du Boccage, Lettres sur l'Italie, translated into English and published in 1770, 2 vv., London, II, 77; [J. F. Cooper], Gleanings in Europe ..., by an American, 2 vv., Philadelphia, 1838, I, 187.

Others who have mentioned the tomb, sometimes surmising as to its authenticity, commenting on the laurel, and so on, are Scipione Mazzella, Descrizione del regno di Napoli, Napoli, 1586, fo. 13; English Faust Book of 1592, ed. H. Logeman, Amsterdam, 1900, 54 [Recueil de travaux publiés par la Faculté de Philosophie et Lettres de l'université de Gand, fasc. 24]; Christopher Marlowe's Doctor Faustus, ed. Sir A. W. Ward and C. B. Wheeler, Oxford, 1915, 28; J. J. Boissardus, Antiquitatum Romanarum libri, 2 vv., Francofordii, 1597–1602, I, 56; Henri, Duc de Rohan, Voyage faict en l'an 1600 en Italie ..., Amsterdam, 1646, 99; Itinerarium Italiae totius ... editum studio et industria trium nobilissimorum Germaniae Adolescentum ..., Coloniae Agrippinae, 1602, 186; Giulio Cesare Capaccio, Neapolitanae Historiae ..., Napoli, 1607, 391 f.; Journal d'un Voyage de France et d'Italie fait par un gentilhomme françois ..., Paris, 1667, 567; Richard Lassels, The Voyage of Italy ..., 2 parts, Paris, 1670, II, 289; Raccolta di varii libri, over opuscoli d'Historie del Regno di Napoli ..., Napoli, 1680, 12 ff.; le comte de Caylus, Voyage d'Italie, 1714–1715, ed. Amilda A. Pons, Paris, 1914, 253; Joachim Christoph Nemeitz, Nachlese besonderer Nachrichten von Italien ..., Leipzig, 1726, 281; Georg Christian Adler, Reisebemerkungen auf einer Reise nach Rom, Altona, 1784, 238; Karl Philipp Moritz, Reisen eines Deutschen in Italien in den Jahren 1786 bis 1788 ..., 3 vv., Berlin, 1792–93, II, 28.

28. G. C. Capaccio, La vera antichità di Pozzuolo, Napoli, 1607, 12; G. Sandys, Travailes ..., 206, translating from "M. Am. Flam."; Massmann, Kaiserchronik ..., 442, with reference to Bulwer Zancai.

29. On the Grotta di Virgilio see Ludovico De la Ville sur-Yllon, La grotta di Pozzuoli, in Napoli Nobilissima, IX (1900), 19 ff.; R. T. Günther, Pausilypon . . ., 15 ff.; F. d'Ovidio, Benvenuto da Imola . . ., 208 ff.; F. W. Kelsey, The Tomb of Virgil, 264 ff.

30. On the Grotta di Virgilio see Fazio degli Uberti (d. ca. 1370), Dittamondo, Firenze, 1501 [first ed. Milano, 1474], Book III (cf. C.–B. 354); Octavien de Saint-Gelais [and André de LaVigne], Le vergier dōneur . . . De l'entreprise & voyage de naples . . ., Paris, 1520?, fo. G i; Hieronnimus Turlerus, De Peregrinatione et agro Napolitani, Strasburg, 1574, 92 f.; Benedetto di Falco, Descrizione dei luoghi antichi di Napoli, Napoli, 1535?, fo. B ii, v° f.; English Faust Book of 1592, ed. H. Logeman, Amsterdam, 1900, 54; Christopher Marlowe's Doctor Faustus, ed. A. W. Ward and C. B. Wheeler, Oxford, 1915, 28; G. Sandys, Travailes . . ., London, 1615, 205; Josephus Mormile, Descrittione della città di Napoli . . ., Napoli, 1625, 38; Carlo Celano, Notitie . . . di Napoli per i signori forastieri, 6 vv., Napoli, 1692, Giornata III, 190 ff., Giorn. IX, 45 f., Giorn. V, 77 f.; Joseph Addison, Remarks on several Parts of Italy . . ., London, 1705, 217; John Breval, Remarks on several Parts of Europe . . ., 2 vv., London, 1738, 67; Johann Georg Keysler, Neueste Reisen durch Deutschland . . ., translated into English and published in 4 vv., London, 1756–57, II, 435; the abbé Coyer, Voyage d'Italie et d'Hollande, 2 vv., Paris, 1775, I, 217; John Moore, A View of Society and Manners in Italy . . .⁴, London, 1787, 294 f. [first ed. 1781]; Lorenzo Giustiniani, La Biblioteca storica e topografica del regno di Napoli, Napoli, 1793, 47.

Other writers who have reported the popular belief in the legend are G. Braun and F. Hohenberg, Civitatis orbis terrarum, 6 vv., Cologne, 1523 [1573?]–1618, V, 65, v°; J. J. Boissardus, Antiquitatum Romanarum libri, 2 vv., Francofordii, 1597–1602, I, 56; F. Schotto, Itinerarii Italiae Rerumque Romanorum libri tres, Antwerp, 1600, 374; Ioan. Francisco Lombardi Neapolitani ΣΥΝΟΨΙΣ. Eorum quae de Balneis, aliisque miraculis Puteolanis scripta sunt, in G. Barrius, De antiquitate et situ Calabriae [Italiae illustratae . . . scriptores

varii], Franckfurt, 1600, col. 799; J. Rigaud, Recueil des choses
rares d'Italie, Aix, 1601, fo. 73, r°; Itinerarium Italiae totius
. . . editum studio et industria trium nobilissimorum Germaniae Adolescentum . . ., Coloniae Agrippinae, 1602, 188;
G. C. Capaccio, Puteolana Historia . . ., Napoli, 1604, 188;
same author, La vera antichità di Pozzuolo . . ., Napoli, 1607,
20 f.; J. W. Neumair von Ramssla, Reise durch Welschland
und Hispanien . . ., Leipzig, 1622, 319; Joannes Henricus a
Pflaumern, Mercurius Italicus, Augustae Vindelicorum, 1625,
362; Jodocus Hondius, Nova et accurata Italiae hodierne
descriptio . . ., Amsterdam, 1626, 237; William Lithgow, The
Totall Discourse of the Rare Adventures and Painefull Pere-
grinations of long Nineteen Yeares Travayles (1609–1629),
London, 1632, 21, 404; Martin Zeiller, Itinerarium Italiae
Nov-Antiquae . . ., Franckfurt, 1640, 166; Philip Skippon, An
Account of a Journey made thro' . . . Italy . . . [5], in A. and J.
Churchill, A Collection of Voyages and Travels [3] . . ., VI,
London, 1746, 603 [Skippon was in Italy in 1663]; Matthias
Puel, Reisen und Seefahrten von der Stadt Steyr . . ., Nürn-
berg, 1666, 69 f.; C. d'Engenio Caracciolo, Descrittione del
regno di Napoli, Napoli, 1671, 30; [Ottavo Beltrano], Breve
descrizione del regno di Napoli . . ., Napoli, 1670, 30; Raccolta
di varii libri, overo opuscoli d'Historie del Regno di Napoli
. . ., Napoli, 1680, 11 [= account of B. Falco]; Pompeo
Sarnelli, Guido de' Forestieri . . ., Napoli, 1685, 2 f.; Topo-
graphia Italiae, Das ist: Warhaffte und Curiôse Beschreibung
von ganz Italien, Franckfurt, 1688, 70; Maximilien Misson,
Nouveau Voyage d'Italie, La Haye, 1691, 317; Tegenvoordigen toestand van de Pausilype Hof nevens alle andere Hoven
. . ., Utrecht, 1697, 193; Curieuse und vollstandige Reiss-
Beschreibung von ganz Italien . . ., Freyburg, 1701, 154;
Rogissart et H[avart], Les Délices de l'Italie . . ., 6 vv.,
Leyden, 1709 [first ed. Amsterdam, 1700], IV, 85; Domenico
Antonio Parrino, Napoli città nobilissima, Napoli, 1700,
146; Joachim Christoph Nemeitz, Nachlese besonderer Nach-
richten von Italien . . ., Leipzig, 1726, 287, note; [Guyot
de Merville], Voyage historique d'Italie . . ., 2 vv., La Haye,
1729, II, 388; A True Description and Direction of what is

most worthy to be seen in all Italy . . ., in Harleian Miscellany, V (1744), 31; Mme. Fiquet du Boccage, Lettres sur l'Italie (ca. 1757), translated into English as Letters concerning England, Holland, and Italy, 2 vv., London, 1770, II, 77 f.; A new and complete Collection of Voyages and Travels . . ., London, for J. Coote, 1760, 259; Paolo Antonio Paoli, Antichità di Pozzuoli, Napoli, 1768, fo. 10; l'abbé Richard, Description historique et critique de l'Italie . . ., 6 vv., Paris, 1766, IV, 153 f.; P. J. Grosley, New Observations on Italy . . . by Two Swedish Gentlemen . . ., 2 vv., London, 1769, 225; D. J. J. Volkmann, Historisch-kritische Nachrichten von Italien . . ., Leipzig, 1771, III, 211; Dictionnaire historique et géographique portatif de l'Italie . . ., 2 vv., Paris, 1775, II, 273 f.; Lady Anna Riggs Miller, Letters from Italy . . ., 3 vv., London, 1776, II, 333 f.; Dr. Burnet, in John Hamilton Moore's A new and complete collection of voyages and travels . . ., London, 1780, 908 [Burnet says that the vulgar people attribute the tunnel to the devil]; J. J. Björnståhl, Rese til . . . Frankrike, Italien . . ., 6 vv., Stockholm, 1780–84, of which I use the Italian translation by B. D. Zini di Val di Non, published in 6 vv., Poschiavo, 1782–87; Friedrich von Stolberg, Reise in Deutschland, der Schweiz, Italien, und Sicilien, 4 vv., Königsberg and Leipzig, 1794, III, 303. Cf. C.-B. 262, 278, 353, 373 f.

31. [J. Clenche], A Tour in France and Italy, made by an English Gentleman, 1675, London, 1676, 95; Tegenvoordigen toestand van det Pausilype Hof . . ., Utrecht, 1697, 194; Maximilien Misson, Nouveau Voyage, 317; Curieuse und vollstandige Reiss-Beschreibung von ganz Italien . . ., Freyburg, 1701, 154; A. de Montesquieu, Voyage en Italie, Paris, 1896, II, 8.

32. Cf. G. C. Capaccio, Puteolana Historia, Napoli, 1604, 188; Carlo Celano, Notitie . . . di Napoli . . ., Giornata V, pp. 77 f.; Domenico Antonio Parrino, Napoli città nobilissima, 94 f.; Paolo Antonio Paoli, Antichità di Pozzuoli, Napoli, 1768, fo. 10; De La Lande, Voyage d'un François en Italie, VI, 147.

33. On the piscine at the Castel dell' Ovo, cf. F. Nicolini,

La Lettera del Summonte, in L'Arte Napoletana del rinascimento, Napoli, 1925, 175; Pompeo Sarnelli, Guida de' Forestieri . . .³, Napoli, 1692, 27 f.; Domenico Antonio Parrino, Napoli città nobilissima, 94 f. On Niccolò Pesce, see Benedetto Croce, La Storia popolare espagnuola di Niccolò Pesce, in Napoli Nobilissima, V (1896), 65–71, 85–89, 141–143.

34. Benedetto di Falco, Descrizione dei luoghi antichi di Napoli, Napoli, 1535?, fo. K ii; Jérome Maurand, Itinéraire d'Antibes à Constantinople, ed. Léon Drez, Paris, 1901, 88 [Schefer et Cordier, Recueil des Voyages]; Lucien Marcheix, Un Parisien à Rome et à Naples en 1632: D'après un manuscrit inédit de J.-J. Bouchard, Paris, 1897, 107; James Howell, Parthenopoeia . . ., London, 1654, 2 f.; Topographia Italiae, Das ist: Warhaffte und Curiöse Beschreibung von ganz Italien, Franckfurt, 1688, 72.

35. On the ruins at Gaiola, see R. T. Günther, Pausilypon, the Imperial Villa near Naples . . . with observations on the Tomb of Virgil . . ., Oxford, 1913, 3, 141 ff. [includes excellent pictures]; for references to the legend, see Carlo Celano, Notitie . . . di Napoli . . ., Giornata IX, p. 83; Domenico Antonio Parrino, Napoli città nobilissima, 155 f.; same author, Di Napoli, Il Seno Cratero . . ., Napoli, 1700 [= part 2 of Napoli nobilissima], 168; same author, Nuova Guida De' Forestieri per l'Antichita Curiosissime Di Pozzuoli . . ., Napoli, 1709, 131; le comte de Caylus, Voyage d'Italie, 252; Johann Georg Keysler, Neueste Reisen durch Deutschland . . ., II, 434; Friedrich von Stolberg, Reise in . . . Italien . . ., III, 308; Elisa von der Recke, Tagebuch einer Reise durch einen Theil Deutschlands und durch Italien, in den Jahren 1804 bis 1806, 3 vv., Berlin, 1815–17, III, 172; Hans Ferdinand Massmann, Der Keiser und der Kunige buoch, oder die sogenannte Kaiserchronik . . ., 441₃; Ampère, L'histoire romaine à Rome, in Revue des deux mondes, 1 nov. 1866, 70; C.-B. 348₂₂, 372.

36. F. H. von der Hagen, Briefe in die Heimat, Breslau, 1819, III, 184 ff., IV, 118 ff., is perfectly genuine in thinking that he has the real thing, and so presumably is Rachel A. Busk in the Virgilian legends which she included in The Folk-

lore of Rome, London, 1870, though both got "guide-lore."
Such is not the case, I think, with Willibald Alexis [pseu-
donym for Georg Wilhelm Heinrich Häring], Der Zauberer
Virgilius, ein Märchen aus der Gegenwart, Berlin, 1851,
with Marc Monnier, La légende de Virgile à Naples et en
Sicile, in Les contes populaires en Italie, Paris, 1880, 51–59,
nor with Matilde Serao, Virgilio mago, in Leggende Napoletane, Modena, 1891. For Leland's remark, see his The Unpublished Legends of Virgil, London, 1899, 47; cf. the review by
Lionel P. Johnson in The Academy for Feb. 10, 1900, reprinted
in his Post Liminium, Essays and Critical Papers, ed. Thomas
Whittemore, London, 1911, 223–229. I suppose that I should
divulge here my own "unpublished" legend. In May, 1931, a
guide at the Baths of Agnano, near the Dogs' Grotto at
Naples, told me in response to a leading question that Virgil
had made not only the baths there, but also the Styx and Lake
Avernus. Nobody will deny, of course, that such a method as
Leland's may — as it actually did — bring in valuable material; but what is of value is the by-product rather than the
tales asked for.

CHAPTER XII

1. The passages on magic and the like are conveniently
collected and discussed by Mario Belli, Magie e pregiudizii in
P. Vergilio Marone, in Archivio per lo studio delle tradizioni
popolari, XXIII (1907), 5–23, 144–165, 267–290. Cf. Eugene
Tavenner, Studies in Magic from Latin Literature, New
York, 1916, 24 ff. [Columbia University Studies in Classical
Philology]. William Godwin solved the riddle by calling on
the Eighth Eclogue — Lives of the Necromancers, London,
1834, 119 ff.

2. The Vita Donatiana, Donatus Auctus, and several other
biographies are edited by Jakob Brummer in Vitae Vergilianae, Leipzig (Teubner), 1912. Cf. Ernst Diehl, Die Vitae
Vergilianae und ihre antike Quellen, Bonn, 1911 [Kleine Texte
für theologische und philologische Vorlesungen . . . 72].

3. For instance, the excellent work by Vladimiro Zabughin, Vergilio nel Rinascimento italiano, 2 vv., Bologna,

n. d. (1921–23) refers only once or twice to the necromancer, and Alice Hulubel, Virgile en France au XVIᵉ siècle, in Revue du seizième siècle, XVIII (1931), 1–77, does not need to mention him. Cf. Duane Reed Stuart, Biographical Criticism of Vergil since the Renaissance, in Studies in Philology, XIX (1922), 1–30, and Anna Cox Brinton, Maphaeus Vegius and his Thirteenth Book of the Aeneid, a Chapter on Virgil in the Renaissance, Stanford University Press, 1930.

The best collection of materials on Virgil's literary reputation is still G. Zappert, Virgils Fortleben im Mittelalter, Wien, 1851 [K. Akademie der Wissenschaften]. The attitude toward the Seven Liberal Arts, and hence toward Virgil, is well understood by J.–A. Lalanne, L'influence des Pères de l'Église sur l'éducation publique pendant les cinq premiers siècles de l'ère chrétienne, Paris, 1850; cf. M. Roger's chapter on Les Pères de l'Église et les lettres classiques, in his L'enseignement des lettres classiques d'Ausone à Alcuin, Paris, 1905; Raymond Thamin, Le Christianisme et la culture classique, in his Saint Ambroise et la morale chrétienne au IVᵉ siècle, Paris, 1895; L. J. Paetow, The Arts Course at Medieval Universities . . ., in University of Illinois Studies, III (1910), No. 7.

4. The attempt is in the brilliant dissertation of Kurt Wieser, Die Zusammenhang der Vergilviten, Erlangen, 1926, 35, 49.

James Westfall Thompson, Vergil in Mediæval Culture, in American Journal of Theology, X (1906), 648–662, argues that St. Francis and the Franciscan movement were responsible for Virgil's becoming popular during the Middle Ages, for "knowledge of Vergil was limited in the Middle Ages to the learned, and veneration of him would have continued to be confined to the cloister wholly, if that wondrous reformation of the church and society had not taken place in the thirteenth century, under the inspiration of St. Francis of Assisi. . . . In St. Francis the mind of the Roman poet, by some Rosicrucian mystery, seemed to have rebirth, but purged of its paganism — Christian. But even Francis' Christianity was different from that of his contemporaries. His humanity was deep enough and broad enough to go out unto all men. In an age when chivalry had become a caste, when the church had become an aristocratic corporation, all men were brothers unto him, whether Jew or gentile, bond or free, pagan or heretic or infidel. This is how the reverence for Vergil, to whose heart that of St. Francis was akin, spread from the cultural precincts of the cloisters down among the common people of the Middle Ages." (Pp. 661–662)

The difficulty with this hypothesis is that, as I have remarked before, Virgil's literary reputation remained essentially unchanged from the times of St. Jerome and Macrobius, and, so far as I can see, was affected in no way by the Franciscans in the thirteenth century or later. Professor Thompson cannot believe that St. Francis or his order had much to do with the formation of the Virgilian legends studied in this volume, since St. Francis was born in 1181 or 1182, more than twenty years after John of Salisbury wrote his Policraticus, began his ministrations to the poor and leprous in 1206, after Alexander Neckam, Conrad of Querfurt, and Guiraut de Calanso had made their contributions to the Virgilian legends, and held the first general consistory of the Franciscan order in 1217, after Gervasius of Tilbury had written his Otia imperialia. Thus the legends would seem to have been well launched before the Franciscans were in a position to influence them.

APPENDIX

APPENDIX

Von Virgilio dem Zauberer

(A literal reprint of the unique copy in the University
Library at Munich)

S was zu rom ein zauberer
    virgilius so hieß er
    Wie er aber die zauberey gelernet ye
das wert ir wol vernemen hie
Als er einß tags zu weingart hackt
vnd so tieff in die erden stackt
Mit der hawen auf ein glag [*read* glas]
das selbig voller teüffel was
Er nam das glaß vnd behielt es ebeñ
er meint es solt im frummen gebeñ
Er maint er wolt groß gut do mit gewinnen
wo erß hin trug do sprachen dinnen
Die teüffel auß dem glase
die also dar in verschlossen wase
Virgilij nun laß vnß varñ
wir wollen dich ymmer mer bewarñ
Vorallem laster vnd auch laidt
vnd laß vnß varñ auf die haidt
Wir wollen dich leren künste vill
das wirt dein freüde vnd auch spil
Immer mer vntz an den todt
wan in dem glas so leüden wir nodt
Czwenundsibentzig ist vnser an der schar
das soltu unß glauben für war
Do sprach virgilij zu der schar
wan ich eüch nit getrawen thar
Gebt ir mir der künsten stewer

ich schwer eůch einen aydt vil thewer
Das ich das glas zerprechen wil
lernt ir mich der kůnst so vil
Der ich frummen gewinnen mag
ich schwer eůch noch heůt bey tag,
Das glas muß prechen von meiner hant   [A i, v°]
zu hant die teůffel alle sandt
Lernten in die zaubtrey vil drat [read zauberey]
alß manß noch in der welte hat
Vnd mancher mensch do mit vmb gat
Do er die kunst von in entpfing
zu einem steine er do gieng
Er brach das glas vnd ließ sie varñ
die teůffel all mit yren scharñ
Czu handt gedacht virgilius
wie in die teůffel alsus
Die do warñ geuarñ von hynnen
ich traw mir nun wol gnug gewinnen
Bayde ere vnd anch gut [read auch]
wie wol das meynem hertzrn thut [read hertzen]
Das ich mag haben gut gemach
an arbeyt vnd an hawen schlach
Das ich mag haben gut vnd eres krafr [read kraft]
zu rom versucht er do sein meisterschaft
Ob war wer der teůffel kraft
Czu rom macht er ein staynes weib
von kunst die het ein sollichen leib
Was schelck vnd poser man
wolten zu frumen frawen gan
So gieng der poß vnd vnreine
zu dem selben steine
So wau pey des stainen pildes leib [read wan]
recht sam es wer vou art ein weib [read von]
Nicht fůrpaß ich es sagen soll
dus vbrig wist ir selber woll

Der zauberey treyb er vill vnd genug
dar zu was er vil weis vnd klug
Ich kan es alles nicht gesagen
der warheit mus ich vil vertragen
Er warb wol vmb einer frawen mynne   [A ij]
die was zu rom ein burgerinne
Das sie seynen willen thet
doch was die frawe also stet
Das sie in nicht wolt gewerñ
das er an sie wolt begerñ
Doch ließ er nicht von seinem werbñ
er sprach er mǔst darumbe sterbñ
Ee er von ir wolt lassen
ir myn kam im zu massen
Sie sprach ewer vnsyn eǔch laid gepǔerdt
wdn ich meynen man es sagen wǔerdt [*read* vnd]
Vnd wert ir schoner dan absolon
mein myn ist eǔch versaget schon
Ir solt eǔch an ein andre keren
vnd die eǔch erfǔlle ewer begeren
Ich pyn eǔch dar zu gut vnd zu rain
ee mǔsten prechen perg vnd stain
Warlich ee ich eǔch wolt gewerñ
des ir an mich thut begerñ
Get hin vnd last mich hie an not
oder mein man wirt rǔch thun den tot [*read* eǔch]
Dem wil ichß sagen sicherleich
ewer pit ist gar vnpilleich
Virgilius er nicht ab lies
silber vnd golt er ir verhies
Do er sein werben nicht wolt lan
do gieng die frawe wolgethan
Czu yren wirt vnd sagt im das
sie sprach lieber wirt nicht pys so las
Wie ich behalt meyn guttes lob vnd er

do mit ich meyn weiplich zucht nit verser
Die ich von kintheyt her
mit zucht han behalten
das ich mit eren müg gealten [A ij, v°]
Ob es nun ewer wille ist
nun ratet mir in kurtzer frist
Das ich virgilio entgee
der thut mir not vnd wee
Er wirbet stet woll vmb meyn myn
nun nempt in ewerñ munt vnd syn
Wie ich seyner kunst entgee
das mir mein er vor im bestee
Ir elich man sprach all zu handt
fraw dein laster vnd dein schandt
wer mir von gantzem hertzen laydt
wie wol er ist der kunst beklaydt
So wil ich rathen frawe meyn
vnd das er muß geschendet seyn
Lad in heint pey disser nacht
vnd sprich du habst dich wol bedacht
Du solt im sagen solliche mer
ich sey von dir mit grosser schwer
Geritten vnd mit zoreñ
du habst vmb sunst meyn huldt verloreñ
Sage im er müg nicht schier
in das hause kumen zu mier
Ich hab dich in starcker hut
sprich also es dunckt mich gut
Das ich euch ließ ein korb zu thall
dar ein sest ir ane schal
Die sorg euch do vil gar entpirt
wan sein nyemant ynnen wirt
Ewerñ willen thu ich sicherleich
auff zeuch ich euch krefftigkleich
In den thurn den ich han

ewern̄ willen den wil ich than
So er vernypt die rede dein [*read* vernympt]
so wil er gantz an̄ sorge sein　　　　　　　　[A iij]
was ir der wirt do rieth vnd sagt
die fraw virgilium do tagt
Si sprach seit ir ein kůner degen
das ir wolt meiner hulde pflegen
Das solt ir heint erzaigen.
ich gib mich eůch zu aigen
So kumet heint wol pey der nacht
mein man hat sich nit wol gedacht
wan er mich seer geschlagen hat
darumb so ist das meyn rat
Das ir heint kumpt zu mir
vnd was ir wolt das thun ich schir
Enden wirß heindt zu disser zeit
Mir ist in dissem landt so weit
Nicht laides so mein man
darumb ich im wol laides gan
Do virgilius die red vernam
die die frawe lobesam
Selber můntlich zu im redt
er sprach fraw wie gern̄ ich thet
Sie sprach ich fůrcht die hundt
ich wil eůch raten was ir thunt
Setzt eůch in meynen korb vill schier
ich wil eůch wol herauff zu mir
Cziehen das ist recht gethan
vil gern̄ also sprach der man
wan ich es ymmer verdienen soll
wan ir seyt aller tugendt voll
　　　　Des nachtes do es spat wardt
virgilius der hub sich auff die vardt
Czu der frawen wolgefar
er warff mit einem stainlein dar

In das venster das erhall
do gieng die frawe ane schall   [A iij, v°]
Vnd entschloß das venster do vil schier
ir elich man der gieng mit ir
Sie sach herab vnd sprach also
seydt ir da virgilio
Er sprach ia fraw woll gethon
den korp solt ir herab lon
Da wil ich sitzen in
ir habt daran weisen sin
Den korp sie herab ließ
als sie virgilius hieß
Dar eiu saß er vnd das ist war [read ein]
Sie zoch in auf vnd doch nit gar
Sie zoch in dreyer gaden hoch
nicht fürpaß sie in auff zoch
Sie strickt in an vnd ließ in hangen
sein wil der was do nicht ergangen
Sie beleib do ein reines weib
keůsch vnd schon so was ir leib
Des morgens do es taget
den romern man es saget
Wie es virgilio wer ergangen
er wer an einem thurn̄ gehangen
Do sprach manig man
ich glaub es nicht ich sechs dan an
Nun ist er doch ein als weißer man
das man sein geleich nicht vinden kan
Da von ichs nicht glauben mag
nun was es doch ein gemeine sag
Do giengen vnd ritten die romer dar
vnd nomen seyner not war
Czu iůngst do kam ir elich man
schon zu im geritten dan
Sam er wer von dan gewesen

virigilius mocht kaum̄ genesen [A iiij]
Wan er liedt spot vnd vngemach
yglicher romer zu im gach
Wie ist das kumen virgilius
das ir hie hangt alsus
Virgilius sprach mit stille
es was zwar nicht meyn wille
Do sprach der frawen elich man
wer pracht eůch zu dem thurn̄ dan
Das ir hangt an meyner mawer
ich main es sey eůch worden sawer
Doch ist es mir an eůch laidt
ir habt erlitten schmachaidt
Do ließ der wirt den weisen man
her nyder von dem thurn̄ gan
Do in alles volck ersach
das was im gar ein grosse schmach
Er het sein grossen schmertzen
am leib vnd an dem hertzen
Er begundt gedencken vnd auch trachten
vnd in sein hertzen achten
Wie er dem gethat
das die frawe stat
Layd von im gewůne
vnd auch dar zu als ir kůne
Vnd von dem laidt geschendet wůrdt
das was im gar ein schwer půrdt
Do schuff der vngehewer
das zu rom alle fewer
In der grossen stat erlaschen
das was in laidt vnmassen
Sie mochten nit gepachen
noch kain essen siedent machen
Sie warn̄ nahent hungers todt
Die romer lietten grosse nodt [A iiij, v°]

Do die romer sollich not do lietteñ
hin vnd her sie do ritteñ
Sie kunden nicht betrachten
wie das sie fewer machten
Es was auch niemant zu der stundt
der mocht erdenckeñ einen fundt
Do was ein romer vntter yn
der sprach ich sag eůch meinen syn
Ich rath eůch get zu virgilio
vnd bitten den vil fleissig do
Vnd gewinnen mit schanckung sein gunst
vnd das er do versuch sein kunst
Vnd mach vnß wider fewer
also sprach der romer thewer
Der rath begunt in allen
rechtlichen wol geuallen
Do giengen die romer all zu mal
fůr virgilium mit grossem schal
Vnd sprachen herre ewren rat
wir suchen vmb ein misse that
Sie thut vnß also grosse not
vor hunger můß wir ligen tot
Wir můgen das brot nit pachen
noch vnsser essen kochñ vnd machen
Des müssen wir hie verderben
vnd manig mensch darumb sterben
Nun wissen wir ewerñ weistumb
der ist vnß an masse frumb
Virgilius sprach ich wil eůch sagen
ir mocht der red do stil betagen
Wan sagt ich eůch die warheit
es wůrd eůch an massen leit
Ir leidet ser groß vngemach
Also virgilius sprach   [A iiiij]
Do sprachen sie mit schwer

in der stat die weisen romer
Her es ist sein do nit zu vill
was du freůdt vnd herre wilt [*read* will]
Das thun wir gerñ mit sinnen
das wir feůer gewinnen
Ee wir also verderbeñ
vnd so iemerlichen sterbeñ
Der hunger macht vnß plindt
vnß sterben weib vnd kindt
Er sprach ist eůch der hunger laidt
So schwert mir des do einen aidt
Das ich eůch haiß das thun bezeit
das ir do wider nymer seit
Vnd das ich ewer hulde
hab vmb die selben schulde
Wan ich durch ewern willen hie
zu wegen pring das fewer als ye
Do wurden sie zu rat
es wer frw oder spat
Nymer woltens wider in sein
ob er in thet der hůlffe schein
Vnd ob sich vntter vnß yemat
wider dich verschuldet hat
Das soltu freůndt lossen varñ
wir wollen vnß fůrpaß gen dir bewarñ
Er sprach so schwert mir hie an disser stet
also virgilius het geret
Do schwuren sie im mit laide
yglicher zwen aide
Do sprach virgilius nun wol
seidt ichs mit hulden sprechen sol
so ist eůch niemandt nutz so wol
Der eůch von ewrem laide schaide   [A iiiij, v°]
das sag ich eůch pey meinem aide
Als die fraw sicherleich

die do ist im thurn̄ reich
Do ich mit noten ane hieng
vil mancher noch der frawen gieng
Die ir mag vnd freündt warn̄
die sach man nach ir reiten vnd farn̄
Ir man bracht sie mit flee vnd mit pet
doch vil vngern̄ sie es thet
Do sie zu virgilio nun gieng
gar schon er sie do entphfieng
Er sprach frawe wol gethon
wolt ir die stat nicht lan zergon
Vnd das wolck dar inne
so thut nach meynem sinne
Vnd thut ir nach meinem rat
so gewint man fewer in der stat
Oder ir müst verderben
vnd mit sampt dar inne sterben
Sie sprach lieber herre mein
mocht es mit ewern̄ hulden sein
So liest es thun ein ander gespill
wan ich hab doch von eüch laides vill
Er sprach fraw es mag anders nit gesein
es müst ee trucken wern derrein
Ee ich es ließ für dissen tag
an eüch es nyemantz geschaffen mag
      Die fraw sprach ir solt mir veriehen
wie mir hie sol geschehen
Do mit virgilius sprach
do er die schonen vor im sach
Fraw secht ir dissen stain
auff den do solt ir sten allain
Das gewandt solt ir ab ziehen̄   [A 6]
ab dem stain solt ir nit fliehen̄
Ir solt an haben ein hembdt
andrie klaider seindt eüch frembdt

Vnd solt das affter muder vor
hinden auff lassen gar
Vnd solt auff allen vieren stan
zuhandt sol weib vnd auch man
Czünden vor dem hindern tail
vnd wer da gewint das vnhail
Der von eim andern zünden wil
so würdt in paiden nicht vil
Wan sie erleschen bayde licht
das man sie nymer prünnen sicht
Wollen sie dan aber fewer han
so müssen sie payde herwider gan
Vnd müssen payde zünden
so beginnen sie·darnach lünden
Do sprach die frawe wolgethon
ee wolt ich den leib lon
Ee ich wolt haben solliche schandt
ee wolt ich rewmen alle landt
Do sprach virgilius der weiß man
also mag es nit ergan
Im muß also ich gesprochen hen
geschehen wollet sie freüd sehen
Do das erhortten ire mag
do hetten sie manig frag
Auch hort es ir aigner man
das es anders nicht mocht ergan
Do patten sie die fraw mit pet
wie wol sie es vngern thet
wan sie schampt sich vil sere
yres laydes wardt vill mere
Sie sprach ich laß mich toten ee   [A 6, v°]
ee es ymer also ergee
Do nicht halff tro vnd pet
nun hort wie ir man thet
Er wolt des nicht erwinden

er hieß die frawe pinden
Das gewandt hieß er ir abziehen
des mocht er nit entphlihen
Er stelt sie oben auff den stain
ir scham was nicht zu klain
Do must die fraw mit schall
das fewer geben vber all
wan sie must auff dem stain stan
des wolt man sie nicht erlan
Einer trug kerzen dar
der ander vnschlit das ist war
Der drit ein schaub
der vierd ein puschlaub
Der fůfft ein puchel her
der sechst einen prant schwer
Also zůntten sie allesampt
das was der frawen ein michel schandt
Also must sie es leyden
sie mocht sein nit vermeyden
Sie must die scham vnd die not
leyden sie was nohent tot
　　　Dar nach virgilius trat von rom
vnd pawt ein stat die im wol zam
Als sie noch heůt woll ist bekant
die selbig stat was napplas genant
Mit listen er es alles an vieng
das es nach seynem willen gieng
die stat er an dreů ayer hieng
Das sie noch von im hat die krafft
von seiner grossen meisterschafft　　　　　[A 7]
Wer einß zerbrach die stat versůnck
dar inne alß volck ertrůck [*read* ertrůnck]
Das ay verhut man in der stat so wol
wer iegen dem ay greůffen sol
So ziettert die stat alzemal

vnd die hewser vberal
    Darnach virgilius der herre
der vandt noch list vil mere
Der macht ein pildt dar ein
das was rot gůldein
An dem pilde stundt geschribn̄
mit rot gůldein puchstabn̄
Do ich hin zaig do ist ein hort
wer in begreůft ist an ein ort
Mit seiner armut abkomen
do das die leůt hetten vernomen
ir ein michel teyl die do komen
Igklicher do versucht sein heyl
ob ym der hort icht wůrd zu teyl
Das im der sorgen půrde
also geringert vnd gemindert wůrde
Die ein handt het das pildt
gelegt auf seinen mundt so wilt
Der ander arm stundt im gestrackt
des mancher erfreůdt wart der ander erschrackt
Das pildt zaigen began
mit seiner hende wolgethan
Gegen einem perge der vor im lag
also zaigt es nacht vnd tag
Mit dem finger fůr sich hin
do sucht mancher den gewin
Vnd graben den perck vmbe
der weis vnd auch der thume
Sein vinger im gerecket was   [A 7, v°]
gein dem perck als ich laß
Der ander vinger zaiget an
gein dem pauch den hort an
Das verstundt sich nyemant da
sie furn̄ nach dem vinger sa
Der do stundt nach dem perck

dar in wůrckten sie manig werck
Sie mainten das sie dort
in dem perge funden den hort
Den hort do niemandt sach
einß mals ein trunckner man do sprach
wie lang sol vnß das pilde effen
an dem pildt wil ich mich effen
Vnd auch die andern̄ do pey
nun mercket eben wie im sey
Die leůt die wil ich rechen
das pildt wil ich zu prechen
Er schlug das pildt auff seinen nack
das es auff der erden lack
Sollichen freuel er do pflag
der schatz der in dem pilde lag
Der viel nyder in das gras
dar an so mag man wissen das
wem guttes ist beschaffen
es sein leyen oder pfaffen
Als dem truncken man geschach
der das eren pildt zerprach
Do er heim gienge von dem wein
der west nit das das gut was sein
Vntz er es trug von dannen da
Do wardt er ein reicher man mit mut
im was beschert groß hab vnd gut
wie wol wie sanft es manchem thut
Das er gewinnet seldt vnd hail [*read* geldt]   [A 8]
o wůrde vnß das ein tail
So wůrden wir freůden reich
helff vnß got inß himelreich
sprechent amen al geleich
     Virgilius der het sein kunst allein
vnd die zu rom gar wol erschein
An einem pildt ich verstee

das het er do gemacht vil ee
welliche fraw ir ere prach
das pildt es schwarlich an ir rach
Das pildt das het die kunst vnd macht
das es die fraw zu schanden pracht
Vor aller welt gar offentleich
das solt ir glauben sicherleich
Czwen vinger můst sie do zu stundt
legen in des pildes mundt
Vnd war sie das schuldig sollicher tat
so kam es ir zu vbelm̄ rat
Die vinger must sie dem pilde lan
anderst mogtz ir nicht ergan
Es piß irß ab mit gantzer macht
wie wol virgilius das bedacht
Es wern̄ frawen oder man
sie musten do in schanden stan
Nun wolt ir fůrpaß werden in
wie es zu rom einer keiserin
Er gieng durch iren grossen neyd
vnd den sie an das pilde leid
Sie gedacht in iren synnen wildt
sie wolt zerstoren das selbig pildt
Die fraw die het do gern̄ zerprochen
ir ee sie forcht es wůrd an ir gerochen
wie aber dem dar noch gescha
das werdt ir fůrpaß horen da   [A 8, v°]
Vnd werdt es fůrpaß werden in
wie das die selbig keyserin
Czerbrach do ir weiplich er
an einem klugen ritter her
Alzuhandt nun do geschach
an dem keyser man wachsen sach
Ein horn auf dem seynen haůbt
fůrwar ir mir das gelaubt

Das mut den keyser also ser
er klagt es fürsten vnd auch her
Er klaget manchem man sein not
er sprach ich wolt vill lieber ligen tot
Ich fürcht ich habs von meyner frawen
das horn̄ begundt vil mancher schawen
Er was dort vern geßhalb mer
pey im was mancher fürst vnd her
Ritter vnd auch knecht
edel vnd auch schlecht
Von mannen vnd auch frawen
begunden all das horn̄ schawen
Der keyser do sein rat besandt
er sprach für war es thut mir andt
Das horn̄ macht mir groß vnrue
nun rathen alle wie ich im thue
Er sprach zu einem weisen man
nun gib mir deinen rath vil schan
Wie ich mich rech an meinem weib
ich fürcht sie hab einß andern̄ leib
Sich do heim genomen an
do antwurt im der weise man
Er sprach her es dunckt mich gar ein guter radt
wir ziehen haim zu landt vil dradt
Do erfragt ir euch der mer vil paß
das sprich ich wol an allen has   [A 9]
Der keiser sprach ich wil nicht peyten
hyn wider haym so wil ich reyten
Hyn wider haym stuudt sein begier [read stundt]
zu seinem weib do kam er schier
Er hieß sie zu im kumen her
Er sprach zu ir mit grosser schwer
So sag du mir pey deinem leben
du hast mich mit eim andern̄ vber geben
Du pose schnode valentein

das horn an dem haupte mein
Das trag ich von deiner valschen myn
das kost dir do das leben dein
Dein er vnd auch dein gut
die fraw die sprach auß freyem mut
Gar lieplich sie do lachen kundt
sie antwurt im wol auf der stundt
Sie sprach do für so wil ich schwerñ
vnd wil mich mit dem rechten werñ
Das ich des zigs vnschuldig pin
der kayser sprach nun dar wol hin
Vor einem pildt das muß geschehñ
das es arm vnd reiche sehñ
Dastu must zu schanden stan
vor aller welt auf dissem plan
Sie sprach beschaidt mir einen tag
das ich meyn fereůndt berůffen mag
Das sie alle mügen sehen
das mir vnrecht ist geschehñ
Des traw ich got dem schopffer mein
der keiser sprach nun das soll sein
Der yren freůndt sie entperñ kundt
Sie sandt nach dem ritter zu der stundt
Mit dem sie ir ee zu brochen het
Nu mocht ir horen wy sy redt   [A 9, v°]
Hoer an gesell vnd mich verstee
wan ich für das gerichte gee
Gesel so würf mich vntter dich
ist meyn beger des pit ich dich fleissigklich
Mit armen soltu mich vmb schliessen
des soltu dich nit lan verdriessen
Do mit so vindt ich ainen fundt
das ich bescheůß des pildes mundt
So behalten wir paide des leben
vnd auch eer vnd gut do neben

Der ritter thet als sie in hieß
ein platen er im scheren ließ
Narren klaider schnyed er im zwar
er trat zu forderst an die schar
Do er die edel kayserin an sach
nach ir do wardt im also iach
Er schloß sie in sein arme weis
er knst sie do mit gantzem fleis [*read* kůst]
Das thet er do gar vnuerholñ
vil schleg vnd stoß must er verdolñ
Ir mocht gerñ horñ wie es gieng
vil weißlich sie es ane vieng
Nun merckt eben wie sie sprach
do sie das pilde ane sach
Nun hor an pildt ich muß das recht volfůrñ an
nun hor an pildt vnd vernym mich schon
Ia sten ich hie vmb leib vnd leben
vnd sol der warheyt rechnung geben
An mir do laß chain vnrecht geschehen
ia wil ichs mit der warheit iehen
Nun wart mein gewaltig nie kain man
wan nur der keiser mein elicher man
vnd dar zu der layvige thor
als dan yderman hie vor   [A 10]
Gesehen hat wol zu der stundt
zwen vinger legt dem pildt in seynen mundt
sie sprach schwer ich valsch so mach mich wundt
Das pildt gethorst ir nye
gepeyssen noch gerůrñ ye
Ir mocht woll horñ wes sie gedacht
als sie die vinger vom pilde pracht
Die fraw die sach den keiser an
nun sichstu das meyn lieber man
Ob du mir vil armen dieg
vnrecht thust mit deiner zieg

Schaw mir meyn vinger ob sie icht
wunden haben noch males pflicht
Er sprach das hab ich woll gesehen
das will ich in der warheyt yehen
Darumb so pit ich eŭch an spot
das ir mir hie vergebt durch got
Des gib ich eŭch mein trew vnd eer
es sol eŭch geschehen nymer mer
Sie sprach das wil ich gerñ thon
durch got ich es eŭch varñ lon
Der mag michs als ergetzen woll
der schanden der ich hie muß doll
Der keiser wardt des hornß loß
wan es im von dem haupte schoß
Er badt sein frawen gar mit witzen
das sie zu im solt nider sitzen
Vnd do die fraw den aydt geschwur
das pildt zu tausent stŭcken fur
Es paiß fŭrpaß kainen mit synnen
der kunst begundt ym zu rinnen

Title-page and colophon are missing.
Signatures: A ij [should be A i?], A ij, A iij, A iiij, A iiiij.
There are ten leaves, the verso of the tenth being blank.
The type is black-letter.

INDEX

INDEX

Numbers of pages on which bibliographical details appear are printed in italics.

Chapter I is the key chapter, and constitutes with the Table of Legends on pp. 60–68 an auxiliary index.

CPSIA information can be obtained
at www.ICGtesting.com
Printed in the USA
BVHW011421210820
586983BV00007B/227

9 780766 1869